The Gothic Novels of Mrs. Smith

The Caledonian Bandit;

OR

The Heir of Duncaethal

A Romance of the Thirteenth Century

AND

Barozzi;

OR

The Venetian Sorceress

A Romance of the Sixteenth Century

THE GOTHIC NOVELS
OF MRS. SMITH

THE CALEDONIAN BANDIT; OR THE HEIR OF DUNCAETHAL
A Romance of the Thirteenth Century

AND

BAROZZI; OR THE VENETIAN SORCERESS
A Romance of the Sixteenth Century

Edited with an Introduction by
CATHERINE E. GROH

WHITLOCK PUBLISHING
ALFRED, N.Y.

The Caledonian Bandit; or The Heir of Duncaethal
by Mrs. Smith, first published by Minerva Press, London, 1811

Barozzi; or The Venetian Sorceress
by Mrs. Smith, first published by Minerva Press, London, 1815

First Whitlock Publishing Edition 2017

Whitlock Publishing
www.whitlockpublishing.com

ISBN 13: 978-1-943115-20-4

This book was set in Adobe Garamond Pro on 55# acid-free paper that meets ANSI standards for archival quality.

TABLE OF CONTENTS

Acknowledgements

I would like to thank Dr. Allen Grove for his guidance, instruction, and assistance in editing and researching these texts.

I also thank my parents, Michael and Christine, and my partner, Anthony, for their help and support in this endeavour.

INTRODUCTION

When they were first published in the early 1800s, the works of Mrs. Smith blended into the sea of other Gothic fiction which flooded the literary market. But today, these tales of terror fraught with intrigue, adventure, and romance are like lost treasures. Smith employs nearly every popular Gothic theme, symbol, and motif of the time, making her novels quintessential examples of the genre. Crafted with skill and style, they were well-received in their time and are still enjoyable to read in the present day. Conventional Gothic plotlines make Smith's stories familiar and accessible to an aficionado of Gothic fiction, and those same conventions make them strange and unpredictable to someone new to the genre.

The Authorship of Mrs. Smith

The life of Mrs. Smith is largely a mystery. Her first name is believed to be "Catherine," but she published her books under the name, "Mrs. Smith." It was relatively common for female authors of the early 1800s to use names like "Miss _____" or "Mrs. _____." Sometimes they even identified themselves only as "wife of _____." What little has been pieced together of Smith's life indicates that she was from a wealthy family and acted at Haymarket Theatre in Westminster.

Two books other than *Barozzi* and *The Caledonian Bandit* have been attributed to Mrs. Smith: *The Misanthrope Father; or The Guarded Secret*, by Catharina Smith; and *The Castle of Arragon; or The Banditti of the Forest*, by Miss Smith. Devendra Varma, a renowned scholar of English Gothic literature, made the claim that all four books were written by the same "Catherine Smith." However, there is evidence to suggest that they were written by a different author or authors. The complete scanned text of *The Castle of Arragon* is available through the Corvey Collection. A comarison of the text with *Barozzi* and *The Caledonian Bandit* reveals a range of discrepancies that suggest the works were written by different authors.

The most direct suggestion that *The Caledonian Bandit*, 1811, was the first novel published by Smith comes from her own address in that book. She refers to it as "this first offspring of my brain." That statement seems to be supported by the way her name is presented on the title page: "Mrs. Smith, of the Theatre-Royale, Haymarket." *The Castle of Arragon* was published in 1810, a year earlier. If Smith had written it, it would probably have been mentioned on the title page of *The Caledonian Bandit*. Just as today we see movies advertised as "from the makers of _____," publishers in the early 1800s liked to promote authors using their previous works. Smith's name on the title page of *Barozzi*, 1815, is followed by, "Author of *The Caledonian Bandit*, &c. &c." The "et cetera" symbols are curious, but the fact remains that *The Caledonian Bandit* suggested no previous books by Smith. Furthermore, *The Castle of Arragon* was handled by a different publisher. Its title page reads, "London: Printed for Henry Colburn, English and Foreign Library, Conduit-Street, Bond-Street." Both *The Caledonian Bandit* and *Barozzi* were published by Minerva Press, a then popular purveyor of Gothic fiction.

Varma cited *Arragon* as being published by Minerva Press in 1813, which would place it after *Caledonian Bandit*. *The Minerva Press, 1790-1820*, a book compiled by Dorothy Blakey in 1935 for the Bibliographical Society at the University Press at Oxford, does indeed cite *Arragon* as having been published by Minerva Press in that year. However, the microfiche of *Arragon* from the Corvey collection clearly shows the publication date as 1810 by a different publisher. Varma likely did not have access to this version of the text and assumed, reasonably so, based on the records available to him, that the 1813 Minerva Press edition was the first edition of *Arragon*.

There are also significant differences in diction and content between *Arragon* and the other two novels. For example, the word "ejaculate" (meaning to exclaim) is used twenty-two times in *Arragon*, just three times in *Caledonian Bandit*, and only twice in *Barozzi*. The term "Providence" is used nine times in *Caledonian Bandit*, eight times in *Barozzi*, and not at all in *Arragon*. *The Castle of Arragon* is also twice the length of the other two, and was published in four volumes rather than two. It was highly unusual for authors to write a long first novel and progress to writing shorter ones. It would typically work the other way around. As far as content and style, the plot of *Arragon* moves at an incredibly slow pace compared to the other two novels. It focuses much less on action, and the sentimental aspects of Gothic are far more prominent. Furthermore, the female characters in *Arragon* almost fall by the wayside. While they may feature prominently in the plot, they are not characterized or even humanized nearly as well as those of *Caledonian Bandit* and *Barozzi*. The extent of this difference is too great to be explained away by *Arragon* being an earlier work, as the time between publications was only one year.

Mrs. Smith may have authored novels previous to those republished in this volume, but there is much evidence to suggest otherwise. In any case, *The Caledonian Bandit* and *Barozzi* are more engaging than *The Castle of Arragon*, and they are the two novels which can most confidently be attributed to Smith.

So, while this volume may not, for certain, present the only works of the elusive Mrs. Smith, it does at least present her two finest works.

Minerva Press

Minerva Press, the publisher that handled Smith's novels, made a name for itself turning out Gothic novels in the late 18th and early 19th centuries. Founded in 1790 by William Lane, it was the most prolific publisher of Gothic fiction of its time. Of the more than 800 titles that came out of Minerva Press, most were not critically acclaimed, but they were popular among readers. The famous novelists only wrote so many books; readers hungering for more Ann Radcliffe or Matthew Lewis also enjoyed the less famous but similar novels that came out of Minerva Press. A great many writers tried with varying degrees of success to ride the popularity of Gothic fiction, and readers inclined toward the Gothic eagerly took them up. Thus, Minerva Press grew successful by answering a growing need for quantity over quality of Gothic novels.

Lane was able to pay first-time authors sums as low as £20, and female authors were even more likely to be taken advantage of. The (relatively) small-time authors who took their work to Minerva Press were often so excited to see their names in print that they accepted low payments without much complaint. Minerva Press also sold their books at low prices, and offered chapbooks or bluebooks—cheap paper copies of fictional works—for those who could not afford to purchase hard-bound novels. These were among the first "paperbacks." Printed on flimsy acid paper, in tiny print, with crowded, messy title pages, these books were hardly visually appealing. For the price though, they couldn't be beat.

The 18th century also marked the rise of circulating libraries, which helped put books in the hands of more people than ever. Circulating libraries operated in much the same way as modern libraries, except they charged a fee to borrow a certain number of books. They also tended to contain more fiction than non-fiction, because their selection directly reflected what people were interested in reading—or what the founder was interested in making money on. Lane, for example, founded several circulating libraries to promote and distribute his own books.

Influences on Smith's Writing: The Theater and Ann Radcliffe

For the most part, Smith's acting career remains a mystery, but there is record of her having performed in a stage adaptation of Matthew Lewis's *The*

Monk. Experiencing Gothic fiction in a theatrical setting may have been what sparked her interest in the genre. In any case, Smith's acting experience certainly influenced her as a novelist, imbuing her writing with a flair for the dramatic, as she tends to favor action over description. Many of her contemporaries in Gothic fiction would begin their novels with a lengthy description of setting, perhaps describing an ominous castle, a gloomy convent, or a dark forest. Smith, on the other hand, begins hers either in medias res or with a brief flash-forward to an exciting scene. While her stories possess a Radcliffean sentimentality, they are very dynamic, shifting frequently from place to place, from focus on one character to another, and punctuating emotional scenes with physical action. She does not often wax on about emotion or lose herself in the sublime, preferring instead to captivate her readers with a theatrical—even melodramatic—storytelling style.

Smith's writing unmistakably shows the influence of Ann Radcliffe, the most successful Gothic novelist of the 1790s. In the early 1800s when Smith published her books, it was common for authors to mimic the styles of popular Gothic novelists like Radcliffe and Lewis in order to try and capitalize on their success. Since the publication of Horace Walpole's *The Castle of Otranto* in 1764 (which was arguably the first Gothic novel, although that status has been contested), Gothic novels had been on the rise. While the genre was by no means ubiquitously liked, it had more than enough avid readers to make it a sensation.

So many novels were based on Radcliffe's works that her name has become a descriptor for a certain Gothic style. She specialized in Gothic Romance, and, arguably, she perfected it. Her novels evoke terror while avoiding gore and the grotesque. They contain sustained sequences of terror and danger, but the heroine—or hero—is always able to overcome them without sustaining any lasting physical injury. While horrific events do occur, they are not described in overwhelming detail, they do not physically affect the heroine (except perhaps to make her faint), and they are never the primary focus of the plot. Many things almost happen to the hero or heroine. Almost assassinated, almost imprisoned forever, almost raped, Radcliffe's heroines undergo emotional ordeals to make up for the lack of physical horrors. This is a perfect setup for appealing to readers who want to experience the exhilaration of terror without having to experience—vicariously, through the heroine—the actual terrifying event. Radcliffe's novels, and Radcliffean novels (works based on her style), are escapist in nature. Smith's novels work in much the same way.

Radcliffe works a remarkable level of detail into her novels, with regard to description of setting and characters' relationships with each other. She creates complex family trees, and usually her plots are based on a heroine of mysterious parentage. The heroine is often a commoner of exceeding virtue who is secretly a member of the nobility, one who has been cut off from her family and denied the honors of her rightful title due to a tragic event or events. Smith's novels bear some obvious resemblance to the works of Radcliffe in the use of central plots based on mysterious parentage, fallen nobility, and dark family secrets. Each of Smith's books presents a fallen high-born man or woman who, by the end, reclaims their rightful title. These Gothic conventions go all the way back to Walpole's *The Castle of Otranto*, in which a commoner turns out to be the rightful heir to the Castle of Otranto.

In Radcliffe's novels, seemingly supernatural occurrences typically appear in the heroine's life and are intertwined with the reasons for her misfortune or the means for her deliverance—sometimes both. Those elements are always explained away by the end. The ghost was a person under a sheet with clever lighting. The demon was only a human in disguise. Radcliffe's heroines are rational and intelligent, and reason always triumphs over superstition. Also, moralists of the time—such as those who criticized Lewis for his portrayal of actual demons, rape, incest, etc.—did not look kindly on most portrayals of supernatural occurrences as real. Radcliffean novels play it safe by explaining away the supernatural, not attempting to push the limits of their readers' sensibilities or what society may deem acceptable reading. Smith also explains away the supernatural in her stories.

Historical Context and Gender Issues

Gothic fiction reached its height in England during a time of great unrest in Europe. The dates of the French Revolution (1789-1799) correlate exactly with the decade when Gothic novels grew to extreme popularity in England. The French Revolution was characterized by intense social upheaval as the lower classes overthrew the aristocracy. It was devastating for France and deeply concerning for England as well, as a nation with a similar class structure. Consequently, the French Revolution is often discussed as a source of inspiration for the gloomy and horrific tales written by authors on the other side of the English Channel. British Gothic novelists did not usually adopt revolutionary or rebellious ideals; in fact, most of them wrote from very conservative viewpoints. The influence of the French Revolution is seen more in the mood of Gothic novels. They tend to have an air of uneasiness, often with the presence of an unknown danger. This feeling reflects what most of England was feeling about the horrors going on in France. Gothic novels also tend to feature one or more corrupt aristocrats as the villains—again, directly relating to the French

Revolution. The people of England were frightened and confused, uncertain of the future of their own nation, and looking for some sort of catharsis, which Gothic novels provided in their own way. Set in a far-off time—like the 16th century—and in a far-away place—often a country such as Italy, Spain, or Germany—their tales of terror and horror avoided seeming too close to home. By using such settings to present a mysterious danger and then proceeding to explain and destroy it, Gothic novels were perfectly tailored to give their readers a sense of relief and release from their fears.

Women's and gender issues mark another important context for Gothic fiction, especially in the early 1800s. The concept of the domestic sphere was emerging in England—the idea that the woman's natural sphere of influence should be in the home. The ideal woman, by that way of thinking, was dainty, domestic, and passive. Those terms perfectly describe both the ideal woman in Victorian literature and the classic Gothic heroine. With few exceptions, Gothic plots revolve around a female character—a young, innocent, naïve and faultless girl who is thrown into harrowing circumstances by a twist of fate. On the cusp of womanhood, she must maintain her virtue (her virginity) and survive to marry an eligible young nobleman at the end of the novel. Her activities include looking pretty, playing musical instruments, and embroidering—all hobbies befitting a young highborn lady. Her main defense against those who may wish to do her harm is being so beautiful and pure that even the most hardened criminals suddenly lose all will to hurt her. We as readers are meant to fall in love with her as much as the other characters do, and hold her up as a standard of perfect womanhood.

But as passive as she may be—or appear to be—the Gothic heroine must also be strong in character. The ordeals into which she is thrown force her to act in ways that do not meet the standards of propriety to which she is held. When separated from anyone who might have protected her, she must become the keeper of her own virtue. When kidnapped, she must be assertive and refuse to go along with the demands of those with authority over her. Lastly, she must entrust her well-being to the hero, outright breaking the rules of propriety by allowing herself to be alone with him unsupervised. Feminist readings have interpreted Gothic romances as fantasies of female power because of the way their heroines take charge of their own lives when thrown into desperate situations. All of Smith's heroines must make their own way in this fashion, particularly Matilda in *The Caledonian Bandit*. Held against her will in the castle of a dishonorable thane, Matilda must deny his repeated, aggressive attempts to secure her hand in marriage, at the same time working to uncover the mystery the castle holds.

Feminism as we know it today was just beginning to develop in the early 1800s. Mary Wollstonecraft's *A Vindication of the Rights of Woman*, the first major feminist philosophical book, was only published in 1792. Wollstonecraft advocated for equality of men and women more pointedly than any other feminist of her time, and even she was obliged to talk around the issue of women's rights. For example, one of her main arguments in *A Vindication* was that women should be as educated as men in order to properly educate their children in the home. She was only able to argue for equality without candidly challenging the domestic role of women. In the same way, authors of Gothic romances had to dance around the concept of empowered women. They may present the heroine as the ideal young woman—passive and proper, never stepping out of bounds—but they change the surrounding circumstances to allow her to act outside of her designated sphere of influence. The heroine may seem helpless to a modern reader, but for the early 1800s, she has a remarkable level of agency—which is to say, the ability to make choices and act on her own.

Understanding the Gothic heroine is important, but we mustn't ignore the other side of the coin: the villainess—the mannish female who casts off her womanly virtues and takes what she wants from the world. She is impious, lustful, vindictive, and intimidating, sometimes even taking on the guise of a man in order to fulfill her desires. She is always portrayed in a negative light and always defeated in the end, but even so she drives that fantasy of female power as much as the heroine, if not more. Smith's handling of the villainess in *Barozzi* does something interesting with that fantasy. Normally, characters who seek out revenge are not looked well upon by Gothic writers, for moral reasons. But the efforts of Smith's seeming villainess are richly rewarded. The true identity and morality of the sorceress are left ambiguous until the very end of the story, when the mystery is solved and all is revealed.

The novels of Mrs. Smith showcase classic elements of British Gothic storytelling—the brave young hero or heroine, the mystery of parentage, the intriguing castle or ruin, the compelling villainess... the list continues on. Smith also brings her own flair to the conventional plotlines, keeping her narratives flowing with exciting action, and turning the trope of villainess on its head in *Barozzi*. Even though these stories were penned in the early 1800s, they still possess the potential to surprise and thrill readers in the present day.

~ Catherine E. Groh

BIBLIOGRAPHY

Blakey, Dorothy. The Minerva Press, 1790-1820. Oxford: Bibliographical Society at the University Press, 1935. Excerpts accessed through Google Books.

"British History Timeline." BBC News. BBC, 2014.

Davison, Carol Margaret. Introduction. Caledonian Bandit: Or, the Heir of Duncaethal, a Romance of the 13th Century. By Mrs. Smith. Kansas City: Valancourt, 2010. Print.

Heller, Terry. The Delights of Terror: An Aesthetics of the Tale of Terror. Chicago: U of Illinois, 1987. Print.

Jenkins, James D. Introduction. Barozzi, Or, The Venetian Sorceress. By Catherine Smith. Ed. James D. Jenkins. Chicago: Valancourt, 2006. Print.

Mullan, John. "The Origins of the Gothic." The British Library. The British Library, 26 Feb. 2014.

"Publishing." Book History: Gothic Fiction. Weebly.

Spencer, Jane. The Rise of the Woman Novelist: From Aphra Behn to Jane Austen. Oxford: Blackwell, 1987. Print.

"Spine-chillers and Suspense: A Timeline of Gothic Fiction." BBC News. Consultant: Catherine Spooner. BBC.

Varma, Devendra P. Introduction. Barozzi: Or, The Venetian Sorceress: A Romance of the Sixteenth Century. By Catherine Smith. New York: Arno, 1977. Print.

Note on the Text

I have been faithful to the original texts as much as possible, correcting grammar and spelling only when it was an obvious mistake of the publisher, not an idiosyncracy of Smith's writing. I also standardized the lengths of dashes and types of quotation marks. I kept most archaic and British spellings of words intact because I believe it adds to the authentic reading experience of these nineteenth-century novels.

THE CALEDONIAN BANDIT;
OR
THE HEIR OF DUNCAETHAL

A Romance of the Thirteenth Century

IN TWO VOLUMES

VOLUME I

Author's Address

There are so many motives for writing, that it is usual to satisfy the reader's curiosity, by a statement of the cause in so doing. Reasons the most laudable first induced the author to attempt the following humble pages:

For the liberal encouragement which she received from the publisher, on her submitting the MS. to his consideration, she is truly grateful.

What most she ought to dread, are the reviewers' disapprobation; but they are her countrymen; and though, by habit and education, strict judges of style and composition, they will, in pity, *spare,* if they cannot praise.

Critics, I deprecate your anger; and though this first offspring of my brain possesses neither brilliancy of character, nor beauty of language, I trust, if you cannot let it flourish in the warmth of your smiles, you will in mercy forbear to crush it with your frowns.

~ Smith

CHAPTER I

What needs there
A stronger breast-plate than a heart untainted?
Thrice is he arm'd that hath his quarrel just;
And he but naked, though lock'd up in steel,
Whose conscience with injustice is corrupted.
                                        Shakespeare.

A HEART-RENDING SIGH burst from the fair bosom of the beautiful Matilda, as she cast a rich embroidered scarf of tartan plaid across the form
of the graceful Donald;—"Receive this, beloved youth," said she; "and
when you meet the eye of the fierce and terror-striking Duncaethal, let it inspire
thee with tenfold strength to crush thy foe, and return to thy Matilda, crowned
with the laurel-wreaths of victory." A drop like the dew of morn glistened in
her soft blue eye, as her taper fingers twined the knot which fastened her gift.
"Farewell," said she, "and sometimes, in the battle's rage, remember Matilda."

The youth arose from his knee, exclaiming, while the feeling of his heart
shone in his expressive countenance, "Farewell, sweet maid! and when I face my
enemy, this arm shall prove that he who feels like me is doubly armed—who
fights alike the cause of gratitude and love. The unknown Donald, fierce Duncaethal's scoff, shall prove his heart as brave, and as great a stranger to ignoble
fear, as though he stood acknowledged sprung from princes. And since I am
blest with thy dear love, I envy not the greatest sovereigns of the world!" Thus
saying, he again sunk on his knee, and pressing her hand to his lips, sealed on it
a burning kiss; then tore himself away, followed by his faithful squire.

Matilda hastily ascended the west turret of the castle, following him with
her eyes as he rode through the forest's maze, until its gloom enveloped him
from her sight; quick tears then chased each other down her fair cheeks, as she
again sought her chamber, when sinking on her knees, she offered up prayers
for the protection of the heroic Donald.

Chapter II

Instantly I plung'd into the sea,
And buffeting the billows to her rescue,
Redeem'd her life with half the loss of mine;
Like a rich conquest, in one hand I bore her.
And with the other dash'd the saucy waves.
That throng'd and press'd to rob me of my prize.

Otway.

A low-born man, of parentage obscure,
Who nought can boast but his desire to be a soldier,
And to gain a name in arms.

Home.

EAST OF THE CHEVIOT HILLS, on an eminence, stood the ancient but grand Castle of Bosmora; it seemed to bid defiance to the destroying hand of Time, as it frowned, in sullen majesty, on the surrounding scenery. It had, for centuries, been inhabited by ancestors of the present possessor, who were no less famous for their deeds in arms, than for their benevolence and hospitality. Their vassals were numerous, and, at the call of their laird, were ready to protect his rights with their lives, not for the fear they bore to him, but their love; for while, with the dignity of a baron, he made them remember he was their lord, he never, by severity, taught them to forget their respect for him as a man. About twenty years previous to the commencement of this period, he obtained the hand of Mabel Duncaethal, who was beautiful, accomplished, and sprung from a race as noble as her consort's. The laird, her father, had one foible, that somewhat obscured his many excellent qualities, an immoderate share of ancestorial pride; he doated on his son, the twin-brother of Mabel, as he hoped he would transmit his name to posterity: but Heaven ordained it otherwise—for when he went forth to repel a chieftain with whom his father had commenced hostilities, he fell in battle, and crushed at once the hopes and life of his unhappy father: nor did he alone sink by the weight of grief—the lovely Agnes Maclean, an orphan who had been reared under the protection of his sire, loved him; and when the fatal news arrived that he was slain, she sunk into a profound melancholy—the rose of her cheek gave place to the lily, as she "Sat, like Patience on a monument, smiling at grief."

Long had she loved the youth Alexander, and he returned her passion with all the glowing ardour of a first affection; but when his father heard of his ignoble passion, as he termed it, he treated it with ridicule; and when he found that had no effect, he bade him forget her, or he would cast him out, an alien to his blood; for though he loved him so passionately, he could not give him such a proof as to admit a union with an orphan obscure and poor.

The amiable and lovely Agnes had been placed under the care of the baron by her father, a descendant of the house of Maclean, when on his deathbed: she was the only fruit of an inauspicious marriage; her birth sent her mother to an early grave, and her father survived her but five years. The baron brought home his little charge, and had her placed under his immediate eye, with his own daughter, who was three years more advanced in age. As they grew up, they loved each other with the affection of sisters; Mabel often said she felt not less affection for Agnes than her brother; and Alexander looked upon both equally as his sisters; till age taught him the difference of the sensations he felt for the ward of his father, and those he felt for Mabel: long did he struggle with his growing passion, until he found it in vain, when gaining courage from desperation, he ventured to declare it to his father, when the confession was received in the manner already related. Though the baron was not blind to the good qualities of Agnes, but as Alexander was the heir of his name and titles, he had other views, and hoped to unite him to the heiress of Cathloda, who was equal, not to say superior, in the pride and wealth of ancestry.

While he was thus endeavouring to realize his hopes, Alexander was indulging in all the melancholy of despairing love. About this period the castle was visited by Bosmora, who, being struck with the beauty of Mabel, offered her his hand, which was accepted with joy on the part of her father, and becoming modesty on hers. All was now hilarity and mirth in the castle, save in the breasts of Agnes and Alexander; the ancient halls resounded with songs of the minstrels, as, with flying fingers, they kissed the golden strings of the lyre, and chaunted an epithalamium in honour of the nuptials of Bosmora and the peerless Mabel; who, at the end of a short time, left Duncaethal for the castle of her lord.

A few weeks after, her brother was slain in battle, as before premised. At the commencement of her father's illness, Mabel was sent for to the castle; and, upon his demise, she would fain have conducted Agnes to Bosmora, as Duncaethal now fell to a far-distant branch of the family, and the succeeding heir had arrived to take possession of his rights; but on his signifying he should absent himself for a few weeks, she requested permission to remain for a short time, as she wished to indulge the poignancy of her grief in solitude. Mabel acquiesced, after a promise of her following in a few days.

In the meantime, the former was recovering gradually her usual spirits; for though she tenderly loved her father and brother, she was not of a disposition to mourn beyond measure for what was without remedy. She found in Bosmora a truly tender husband, which contributed to the mitigation of her sorrows, and compensation of her losses; and she looked anxiously forward to that blissful period when she was to produce a living pledge of their mutual affection; though her anticipated joy was severely checked by learning the loss of Agnes, who, in a short excursion into the fields, was precipitantly thrown from her palfrey, who had taken fright from the rushing of a flight of birds, into a roaring flood which flowed near the castle, and met with a premature death. Many tears were shed for the hapless fate of her friend, till Heaven sent her consolation in the being of a lovely son, which weaned her from her sorrows, to taste the most transcendant joys of maternal love.

The castle now echoed with shouts and joyous acclamations, with which the numerous vassals greeted the birth of their future laird; but scarcely had six months elapsed, ere all mirth was converted into grief, by the sudden death of their anxious hope, the new-born heir; the unhappy mother was almost frantic, while the father, though less violent, felt equal sorrow; and summoning all his philosophy, endeavoured to bear his loss with a pious resignation.

At the expiration of a few months, Mabel again proved pregnant; the baron's hopes were once more revived, and he looked forward to the rapturous period with joy undisguised: but, alas! how often human hopes of happiness terminate in sorrow; and we oft anticipate, as the greatest blessing, what, in the end, may prove a curse; thus it was with the baron. While he was fondly indulging the hope of having an heir to his name, he forgot the attendant dangers—what, then, was his distraction, at seeing the death of the lovely and most truly affectionate of wives, in bringing into the world a daughter!—he was frantic and despairing by turns; nor could he be brought to look upon the innocent cause of grief, then so poignantly felt; but shut himself in his apartment, and would see no one except his servant Andrew.

He engaged attendants for the care of his infant daughter, and appropriated the east wing of the castle for her particular use.

Several years passed on in the same gloomy and monotonous manner, when one day, as the baron was crossing the corridor leading to his apartment, he suddenly met his daughter led by her nurse; glancing instantly his eyes upon her infantile countenance, a thousand new and tender emotions were raised in his heart, by her strong likeness to her mother; he caught her in his arms, and, for the first time, imprinted upon her cheek a father's kiss; then took her into his chamber, where her innocent prattle amused, and yet, at times, distressed him, as she would oft make observations which reminded him of her mother's loss. He, however, from this day, grew as fond of her society as he had before avoided it, nor would scarce suffer her to be a moment from his presence; she repaid his affection by a thousand puerile endearments.

As she advanced in age, her necessary tuition would sometimes deprive him of her company, but he felt the loss repaid by her rapid progress in all the studies and accomplishments which adorn her sex.

At the time when she arrived at the age of fifteen years, walking one day in the adjacent forest, and approaching too near a river, which with rapidity sought its course, by quickly turning round to speak to her maid, she lost her equilibrium, and was plunged into the foaming deep; a loud shriek burst from the lips of her terrified attendant, as she looked round in vain for assistance, and seeing no one, left her hapless mistress to her fate. Hastening towards the castle, the first person she saw was Andrew, to whom, as fast as terror would permit, she recounted the dreadful accident; but ere she had finished, her loud sobs attracted the attention of the baron, who, on learning his daughter's dreadful fate, was rushing towards the spot, when he perceived a youth of about seventeen, bearing in his arms the object of his solicitude. He received the insensible form of Matilda, and conveyed her into the castle, where, by proper applications, she was soon restored to her senses, to the great joy of her father.

After a shower of tears, in which she recalled the danger that had passed, she inquired for the youth who had delivered her from her perilous situation; this reminded the baron, that he had failed to reward, or even to thank him for his intrepidity; he now summoned Andrew, and inquired the name of the noble-minded boy, who had saved his daughter's life at the extreme hazard of his own.

"'Tis Donald, so please you, my lord," says Andrew.

"Donald," replied the baron; "and who is he?"

"He is the son of Allen and Jannet, your vassals, who dwell in the white cottage hard by the glen."

"Call him to me," said the baron.

"I will, your honourable lordship," answered Andrew, and immediately left the apartment for that purpose. The baron then ordered the attendants of his daughter to convey her instantly to bed, and seating himself on a couch, waited, with some degree of interest, for the youth's appearance. In the course of a few minutes, Andrew tapped gently at the door, when being desired to enter, he came in, leading by the hand the young peasant.

"Well, young stranger," said the baron, "you have done a brave and gallant action—accept of this as a small token of my gratitude;" at the same time presenting him a purse of gold; which the youth declined, with a graceful bow, apologizing, at the same time, for his refusal, by saying—"My lord, I have done but my duty; I should have acted the same, had it been one of my fellow-vassals, where I was sure of no reward, save the heartfelt satisfaction of having saved a fellow-creature's life; then how much more must my joy be augmented, in preserving the daughter of our noble laird!"

While he delivered thus his sentiments, the baron gazed on him in the greatest surprise; that a poor peasant boy should, when offered, refuse a purse of gold, was, to him, the source of the highest admiration, and that, added to the language which he uttered when declining it, made him conclude he had received somewhat more than a common education.—"Are you the son of Allen and Jannet?" interrogated the baron.

"I am, my laird," replied the boy.

"Wonderful! there are few young men possess your generous ideas; pray who has instilled into your mind such exalted sentiments?"

"If my sentiments are indeed exalted," says he, while a modest blush suffused his cheek, "I am indebted for them to Father Peter, of the convent of St. Andrew; he has, gratuitously, been my instructor, as my parents were too poor to procure for me that knowledge for which I am beholden to his great good-nature; therefore, my laird, if my actions indeed merit the high encomiums you are pleased to bestow, they are due to him who taught me to *know* myself, and love my fellow-creatures."

The baron grew more and more astonished as he contemplated the animated countenance of the speaker; for when he mentioned the name of Father Peter, a tear trembled in the corner of his eye, as, with enthusiasm in his voice and manner, he endeavoured to express the gratitude which he owed him.—"How old are you?" asked the baron.

"Seventeen, my laird," replied Donald.

"It is a pity you should pass your life in the seclusion of a cottage—is it your choice? are you content?" reiterated the baron.

"I wish to bear arms in the service of my country, and would fain leave home to fight the battles of our sovereign; but my fond parents will not consent to it."

"If you can gain their permission, you shall reside in the castle, and be the knight of Matilda, and guard that life which you have so gallantly saved."

Donald dropped on his knee; surprise and joy deprived him of speech, as he respectfully raised the hand of the baron to his lips.

"Spare your thanks—I see what you would utter; receive this ring, and remember, from this time, your name shall be enrolled with the warriors. Andrew shall instruct you in feats of chivalry; and when your studies are complete, you shall depart from Bosmora to the wars, in a manner worthy thy brave and noble spirit."

After endeavouring to express his thanks, Donald arose and left the room; then, swift as the winged arrow from an archer's bow, he sought the cottage of his parents, to whom he recounted the morning's wondrous adventure. Allen and Jannet listened with surprise and wonder, the latter frequently thanking the Virgin for the good fortune of her darling son; and after receiving their benedictions, he left their humble roof for one more suitable to his noble aspiring mind.

Chapter III

Arise, black Vengeance, from th'unhallow'd cell!
Yield up, oh Love! thy crown and hearted throne
To tyrannous hate! Swell, bosom, with thy fraught.
For 'tis of aspic's tongues!

Oh, blood! blood! blood!

Shakespeare.

THE BELL AT THE CONVENT of St. Andrew had chimed the hour of vespers, when Father Peter received a message, desiring his attendance at the castle on the following morning; he was the confessor of the baron, and the latter wished to make some inquiries respecting the youth he had taken under his protection. Upon his arrival, he related many circumstances, which tended to exalt the boy still higher in the favour of Bosmora. When he was departing for the convent, as he crossed the court-yard of the castle, he was accosted by Donald, who had now thrown off his peasant's guise, and appeared in a dress worthy of his exaltation; the father was surprised; he scarcely, at the first glance, recognised his pupil, such an advantage did he derive from his present habiliments, which consisted of a kilt of rich plaid, and a tartan plaid which hung pendant from his shoulder, and, with various folds, encircled his graceful form; on his head he wore a bonnet of Saxon green, on which nodded a plume of black feathers, that gave a shade to his open brow; a girdle of glossy jet leather buckled round his waist, firom which a sword of curious workmanship was suspended, gave a martial appearance to the garb of the beautiful youth. The father contemplated him with tears of joy, as he entertained for him a real affection, almost equal to a parent's; many admonitions did he offer in regard to his future conduct, all of which were received with humble respect and attention by Donald.

A series of time now passed on, without any change in his fortune, save that he grew more in favour with his lord; nor did the fair Matilda view him with an impartial eye; at first she felt for him only gratitude as the preserver of her life; but it soon ripened into a more tender affection, an affection which she dared not confess even to herself.

At the period when she attained her eighteenth year, the baron gave a fête in honour of the event. Numerous lords and ladies assembled at Bosmora on the occasion; among others came Duncaethal, who, since the death of the baroness, had travelled to distant countries, and had but lately arrived at his inheritance, the castle, bringing with him his beautiful lady, the heiress of Monteith. They were welcomed with the usual hospitality of the baron, though he recalled many unpleasant recollections into, his breast by his presence, as the last time he had beheld him was on the death of his lamented lady's noble father, by which he became possessed of the name and fortunes of Duncaethal.

The manner of this chief checked all familiar intercourse; his face wore a gloomy and ferocious appearance; his form, though noble and commanding, was to be remarked more for an air of unbending pride, than any natural dignity. His lady, Margaret, was his counterpart in mind, as she also resembled him somewhat in person; her features were strictly beautiful, though masculine, and ill suited the air of languor which she endeavoured to assume; her piercing black eyes seemed more calculated to command homage, than win admiration; and her person, though at once dignified and elegant, was rather above the common stature;—such she was at the time she paid her first visit to the heiress of Bosmora.

The morning of Matilda's natal day was proclaimed by the songs of minstrels, while the beautiful object of these rejoicings was discovered on an exalted seat, by the right hand of her father; on his left was lady Margaret. There could not be a greater contrast than that exhibited in the appearance of those noble females; a rich bandeau of rubies, set in gold, confined the hair of the latter; while a crimson velvet robe, embroidered with gold, and fastened with rich jewels, gave more than usual dignity to her appearance: Matilda wore a pale blue vest, confined round her sylph-like form by a cestus of pearls; a tiara of the same encircled her arched brow; while her auburn tresses waved on her shoulders in graceful ringlets; her arms were bare, except bracelets of the richest pearl, which were only to be rivalled in whiteness by the snowy skin of the wearer, which they were meant to adorn.

The harpers, at an appointed signal, struck their instruments, and, with inspiring voices, chaunted the following words:—

Hail, flow'r of great Bosmora's race!
Hail, Matilda, young and fair!
In our peerless lady's praise
We chaunt the loud inspiring air.

May she all her days possess
Her mother's beauty—spotless fame;
And her great sire shall ever bless
The fair descendant of his name.

Chaunt still louder, louder praise!
In beauty's cause the song we raise:
Ceaseless honour—endless fame,
Crown Bosmora's mighty name!

At noon the company withdrew to an elegant saloon erected for the occasion, in the eastern wing of the castle; there, seated in a balcony, they were to behold the dexterity of the youths who were about to try their skill in feats of archery. The ladies Matilda and Margaret had the office of presenting the prizes to the victors. The first who approached to claim his reward, was Malcolm, heir of Ross. Matilda, who was to present the first prize, involuntarily heaved a sigh, as she had secretly hoped the victor would have proved Donald.

After the congratulating shouts the spectators raised in honour of the young champion had subsided, the second in skill advanced, and she had the mortification of beholding, at the feet of lady Margaret, Donald himself, who gracefully knelt to receive from her hands the prize due to his skill—it was a beautiful rosary, from which was suspended a rich cross of St. Andrew; an indefinable sensation disturbed her breast, as she saw him gallantly press the gift to his lips; and it was the more augmented, when she beheld the looks of admiration with which he was regarded by lady Margaret; her heart sickened, and she anxiously longed for the commencement of the masque, which was to conclude the festivities of the day.

At the end of the banquet, the visitors retired to assume the characters they intended to represent; when the pavilion being thrown open, glistened with a thousand lights, and admitted the motley group. Donald was arrayed as a knight of St. Andrew, and wore the cross he had received from lady Margaret; he could nowhere distinguish, amongst the crowd of beauties which thronged through the place, the beloved object of his soul, the fair Matilda, and withdrawing to an unoccupied corner of the pavilion, watched anxiously for her appearance. He had not remained long in this situation, when he heard his name pronounced in a low voice, and looking round, perceived, at the left of him, a tall figure, enveloped in a long cloak of plaid. "Follow me, youth!" said the stranger; and instantly issuing from the entrance, and turning into a dark walk overshadowed with trees, suddenly disappeared.

Donald, for a moment, was irresolute, when curiosity gaining the preponderance of caution, he followed his mysterious guide, who proceeded, by a circuitous route, to the left entrance of the castle, and beckoning him to advance, entered an apartment appropriated to the use of some of the visitors, but to whom was to him unknown.

His conductor now being seated on a couch, seemed, for a moment, at a loss to disclose the purport of this nocturnal meeting. In the mean time, Donald remained standing by the entrance of the door, which the stranger had secured: at length the latter seemed to be making a powerful effort to overcome sensations which were evidently painful, and turning to Donald, desired him to be seated, at the same time motioning him to take part of the couch. The stranger then continued—"You are, no doubt, in surprise, at my bringing you here; and perhaps, when I discover who has thus far forgot the dignity of birth, to gain an interview with one unknown, it may be converted into contempt; and yet it lies in your, and only *your* power, to ease the torments of a heart become a burthen to the bosom it inhabits."

The voice of the unknown became agitated with contending emotions, while the sympathizing Donald replied—"Oh, stranger, if it is in the power of so poor a youth as I to allay the sorrows you struggle with, I should feel happy; freely would I sacrifice my life to save a fellow-creature's, nor ever did their miseries by me meet with contempt!"

"'Tis well," said the unknown, "and disguise is no longer necessary;" at the same time throwing up the slouch bonnet –which had concealed her face, and casting aside the cloak which had covered her dress, arrayed in an elegant habit, stood before the astonished eyes of Donald the lady Margaret Duncaethal; his amazement was increased tenfold, when he heard her unblushingly declare for him a passion, forgetful of her own and her husband's honour.

With all the uprightness becoming a man, he withstood the temptation—exhorted her to banish from her breast so guilty a passion, and reminded her of the duty due to her noble lord. She regarded him not, but bent on him ardent looks of love; and finding him still remain cold and inflexible, vengeance flashed from her dark eyes—then endeavouring to stifle the revenge which agitated her bosom in convulsive throbs, burst into a flood of tears. He now endeavoured to sooth and calm her perturbation, when recovering in some degree, she earnestly requested him never to divulge the purpose of the meeting.

"If that will give you any satisfaction, you may firmly rely that I never shall."

"Nay, but swear to me," she urged.

"By what oath would you have me bind myself?" asked Donald.

"Swear to me, by the honour of the knighthood you now bear, upon any occasion whatever, to mortal ears never to mention this meeting!"

"I solemnly swear that I never will!" said he; and raising the cross he then wore to his lips, imprinted upon it a kiss to ratify the vow.

"I am now secure," she exultingly replied; "you dare not break your oath—full well I know you dare not violate it!"

Horrid passions combated in her breast, while her dark features were distorted with marks of vengeance, as, with a tight grasp, she held him by the arm: in dreadful sounds she exclaimed—"Learn, thou proud upstart, that, in rejecting my proffered love, thou hast aroused my bitter hate; and from this moment I will prove thy direst foe, for I will revenge myself for the slight thou hast offered me, in a way that shall rend thy heart-strings, and make thee curse the hour in which you first beheld me! Full well know I the cause of this insult—love for another! Matilda! she is the object of thy *chaste* adoration! Heavily will I wreak on her all my vengeance, and when in vain you seek to save her from destruction, in bitterness of soul you shall utter—'This is the revenge of a disappointed woman, who will not bear an insult with impunity!'"

Her ravings now became so loud, that he was fearful lest she should be overheard by Duncaethal, whose apartment was contiguous, and possibly he might then be within, as he had sent an apology for being unable to attend the masque, by reason of a sudden indisposition. Donald ventured to expostulate, and expressed his fears of her exposing herself to the rage of her lord.

"Thou shallow boy," said she, "dost thou foolishly think that Margaret ever acts by halves? think thou I should venture to procure this interview, if I had not been certain of being free from interruption, and still worse, the interruption of a hated husband?—follow me, and be a witness of my security."

She now led him into the adjoining chamber, where, in a deep sleep, lay Duncaethal, unconscious of his dishonour. Donald was going to recede, but holding him by the arm, with a frowning look of contempt, she exclaimed—"*Coward!* what, art thou afraid to approach, when thou seest no terror mark my cheek? he shall not wake till I command!" then lowering her voice—"and if I will it so, he shall sleep for ever!—Now begone! and learn from this, that I have both the will and power to execute my threats!" Thus saying, she led him to the entrance, and closing the outer door, in a voice that struck to his heart, bade him *remember his oath!*

Donald could scarcely believe but that all he had been a witness of was only the effervescence of an imagination proceeding from an oppressed mind; but as the sound of the last words of Margaret, sounding in his ears, recalled to him the remembrance of the dreadful threats she had vowed against the innocent

Matilda, and though he would fain persuade himself that she would not dare to put them in practice, yet it cast upon his mind a gloom, which he in vain endeavoured to dispel.

In the mean time, the idol of his soul was endeavouring to account for the reason of his absence from the entertainment, which was on the point of concluding, when he again entered the pavilion, where he beheld the lovely Matilda habited as a nun, (a character she had assumed by reason of its requiring so little spirit to support, being a stranger to that gaiety with which she was surrounded).

Donald now approached, and, in a voice of tender solicitude, inquired if he should conduct her to her apartment, as she appeared unwell? when giving him an assenting smile, and presenting her hand, he proceeded with her to the door of her antichamber, and then gracefully bowing, retired.

Matilda had not been there many minutes, ere she was attended by her woman, Venella, who, perceiving her mistress look pale, inquired if she was ill?

"Rather indisposed," replied the former. "Go to the baron, and inform him that I have retired for the night."

"I will, my lady," said the latter, and withdrew for that purpose.

On the departure of her maid, Matilda relapsed into a train of thoughts but little calculated to tranquillize her troubled spirits. Her reverie was interrupted by Venella, who returned with the baron's and complimentary wishes of the guests for her recovery; which, when she had delivered, with a look of vast importance, and in a tone of half whisper, said—"You know, my lady, you asked me, when you was dressing for the masque, if I had seen sir Donald. I had not seen him then. Madam, but I have since—and where do you think it was, my lady?"

"Nay," said Matilda, as she listened, with the greatest emotion to the chattering Venella, "I know not."

"Why, my lady, he was in the apartment of lady Margaret."

"Impossible!" said Matilda; "what should he do there?"

"Ah, my lady," said Venella, "that's what I should like to know myself. I would not have the sins of some folks to answer for—no, not for that beautiful blue robe I put on your ladyship to-day."

Matilda could scarcely help smiling at the conclusion of this speech of her attendant, though she endeavoured to check her free observations on the lady Duncaethal, by saying she must have mistaken some one else for Donald.

"What! does your ladyship think," said Venella, "that I have lived all these years in the same place, and not know him when I see him?—why, my lady, I should have known him in the dark—and besides, he had on that fine beautiful cross he won to-day by shooting at the mark—the one which lady Margaret herself hung round his neck. Ah! she looked then just for all the world as if she was in love with him;—I thought so, and it seems I thought right.—Ah, said I to myself—"

"Silence, I desire you!" exclaimed Matilda.

"Why, holy Virgin! my lady, do you think sir Donald would have gone if he had not been sent for?—No, I am sure he would not; and I saw lady Margaret her own self lead him to the door; she had a taper in her hand, and laying her arm upon his, she said something to him—what it was, I don't know, but I thought to myself, at the time, it was no good, and so—"

"And pray where did you behold all this without being seen yourself?" inquired Matilda, wishing to find the tale untrue, and yet she felt inwardly convinced there was no mistake on the part of Venella.

"Where did I see it, my lady! why I was going through the garden, to take a peep at the fine doings that were going forward in the pavilion, when I heard someone open the door of lady Margaret's chamber; so I stepped behind a pillar of the corridor; I should not have done this, only that I saw sir Donald, and I thought I should hear what he said; but for once I was out in my reckoning, for he never said one single word—no, not one, but walked through the garden; why I was close behind him, my lady, and saw him come up and speak to you, and then lead you to the castle; why, my lady, I wondered to myself how he dared come to a lady so chaste, and so beautiful, and so handsome as yourself, when he knew he had just visited that good-for-nothing, shameless, and—"

"Peace!" said Matilda; "you forget you are talking of my relation."

"Why then, my lady, don't she behave like you? would you have had a man in your chamber at midnight?—no, my lady, that you would not: besides, she has a husband; and though my lord Duncaethal does look so fierce, he is a handsome man: besides, what matters if he is a little older than his lady?—you know he is a baron, which argufies a great deal, my lady; for though we are all ordered by your ladyship's honourable father to call the son of old Allen and Jannet *sir* Donald, yet he is *but* the son of Allen and Jannet; therefore I think the lady Margaret the more to blame, my lady: now if it had been a lord, or an earl, indeed, why it would not be half so shameful; but to act as she has done with a poor peasant, 'tis very shameful indeed—don't you think so, my lady?"

"What then," said Matilda, "you would not think her conduct blamable if Donald had been a lord?—oh, fie, Venella!"

"Oh no!" stammered she; "but I meant if she had not been already married, my lady."

Matilda smiled at the confusion which she perceived in the countenance of her loquacious attendant, who remained silent till she was asked if she had mentioned this affair to any one else?

"No, my lady, not to no living soul: why I have seen no one but the baron your father, and your ladyship is sure I should not mention it to him."

"Then," said Matilda, "you would oblige me very much, by never hinting the subject to any one."

"That I am sure I will not, my lady, if you desire it, for perhaps my lord Duncaethal might call sir Donald to account, for being alone with his lady at that time o'night; now it is a chance if he could account for it, much to his own credit, or to lady Margaret's either—therefore, my lady, it will be best to say no more about it, though I am sure I need not be silent for the sake of sir Donald, for he never said a civil thing to me in his life—no never! so I am sure I have no occasion to like him."

"Why I thought I often heard you say you had a great affection for me," said Matilda.

"Oh, the Virgin! and so I have, St. Andrew be my witness!—but I did not know because I loved you, my dear lady, I was obliged to love sir Donald too."

"You seem to forget," said Matilda, piqued at the remark of her attendant, "that sir Donald saved my life, when, walking with you, I unfortunately fell into the stream, and must inevitably have perished, but for the intrepidity of him you speak of so slightingly."

"I speak slightingly! Oh, St. Andrew forbid! no, indeed, not I. To be sure, I forgot—yes, my lady, he did indeed save your ladyship's life, when I was terrified out of my wits, and left you, to run to the castle for assistance; but you would have been lost, my lady, ere I could return, but for sir Donald, who was returning from the convent of St. Andrew, and was just passing the old oak, when he heard my screams, and I believe he called to me, but I was so frightened, that I dared not look back. Then, to be sure, it was very brave of him to jump into the water, for all the world just like Juno the great dog but then he knew he could swim: then, my lady, old Andrew scolded me for leaving you, to run so far as the castle—but what could I do? I saw no one near; and if I had jumped in after you, my lady, and caught you by the robe, which I at first thought of doing, I remembered me I could not swim, therefore we should have both gone to the bottom together;—so, in spite of what Andrew said, I think I showed better judgment in flying to the castle; don't you think so, my lady?"

"A very safe one, at least," replied Matilda, smiling.

"Oh, as to that, my lady, if I had been sure of saving your ladyship's life, I would have done my best; but as I knew that was impossible, why I thought it would do no good to drown myself too."

"Very true," said Matilda, who, in spite of the depression under which she laboured, could not refrain indulging in a fit of laughter, at the wise rhetoric of her attendant, whom she now desired to assist in undressing her, and then dismissed her for the night.

Matilda, now left to herself, recalled to herself the wonderful communication made by her attendant, whose veracity she could no longer doubt; now did she fatigue her mind with fruitless conjectures of the purpose for which the visit of Donald could be made to the chamber of Margaret in that mysterious manner, and at that secret hour of night, when the castle was supposed to be entirely evacuated, all the company being assembled in the pavilion; in vain did she endeavour to find some plausible pretext for this conduct; she would have given worlds to have cleared her breast of the painful suspicions with which it laboured; but after a long time spent in ruminating to no purpose, she was obliged to conclude her reflections, very little in favour of the honour of lady Margaret.

Morpheus now cast over her his somniferous veil, and she awoke not till a late hour the next day.

Chapter IV

Ha! soft!—'twas but a dream;
But then so terrible, it shakes my very soul;
Cold drops of sweat hang on my trembling flesh;
My blood grows chilly, and I freeze with horror!

Shakespeare.

DONALD RETIRED TO BED as soon as he had left Matilda, but not to rest; no sooner had he closed his eyes, than horrid images flitted across his imagination—the fiend-like looks of lady Margaret, with her dreadful vows of revenge; sometimes he beheld Matilda in the grasp of her unrelenting enemy, calling for his aid in vain; for when he would have flown to her rescue, an unknown power rivetted him to the spot; he then beheld the keen poniard pierce her snowy bosom, and her soft blue eyes closed in eternal sleep.

A deathlike shiver pervaded his whole frame, as he endeavoured to shake off the poppy influence which reigned over his senses; then starting from his couch, repaired to the window of the apartment, and opening the casement, the picturesque view which met his eye in some measure caused the perturbation of his spirits to subside: to his left arose the lofty hills of Cheviot, meeting the first kiss of the ruddy goddess, as she peeped forth from her rosy chamber—it was a fine clear morning, and her disk appeared a bright orb, darting forth rays of refulgent glory, the radiant brightness of whose splendour confounded the curious eye which would discover the spots philosophers maintain are on that heavenly luminary; flocks innumerable cropped the grassy carpet of nature, and, by their gambols, seemed to greet the opening day with that gratitude to the Omnipotent, too often neglected by the part of the creation he has stamped with his own godlike image, and endowed with the divine attribute of reason, and pour forth their thanks to the great Dispenser of all things.

Donald now closing the casement, prepared to attire himself, and walk forth to enjoy more fully the beauties of the morn; he strolled towards the cottage of his parents, as the duties which he owed them he never failed to pay. In his way he passed by the spot where he had rescued Matilda from a watery grave; the feelings of delight rushed into his breast, as he praised the dispensation of that Providence who had made him the instrument of preservation to that lovely maid. A horrid idea now rushed across his imagination, as the recollection of lady Margaret again obtruded itself.—"And have I," exclaimed he, "preserved the most lovely of her sex from a fate like this, to meet a still worse from the unjust rage of a fiendlike woman, the disgrace of herself and her lord—forgetful of the sacred ties of honour and religion! Shall she presume to rule the destiny of the angelic Matilda! no; perish such a thought! I will instantly unfold the—" He started; for, as he raised his hand, in an energetic manner, it came in contact with the cross he wore suspended from his breast, and seemed to say, in a language more powerful than speech—"Remember your oath!" His blood ran cold, large drops bedewed his brow, and his trembling limbs could scarce support him, as, in a low voice, he said—"Yes, I must be silent;" and recalling his scattered spirits, he proceeded to the cottage, and was redeemed with all the parental tenderness the authors of his being never failed to express.

When Jannet, for the first time, beheld that beautiful cross—"Oh, holy Virgin! where did you get that? Look," said she to Allen, whose eyes were also rivetted on it, "if that is not the very jewel which—"

A forbidding look from her husband stopped her prattle, to the disappointment of Donald, who asked if she had ever seen the jewel before?

"Not that I know of; for, now I look again, it is not the same I thought: but how did you come by it, son?" again asked she.

He now explained the means by which he possessed it. "Oh, holy Virgin! that ever I should live to see you excel all the young knights in feats of archery! So pale and thin as you looked, when I saw you with that cross hung on your neck, and—"

"Silence!" said her husband, angrily; "hast forgot what thou art talking of?"

"I believe I have," said Jannet, in confusion. Donald, all this time, stood in the greatest surprise, but as he saw his father wished to drop the subject, he forbore further question; though Jannet's unguarded words aroused his curiosity, and he was determined, at a fit opportunity, to find out the meaning to which she alluded.

He soon after took his leave, and returning to the castle, arrived just as the company were sitting down to their morning repast. At table he beheld the lady Margaret; when he perceived her gentle demeanour, and heard the languid tone of her well-modulated voice, he could scarce persuade himself it was the same being, who, by the violence of her passions, had caused him so much uneasiness. While these thoughts passed, in quick succession, across his mind, and he was gazing at the object who had caused them, he turned and beheld the lovely eyes of Matilda earnestly rivetted on him; as soon as she perceived herself observed, she withdrew them in the greatest confusion; a vermilion tint heightened the colour of her cheek, as, quickly turning, she addressed some question to her father, at whose side she was seated. Lady Margaret paid her more than common attention, like the concealed snake, that waits a proper opportunity only to sting the deeper. Secretly did Donald rejoice, as he heard Duncaethal name the following day for their departure; and when Bosmora, in the voice of friendship, requested their longer stay, earnestly did he pray the invitation might not be accepted; his wishes were propitious, for he heard Duncaethal say he had business which could no longer be delayed, and turning to his domestic, bade him make preparation for the journey.

Heavily did the hours lag on till that period arrived, when Donald, with a joyful heart and ready hand, assisted lady Margaret to mount the steed which was to convey her from Bosmora.

What a weight was lifted from his heart, when he once more saw the castle free from visitors! Now did he again enjoy the sweet society of Matilda, either by rambling in the adjacent forest, or, when seated by her father, she charmed his enraptured ear, by playing, with a skilful hand, harmonious strains upon the sweet-sounding lute. Often, in their walks, was she on the point of breaking into the subject of his visit to lady Margaret, but the words died upon her lips, as an innate shame prevented her utterance; and, at length, she almost forgot the occurrence, as she felt convinced Donald could not be guilty of any action base or dishonourable.

Several months passed on with the usual serenity, when one evening a messenger arrived at the castle, with information that the father of Donald lay apparently at the point of death. The youth flew, in the greatest agitation, towards his parent's cottage, and, sinking on his knees by the side of the bed, on which sat the weeping Jannet, he seized the hand of his father, and pressed it fervently to his lips, as the quick tears that chased each other down his cheeks deprived him of the power of utterance.

"My son," said Allen, "I feel the approach of death; and I cannot depart in peace, till I have disclosed a secret on which your future welfare must, in a great measure, depend; for I never so easily should have given my consent to your residing at the castle, had I not thought you had some claim to the exaltation which, by our noble baron's munificence, you now possess; for know that I have no natural claim to your duty—you are not my son!"

"Not your son!" said Donald. "Oh, my father! then will you, on your deathbed, disown me?—you surely are my sire; for since my earliest days, you have tenderly loved me!"

"Indeed, dear youth, I am not," said Allen; "nor can I tell who are your parents; but whatever I know upon the subject shall not be concealed from you."

Donald now sat, with an attentive ear, while Allen proceeded in the following words.

"About twenty years since, I resided in a vale some miles distant from this place. One evening, as the rain poured down in torrents, the rushing waters from the hills overflowing all beneath, and tremendous peals of thunder shook the firmament, a loud knocking was heard at the door of our hut. 'The Holy Virgin protect the wretched being who is obliged to wander such a dreadful night as this!' said Jannet, and proceeding to the door, admitted a man, bearing in his arms a babe about a month old—I need not add you was that child. The stranger seemed almost sinking with fatigue, and delivering you into the arms of Jannet, who stood ready to receive you, requested lodging for the night.

'Marry! I have but sorry accommodation,' said I; 'but you shall have the best that I can afford.'

'Well, 'tis no consequence; for when I have quenched my thirst, and refreshed my limbs a little,' said he, 'I will pursue my journey'

'But you will not think of taking this poor babe out such a night as this?' said Jannet.

"The stranger considered a moment, then said—'Good woman, you appear affectionate—will you take this child to nurse? you shall be paid for it annually, receiving the first year in advance.'

"My wife looked at me with a beseeching eye; we had never been blessed with children, and that, together with the pity I felt for your helpless state, made me resolve to accept the proposal; when producing a well-stocked purse of gold, he put it in my hand, with a promise, that, at the end of the year, we should receive another, if you lived, which was rather doubtful, as you appeared sickly and declining: the stranger then kissing you, was about to depart, when a rich cross, which was fastened round your neck by a string of small beads, attracted his attention; he seemed to ruminate earnestly for a few moments, then quickly seizing the necklace, he separated the jewel from it, and bore it away with him; whether this was for fear it should, by any means, lead to a discovery of who you were, or that he was afraid to entrust such a valuable ornament in the hands of poor people like us, I know not, but *thought* the latter.

"In the mean time, you improved in health and beauty. The stranger expressed great satisfaction at your altered appearance, when he again came, which he did at the expiration of the promised time: he asked how we had accounted for your sudden appearance to our neighbours? We told him we had said you was the child of a distant relation of Jannet's. This did not seem to satisfy him, so fearful was he of a discovery; and he begged we would remove to a distant part, to rear you as our own, at the same time exacting from us an oath of inviolable secrecy, with a promise of a satisfactory and ample reward. We then left our dwelling and came to this cottage, which we let him know by my meeting him at a spot appointed for that purpose.

"Year after year rolled away, and we never saw or heard of the stranger more. We loved you as if you were indeed our son; and I often regretted that it was not in my power to give you learning equal to what I felt inwardly convinced your birth demanded:— how joyful was I then, when you gained a friend in father Peter, that good man who is now no more! I was many times on the point of disclosing the mystery concerning you unto him; but the remembrance of my oath, and the hope of once more seeing the stranger who had consigned you to my care, restrained me. Nineteen years have now elapsed; during that I have never again beheld him; then judge, my dear child, how great must have been my astonishment, when you visited us the morning after our young lady's birth-day, to behold on your neck the very cross which the stranger took from your infant bosom, when you was first entrusted to our care! I doubt not but you recollect the astonishment Jannet betrayed when it first met her wondering eye; and how it should come into the hands of lady Margaret, is a source of surprise, that only serves to convince me that I am right in my conjectures in supposing you are the offspring of some noble family, who, for unknown reasons, disclaim you, and withhold from you your rightful inheritance."

Allen now ceased, being quite overcome by the disclosure he had made to Donald, who sat quite absorbed with surprise and wonder; yet he could not help thinking they had made some mistake in regard to the ornament he had worn when they first beheld him, and the one presented him by lady Margaret; but he was determined to make inquiries, on his arrival at the castle, of the baron, who, he believed, had given the prize for her to present; but the illness of Allen would not allow him to leave the cottage that night, for he loved the old man with all the filial duty of a son, and therefore was determined to watch by his bedside during the night, as the aged Jannet was ill calculated to bear the fatigue.

Towards morning Allen fell into a slumber, and awoke, about noon, in a state of convalescence, to the great joy of Jannet and the affectionate Donald, who, soon as the glow of health appeared on his cheek, took his leave, to return to the castle, where, on his arrival, he requested a private audience of the bar-on, to whom he unfolded the wonderful relation which had been disclosed to him, at the same time producing the row of small beads, (as Allen had called them, and which, in reality, were fine pearls,) to corroborate the truth of what he had spoken. The baron listened with silent attention, and, at the conclusion, expressed his great surprise; but agreed with Donald in saying that Allen was mistaken in respect to the cross, which, he affirmed, had belonged to his late lady, the baroness, and, at the important period mentioned, was in the castle;—"Though," added he, "I have no doubt but that you are the descendant of some noble family, who, for selfish and unknown reasons, have thus shamefully deserted you: but be not dejected, sir Donald," added he, "for Heaven will, no doubt, one day or other, discover the mystery which envelopes you; and remember you have a friend and father in Bosmora."

"Oh, my lord," said the grateful youth, "you have indeed ever been a parent to me, when those on whom I had a natural claim cast me out, an alien wretched and forsaken!" A tear forced itself into the corner of his eye, as he continued—"Oh, may it one day be in my power to prove how gratefully the remembrance lives in my heart!"

At that instant a slight rap at the door announced the approach of some one, and, on its being opened, there entered the lovely Matilda. She blushed on beholding Donald, as she was unacquainted with his being in the castle; and when she perceived that he had been in earnest conversation with her father, was about to retire; but the baron requested her stay, and, on her being seated, he recounted to her the tale of Allen. During the recital, numberless sensations arose in her breast, the foremost of which was joy to think that her preserver was not the offspring of a peasant; and she flattered herself that if the veil which now obscured his origin was once removed, her father would gratify the hope she had long cherished in her bosom; for she was convinced that Donald long had loved her, and had only been restrained from declaring his passion, through the hopelessness of ever obtaining her hand, knowing that the baron, how much soever he might esteem him for his virtues, would never consent to bestow on a peasant's son the heiress of Bosmora.

CHAPTER V

I am too sore enpierced with his shaft
To soar with his light feathers, and so bound
I cannot bound a pitch above dull woe;—
Under love's heavy burden do I sink.

Shakespeare.

But let each bind on his mail, and each assume his
shield—let every sword be unsheath'd, for the foe returneth
in his strength.

Ossian.

MONTH AFTER MONTH PASSED ON, but still nothing occurred by which Donald could gain any clue by which he might come at the knowledge of his birth. Allen had perfectly recovered, and was each day visited by his son, as he still continued to call him, who, trusting in Providence to aid his cause, and bring to light the authors of his being, felt resigned to his fate, and once more recovered his usual serenity.

One night, as the castle-clock loudly announced the silent hour of midnight, a tremendous knocking at the gate alarmed its peaceful inhabitants. Old Andrew, repairing the portal, demanded who was there, and their business at that unreasonable hour?

"'Tis Dargo," answered a rough voice; "I have brought a packet for the baron, which must be immediately delivered."

Andrew, knowing the speaker to be one of Duncaethal's servants, unbarred the gate and instantly admitted him.

"I had been here by noon," says he, entering, "had it not been for the freaks of my horse; confound the jade! she took fright, and ran out of the way some miles with me, nor would have stopped till now, I suppose, if her career had not been arrested by a shepherd catching the reins. I was to have delivered this packet to the baron by noon, as I expect my lord Duncaethal will be here tomorrow."

"Lack-a-day!" said Andrew, "we shall be sadly harrassed for want of proper notice, as I suppose he will bring a score attendants with him."

"Not he, indeed; he does not want so many now, since he has lost his lady."

"Lost the lady Margaret!—why where is she gone?"

"Gone! why to the tomb of her ancestors."

"Oh, gramercy!" said the astonished Andrew; "what, is she dead?"

"Why dost think a lady of her spirit would go there while she was living? or, mayhap, you did not know her so well as I."

"Ah, Dargo, thou wert always a joking knave; but come in, and I will deliver your packet to my lord." Dargo now followed to the hall, where some remaining embers, which Andrew blew into a flame, and a flask of wine, which he placed on the table, made the former completely happy. The old man then repaired to the chamber of his lord, whom he found anxiously expecting him— "Now, Andrew, who is it?" said he.

"Marry, my lord, 'tis only Dargo; he has brought this packet for your honourable lordship; and the reason he came at this unseasonable hour, is because his horse ran away."

"Well," said the baron, "go and make him welcome, while I peruse this packet; and when he has refreshed himself, conduct him to a chamber."

"I will, your honourable lordship," said Andrew; and leaving the room repaired to the hall, where seating himself and filling Dargo a bumper, he said— "Do tell us where lady Margaret died, how long it is since, and of what complaint?"

"That I will, Andrew," said his companion, drinking off his bumper; "for I know you love to have your curiosity satisfied:—as to the when, why 'tis since you last saw her; as to the where, why in bed; and as to the how, why it was e'en by the stoppage of her breath."

"Pish!" said the disappointed Andrew; "why, thou madcap, canst not be serious for a moment?"

"Well then," said Dargo, "about four months since, she died of a disorder sudden as it was violent—a raging fever, which carried her off in a few hours; and of so malignant a nature, that my lady's confessor, a priest of the monastery near Duncaethal, would scarce suffer her to be approached by any but himself; and, soon as her eyes were closed, she was put into a coffin, and conveyed to Monteith by my lord, who saw her deposited in the tomb of her ancestors; when, after spending the last three months in mourning for his departed lady, he called me into the chamber yesterday, and put in my hands the packet which I brought tonight; but though he did not condescend to acquaint me with the contents, why I think I can partly guess: but come, let us have another cup of wine, for sorrow and talking together makes me thirsty."

"Ah, so it does me," said Andrew, filling up a goblet, and lifting it up, said—"Here's to the health of lady Matilda, my lord's daughter!"

When Dargo exclaimed—"I will pledge you—there's to the health of Matilda, my lady that is to be."

"What!" said Andrew, dropping the uplifted goblet, "is our baron's daughter to be your lady? Marry how?"

"Why by becoming the wife of my lord, to be sure," answered Dargo.

"Matilda the wife of your lord! that she will never be. Why dost think she'd marry a man old enough to be her father?—no, no!"

"That will be as her sire commands," said Dargo.

"And dost thou imagine my lord will ever command her to marry a man she does not love?—ah, you don't know him!"

"Not much of him," said the other; "and yet I think he will not refuse a powerful nobleman like my master."

"Powerful! who made him powerful? why the death of Matilda's uncle; for had it not been for the unfortunate end of Alexander, he never would have been lord of Duncaethal; previous to the possession of which he was poor enough, I believe, for he was of a very distant branch of the family; and if, after his son's death, the old baron had lived to have another heir, why it would never have been his."

"Ah well," said Dargo, "we shall soon see who's right; in the meantime, I wish you would let me lie down a little, as that jade of a horse has made me feel the effects of her mad ramble through the forest."

Andrew, now taking a taper, preceded Dargo to a chamber, and seeing him in bed, betook himself to his own, to finish his night's sleep.

Not so his lord; for the packet he had received from Duncaethal at once astonished and perplexed him—it contained an offer of himself and fortune to the fair Matilda; concluding with an intimation that he himself should follow in the morning to receive his answer personally: it was couched in language almost amounting to haughtiness. This irritated the baron, who was used to receive the most servile adulation from him, when formerly he wished to ingratiate himself into his favour. As yet, no one had ever presumed to offer themselves as candidates for the hand of the heiress of Bosmora, even in the most respectful manner; yet did this upstart lord, who was indebted to the family for the honours which he bore, disdaining solicitations, dare to proceed in terms which seemed to say—"I will not be refused!" The baron formed an instant resolution not to consent to this preposterous union, which was but at the best a sacrifice, in   consigning his young and lovely daughter to a man in age equal with himself. He had, moreover, often thought of presenting her hand to Donald, as he long observed a mutual passion between them, should the latter ever attain that elevated rank which he was inwardly convinced was his due by birth.

In the morning he sent for his daughter, and informed her of the death of lady Margaret, with the subsequent offer of Duncaethal; when a sudden flood of tears which gushed from her lovely eyes, and streamed down her now pallid cheek, convinced the baron of the repugnance she felt at the proposed union.

"My beloved Matilda," said he, taking her affectionately in his arms, "dry your tears: my dearest child, I did not say I had any intention to give Duncaethal hopes, or that I should to (I will not say) his solicitations, for he has almost dared to demand of me your hand; add to which, I think that you have not the least liking for him, but, if I mistake not, entertain a secret passion for another."

During this speech, he fixed on her a penetrating eye, while her lovely face underwent alternate changes from the rose to the lily: then hiding her blushing countenance, she convinced him that he was right in his conjectures; when pressing her with a parent's fond embrace, he thus continued—"'Tis Donald, my child, whom you love."

"Oh! my dear, honoured father!" dropped, in sounds almost inarticulate, from her trembling lips.

"Compose yourself, dear Matilda," added he; "I am not displeased with you; but tell me, has he ever made to you any professions of love?" As he spoke, a slight frown passed across his features, lest Donald had so far presumed upon his bounty and benevolence.

"Alas! no, my lord, it is utterly unknown to me whether he has ever thought of me at all, but with respect, as the daughter of his benefactor."

"'Tis well," said Bosmora; "I have, for a moment, wronged the noble-hearted youth; and yet, my child, I am convinced he tenderly loves you; I have long observed it, but cannot say the   discovery just made of your returning his passion at all offends me; for should he, by the goodness of Providence, ever be discovered and acknowledged by his race, I will not withhold my consent to your union; but while the least mystery involves him, and conceals his birth, I cannot, in respect that is due to mine, bestow on an unknown youth the heiress of Bosmora. The first opportunity that occurs, after the departure of Duncaethal, I shall make him acquainted with my sentiments in his favour; and, in the interim, I shall expect that your conduct will bear the usual marks of polite reserve towards him."

Matilda spoke not; a thousand tumultuous but grateful thoughts prevented her utterance, and respectfully taking the hand of her father, she pressed it to her lips; then flying to her apartment, threw herself on a couch, and, for a considerable length of time, indulged the most delightful sensations she had ever experienced.

Donald had risen at an early hour, and directly seeking out Andrew, with whom he was a great favourite, inquired the reason of the knocking at the castle-gate on the preceeding night, which had disturbed all its inhabitants?

"Oh," said Andrew, "what reason indeed! why a very pretty one, if you did but know all;— why would you believe, the lord Duncaethal is coming here to-day, to offer his hand to the lady Matilda—yes, indeed, to my dear young lady; and sent his servant forward with a packet to my lord, containing his intentions.—Oh that ever—"

"Impossible!" said Donald, interrupting him; "why he is already married!"

"He was, you mean, sir Donald," answered the other, "but the lady Margaret is dead."

"What did you say?" asked the latter. "Why I say that she is dead—defunct," replied Andrew, with a look of the greatest communication.

"Indeed!" said Donald; "how long since?" "Why," returned he, "Dargo says 'tis about four months since; and, marry, I think he must be main fond of matrimony, when he is in so great a hurry to marry again; but I think he had better seek elsewhere, for I am sure our sweet young lady will never be happy with such a man of his age—No, no! I know better than all that: I have not lived as long, but that I can tell what's what!"

"No," said Donald, as a heavy sigh escaped him, "the lovely Matilda was never formed to be the wife of a man like Duncaethal!"

"Ah, well," said Andrew, "perhaps my lord never may consent to give her hand to a man that she does not love—and I am sure she does not love him."

"Ah!" said the former, "how do you know, pray?"

"Why, marry, because I know who she does love, sir Knight;" at the same time fixing his eyes upon the face of his interrogator, and seeing the colour rush into his cheeks, he added—"Ah! and so do you, sir Donald!"

"Indeed I do not," said the still more confounded youth.

"Don't you? why then you can give a pretty shrewd guess," said the other. "Well, well! you saved her life; and though she is richer than you, yet her riches would have been of no use without life to enjoy them, and—"

"Andrew, you are mistaken," said Donald, earnestly, "if you suppose that—"

"Ah! ah! you are afraid that I should tell!—ah! ah! ah! marry, that will I not; but you must not think to deceive old Andrew; for though I am not in love myself, I can tell who is, and in those affairs I can see as far as most folks."

"I have the greatest respect in the world for your penetration, Andrew; in this, however, I repeat that you are mistaken," said he, emphatically.

"Ah! ah! go to, go to! I did not suppose you were such a novice as to kiss and tell. Ah! ah! when I was your age, I was a wag myself;" and went off, exulting in his skill of penetration, singing—"I once was young and gay, but now am old, &c." leaving Donald in the deepest vexation, fearful lest his garrulity should bring upon him the anger of the baron.

When he had in some degree recovered from the surprise which the strange intelligence just communicated had thrown him into, recollection brought to him the death of lady Margaret,   and he felt a sensation of pleasure, which he thought it impossible ever to experience in learning the loss of a fellow-creature; for though a long time had elapsed since the night she met him at the masque, he had not once forgot her horrid looks and fiendlike vows; nor did he ever pass near the fatal chamber, but that a cold shiver would run through his veins at the bare recollection.

He now sought his chamber, and in solitude ruminated on the morning's unwelcome intelligence; a heavy weight oppressed his spirits, as he found the hopes which he had so long cherished within his breast for ever crushed by the object of his soul's adoration becoming the wife of another.

A loud noise in the court-yard aroused him from the reverie into which he was plunged, and stepping towards the window, he perceived Duncaethal had already arrived, who, surrounded by a train of attendants, was making his way into the castle. "Oh!" faintly ejaculated Donald, "when he departs, he will bear away with him as his bride the angelic—the peerless Matilda! Oh, happy, enviable man! to enjoy a bliss which gods might envy, and the greatest monarchs contend for! while I, the unfortunate Donald have been prevented declaring my adoration, by the inexplicable veil my adverse fate has thrown on my birth! Oh! I had still remained happy, had I never beheld her lovely form; but to feel the dreadful pangs of secret love is more than I can bear. Oh Heaven! give me fortitude to endure those painful ills with a becoming resignation!"

Thus did he soliloquize, till the bell rang which summoned him to attend the banquet, in the saloon where sat Duncaethal on the right of Bosmora. When he entered, he expected the baron would arise from his seat, and present to him the future husband of Matilda; but no such movement being made, he fondly began to hope that he declined the offer of marriage made by Duncaethal; a thousand palpitations agitated his breast, which, by turns, felt the most lively hopes and the dreadful torture of despair. His fears were again aroused, when the latter broke the silence which prevailed, by saying—"My lord Bosmora, time wears apace, and I wish to receive your sentiments on the subject already proposed; will you grant me a private audience, or is sir   Donald so great a favourite, that you have no desire to conceal from him the purport of your intentions?"

The latter part of his speech was spoken in a tone so malevolent, that Donald, instantly rising from his seat, and bowing respectfully to the baron, requested permission to retire.

"You need not," said the latter, mildly, "as I will attend lord Duncaethal to a private apartment."

The two chiefs arose, and repairing to the study, Duncaethal impatiently demanded of the baron, if he consented to his proposal of the alliance between himself and Matilda? To which, in a voice of restrained anger, the latter replied—"My lord, the abrupt, not to say haughty, manner in which you first made the proposal, would almost determine me to refuse, even if it had met the acceptance of my daughter; but as she feels an utter objection, you will excuse me, if I say I must decline the honour you intend me."

"You refuse me then? 'tis well!" exclaimed the offended chieftain; "you then refuse me your daughter, to bestow her on an unknown?—I perceive your views— you would unite her to Donald—an outcast, as dishonourably born as the tale of his consignment to Allen false, which he has deceived you with, in hopes of your bestowing on him your daughter, and so enrich himself, with the old dotard who forged the lie, at the expence of your credulity: but, my lord Bosmora, do not suffer yourself to be imposed upon, which, if you will, beware how you refuse me! Now I again make the offer— beware!"

"How!" replied the baron; "beware!—beware of whom? and darest thou add threats to thy presumption? Know, thou proud lord, Bosmora can be as quick in resenting an injury as thou art in giving one; and, further, know I alike despise thy friendship or thy hate!" Then ringing the bell, he ordered Andrew, who attended, to summon Donald and his daughter to his presence, and turning to the enraged Duncaethal, continued—"Sooner would I give her to that *unknown wretch,* as you are pleased to term him, even if I was assured he was no other than the ofispring of a peasant, rather than link her to a man, who, from his pride or his passions, seems so little calculated to render her happy."

The door now opened, and he was interrupted by the appearance of his daughter, who entered the room with trembling apprehensions, fearing that Duncaethal had won her father over to his wish; she was closely followed by Donald, who imagined he was about to see the beloved object of his heart consigned for ever to the arms of another. "Ah!" mentally exclaimed he, "the baron little knows the feelings of this breast; for he is too noble to think of adding to my miseries, by making me a witness of a scene like this." What then could equal his joy and surprise, when Bosmora addressed him in the following words—"Approach, yoimg man; behold this maid, my daughter— the heiress of a noble house—receive her from my hand as your destined wife; take her, for she is yours: nor do I give her to you more to recompense your many virtues, than to convince this haughty lord that I defy his utmost malice."

Duncaethal hastily arose, rage sparkling in his eyes; and uttering the most dreadful threats of revenge, hastily left the castle.

Matilda and Donald cast themselves at the feet of the baron, to pour forth their gratitude, and receive from him his blessing, which he failed not to bestow, and then addressed them in the following manner—"My dear children, the conduct of the haughty lord Duncaethal has compelled me, in some measure, to adopt the method I have now taken; but I feel perfectly assured the high mind of Donald is too noble to wish to unite himself to my daughter, until he has obtained some clue to the mystery of his birth: in the meanwhile, until that period arrives, which I hope, through the help of Heaven, will not be far off, you have my permission to look upon Matilda as your destined bride; and I doubt not but that your future, as well as your past conduct, will merit that title. In the mean time, it will be necessary to adopt proper measures for repelling any attack which may be made on the castle; for I have no doubt that Duncaethal, from the threats he uttered, will commence a feud, to revenge the affront he supposes he has this day received; therefore it will be wisest, at all events, to put the castle in a state of defence."

He was interrupted by a billet from Duncaethal, in which he informed him that if he did not send his written consent by the following day, to prepare to meet him as his foe.

Orders were now issued to make speedy preparations for resistance; a centinel mounted the watch-tower, which commanded a view of the adjacent country; the vassals now, with an alacrity that evinced the love they bore their laird, made preparations; the armourers began to repair the long-neglected shields and helmets; the archers their arrows; all within the castle was a busy stir, attended with the clank of arms; the drawbridge was raised; the ramparts filled; and Bosmora, that had so long wore the smiling face of peace, now assumed the terrific look of war.

Chapter VI

Take thou thy armour, and rush to the first of thy bat-
tles!—be thy course in the field like the eagle's wing! Why
shouldst thou fear death, my son? The valiant fall with
fame—their shields turn the dark stream of danger away—re-
nown dwells on their aged hairs.

Ossian.

THE UTMOST VIGILANCE WAS CONTINUED within the walls of the castle;
but nothing in particular occurred to disturb the peace of its inhabitants, until the evening of the fourth day after the departure of Duncaethal, when the centinel stationed on the watch-tower that commanded the
forest gave notice of the approach of a band of armed men seemingly towards
Bosmora.

Donald, to whom this intelligence was communicated, immediately
mounted the parapet, where, at a distance, he beheld the clan of Duncaethal,
with martial step, winding through the intricacies of the forest; for some time
they were hid from view, within its labyrinths; then suddenly again appearing,
the red bright rays of the departing sun, gleaming upon their bright helmets
and polished shields, made their appearance at once glorious and terrific.

Donald now retired to the armoury, and equipping himself with a helmet
and breastplate of steel, drew forth his two-edged trusty sword, and waited, in
anxious expectation, their nearer approach. He was joined by the baron, who
had been informed by Andrew of the enemy's appearance.

When they arrived nearly within bowshot of the castle, a herald stepped
forth from the opposing army, and, with gigantic strides, advanced to the foot
of the drawbridge; with heavy strokes he thrice struck the ponderous shield of
war, whose sonorous sounds made the castle ring, and surrounding glens re-
echo back its martial clash; he then, in the name of his lord, loudly demanded
a parley; which being granted, he thus addressed Bosmora:—"In the name of
the most noble and illustrious baron Duncaethal, I, his honoured servant, now
stand forth, and, speaking with his mouth, propose saving the effusion of blood,
which must this night be shed, should he proceed in his intention of attacking
this fortress; and as our brave and humane lord would fain spare the lives of the

31

unoffending vassals, he challenges Donald, son of Allen and Jannet, to single combat; and though he is so much inferior to our great lord in birth, yet he will descend, for once, to wave his dignity, and meet him in the field on equal terms. Should this proposal be accepted by Donald, let him so signify, and to-morrow, at sunrise, our lord shall meet him, to prove, by force of arms, his claim to honour, attended only by his armour-bearer, and Malcolm, earl of Ross, who shall play the umpire between the challenger and challenged. If this arrangement satisfy not Donald, and he does not confide in the impartial arbitration of lord Malcolm, he is at liberty to bring whom he chooses, provided he is a man of unstained honour, and bears the dignity of knighthood. The spot proposed for the combat is the vale of Aldo. Long live our noble lord Duncaethal!"

The herald now ceasing, the baron stepped forth, and thus answered for Donald—"In the name of the saint of whose order he has the honour of bearing the dignity of knighthood, sir Donald, the future son of Bosmora, shall accept the terms; and I, the baron, will accompany him to the fight: bear back from me this message to thy haughty lord."

The herald departed, and returning to the clan of Duncaethal, delivered the acquiescence of Donald; and, after a pause of a few minutes, the clan then wheeling round and clashing their shields, with warlike sounds and martial steps returned through the forest.

In the mean time, Donald, with his utmost eloquence, endeavoured to dissuade the baron from accompanying him to the combat, adding—"My lord, I can fully confide in the honour of earl Malcolm; and as the faithful Robert will accompany me, there will be no fear but I shall meet with justice:—if I conquer, I shall at once revenge the insults offered to my benefactor and myself—if I fall, it will be in the cause of gratitude and love; for since I have received the sanction of my honoured lord to love Matilda, I will maintain the glorious claim, while life remains, or perish in the cause."

Bosmora being, at length, convinced of the inutility of himself attending, consented to his departing only with Robert. The intervening time was spent by Donald in visiting Allen and Jannet, and preparations for the important moment, when, for the first time, he was to prove his prowess in deeds of arms. When the hour drew near, he went to bid Matilda and the baron adieu, when the former, being agitated by the ceremony, gave utterance to the words as recorded in the first chapter; and, soon after, he bade farewell to the inhabitants of the castle, whose good wishes for success went with him.

Frequently did Matilda, on her knees, offer up her earnest prayers for his safety; and often did she send Venella to the turret, to see if she could descry his appearance— but in vain; hour after hour passed away in the most torturing suspense, and yet no signs of his return: Sometimes thinking Venella did not look carefully, she would ascend the castle walls, and partake with her a station on the turret, till the gloomy approach of night, and the fast-falling dews, which descended in thick clouds of mist, prevented her anxious eyes from distinguishing objects at the distance of a bow-shot from the castle; she then sought her chamber, and seating herself at the window, which looked over the court-yard, with palpitating heart, agitated with hope and fear, then listened, with eager ear, for the notice of his arrival. As every tedious hour was proclaimed by the castle-clock, she would exclaim—"Ah! he has too surely perished!" At length the bell sent forth the lengthening sound that announced the hour of midnight, when being no longer able to contain her fears, she rushed down to the apartment of her father, and throwing herself upon his bosom, exclaimed—"Oh! my dear lord, he has too surely fallen a victim to the treachery of Duncaethal! for had he perished in the fight, Robert, ere this, would have returned. Ah! little did his noble spirit consider the wily nature of his foe! Wretched Matilda! well, well did my heart forebode that I had beheld him for the last time! It is for me—for me he has perished! for had it not been for this wretched form, he never would have encountered the vengeance of the fierce Duncaethal!"

Thus did she indulge in the most frantic grief, unrestrained by the presence of her father, who in vain endeavoured to console her. He said he had sent some vassals in search of him at the approach of night, fearing lest some false play had been offered.

He was interrupted by a loud knocking at the gate; the breast of Matilda now beat high with trembling expectation, when Andrew, entering the apartment, acquainted his lord that they had searched every avenue of the forest in vain, and had proceeded to the vale, where there was no signs of any combat having been fought that day.

Bosmora now felt convinced, by Matilda's conjectures, that Donald had doubtless fallen into some snare laid for him by his deceitful enemy: summoning Venella, he ordered her to conduct her sorrowing mistress to her chamber; then turning to Andrew, bade him prepare his arms, and summon the vassals—"As," said he, "at the break of day, I myself will march against Duncaethal, and demand the youth, whom, I have no doubt, he unlawfully detains."

Andrew retired, with a heavy heart, to obey his lord's commands; and ere sunrise, the loud clang of arms gave notice to the baron that his faithful clan stood ready to attend him; and, buckling on his armour, he proceeded to bid his daughter farewell, who offered to the Virgin prayers for her dear father's safety and speedy return. The baron, tenderly taking her in his arms, kissed her faded cheek, and bidding her trust in the all-ruling power of Heaven, tore himself from her embrace. Andrew now informed him all was ready for his departure; and mounting his black steed, he moved towards the residence of the foe.

Towards evening they came within sight of the castle, which, to the astonishment of the baron, wore the smooth appearance of peaceful serenity. "What!" exclaimed he angrily, "did this haughty lord suppose Bosmora would fail to resent the injury done him, that he thus hugs himself in fancied peaceful security!" Then spurring forth his courser, he quickly arrived at the foot of the drawbridge, which was raised, and ordering his squire to strike loudly upon the shield, he demanded of a domestic who appeared to answer the summons an immediate interview with his lord. The servant retired, and, in a few moments, Duncaethal appeared upon the parapet, and demanded the cause of this warlike appearance; adding—"Is it possible the lord Bosmora has so little honour as seemingly to consent to my condescending proposal, in offering to terminate the breach by single combat with the peasant Donald, to save the lives of your vassals?—was this the mean subterfuge, that he might attack me unprepared? Say! was it well done, baron, to accept my challenge, and then, when I arrived at the appointed spot, to find no foe, who, from cowardice or policy, failed to meet me?"

Bosmora was thunderstruck; but in a moment recovering himself, he thought it was an artful evasion of the speaker to disguise his knowledge of Donald's disappearance; and again addressing him, he said—"Dost thou then pretend to me the brave Donald did not meet thee, thou stain of knighthood?— it is on his account I now appear;—where is he, and by what black treachery has he been prevented returning to Bosmora?"

"My lord," replied Duncaethal, "you are too hot—let your better judgment," continued he, with apparent calmness, "gain the preponderance for a moment, and you will soon perceive the fallacy of your accusation. If I had so far forgot my honour as to make use of stratagem to secure the person of Donald, think you I should have failed to have had my castle filled with soldiers, to repulse the attempt you would, no doubt, make to free the captive?—but I am unprepared—no armed vassals appear upon my walls—and will Bosmora attack a chieftain with such unequal numbers?"

The baron was loath to admit a thought which conveyed with it the bare suspicion of an action disgraceful or derogatory to the dignity of a knight; and the deep sophistry of Duncaethal confounded him; nor could he fail to admit the plausibility of his reasoning—when once more turning to him, he said— "My lord Duncaethal, dare you swear by your sword you met not Donald in the field?"

"I dare, my lord!" then directly unsheathing it, raised it to his lips with great solemnity. "Now, my lord Bosmora, should you still retain an idea of my having used deceit, I refer you to earl Malcolm of Ross, who attended me to the spot, and is a witness I waited upwards of three hours in vain, and at length returned, accompanied by him, to Duncaethal."

If the baron failed to be convinced, even by the asseveration of the former, this ready reference to earl Malcolm, whom he knew to be a man of strict honour and undoubted veracity, at once brought with it a painful conviction; and turning round his horse, he, followed by his faithful clan, bent his way back to Bosmora, and communicated this distressing intelligence to his wretched daughter. 119

We will now leave them, and return to Donald and his squire. Soon after his departure from the castle, he reached the outskirts of the forest; a loud shout close to his heels affrighted his proud mettled steed, when being restrained by the reins, and eagerly struggling to be free, he stumbled, and, by the violence of the motion, precipitated his master from the saddle, who was preparing to rise, when he found himself surrounded by a troop of armed men, who, seizing him and confining his arms, conveyed both him and his squire, whom they had bound in the same manner, to a carriage, which had been hitherto concealed by a thick clump of trees. During this action, which was all executed in the space of a minute, Donald was so confounded, that he had not power to utter a word; but recovering a little from his surprise, he demanded the reason of this cavalier treatment; but not a word did they deign to answer, though he repeatedly interrogated them; nor could he gain the least glimpse of their faces, their visors being kept continually closed.

He was now silent, and waited patiently for the conclusion of this strange adventure, as all efforts of resistance would be fruitless: they had taken the necessary precaution of disarming him; at last he thought total silence would be the best policy.

Not so his squire, for he loudly clamoured forth his complaints in the following words—"Here's a pretty end to a battle, indeed! to be seized and cooped up in this rumbling thing, just like a couple of wild-geese in a market-woman's basket! and then to interrupt me too, just as I was composing a long speech which I intended to speak to Dargo, the squire of my lord Duncaethal, when you should have disarmed his master, which I plainly foresaw, my lord, you of course would do—'Dargo,' says I to myself, 'you see it was a mighty foolish whim of your lord, to suppose he was sure of gaining a victory over my master, sir Donald— Ah! ah! Dargo,' says I, 'I plainly foresaw he was playing a losing game; for though he has fought many more combats than my master, yet my master was in the right cause, and consequently our patron, St. Andrew, would aid him in the fight, and make him the conqueror; for I foresaw—"

Donald now impatiently interrupted him, by saying—"I wish the wonderful foreknowledge you so abundantly seem to possess had caused you to foresee this strange conclusion to our enterprise."

"Ah! sir Donald," answered Robert, "Saint Andrew grant that I had! then would not I have helped to dissuade the good lord Bosmora from accompanying us. Ah! what will the lady Matilda say? and what will Venella, her ladyship's maid, say? ah! how disappointed will she be! good lack! good lack! for," said I, to her, 'Venella,' says I, 'when we return, and while my master is giving your lady an account of the fight, you and I, Venella,' says I, 'will have a cup of good wine comfortably together; and while we drink their healths, I will,' says I, 'tell you the share I took in the encounter; what my lord said to the lord Duncaethal, which,' says I, 'I plainly foresee he will, when he, after disarming him, returns him his sword; then,' says I, 'what a graceful bow he will make to the lord Duncaethal, who will, of course, look fierce and malicious at being overcome! and how I should crow and strut over Dargo, because we had got the day! Now, instead of all this, sir—instead of my eating ragout and drinking wine with Venella, perhaps some of these clumsy-fisted fellows which surround the carriage may make mince-meat of me! Oh that I was once more safe at home in the castle of Bosmora! Oh that I could again taste those happy joyous days we enjoyed, before lord Duncaethal took it into his mad head to demand our sweet young lady for his wife! Now 'tis very strange these bandits never rummaged our pockets, to see if we had a purse for them, or anything worth their taking. Good lack! now it strikes me, I should not be at all surprised if they acted by the command of some lady who has taken a fancy to our persons— what do you think, sir Donald?"

"Think! why that thou art an ass to suppose any such thing."

"Nay, my lord," replied the mortified squire, who imagined that Donald was offended at his ranking himself as an object to be seized by violence, "I did not mean to insinuate that I thought I was so comely and handsome as you are, my lord; but yet, you know, my lord, if they had not been ordered to bring me too, why you know they might have let me gone home again about my business, which I should soon have done, in spite of the honour intended me by the fair one, whoever she is. Venella has often told me that I had a pretty smirking face, but really I never had the vanity to suppose I was so handsome, that any woman would ever proceed to violence to obtain me."

Donald now, in spite of his great chagrin, burst into a loud fit of laughter, at the conclusions made by the simple vanity of his foolish squire, at the same time saying—"Robert, does not thy miraculous foresight inform thee we are in the power of Duncaethal, who, by this treacherous conduct, has us completely in his clutches?" Then pausing a moment, he continued—"Cannot thy shallow brain perceive he will now attack the castle, and carry off the angelic Matilda, now I am absent, and our noble lord is unprepared for his reception? Oh! villainous traitor! Oh that I had some method of escape! but, alas! there's none!—the carriage is surrounded, and the most distant hope is vain!"

The simple squire now being convinced of the truth of his master's suspicions, sunk into a profound silence, and thought no more of amorous ladies or love-sick damsels; nor did he ever   once disturb the painful reverie into which Donald had fallen.

Their taciturnity was, at length, interrupted by the sudden stopping of the vehicle, and a demand from one of the men who opened the door, if they would alight and take some refreshment? Donald was on the point of refusing, when an imploring look from Robert, who, with all the misfortunes and disappointments of the day, could not resist the powerful attacks of hunger, made him comply; and alighting, a wallet of cold provisions, and a keg of liquor, were spread upon the grass, of which they were rudely invited to partake; it was immediately accepted by Robert, without the least hesitation, who did ample justice to the viands and keg of liquor. Donald refused tasting either, till one of the men, producing a bottle of wine, which, he said, was of a most excellent quality, earnestly pressed him to take a cup; then offering the same to Robert, who, nothing loth to refuse, drained it to the bottom; and turning round to present the empty goblet, he fixed his eyes on the face of a man who sat at some distance, and, after a moment of surprise, exclaimed—"What, Dargo! ah! it is Dargo!" and directly approaching him, said—"Do, good Dargo, tell us where we are going?"

A morose reply from the latter to command silence, prevented Donald, who was going to make the same question, from speaking; but Robert, not regarding him, continued—"Ah! little did I think, when I was regaling you at the castle with some of my lord Bosmora's best wine— little did I then dream of your playing me and my master such a scurvy trick as this! Ah, Dargo! I cannot help saying that you are a confounded great rogue!" The enraged Dargo, now drawing forth his sword, presented it to the breast of the terrified squire, who stammered out—"Nay, nay, I did not mean to say that you, good Dargo, was a rogue, for you only act by the orders of your lord, as every good servant, you know, ought; though, I must confess, when you was drinking to my success, and calling me your dear friend, I never thought you would turn out such a villain!—I beg your pardon, I mean I little supposed that your master would command you to hold a sword to my throat; but we poor servants must obey orders, and if my master was to bid me cut yours, why I should do it with pleasure—No! I did not mean that, dear, dear Dargo—only meant, my good friend, I should be obliged to fulfil his commands."

They were now rudely bid to re-enter the carriage; and soon after, loud snores from Robert gave notice to his master he had now sought repose in the arms of Somnus; and a heavy drowsiness, which he, at the same time, felt creeping over his own senses, convinced him that there had been infused some powerful soporific mixture into the wine which he so incautiously had swallowed; and, after a long struggle with its influence, which proved vain, he was compelled to submit to its potency; and when, at length, he opened his eyes, he beheld a sight that horrified every faculty; suspended from the top of a loathsome dungeon, in which, on a truss of straw, he found himself reclining, was a rusty iron lamp, from which arose a glimmering flame, whose feeble rays were nearly obscured by the unwholesome damps which exhaled from its trickling walls. He tried to raise himself, when a stiffness which pervaded his limbs, painfully convinced him he must have slumbered, in that wretched situation, a considerable length of time. "Oh, my dearest Matilda," said he, "shall we never more meet? have I but just possessed the precious knowledge of thy love, to be separated for ever! Alas! too surely it is so! I am destined to meet a horrid lingering death! no more to taste the sweets of liberty, and, what is far dearer, thy delightful society, without which life were not worth retaining!"

"He again cast himself on his straw, and indulging in the most poignant sorrow, abandoned himself to despair. A loud rattling now attracted his attention, occasioned by the unbarring of his cell door; and he waited in the horrible expectation of seeing his murderer enter to complete the vengeance of Duncaethal. Dargo now appeared, bearing a basket of provisions, a pitcher of water, and a fresh supply of oil for the lamp, which settling down, and turning to Donald, he inquired if he was ready to receive a visit from his lord?

"I am," replied he, "for fain would I see the wretch who has so far forgot his honour as a knight, and humanity as a Christian."

Dargo, without again speaking, retired, and shortly after re-entered, preceded by Duncaethal. "Well, valiant sir," said he, tauntingly, "I fancy you little expected this commodious apartment? No! no! you thought to be enfolded in the arms of the love-sick Matilda, and triumph over Duncaethal by recounting his fall! Vain wretch! couldst thou, even for a moment, suppose that I would oppose myself, in fight, with an impostor, the grovelling ofispring of Bosmora's vassals? Know, thou weak boy, it was a stratagem to check thy pride, and teach thee to know the difference of a peasant's son, ignobly born, and the dignity of Duncaethal!"

"Yes, thou proud wretch! I know thee well, a stranger alike to honour or to valour—thy heart cowardly as it is treacherous! Rapacious, cruel, and bold, amidst thy villanies—"

"Rail on, disappointed boy! 'tis all thou canst now do; yet know I am come to prove to thee I am not cruel; consent to whatat I shall propose, and thou shalt have safe conduct from the castle."

"Name your terms," said Donald; "but, mark me, I will consent to nothing that will, in the least, sully my fair name, or cast the slightest stain upon my hitherto unimpeached honour."

"Nothing which I propose shall wound the name you now possess," said he, equivocally; "The first condition is, that you quit Scotland, never to return; the second, that you resign all claim to Bosmora's heiress; and the third, that you signify the same by returning that scarf which now adorns you, by a messenger of my providing, and in a manner that I shall direct."

"I disdain the terms," said the indignant youth. "Did not thou say, thou wouldst propose nothing that might stain the fairness of my name?"

"Nor have I," returned the other. "The name you now bear is that of a base coward, who first accepted of the fair challenge that I gave, and then, with ignoble fear, fled, not daring to face me; and such, Bosmora is informed thou art, for he has been here already to demand thee; but being convinced thou art no longer worthy the high honour which he intended thee, has returned with the intention of forgetting you for ever; therefore, by consenting to my prop-ositions, you will not only save your life and regain thy liberty, but might, in return, forget Matilda."

Donald, no longer being able to contain his resentment, exclaimed—"Oh! thou vile traitor! that dares thus, with unblushing front, stand before the victim of thy base insidious arts! Had I but my sword, I would prove, on thy coward head, the falsehood of thy damned insinuations! but threats are vain; and, since my fair fame, by black deceit, is gone, I defy thy utmost power, for I will die in the full assurance of my honour being unstained."

The enraged Duncaethal, now turning to depart, said he gave him to the following night to consider of it, when, if he still refused, he might expect his fulfilling his utmost vengeance; then quitted the dungeon, followed by Dargo; the latter, placing a bar of massy iron against the door to keep it secure, once more left him to indulge his thoughts uninterrupted.

CHAPTER VII

*The foe came on like a stream! the mingled sound of death
arose! man took man—shield met shield—steel mixed its
beams with steel—darts hiss through the air—spears ring on
mails—swords on broken bucklers bound! As the noise of an
aged grove beneath the roaring wind, when a thousand ghosts
break the trees by night, such was the din of arms!*

Ossian.

MATILDA HAD RETIRED TO HER CHAMBER with a heavy heart; it was now the third night since the departure of Donald; no clue had yet been obtained to the cause of his extraordinary disappearance, and the baron had, for farther conviction, rode to the castle of Ross, to interrogate sir Malcolm, who corroborated the account made by Duncaethal; yet she could not believe but he had been the victim of treachery; that cowardice was the cause, she banished the ignoble thought; nor would she, for a moment, give room to an idea so basely injurious to the honour of her heart's beloved.—"Ah!" said she, "he is too surely in the power of the wily villain Duncaethal! Holy Virgin protect and deliver him from his remorseless enemy!"

Her prayer was interrupted by the sound of a tremendous crash, and a moment after, by the entrance of Venella, who, pale, agitated, and breathless, seemed unable to recount the dreadful subject which laboured for utterance. "Oh! my lady, my lady! we are lost! we are lost!"

"What dost thou mean?" asked the trembling Matilda.

"Oh, my lady! the castle is attacked by the clan of Duncaethal!— hark! my lady, how their arms clash on the walls! Oh, the Virgin protect us! we shall be all killed!" Now the dreadful bursting of the castle gates caused a noise still more terrible than the first. "Oh, my lady! they are in the castle! oh! let us fly!"

"Alas, whither?" said her mistress. "Oh, my father! my dear father! perhaps thou art, at this moment, breathing thy last! Oh, let me haste to save thee, and resign myself into the power of Duncaethal!" She now essayed to leave the chamber, when she sunk down in a swoon upon the ground, occasioned by the fright that now had overpowered her before agitated spirits.

Loud terrific shouts sounded through the lofty halls of Bosmora, as the ferocious besiegers followed their flying victims through the various apartments of the castle; the gleam of wildfire that was thrown in by the dreadful foe, gave a partial light, at intervals, of the accumulating horrors which, at every turn, met the terror-struck eye of the besieged, who had been surprised unawares, at a time they were, for the greatest part, buried in profound sleep, little dreaming of the enemy's black treachery. Loud piercing shrieks from the terrified female domestics, that sought, in vain, for refuge, rent the air, and bursting the caverns of night, told the dangers with which they were surrounded. Horrid War, with rapid and gigantic strides, rushed forth, marking his fatal track with murder! bloody, remorseless, sanguinary murder!—man against man, breast to breast, fought dreadful, tugging hard for victory! Bravely did the faithful but unprepared clan of Bosmora defend their lord; till at length, overpowered by the superior number of the foe, they sealed their fidelity with their lives. Bosmora dealt death around him, but, at last, being surrounded, a blow laid him prostrate on the earth at the feet of his ferocious enemy, who now went to seek the lovely object which had caused this dreadful havoc. He directed his course to   the apartments of the unoffending and beauteous victim, leaving his remorseless crew dealing ruin and devastation to all around them. Finding her chamber vacant, imprecations burst from the lips of the disappointed chief; and, on meeting the frightened Venella, he loudly demanded her mistress, and threatened instant death, if she refused to tell him the place of her concealment; in vain did she endeavour to convince him she knew nothing of her—terror preventing her speech; while Duncaethal, thinking her stammering a stratagem to delay time for her further escape, proceeded again to threats, when Venella exclaimed—"Indeed, my lord, you terrify me so, that you prevent me telling the truth."

"Well, then, proceed," said he, more mildly, hoping, by gentle means, to gain that information which passion in vain endeavoured to extort.

She now said—"Indeed, my lord, I was almost frightened out of my wits, when I saw my lady fell into a swoon, and I ran to get some water to sprinkle her face; but when I returned, she was gone, my lord."

"Impossible! how could she leave the apartment if she was in a swoon?"

"Why, my lord," said Venella, "somebody has carried her away, I dare say."

Duncaethal now supposed some of his party, during the battle, had conveyed her to a place of security, as he commanded them all to strict care she did not escape. Summoning them to his presence, he inquired if any had secured her; but not one could give the least account. He then ordered a strict search to be made through the castle, and took himself an active and vigilant part for the recovery of his devoted victim.

Matilda, on recovering from the insensibility into which she had fallen, found herself in the arms of a man, who hurried her on with an amazing rapidity; a scream burst from her lips, when a poniard, which he presented to her breast, made her silent, and caused her again to relapse into forgetfulness. At length, when recollection again visited her, she found herself in a subterraneous apartment; over her stood a tall figure, gazing upon her most stedfastly; his dark scrutinizing eye was fixed full upon her face, with an expression gloomy and terrific, which caused a shuddering throughout her whole frame; scarcely could she consider his dress, which was altogether strange as himself; on his head he wore a casque of polished steel, the crown of which supported a large plume of blood-red feathers; a heavy cuirass, and cuish of iron, defended his breast and the lower parts of his body; a broad leather belt girted his waist, and contained various weapons of destruction; gauntlets clothed his hands, in one of which he held a lighted flambeau, whose glare, reflecting on his arms, gave him an appearance most horribly terrific.—"Matilda," said he, in a sepulchral sounding voice, "arise, and follow me!"

"Alas!" said the wretched girl, "where am I, and whither would you convey me?"

"To safety!" replied he.

"How can I be assured of that?" returned she; "thy appearance is not cal-culated to inspire confidence; and the mysterious manner in which I have been conducted hither, convinces me that thou art an agent of the tyrant Duncaethal. Oh, Donald! why art thou not here to protect thy unhappy ill-fated Matilda!"

A frown passed across the features of the unknown, as he pronounced—"La-dy, your unjust suspicions wrong me—we are not yet without the walls of Bosmora; I repaired here, amidst the confusion of the fight, to save you, and sought your chamber for that purpose, when your insensible state prevented me explaining my intentions; I took you in my arms, and, by a private passage, brought you to this place, which is a subterranean of the castle, and through which I intended to make our escape, but was obliged to rest, till you recovered and became able to proceed."

A loud noise now resounding through the vaults alarmed the stranger, and seizing a long plaid cloak which he had cast off on his entering the cavern, hastily threw it around him; then exclaiming—"Farewell—it is too late! by your foolish scruples you have prevented my intentions of securing you from the tyranny of Duncaethal, whose agents now indeed approach;—bitterly will you repent refusing the proffered kindness of the bandit Darthalgo!"

He retreated through a passage on the right, leaving the hapless Matilda in the power of her remorseless pursuers. Duncaethal at that moment entering, or-dered them to convey their wretched victim to a carriage, which was in waiting on the outside of the castle, when sinking on her knees, she begged to see her father ere she departed. The ferocious chief, who did not wish her to be made acquainted with his fall, answered evasively, she should behold him at the end of her journey.

"Ah," shrieked she, "he's murdered! avaunt, thou homicide! off! touch me not—thy hands are stained with blood! the lifecurrent of my venerable father now encrusts thy dagger's point; but heavily shall the vengeance of Omnipotence revenge his death, while the never-ceasing remorse of a guilty conscience shall make thee curse thyself, in bitterness of despair and misery of soul!"

"Seize her!" cried the enraged Duncaethal to his followers; "do the ravings of a weak girl intimidate you, that you all stand aloof, gaping like lifeless statues? Instantly lay hold of her, or this sword shall enforce my commands!"

The soldiers now rushed forward, and conveying her through the court-yard, forced her into a carriage, in which Venella was already confined, who sat wringing her hands, and loudly expressing her sorrows; and when her mistress was seated by her, she cried—"Ah! my dear lady, then they have found you at last!—oh! the Virgin! how earnestly did I pray that you might have fled beyond their reach! for then this surly centinel who guards the carriage perhaps would have let me go home to my father and mother. Ah! woeful was the time I left our happy cottage for Bosmora! Ah! never shall I see my dear parents again, nor dance on the green before the door to the sweet-sounding pipe! Oh that I was once out of this carriage, that is now conveying us I know not whither! for I suppose my lord Duncaethal will do just as he pleases with us, now sir Donald is lost, and the good baron is no more."

"No more!" shrieked Matilda, with horror at the truth of what she already feared; "art thou sure my father is no more?"

"No, no! not quite sure," replied the incautious Venella; "I only saw him stretched out on the hall floor; but you know, my lady, he might only have swooned like yourself."

Matilda heard not the conclusion of this speech, but sunk down insensible at the foot of the carriage. All the screams for assistance made by Venella failed of effect, for the unfeeling wretches who guarded them never once offered to stop, thinking her cries were only intended to attract the attention of any traveller who might aid their escape; therefore, instead of lending the least help, they threatened to stop her mouth, unless she was instantly quiet.

At length she had the pleasure of seeing returning animation visit the form of her wretched mistress; and a heavy shower of tears, which, in a torrent, flowed from her lachrymal eyes, chased each other down her sorrowing cheek, gave some relief to her bursting heart; and with an earnest prayer to Heaven for her safety, endeavoured to compose herself and was patiently resigned to the wretched fate which, she had no doubt, awaited her; and, at last, sunk into a profound silence, which Venella, at intervals, interrupted, by declaring the jolting of the carriage would kill her before she reached the end of her journey: but at last they came in view of the castle of Duncaethal, and passing over the drawbridge, which was lowered for that purpose, the vehicle stopped, and they were handed out by Dargo, on whom she discharged a volley of reproaches; nor could she scarcely be silenced by her lady, who endeavoured to convince her that he acted only by the orders of his lord.

They were now conducted to an elegant apartment, where they found a table spread with a rich collation of the choicest viands, of which they were invited to partake by Dargo, who, in a moment after, left the room. When Venella saw the magnificence of the place, she could not contain her joy, and, in ecstasy, exclaimed—"Oh, what gay furniture, and what a rich supper!—well, how comfortable! instead of being conducted to a gloomy prison, which I thought we should, to find ourselves in the grandest place I ever saw in my life!—Oh! do, my lady, taste of this nice cake or this wine," at the same time taking a glass herself; but Matilda heard her not, for, regardless of surrounding objects, she was plunged in a train of melancholy thoughts, and recalled to herself the dreadful horrors of the late scene, in which she had borne a principal part. The mysterious being who would have saved her, his terrific appearance, and his evident knowledge of Bosmora Castle, what motive could he have for the interest he took in her fate? he who had called himself, and whose person corroborated his words, a bandit! how could he know what was to take place that very night, and why wish to save her, when a person of his calling might have so easily seized on the valuables which, in the confusion, lay neglected?

All these ideas rapidly crossed her recollection, and she earnestly wished she had accepted his proffered kindness;—"for," thought she, "I could not have fallen into the hands of a greater ruffian than Duncaethal, even in those of a professed bravo."

She was interrupted by the opening of the door, and the entrance of an old woman, who, approaching with a low curtsey, asked if she should shew her to those apartments which were expressly designed for her sole use? Matilda answered that she was ready to attend; and arising, followed the old woman to an antique but elegant bed-chamber, ornamented with many portraits of knights and ladies; one of the latter, arrayed in a white robe, particularly attracted her attention. "Whose likeness is that?" asked she.

"Ah, my lady!" answered her conductor, "that was the bonny Agnes Maclean; ah, sweet good lady! she was lost on the outskirts of the forest; her horse taking flight, plunged her in the river that flows near, and she was never more heard of: but see, madam, that young knight next to her, that looks so handsome, is the brave Alexander, the noble heir of Duncaethal, who was slain in the wars, and, by that means, broke the heart of our good old lord. Ah, my lady! the bonny Agnes loved him, and he loved her too—but our dear old lord would never consent to their union;—ah! her death was a relief to her sorrows; for when she was left in the castle with old Peter the steward and myself, she used to mope about just like a ghost, and would sit gazing at this picture of our young lord for days together: at last Peter thought she injured her health, by giving way so much to grief, and prevailed on her to ride in the adjacent valleys, which she did: Peter, at first, attended her, but on her wishing to be alone, and he not supposing any danger would happen, let her go out by herself. Ah, wretched day! the steed on which she rode returned neighing to the castle, but we never saw the bonny Agnes more." The affectionate Gertrude now wiped the tears fix>m her eyes, and directing the attention of Matilda to the opposite side, said—"Look, lady, there is the peerless Mabel Duncaethal."

"Merciful powers, my mother!" said she.

"Your mother, lady!" inquired the astonished Gertrude; "are you the daughter of lord Bosmora?"

"I am that wretched orphan," said she.

"Orphan!" reiterated Gertrude; "is the noble baron dead?"

"Alas, yes!" sighed forth Matilda; "he was last night inhumanly murdered by the tyrant Duncaethal!"

"What!" screamed Gertrude, "did Duncaethal murder the husband of his cousin? Ah! little did I think, when I saw the beautiful Mabel leave this castle for that of her lord, your father—ah! little did I think that I, so old even then, should ever live to hear of his murder—and that too by a descendant of her own family. Ah! when I was ordered to prepare the apartments of the late lady Margaret, for one who was coming to be my lord's bride—ah! little did I think it was the daughter of the sweet Mabel; and is it indeed, my lady, true that you are to be his bride?"

"Bride! thinkst thou," said Matilda, "this breast shall ever receive the murderer of my father? No! sooner would I bare it to meet that dagger's point which pierced his honoured breast, than Matilda Bosmora should become the wife of the murderer Duncaethal, that ferocious homicide!"

"Ah! my dear lady, but will you be able to escape firom his power?" asked the other.

"Ah! good Gertrude, could not you assist me?" inquired Matilda; "and I will fly to my sovereign, fall at his feet, and implore protection from your tyrannic master."

"Alas, my lady, 'tis not in my power; old Peter is dead; and Dargo, who keeps the keys, is no fiiend of mine."

"Then I have no resource," cried the miserable Matilda, "but to trust in that Providence whose attribute is to watch over unprotected innocence!" and turning to Gertrude, continued—"Did you not say these were the apartments of lady Margaret?"

"Ah, Madam," said she, "here, on this very bed, she breathed her last; I saw her myself when she was dead— she was a handsome lady, but not the sweet temper of bonny Agnes;—my lord and she had often high words, and when she died, I think he did not mourn for her so much as he would have it believed he did."

"I fancy not," said Venella, who, for a long time, had, much against her inclination, been silent; "he never cared much for her, and I am sure there was no love lost, for when she was first at Bosmora, she—"

"Silence, Venella," cried Matilda, "what are you thinking of?"

"Oh! I beg pardon, my lady," answered the other; "she is dead, and they say you should never speak ill of the dead; and as I cannot say any good of her, why I'll e'en hold my tongue."

"Aye, pray do," returned her mistress; "and don't allow yourself so much freedom."

"Dear heart, my lady, I am sure I spoke no harm!" and then addressing herself to Gertrude, Venella inquired if she was to sleep in the same room with her mistress?

"No," answered the other; "there is a bed prepared for you in the antichamber."

"Oh lord! I dare not sleep there by myself."

"Why not?" said Gertrude; "I have slept there many nights, for, unconscious of ever having injured any one, I thank the Virgin I possess a quiet conscience."

"Marry, indeed!" said Venella, pertly; "I dare say I am as righteous as yourself;" and she was now determined to assume a degree of courage she did not possess. The clock now proclaiming a late hour, Gertrude, with a low curtsey, left the apartment, wishing a good repose to Matilda, who, shortly after, dismissed Venella for the night; then being by herself, with weeping eyes, fell on her knees before the picture of her mother, and gave utterance to the following words—"Oh thou, whose beatified spirit now dwelleth in realms of eternal glory, regardless of this terraqueous globe of misery and woe, if it be so permitted, look down upon thy unhappy unprotected child; and when the unrelenting hand of cruelty is raised to end my wretched being, step forth, and, by thy presence, strike terror to the heart of my dear father's cruel murderer!"

At this moment a hollow groan seemed to proceed from the picture, and Matilda, fixing on the canvas a gaze of terror, each moment expected to see it move; but all was still, and casting a look of fear and wonder round the apartment, all remained as before. She now fancied she had been deceived, and it could be nothing more than the moaning of the hollow blast forcing its entrance into some chasm of the castle; and yet the sound seemed so distinct—so like what they say breaks from the troubled spirit, who, wandering, expiates the crimes done in the days of its mortality, she once more raised her eyes to the portrait, whose mild countenance seemed irradiated with maternal love—"Ah, my mother, thy child never experienced thy tender care; yet she had a father!—oh, Heavens!"—Her voice now became convulsed as she recollected she had not now left one parent, and casting herself on the bed, gave way to the most poignant and unrestrained sorrow. At length nature being entirely exhausted by incessant fatigue, she sunk into repose.

Chapter VIII

Duncaethal, on the evening he had quitted the dungeon of Donald, proceeded to an apartment with his trusty minister Dargo, to consult how they might induce the former to resign his claim to Matilda.—
"Might I be allowed to speak," said Dargo, "I think I have hit upon an expedient."

"Say on, my trusty fellow," replied Duncaethal; "and if thou canst devise any method, propose it, if it will aid me in gaining Matilda, and disposing of that minion who has presumed to rival Duncaethal."

"If your lordship would be ruled by me," answered the villanous Dargo, "I would seize on the lady Matilda by force; and as to Donald, your lordship already knows I have a dagger very   much at his service; and I defy him ever to escape from his prison without my permission."

"Your counsel in regard to the latter likes me well; but by what means can I seize the former and convey her here, for she never suffers herself, even for a moment, without the walls of Bosmora?" said Duncaethal.

"My lord," returned Dargo, "your faithful vassals, by my persuasions, convinced that you have been vilely insulted, in being refused by the baron the hand of Matilda, burn with impatience to revenge your cause; now, my lord, as you treated Bosmora so seemingly fair when he was here to-day, and as you made no mention of his daughter, he will, of course, conclude you have given up the pursuit, and, by that means, will grow remiss in his wonted vigilance, consequently somewhat off his guard: now, my lord, I would have you secretly march your clan to the forest near Bosmora, and there ambush till darkness obscures our motions—then suddenly attacking the castle, when the greatest part of its inhabitants are buried in sleep, then will Matilda become yours by certain conquest, for what can avail the few unprepared domestics, opposed against our numerous party?"

The counsel of this wily wretch met the approbation of his villainous lord, who immediately put his infernal advice in practice, by communicating his intentions to the misled vassals, whose alacrity and eagerness exceeded his most sanguine expectations.

Dargo, previous to their leaving the castle, proceeded to the cell of Donald, taking with him a large basket of provisions; and informing him he should not return to him again for the space of two days, bade him husband them out.

Donald, in a gentle voice, begged him to tell him what had become of his squire?

"He is safe enough," said Dargo, smiling maliciously.

"Is he alive?" asked Donald, earnestly.

"Alive!" returned Dargo; "ah, that he is; the empty basket that stands at the door of his cell will answer for his being alive; this is the third morning he has been here, and, notwithstanding he is in a dungeon, he has eaten more than any one in the castle. I have often heard that sorrow made folks dry, but I never knew before that it made them hungry; however, he has evinced that it sometimes is the case, for I really think the more he moans, the more he eats."

"The third day, did you say?" inquired Donald; "surely I have been here but two mornings," said he, musing.

"Oh, sir," said Dargo, smiling, "you took such a long sleep, and, by that means, the first day past more agreeably than the next."

The cool satirical manner in which the knave spoke, provoked Donald to such a degree, that he angrily bade him quit his presence.

"Ah, that I will," said Dargo; "for I promise you, this gloomy apartment suits not with my elevated notions and aspiring ideas;" and ironically bowing, with a look of the utmost effrontery, withdrew, closing the door on the outside.

Donald now paced his dungeon with agitated steps, ruminating on his dreadful fate; then reclining on his straw, considered within himself, if there was a possibility of devising any method of escape; then arising, anxiously looking round his prison for some chasm through which he might extricate himself—but in vain; at one corner was a small arched door, thickly covered with iron bars closely rivetted, and seemingly fastened on the outside by means of a bar; often had he examined this entrance, with an earnest wish of being able, by some means, to unfasten it—often had he exerted his utmost strength to force it; it now struck him, that probably the dungeon might contain some secret trap, and moving the straw which composed his bed, commenced a strict search; a cold iron ring that met his hand, gave him hopes, and exerting his strength to the utmost, endeavoured to raise it; but not being able to succeed, he took the lamp and examined it more closely, when his disappointment was unequalled by discovering several links of a chain, by which he concluded some unhappy wretch had been fastened to the ground; his spirits, which a few moments before had been raised by hope, with this new disappointment entirely forsook him; and quickly throwing the straw again on the place, he cast himself upon it in all the bitterness of despair; till at length sleep kindly sealed up his eyes, and gave a short respite to his misery.

He had not long remained in this state, ere a sudden noise awoke him, and caused him to look round, and to his utter astonishment, the door which he had so long vainly endeavoured to force stood wide open; at first he could scarcely believe but that he was in a dream, till he heard a rustling on the outside, when, by a sudden impulse, he started up, and rushing forward, passed through the entrance; a glimmering light and receding steps convinced him some one fled his approach; he, swiftly as the winding of the passage would permit, pursued, and caught sight of a figure bearing a lamp; he was on the point of overtaking it, when staggering over a step, it stumbled, and the lamp was extinguished; Donald fell over the prostrate stranger, and seizing him by the throat, with a firm grasp, demanded who he was?

"Oh, St. Andrew save me! mighty sir, I shall be choaked; release me, and I will tell you all, sir!"

Donald instantly quitted his hold, for, to his great surprise, he recognised the voice of his faithful Robert.—"Robert," said he, "for mercy's sake tell me how you came here?"

"Why, is that you, my dear master?" eagerly inquired he.

"It is," said Donald; "but where are we?—can we escape from the castle?"

"Alas! not that I know of," returned the other; "for I don't even know the way back to my dungeon, now the lamp is out, for it is dark as pitch."

"Hush!" said his master; "let us endeavour to grope our way back to mine, where there is a lamp burning."

They now felt their way, Donald going first. After many stumbles, he caught a glimpse of the flame which the lamp emitted; it enabled them, at length, to gain the cell, when, immediately upon their entrance, Donald requested Robert to tell him for what purpose he had sought him, and why then fled?

"Alas! sir," said the poor terrified squire, "I thought I would try and give my friend Dargo the slip, as I chanced to find a small door behind an old chest which stood at the head of my miserable couch; and taking an opportunity to raise it when he was gone, I found that I could easily pass through; and when I thought all was still, I took my lamp, and cautiously quitting my cell, endeavoured to find some outlet, that might favour my escape; when, after turning a long passage to the right, and another to the left, came to this door, and, after removing the heavy bar that fastened it, threw it open, when a light burning, and the noise you made in starting, led me to suppose I had broke in upon some enemy, and I fled, with a view of gaining my prison ere I might be perceived; for I never supposed, in the least, my lord Duncaethal would confine you in such a miserable place as this!"

Donald now proposed that they should both reconnoitre the passage, which being agreed to, they left the dungeon once more, in hopes of emancipation;

they recovered the lamp of Robert, and trimming it, they proceeded down a turning on the right, examining it on both sides with great care, hoping to find some door, which, at length, to their great joy, they discovered, with a key in it; this made them conjecture it might be a prison like their own, but, at all events, they were determined to open it: for a long time their united efforts proved fruitless, for, with their utmost strength, they were unable to turn it; till at last Robert bethought himself of a project that flattered them with hope; he took the oily wick from one of the lamps, and thrusting it into the keyhole, softened by that means the cankerous rust which prevented it from moving; success crowned their endeavours; and cautiously opening it, for the hinges loudly grated, to their great joy they discovered a steep flight of stone steps, which seemed to terminate with the upper part of the castle; they gained their summit, and found themselves in a spacious passage leading to a suite of apartments, the dilapidated appearance of which plainly evinced that they had not been inhabited for a considerable length of time: they set down the lamp, as the painted windows admitted the glorious rays of the sun, which, at first, dazzled their sight; but a short time reconciled their eyes to its golden beams, and, from its meridian splendour, proved it to be about the hour of noon. They were on the point of entering a chamber on the right, when a distant sound of footsteps which resounded through the arched ceiling caused them to look up, and, at the extremity of the passage, they beheld Dargo! Donald instantly slipped behind a friendly buttress, and his example was followed by the trembling Robert, who feared that he had been   discovered. Dargo passed the very spot where they were concealed: they expected he would instantly perceive the lamp, and, by that means, discover their hiding-place; but as it was, by the projection of a pillar, half-concealed, and nearly extinguished by the sunbeams darting fully upon its feeble flame, it escaped his notice, and he went carelessly on.

Soon as he was out of sight, they stole from their hiding-place to the stairs, and making their way down them, turned the key of the door; they then consulted how they should proceed. Donald proposed returning to their cells, and waiting till the inhabitants of the castle had retired to rest, ere they should again venture to explore the several apartments they had perceived at the end of the passage. Robert agreed, and raising the wick of the lamp, they returned to the cell of Donald.

Robert now proposed remaining with his master till night, but the latter reminding him Dargo had not yet left the castle as he had hinted, requested him to go back to his dungeon, lest their jailor should return in the course of the day, which, in all probability, he might. Robert could not but admit the truth of sir Donald's remark, and prepared to leave him; when it was farther agreed between them, that, when the latter thought it a fit time for their enterprise, he should repair to the trap door, and give a signal by striking it with his hand thrice; and Donald stepped with him through the passage, to ascertain the exact spot it was placed in. After satisfying himself in this particular, he left his attendant, and entering his own dungeon, pulled to the door, and reclining on his straw, anxiously waited the evening's approach.

"Oh, my beloved! could I but once again behold thee, that I might be able to clear my fame, I should die content! but to be thought a base coward, and die, conscious of the foul aspersion, is more than I can bear!" Thus did he soliloquize. The words of Duncaethal now recurred to his recollection, who said he should return that night to hear his final determination to what he had proposed. This had escaped him in his interview with Robert, and he feared he must forego his enterprize till another opportunity. Bitterly did he reproach himself for not remembering this, previous to the departure of the latter; and dreading the consequence of a discovery, he sallied forth to acquaint him with the circumstance; he succeeded in finding the place, and briefly told him his apprehensions, should they venture forth that evening. Robert acquiesced in the prudence of Donald's objections, and they determined to keep in their respective cells till the time mentioned by the latter, which was to be, as near as they could possibly guess, about the hour of midnight. Donald once more retraced his steps to his dreary abode, with intention of waiting patiently for the appointed hour.

Time moved on with leaden and sluggish steps; tediously did he wait in expectation of Duncaethal's appearance; but he came not; and on Donald's awaking from a heavy slumber, which he had imperceptibly fallen into from intense watching, he concluded it was morning; and that, from some unaccountable motive, his enemy had failed to torment him with his presence, so hateful now to his sight. Happily he did not know, that, during the hours which he had slept, his benefactor had fallen a victim to his unrelenting cruelty, or that his beloved Matilda was safe in his power. He arose from his bed of straw, with a determination of making his way to the passage, to judge, by the sun, how far the day had advanced, and proceeded to the friendly door with that intention, when the jingling of keys announced the approach of some one; instantly throwing himself down, he awaited, with all the composure he could assume, for the appearance of this unwelcome visitor.

The door was now opened, and, to his surprise, he beheld Dargo.—"Ah," said he, "I did not expect to see you this morning."

"This morning!" returned the other; "marry, time must pass merrily with you, I think, that you take it for morning!—why 'tis now near twelve o'clock at night!"

Donald felt convinced it must have been near day before he had fallen asleep, and turning to his gaoler, replied—"Why I thought you said you should not visit me again for a day or two."

"So I did," returned the other; "but I come for the purpose of bringing you glad tidings;—the fair Matilda is now in the castle."

"Here!" said Donald, starting; "to what purpose?"

"Why," returned the other, with an ironical look; "why to become the bride of my lord, to be sure."

"Thou liest, villain!" exclaimed Donald, in wrath; "the baron would never consent to it."

"He silently consented," said Dargo.

"Impossible!" returned his agitated prisoner.

"Ah, but he did," replied the other, "for a very good reason."

"What reason?" eagerly demanded the other.

"Why because he could not say anything against it."

"Could not! what dost thou mean?"

"Why because he had not a word to say for himself—he's dead!"

A cold shivering rushed throughout the frame of the horrorstruck Donald; as he exclaimed—"Then he is murdered!—inhumanly murdered!"

"Not he," replied the other, with great seeming coolness; "he fell by the chance of war. Last night we attacked Bosmora; the victory was ours, and the lady Matilda became the lawful prize of our lord; I conducted her here myself, and scarcely an hour has elapsed since we arrived."

Donald now became almost frantic, but, after a pause, it, for the first time, struck him, that, perhaps, by the power of a bribe, he might gain over his gaoler to suffer his escape;—then addressing him, said—"Dargo, you cannot be ignorant of the baron's intentions when living to make me the husband of Matilda; and I flatter myself, if I was once at liberty, I should directly be united to her, and, consequently, be equal in power with your lord; if, therefore, you suffer me to gain my freedom, and aid me in procuring Matilda's also, I swear to you, by the honour of a knight, to reward you amply, and place you in a much superior situation than ever you will be by Duncaethal."

"Why," returned Dargo, "you promise greatly."

"Nay," replied the other, "I will perform—I swear it! and, as an earnest of my future favour, accept this," taking from his neck the rich cross presented him by the lady Margaret, which he constantly wore, "which is the only valuable I now possess."

"Sir," said Dargo, "you are very complaisant, and there is no withstanding your offer; so I must, perforce, accept it;" then receiving the ornament from the hand of Donald, made a low bow, and conveyed it to his pocket, at the same time saying—"I am much beholden to your liberality, and shall never forget the obligation; but as to freedom, never let that trouble you, for I have it not in my power, even if I was inclined to grant it."

"Why, wretch! didst thou not say thou accepted my offer?" said Donald.

"Änd so, sir, I do; believe me, I am truly grateful for this mark of your favour," said the other sarcastically bowing, "and, in return, I have the pleasure to inform you, that you will have the felicity of ending your days in this agreeable place, where it could not possibly be of any service to you; so if you had not good-naturedly made me a present of it, why perhaps I might have been tempted to help myself; for it really is too pretty, and a great deal too valuable, to be buried beneath the surface of the earth, so long as there remains any one above to make use of it."

"Why, villain!" said Donald, "will you break your promise?"

"Promise!" returned the other; "I break no promise; I only said I accepted your proffered kindness; beside, you promised me more than you would ever be able to perform; so I think that you ought to thank me for preventing you from ever having the very disagreeable reflection of forfeiting your word; for when the lady Matilda becomes the bride of my lord Duncaethal, all your hopes will have an end, and so would your promises too."

"Wretch!" returned the other, "torture me no longer with thy hated presence and detested falsehoods! Quit my sight!"

"Oh, sir," coolly replied the other, "don't be in a rage, for really I don't want to force my conversation; so, sir, a good rest to you."

The villain now withdrew, and closing the door, left the miserable Donald cursing his folly, for suffering himself to become the dupe of such an unfeeling monster; and throwing himself upon his straw, once more gave up to despair.

Chapter IX

Sure 'tis
The echo of some yawning grave,
That teems with an untimely ghost!

Take any shape but that, and my firm nerves
Shall never tremble.

Shakespeare.

ATILDA, AFTER A NIGHT'S SLEEP, disturbed by frightful and horrific dreams, arose, feverish and unrefreshed; then summoning Venella to assist her in dressing, which, after finishing, they repaired to the apartment they had left on the preceding night, where an elegant breakfast had been set forth by Gertrude, who, shortly after, made her appearance.

"Ah, lady," said she, in a tone of sympathy, "those pretty eyes plainly tell me that you have had but an indifferent night's rest: ah! I am sorry for it, lady—indeed I am!—but do try and eat something—do, my dear lady! I have prepared the best breakfast for you that the castle could afford."

"I am very much obliged to you for your kind attention," said Matilda; "but I am really very ill, and feel it utterly impossible to avail myself of it."

"Ah, dear lady," answered Gertrude, "I am sorry for it, very sorry, and I fear I bring you news but little calculated to restore your health—my lord Duncaethal bade me inform you he intended to visit you in the evening, if you would grant him permission."

"If I would permit him!" exclaimed Matilda; "why does he thus insult the wretchedness he has himself caused, by this mockery of complaisance? He can, no doubt, if he chuses, visit his miserable prisoner without her consent; then why thus seemingly request it?—but you may tell him I am ready to receive him, if he has the boldness to meet the indignant eye of the unhappy daughter of the murdered Bosmora."

"Alas, madam," said Gertrude, "I dare not tell him what you have said, for the world."

"Well then, you may deliver to him what message you think fit to that purport," said Matilda, mildly.

Gertrude, making a low curtsey, withdrew, followed by Venella. Matilda, striking the chords of lady Margaret's harp, which never, since her demise, had once been removed, but still remained in all its pristine excellence, sought to compose her agitated spirits by music; sweetly did the enchanting sounds float upon the air; and tuning her syren's voice, she began a melodious strain, but had not proceeded far, ere she recollected that it was the same that had so often charmed the ears of her father and Donald, in those days of happiness spent at Bosmora. This recalled to her perturbed mind her father's dreadful fate, with a train of horrid ideas that tortured her to madness; in frantic accents she called upon Donald to rescue her from the power of the murderous Duncaethal, until, exhausted by the violence of her ravings, she sunk upon the floor in a state of total insensibility. Venella then luckily coming into the room, conveyed her unhappy mistress to bed. The poppy influence of Morpheus once more visited her weary eyelids; and, after a few hours of undisturbed repose, she awoke, much recovered, and returned to the apartment, tranquillized and composed; she inquired of Venella, if Duncaethal had been to pay his visit, or if he was acquainted with her sudden indisposition? Venella replied, Gertrude had informed him, and he intended to postpone his visit till the evening.

Matilda now, for the first time since her arrival, took some refreshment, and dismissing her attendant, with an order of being within call if wanted, seated herself at a large gothic window, and waited reluctantly for the dread approach of Duncaethal. It was rather late in the evening; the sun had already sunk beneath the distant horizon, and the gentle zephyrs played upon her pale cheek. Darkness was swiftly approaching, when closing the casement, and arising to summon Venella for a taper, she heard her name pronounced, and quickly turning round, beheld at her elbow the mysterious figure which she encountered in the subterranean of Bosmora. A loud shriek was just bursting from her lips, when raising his hand, he motioned her to silence, and, in a low tone, thus addressed her—"Matilda, fear not! thou shalt not fall a victim to Duncaethal:—thou art reserved for another fate! I tell thee so—I, the bandit Darthalgo! Hadst thou accepted my proffered protection, long ere this, thou wouldst have been free from sorrow—but I perceive my appearance offends you; girl, trust not to that! for I could so far change myself, that, in some eyes, I might even appear prepossessing—I am not what I seem!"

"Indeed!" said the terrified Matilda, who now, for the first time, had recovered the use of speech, of which his sudden and terrific appearance had deprived her, "indeed!"

"Nay, I swear I am not, lady! I will save you; to-morrow I will return, and, in the mean time—" A voice in the antichamber interrupted him, and instantly snatching a mantle from the shoulder of Matilda, he cast it over her face; and ere she could remove it, not the least trace remained of her mysterious visitor.

Duncaethal now entered the apartment, and, in a voice of studied complacency, asked if she was better? at the same time remarking that her cheek retained all the lovely carnation, as when first she enslaved his heart.

"Monster!" said Matilda; "if that colour does indeed appear in my face, it is to express the indignation which I feel at beholding the murderer of my father. Would I could arm those eyes with avenging lightning, to strike thee dead!"

"Lady, spare your rage," said Duncaethal, coolly; "it will not avail thee half so much as gentleness. If thou wilt hear me patiently, I may remember the respect and dignity due to your sex and rank; but if, by ill timed rage, you scorn my offers, it will but hasten the fate prepared for stubbornness." Then kneeling before her, he thus continued—"Lovely Matilda, behold me at your feet!—me whom you have for ever enslaved, to beg for your pity, which can alone make me happy! 'Twas for the great felicity of calling you mine, that I rushed into fatal war, to gain that prize which courtesy solicited for in vain!"

"And didst thou, mistaken wretch, think the heart of Matilda was to be won by imbruing thy hands with the blood of my father? Hear me, Heaven, as I hope for mercy at thy great judgment- seat, never will I become the wife of a homicide!—never will I call the murderer of my father, husband!"

"'Tis well, madam," said Duncaethal, while rage shot from his fierce dark eye, "'tis vastly well; but if you care not for your own life, I have yet another hold on you—your minion, Donald, he is in my power, and amply will I revenge myself in his death, for your scorn and haughtiness!"

Duncaethal had attained his point. Matilda, who feared not for herself, when she heard her heart's beloved was within his grasp, all the woman's tenderness arose, and sinking on her knees at the feet of her remorseless tyrant, in piteous accents, implored him to save the life of the unoffending Donald.

"What!" said he, exultingly, "can the proud imperious Matilda descend so far as to prostrate herself before a murderer, whom her eyes would fain strike dead! and, in humiliating language, can plead for the life of a wretch beneath her regard!—but I pity your weakness, and will spare his life, if you will consent to become mine; but if you still reject me, I will wreak on his head my utmost vengeance, in which I am irrevocably fixed."

The agitation of Matilda almost amounted to madness, as she struggled between fear for herself, and dread for the life of Donald, which, to preserve, she was nearly on the point of consenting to his wishes, when suddenly she recollected the words of the bandit—'Thou shalt not fall a victim to Duncaethal—I will save you!' "If," thought she, "he can rescue me, he might also be able to preserve Donald." Gathering courage at this idea, she hastily arose, and exclaimed—"Never, never will I become the wife of the murderer Duncaethal!"

"Indeed!" said he, instantly seizing her in his arms; "you have now, haughty madam, signed the fiat of your own destruction; I will not again sue for the happiness which is already mine by right of conquest, and force shall procure for me what I have so long solicited in vain."

A loud shriek burst from the lips of Matilda, as she endeavoured to extricate herself from his loathsome kisses and rude embrace, when a dismal and hollow groan, sounding through the apartment, caused him instantly to quit his hold, and a voice, in sepulchral tones, cried—"Murderer, forbear!" The room, which, till now, had been almost dark, was instantly illuminated by a flaming lamp, that was borne in the hand of a tall spectral figure; a deep wound appeared in her breast, from which the sanguinary stream still seemed to flow, while, in hollow accents, it thus addressed the terror-stricken Duncaethal—"Behold me, thou homicide! long shalt thou not flourish amidst thy horrid crimes; thou shalt fall by the hand of one, who, by thy blood, must give peace to the suffering spirit of the murdered Margaret!"

The conscience-smitten Duncaethal sunk to the floor, as the figure, approaching him, uttering a dismal groan, slowly disappeared. Matilda fell upon a couch, in a state of total insensibility, for she beheld, in the pale countenance of the spectre, the features of the departed lady Duncaethal.

Venella, who was, with great anxiety, longing to know the result of the interview, and not being able longer to resist, advanced to the door of her lady's apartment, and placing her ear to the key-hole, as was her usual custom, when she wished to gratify her ardent and irresistible curiosity, she was greatly surprised at not hearing any one, and, after waiting a considerable time, was tempted to open the door, and, to her great surprise, beheld them both in the state already described; she loudly called for assistance, and, in a moment after, Gertrude made her -appearance, followed by Dargo, who, with looks of astonishment, beheld the prostrate situation of his lord, and summoning another domestic to his aid, conveyed him from the apartment, while Venella and Gertrude were both endeavouring, by all possible methods, to recover Matilda, who, on opening her eyes, uttered many incoherent expressions relative to the strange sight which she had so lately witnessed, not a word of which was understood by her hearers, who concluded she was delirious. After a pause, she asked Gertrude if she had ever beheld the ghost of the departed lady Margaret?

"Who, I, my lady? No, the Virgin forbid! why, have you, madam?"

Matilda then recounted the cause of her fainting; and minutely described the figure she had beheld; when she mentioned the wound in her breast, Gertrude shook her head, and said—"Ah! I fear that there has been sad doings, in some respects; but I do really think it could not be the ghost of lady Margaret, for I saw her lie dead, with my own eyes."

Matilda was surprised, and yet she felt convinced it bore her likeness; and the words she uttered striking so forcibly on Duncaethal's guilty conscience, corroborated her suspicion of Margaret's having been basely murdered; but not being able to develop the mystery, she endeavoured to change the subject, inwardly blessing that Providence which had, by its heavenly interference, saved her from a fate worse than death.

She now interrogated Gertrude respecting what prisoners there were in the castle, and if the person of a young knight was amongst the number? hoping that Duncaethal had only made use of artifice, by saying Donald was in his power, to intimidate her with the fear of his vengeance falling upon him, which she now began somewhat to suspect.

Gertrude replied—"Alas, my lady, I know not indeed! but I suppose there are several confined in the dungeon, for Dargo frequently carries several baskets of provisions from the hall, which I know not how he disposes of, except for the use of prisoners: I once had the curiosity to inquire, but he surlily bade me mind my own business, and not question him. Ah, madam! this castle is not like what it was in the time of our good old lord, your noble grandsire! Ah! he little supposed this old mansion, which was the seat of benevolence and hospitality, would ever be converted into a prison! but when our present lord came to be possessor, he dismissed a great many of the ancient domestics and bards, who had, for many years, eaten the bread of our good old baron; but when he returned from his travels, and brought home his bride, lady Margaret Monteith; it became again enlivened by the resort of company, for she was never easy but when having revels and masks; and I believe, by her extravagance, wasted much of my lord's substance; and since her death, the castle has been solitary enough, for my lord seemed to make amends for her profusion by his parsimony, my lady:—but, lack-a-day! I am talking away my time, when I ought to be in the hall; and so, my dear lady, if you are better, I will leave you with your maid."

Matilda assured her that she was perfectly recovered; the kind old woman, making a low curtsey, and desiring she might be called if her illness should return, modestly withdrew, leaving her to the care of Venella, who was terrified to death at the idea of ghosts and apparitions, declaring she should never be able to remain alone after dark, or sleep again by herself, long as she lived, for fear of being visited by some supernatural intruder.

Matilda now recurred to the words of the mysterious Darthalgo—"I am not what I seem, and could appear prepossessing." She thought it might be a friend in disguise, who had some particular motive for his strange conduct, and offers for her service. Then formed the resolution of trusting herself under his protection, if ever another opportunity should occur; and after earnestly returning her thanks again to that Providence who had, in such a mysterious manner, delivered her, she offered to Heaven a petition for the safety of Donald; but feeling no inclination for sleep, she took up a book which lay in the room, and sought to beguile her time by reading; she accidentally opened it at the commencement of the following tale:—

"Deep in a glen, obscure and lowly, dwelt the lovely and innocent Mora; sweetly glided her days till she was seen by Rothma, lord of the castle, which, in proud majesty, frowned upon her clay-built cottage. Loudly had the horn of the hunters sounded through the winding of the vale, as the fleet hounds swept away the pearly dew-drops from the grass, when the proud-mettled steed threw his lord near the gate of Mora. Her father, with a ready hand, assisted him to their dwelling, and he departed not for several days, but, like the fiend, lingered, with many evasive excuses, until he triumphed over the virtue of the innocent Mora. The poor deserted one pined in secret, till the damask hue which had once blushed upon her cheek changed to a death-like paleness, as, with rapid steps, she was hastening to hide her shame under the green sod which covered her heart-broken father.

"Not so the proud Rothma; he forgot the daughter of Carlina; and his bridal day, in all the pomp of lordly pride, quickly followed the destruction of Mora. Loudly sounded the harp in his halls, and the banquet board sunk under the weight of the rich viands which composed the feast. In the midst of the revels, a wandering minstrel approached, and bowing gracefully to the bride, skilfully struck the lyre, and, with a melodious voice, sung the following legend:—

> 'List, sweet lady, to my ditty—
> 'Tis of Mora fair I sing;
> Prythee drop a tear of sorrow.
> While I gently touch the string.
>
> 'Lovely Mora, in a cottage.
> Sweetly pass'd each fleeting day;
> 'Till lord Carril, like a canker,
> Grop'd this flow'r and fled away.

'Many days, in silent anguish,
Gentle Mora pass'd away;
Many tears of briny sorrow
Damp'd the pillow where she lay.

'Now the merry bells are ringing
Through the vale with clamour wide.
Tell poor Mora, the deluder
Basely has receiv'd a bride!

'Mora now, in strange attire,
Seeks the castle where he dwells.
And, as in a minstrel's legend,
To the bride her story tells.

'Yes, fair lady, that is Carril!
I am Mora the betray'd!
Thou'rt the bride that have with patience,
Listen'd to the ruin'd maid!'

"She was silent, while all within the hall cast their eyes upon the proud Rothma, who in vain endeavoured to hide the stings of guilt, as the minstrel earnestly fixed on him her penetrating gaze; when, at length, endeavouring to recollect his scattered spirits, he loudly exclaimed—'Seize that vile impostor, and bear him instantly to a dungeon!' The domestics approached, and the minstrel in a moment vanished, when, in his place, stood a meagre spectre! All started aghast, and Rothma gazed in wild affright, while the spirit of the deserted Mora thus addressed him—'Rothma, my bridegroom, haste! quit that form, and come away!' In a moment the flesh faded, and the noble person of Rothma sunk into a loathsome skeleton! loud thunders shook the battlements, as, enclasping him in her arms, they both disappeared from the view of the astonished assembly!

"The castle was deserted for ever! and as the hind nightly seeks his peaceful cot, he hies him swiftly by the gate; for as the bleak wind whistles past him, he hears, or fancies he hears, the sigh of Mora borne on the shrilly breeze."

Chapter X

She lives; but wastes her life in constant woe—
Weeping her husband slain—her infant lost!
Home.

DONALD, AFTER IN VAIN reproaching himself for resigning the jewel, and his tumultuous passions had somewhat subsided, endeavoured to rally his subdued spirits, and resolved to make another attempt, if possible, to procure his emancipation. He cautiously proceeded to the door of Robert's cell, and giving the appointed signal, the latter gently raised the friendly trap, and, in a moment after, joined his master. They both repaired to the staircase, and opening the door slowly, found themselves once more in the passage or corridor. Donald, with great precaution, entered the chamber on the right, whose ruinous state proved that it had long been uninhabited; and, after searching in vain for some outlet, returned to Robert, who remained in the passage, to give a signal if any person should approach.

They now perceived a flight of stairs, which had escaped their notice on their first entrance, and, with renewed hopes, both ascended them; but to their disappointment, found they communicated with the roof, and had been erected for the purpose of a quick ascent to the parapet; but the top was closed up. Being dejected with this disappointment, they descended, and were debating whether they should return to their cells, as there seemed to be no chance of success; but Donald was determined to search every cranny, ere he quietly resigned himself to his fate.

At this moment a voice, seemingly in earnest supplication, attracted his attention, and motioning to Robert for silence, he followed the sound through a chamber to a door at the end of it which was barred on the outside; he proceeded to unfasten it, in spite of the fears of Robert, who sought to deter him, by saying they possibly might break in upon some of the ministers of Duncaethal. His master felt convinced it was some poor captive, or else, for what reason should the entrance be secured? He soon succeeded in his attempts to remove the bar, and opening the door, found it was the antichamber of another apartment. An earnest prayer, which a female voice was offering up to the Virgin, encouraged them to proceed; their approach did not alarm the supplicant, and gave time, ere she perceived them, to contemplate her strange appearance. A long black vest was fastened round her waist, from the girdle of which hung a rosary; her long hair waved negligently on her shoulders, and her arms were crossed upon her bosom, in the posture of adoration; her fine blue eyes seemed irradiated with pious fervency, forgetful of all sublunary objects.

Donald knew not whether to advance or recede, so fearful was he of disturbing the devotions of this mysterious recluse. She now arose, and turning, beheld the two intruders—"Ah!" she exclaimed, "is my tyrant, at last, determined to extirpate my wretched existence? but I am prepared—so, murderers, advance, and execute his bloody purpose."

Donald, gracefully bowing, said—"Lady, you are deceived; we are not assassins, but almost strangers here."

"Ah!" exclaimed she, "by what happy chance come ye?" and falling at their feet, continued—"I beseech ye, for Heaven's sake, to conduct me from this prison. Not for myself I sue, but I would learn the fate of a being far more dear to me than my wretched life."

"Alas, madam," replied Donald, "I regret 'tis not in my power, for, like yourself, I am but a prisoner; and it was in hopes of gaining my liberty that brought me here."

"Are you then in the power of Duncaethal?" said she, sympathetically. "I am," returned Donald.

"Then, stranger, I pity you; for you are in the fangs of a lion, from whom escape is impossible. Many years have I wretchedly lingered here; yet bless my fate that I have not, ere this, fallen a victim to his rage, and still remain in this world of woe."

She now inquired of Donald how he had contrived to leave his dungeon? He informed her briefly as possible, at the same time saying he must return, lest his gaoler should, by chance, visit his prison and find it vacant. The lady agreed with his observation, and bidding him farewell, added—"Stranger, if you could again contrive to visit me to-morrow night, you shall be made acquainted with the sad events of my wretched life; and if you should ever escape, may seek out one I shall mention, and inform him of my hapless fate."

The castle clock at this moment proclaimed the hour of two; and supposing the inhabitants were all buried in sleep, he said—"Madam, the interest I feel for your wretched situation, together with the hope I may, by the help of Heaven, have it in my power to serve you, makes me resolved to seize the present opportunity, lest another should not occur, to know in what manner I can effect it."

She pointed to a bench, when being seated, she began her wretched narrative.

"In me you behold the sad remains of Agnes Maclean."

Donald started; she marked his emotion, and said—"Why start you, stranger?"

"I had heard," Donald replied, "she perished in a flood, and was never heard of more; but I beg pardon, lady—proceed."

She continued.—"My father, on his deathbed, entrusted me to the care of the former baron of Duncaethal, who acted the part of a tender guardian, and reared me with his own son and daughter. For the lovely Mabel I felt all the affection of a sister; but the youthful Alexander won my virgin heart, and he returned my affection by a passion amounting to adoration. He disclosed his love to his father, without hopes of success, for family pride cast a shade upon a character otherwise generous and benevolent.

"About this period lord Bosmora visited the castle, and being smitten with the beauty of Mabel, married her, and bore her away from Duncaethal. 'Twas now that her brother's flame for me burst forth, and pleading his passion in the most glowing terms, urged me to consent to the solemnization of a private marriage. This I constantly declined till he was on the point of going forth to terminate a feud, existing between his father and a neighbouring chieftain; when, won by his parting solicitations, I gave him my hand, and consented to his making me his wife, ere he quitted Duncaethal. We concerted that I should walk out alone, as was my custom, and he should meet me at an appointed spot. Every thing succeeded to our wishes, and we repaired together to a neighbouring monastery, where my beloved lord bribed a father of the place secretly to unite us. A woman who had attended me from my infancy, was a witness and confidant of this inauspicious marriage. Two days after he left me, to meet his death, for never did he return until his eyes were closed in lasting sleep. Wretched woman as I am, how did I ever survive this blow, as fatal to my peace! but, alas! my cup of misery was not yet full.

"The news of his son's death smote the old baron to the heart's core, and he speedily closed his sorrows in the grave. Oh, would that his fete had been mine! Mabel came to close the eyes of her father, and would fain have conducted me to the castle of her lord, which I was on the point of consenting to, when the present possessor of this castle arrived, to invest himself with the rights of possession; but on his saying he should leave the place for a few weeks, I requested of Mabel permission to remain for a short time, and wear off the poignancy of my grief in solitude. She consented, and I saw her depart, with a promise of my following shortly after.

"One day, as I was riding in the adjacent forest for the benefit of the air, I recalled to my afflicted mind how often I had, in that very spot, accompanied my departed lord. The tears unbidden rushed in torrents down my cheeks, when turning my steed, I was about to quit the place; but the reins were suddenly seized by a ruffian, who commanded me immediately to dismount and follow; I was forced to comply, and another fierce-looking man assisted me in so doing. They now proceeded into the thickest part of the forest, and seating me under a tree, waited for approaching evening. Resistance was in vain, for they threatened me, on their first appearance, with instant death, if I attempted to make the least noise.

"When they thought it sufficiently dark, they reseated me, but on another horse, (for they had left mine to retrace its way back to the castle, and, by that means, to cause its inhabitants to suppose I had perished,) and placing a bandage over my eyes, swore, if I uttered a single word, that moment should be my last. We now proceeded, and, after an hour's riding, near as I could guess, they stopped, and lifting me from the horse, conveyed me up some steps, where being unbound, and the bandage taken from my eyes, I found myself in the adjoining chamber to this: I knew not then that it was the castle of Duncaethal, for this wing being in a ruined state, the old baron had always kept it closed up.

"I now inquired for what purpose I had been brought hither? They replied I should soon be informed, and left the room, closing the door, and securing it on the outside. When left to myself, I revolved within my mind the strange motives for this unaccountable procedure. That they were not robbers was evident, for they neither demanded my purse, or any valuable about me, or offered the least violence to my person; what could they be?

"My ruminations were interrupted by the appearance of no other person then Duncaethal himself. Surprise bereft me of the power of speech, while he thus addressed me—'Lovely Agnes, behold before you the man whom the power of your charms has compelled to act thus forcibly against his inclinations; but consent to be mine, and you shall reign in this spacious and noble domain with unbounded sway. 'Tis not in my power to espouse you, but, as my mistress, you shall command a heart that pants with adoration.' Then kneeling at my feet, he continued—'My soul's idol, let me only call you mine, and my happiness will be complete.'

"I now interrupted him by saying—'Arise, lord Duncaethal, and insult not mine ears by your detested passion, but instantly tell me where I am, and by what authority you have dared to seize my person, and convey me from my friends?'

"'I have no authority' said he, 'but love: I must also be so free as to tell you, that, unless you consent to my wishes, you have tasted liberty for the last time. You are in my power, and the whole world shall not compel me to resign you.

My plans are securely laid; no one but my trusty emissaries knows of your being here; the old stupid servants of the castle are lamenting you as lost, by supposing that you were thrown into the flood near the forest; and every precaution has been made to prevent your escape. You can only impute all that I have done to the effects of passion, ardent and irresistible. I have loved you from the moment I first saw you, which was at the death of the baron; and my pretence of leaving Duncaethal was a stratagem to get you into my power. I have beheld you when you thought yourself in solitude, and every glimpse I caught of that lovely countenance served only to rivet my chains, that were already galling, and I found it was in vain to resist the force of charms ordained to enslave my heart—therefore, lovely Agnes, consent to my happiness, and, in a distant land, we'll enjoy the bliss of love, uncloyed by the trammels of the canting priest.'

"He now paused, and I replied—'My lord, I have heard you with patience, but am at a loss to account for the motive of this insult, or what part of my conduct could ever induce you to suppose that I should listen to the offer of an illicit connexion; nor can I imagine how you could so far insult the unstained honour of a descendant of the house of Maclean—of one who, though poor, has the claim of noble birth. That I possess not riches, is my fault, not my misfortune; for know, thou insulting wretch, I have a legal right to those which you enjoy, and it was only with a view to forget my sorrows that I withheld my claim; and may it strike terror to thy soul, as I now inform you that I am the lawful wife of Alexander, the deceased heir of Duncaethal!'

"These words, for a short time, seemed to petrify the wretch; the pale cheek was blanched with fear and surprise; but recovering himself, he said—'Well, if it really is so, why I have a double cause then to retain you: but fear not, for I shall no longer persecute thee with my passion;—my heart, which burnt to possess the virgin, is cold towards the widowed wife.'

"He now, coldly bowing, left the room, regardless of the entreaties which I made for liberty.

"On the following morning he returned, leading in Peter and my woman; I fell upon my knees before the old steward, and besought him to rescue me from this wretched place. I was rudely raised from the floor by Duncaethal, who told me prayers were in vain; and if I made such ill use of his indulgence in allowing me servants, he should find means to make me wait upon myself. He then left the room, when old Peter informed me the tyrant had returned to the castle on the evening that I was missing, and pretended to take an active part in the vain search that was made for my recovery; but finding my mantle, which, it seems, had been purposely left in the forest, asserted that I had been thrown into the river, and caused Peter to send a messenger to that effect unto

Mabel. He then visited me, in hopes of gaining my consent to his infamous proposal, when making a discovery so little expected, his love was converted into fear, and he determined to make this place my eternal prison. Upon leaving me, he summoned Peter, and Beatrice, my woman, from whom he extorted a dreadful vow never to divulge what he should disclose to them, at the peril of their lives; at the same time insinuating to them, that if they acted faithfully, they should be rewarded amply. They had no resource but compliance; and after administering to them the oath of fidelity, which, in its form, was truly horrid, as he acquainted them with his securing me, and his purpose in so doing, until a recent discovery had caused him to alter his project, which required their service to perform, in attending me and preventing my escape. To this, with reluctant hearts, they were compelled; then giving them notice that he should be absent for a considerable length of time, he renewed his threats and promises, as their conduct might merit; and departed from the castle, accompanied by the ruffians whom he calls his domestics.

"I had not been long imprisoned, ere I found that I was fast approaching to that period when I should produce a living pledge of the unhappy loves of Alexander and myself. I implored Beatrice and Peter that, if they could not save me, they might my child, as their oath extended no further than to myself. Both of them consented to my request of placing my infant beyond the power of Duncaethal, should the time of my accouchement arrive before his return, who, happily for me, had not suspected my pregnancy.

"At length the important moment approached; and here, imprisoned and unknown, I gave birth to the rightful heir of these rich domains. The very day after, Peter received notice from his master, that he should return in about five weeks. They suffered me to retain my babe the space of a month; when deeming it no longer safe, lest his lord should come unaware, Peter prevailed on me to resign it to him, for the purpose of conveying it to some safe retreat. With a breaking heart I was forced to comply with his prudent advice; and, with many tears, I kissed his infant cheek, and consigned the precious charge to his care.

"I now recollected that I was entirely bereft of money, and knew of no person that, without reward, would receive an unknown child, when the good old Peter, producing a purse of gold which contained nearly half of what he possessed, quieted my fears in that respect; and again embracing, for the last time, my darling infant, I fastened round his lovely neck the only valuable in my possession, which was a string of small pearls, from which was suspended this cross;" at the same time drawing from her bosom the exact counterpart of the jewel given to Donald by lady Margaret, and which he had that night resigned to the villain Dargo.

"God of mercies!" exclaimed he, soon as it met his astonished sight; and thrusting his hand into his breast, drew forth the necklace given him by Allen; he said, in broken accents—"Ah! it is! the pearls—the cross!" and sinking on his knee, exclaimed—"Oh, mother! mother!— bless your child!" But she spoke not; surprise and joy overcame her, and she sunk senseless into the arms of the agitated Donald.

Robert, who had been a silent spectator of this moving scene, wept with joy, and jumping frantically about the room, cried—"My dear master is a true baron! oh dear, how glad I am!"

"Hush," said the youth; "your noise will betray us. Calm your transports, and assist me to recover my mother:—mother! oh thou name revered! but that it should be my unfortunate lot to discover my parent in a prison, damps the joy I feel. Oh, mother! dear mother!"

The name seemed to bear with it a powerful charm, for the poor Agnes once more felt returning life; and once more falling on his neck, crying—"It is—it is my long-lost child!—my dearest Alexander!" she now endeavoured to tranquillize her much-agitated frame, and addressing him, said—"Tell me, my son, how thou hast fared since the fatal day when Peter saw you for the last time?"

Donald, with all the brevity possible, gave her a sketch of his eventful history; which concluding, begged her to proceed with her wonderful narrative, which she did as follows:—

"Peter, on his return, informed me that he had, with safety and great secrecy, consigned you to the care of an honest well-meaning peasant; at the same time returning me the cross which I had fastened round your neck, gently reproved me for risking a discovery, by so remarkable an ornament: it had been presented me by your father, who, on the departure of Mabel, gave her one also, that bore, in every respect, a resemblance and caused the mistake of the good old peasant Allen.

"Shortly after my painful separation from you, the usurping tyrant once more shocked me by his hated presence; but finding I bore my confinement with seeming fortitude and resignation, expressed his approbation of the care of Peter and Beatrice, and seldom troubled me.

"About a year after his return, the good and faithful Peter acquainted me with the death of Mabel, who had left an infant daughter. He had learned these tidings from old Allen, whom he had persuaded to retire to a cottage near the castle of Bosmora, to whom he presented a second purse, containing all that he possessed in the world, promising a renewal of his visit at the end of another year; but ere the expiration of that period, I lost both my faithful servants;

and since that time have been attended by the villain Dargo, who inhumanly prevented both old Peter and Beatrice from obtaining a confessor, fearing, I suppose, lest, on their deathbeds, they should disclose the place of my confinement. Duncaethal never supposed that I had ever given birth to a child; and since the deaths of my attendants, I only have mentioned your name in my orisons, imploring for you the protection of Heaven.

"A long series of years have I now passed, without seeing a human being, except Dargo, whom his cruel master left to guard his hapless prisoner, who every week generally brings me a supply of food, during his travels. Upon his return from them, he brought with him a bride, as I was told by my unfeeling gaoler; nor since that time have I ever heard of him; and when I to-night saw you in my prison, I supposed he was agitated by some new fear of discovery, and had employed you to put an end to my then wretched experience. Little did I suppose I then beheld my son!—that son for whose safety I had daily offered up my constant prayer!" and again embracing, said—"We are now both in the villain's power; but fear not, my child—the omniscient Being who has been graciously pleased to let me once more behold you, will still preserve you from the murderer's poniard, to add lustre to the name and virtues of your noble sire."

The hour of four now loudly sounded, and the streaks of approaching day warned them to separate, lest a discovery should take place by a visit from Dargo. Robert now relighted the lamp; and ere Donald left his mother, she earnestly besought him, however he might be incensed by Duncaethal, not to let drop a hint relative to his real name or title. This he promised; and repeatedly embracing her, tore himself away, after agreeing to a proposal of his venturing to return on the following night.

Robert then assisted him in fastening the door as they at first found it; then repairing to their separate cells, Donald again beheld himself in a place now become doubly disgusting, by his knowledge of the real claim he possessed to an elevated rank, by being the rightful heir to the castle of Duncaethal.

END OF VOL. I

THE CALEDONIAN BANDIT;

OR

THE HEIR OF DUNCAETHAL

A Romance of the Thirteenth Century

IN TWO VOLUMES

VOLUME II

CHAPTER I

Oh that my head were laid, my sad eyes clos'd
And my cold corse wound in my shroud to rest!
My painful heart will cease to beat,
Will never know a moment's peace till then.

Rowe.

MATILDA, THE NIGHT SHE HAD WITNESSED the strange appearance that had struck terror to the guilty soul of Duncaethal, undisturbed by the remorseless pangs of the latter, slept tranquil and secure until a late hour the following day. Gertrude then made her appearance, and informed her, among other circumstances, of the severe indisposition of her master, who, she said, was unable to leave his chamber. That day heavily passed on, unmarked by any change favourable to the lovely captive; but on the evening of the second, as she was reclining on her couch, a loud sigh, seemingly close to her, caused her to start, and at her elbow she again beheld the mysterious bandit!

"Well, lady," said he, "once more chance has given me an opportunity of serving you; will you avail yourself of it, or must I again deprive myself of the satisfaction of conveying you to a safe retreat?"

"Alas!" said Matilda, "your appearance is doubtful, not to add forbidding; therefore be not offended at my objections; for how am I certain but that I may, perhaps, change my miserable situation for a still worse?"

"Worse!" exclaimed the bandit; "thinkst thou there can be a worse wretch in existence than Duncaethal, or dost thou entertain suspicions of my injuring thee? If that were my motive, have

I not now an opportunity? and if thy life was my object, have I not the power now to take it?"

As he spoke he presented a poniard to the breast of the terrified Matilda; then, instantly replacing it, continued—"Foolish girl, are you now convinced? If so, banish your timid fears, and say whether I shall depart alone, or will you confide in the honour of the bandit Darthalgo?"

"I will entrust myself to your care," said she, tremblingly, "for you seem to take great interest in the wretched fate I endure, and will place myself under your protection."

"You are right, lady; no one living takes a greater interest in the fate of Matilda than myself."

An indefinable expression crossed his features as she uttered—"Mysterious being! what art thou?"

"Lady, I repeat to you that I am not what I seem; follow me, and, ere this hour to-morrow, you will be convinced of the truth of my assertion."

He now seized her half-reluctant hand, and pressing a secret spring at the side of her mother's picture, it flew back and discovered a large aperture, through the cavity of which they proceeded, when Matilda found herself in a dark narrow passage (the manner of their escape from the room fully explained to her the method by which the bravo had made his nocturnal visit, and accounted for his sudden appearance): at the end was a door, where taking up a lamp that had been left burning, and shading the flame, they moved slowly on: at length they arrived at a trap in the floor, so cunningly contrived, that not the least appearance of such a device could be detected by any one unacquainted with its construction; The bravo placed his feet on a particular board which composed it, when he instantly sunk from the sight of the wondering Matilda; but, in a moment after lifting up his head, bade her act as he had done, and she would soon find herself in the under apartment. The trap now arose, when she, with a palpitating heart, followed his directions, and found herself, after safely descending, in a spacious room; the damp air instantly chilled her whole frame. The bandit now seemed to think himself beyond the reach of detection, and, with a ghastly smile of exultation, he proceeded with a quick pace, leading by the hand his trembling fugitive, through the intricacies of a winding passage, when arriving at the extremity, and striking with his hand three distinct times upon a small door, he was answered, in a rough voice, by a signal of "Liberty and Darthalgo!" He now withdrew a bolt and threw it open, and pulling Matilda along, entered a small cavern, where three rough-looking men appeared to be in waiting.

One of them, in a discordant voice, said—"Darthalgo, we have tarried for you a long time; if we are not speedy, day will break ere we arrive at the end of our journey."

"Fear not," replied Matilda's incomprehensible conductor; "here is the lady, and our horses are swift of foot."

She was unable to conceal any longer the fear which the sight of these ferocious men had excited, and falling upon her knees, she besought Darthalgo to inform her whither he intended to convey her.

"Rise, madam," said he, in a voice more stern than what he ever before addressed her in; "have I not sworn to free you from your troubles, and yet still do you fear. Cannot you confide in my oath?—Are our horses ready?" said he, to one of the men.

"They are," answered another; "all is prepared."

"'Tis well," said Darthalgo, "and we will make no longer delay."

"Lady, you must consent to my placing this bandage over your eyes, a ceremony which we never omit when a stranger is admitted into our dwelling."

Matilda tremblingly consented to this strange request, which being performed, she felt herself in the arms of a man, who bore her a considerable distance, and placing her on a horse, mounted himself, without speaking a word to his companions, whose horses feet she could plainly hear. He now spurred on his courser, and riding briskly for a long time, a voice cried out—"Halt!" in a tone she recognized for the bandit's, and another gave the signal, by saying, "Liberty and Darthalgo!" which was answered by "'Tis well! all is in readiness!"

Matilda was lifted from off the horse, and being desired to stoop, was conducted through a very narrow aperture; then descending several steps, and turning into a winding passage, proceeded onwards, when a door, which grated on its rusty hinges, was opened; and the bandage being removed, she found herself in a large dismal apartment, hung round with various weapons; a lamp burning on the table, round which were seated a group of men, discovered to her their savage features and uncouth appearance, which plainly spoke their dreadful calling.

"Oh Heavens!" mentally ejaculated she, "Darthalgo has betrayed me!"

She was that very moment addressed by him, saying—"Lady Matilda, be seated and partake of our cheer; we shall shortly have breakfast."

She declined the invitation; when one of the men at the table said—"Don't be alarmed; you need not fear us, my pretty dear."

"No, no," said a second; "we have too much respect for the fair sex, to offer them any injury."

"Aye, aye," said a third; "we love a pretty girl as well as other people, who call themselves honest—don't we, my boys?"

"Aye, aye, that we do," returned the others.

"But," said the first, "the lady don't seem to relish our freedom; mayhap she's weary. Call old Peg, and let her conduct her to bed."

Darthalgo till now had been silent, when, in an authoritative tone, he said—"Go, one of you, and desire that old grumbling harridan to come here."

Matilda felt somewhat easy when she heard that a female was in this strange habitation, as she hoped to experience from her some small commiseration; but her hopes vanished when she beheld the entrance of an old withered hag, whose wrinkled features betrayed evident marks of ill humour, as, in a harsh voice, she demanded their business with her.

"Here," said Darthalgo, "take this lady, and conduct her to a couch."

"Marry," said she, eyeing Matilda with looks of great dislike, "her fine tender joints will rest ill enough upon any couch of ours; she has been used to sleep upon down, I have no doubt. What does she do here, I wonder?"

"What's that to you," returned the former; "go, prepare the best apartment you have, and never ask questions about what you have no business."

"Marry but I have business," said she, "and will have business, let me tell you. You take too much upon yourself, Darthalgo; our chief, Morven, never gave himself any such airs—no, never. Heaven send that he was once more amongst us! I should have cured his wounds long before this, had he entrusted me; but he must suffer himself to be advised to stay among a parcel of strangers, quotha! and invest his command upon one, the newest of our gang. Why did he not appoint Hugh or Gilbert? for I promise you, I care not for Darthalgo; and when Morven returns, I will tell him how you have endangered our community, by bringing among us this young strange minx. She, marry, must have attendance; she is not like me."

"No, no," said one of the band, "that she is not; we can see that with half an eye."

"Don't mind her, my pretty dear." said another; "she hates the sight of any one young or handsome; for it reminds her that it is not her happy lot. Does it not, old Peg?"

"Wretch!" muttered the hag, "I defy—"

"Peace! No more of this jangling," said Darthalgo; "get a bed ready for the lady, or, by St. Andrew, I'll punish this audacity."

"You punish!" returned the hag, "I should like to see you—ha, ha, ha! But come, my fine madam, follow me."

She then quitted the cavern, and Matilda, at any rate willing to leave the company she was in, patiently measured her steps after her, and arriving at a flight of steps, which on ascending she found herself in a spacious room, tolerably decent. An old arched painted window, through which the moonbeams gleamed, made her suppose it was the ruins of an old monastery, which this banditti had converted into a rendezvous. She now sunk upon a couch, to which the old woman pointed, and, muttering, left the room.

Matilda, when alone, was bewildered by painful conjectures what strange motives the mysterious Darthlago could have in rescuing her from the power of Duncaethal, only to expose her to the insolence she endured from a rude band of robbers; till at last she gave herself up as lost. "He has deceived me!" thought she; "his conduct is at once inexplicable and dangerous!"

The door was at this instant opened, and the object of her thoughts made his appearance. She started hastily from the couch, and, in a dignified tone, demanded the reason of this intrusion?

"Intrusion, lady! I hoped that the conduct of Darthalgo had merited permission to break in upon your solitude at any hour."

As he spoke, a dark meaning lurked in his eye; and now, for the first time, the horrid idea was suggested by Matilda, that he entertained for her a wicked passion. Her heart sickened at the thought; a sigh burst from her agitated bosom; and the tears rushed down her pale cheek, as she uttered, in broken accents—"Mysterious being! I implore, I beseech you, to tell me what the motives are for your incomprehensible conduct?"

He seemed for a moment at a loss for a reply, and after a short pause, said—"The motive that first urged me to act as I have done, was love."

"Oh, Heaven!" exclaimed she, "Love! You love me! A bandit!—the outcast of society! Oh God! for what dreadful fate am I reserved? Thou base deceiver, didst thou not say thou wert not what thou seemest?"

"I did," said he, "nor did I speak false; for I appeared *disinterested,* but I was not; and know, thou weak girl, though I am determined to make you mine, 'tis not so much to gratify my love, as it is my revenge!"

"Revenge! revenge on whom?" said Matilda.

"On one whom I hate; on one who is the bane of my life—Donald!"

"Oh, Heavens!" shrieked she, "how has he offended thee?"

"How offend me! Has he not given the worst cause of offence—deprived me of my love?"

"Deprived *thee!* Dost think, vain man, Matilda Bosmora would have ever listened to a bandit?"

"Matilda's credulity confided in the honour of a bandit," said he, scornfully, "to gain your freedom; but know, shallow girl, I did only free you from Duncaethal, to be the more able to gratify that passion which preys upon my very vitals. Here will I refine upon cruelty, and vainly shall my victim seek for help; for revenge, that so long lay smothered, shall break forth in flames, and deal destruction on thy head, thou puny lovesick girl!"

A loud shriek burst from the lips of the terrified Matilda, as Darthalgo, unsheathing a poniard, pointed it to her bosom; but suddenly returning it, he cried—"No! by this my vengeance will be but half complete; I could long since have had thy life; I must glut on revenge, by making Donald witness thy death!"

He left the room, and the undone, the deceived Matilda, bitterly reproached herself for her credulity, in trusting herself to the power of a remorseless bandit. At length, thought she, "I might very well suppose that a wretch, whose business it is to live by rapine and plunder, could be no protector to a helpless girl." His threatening words still rang in her ear—"Here will I refine upon cruelty!" "Who is he, or what can he be? A robber he acknowledges himself; but where can he ever have seen me, that he should entertain in his breast such horrid passions? for never did I behold him until the fatal night when Bosmora fell a prey to a treacherous foe. Oh, Donald! art thou too in his remorseless power? Has he beguiled thy unwary feet into the snare? Alas, it too surely is so! For did he not say thou should behold me perish? Wretched, wretched Matilda! but six months since, and I was the happiest of the happy. A beloved father anticipated my most distant wishes, while Donald existed but upon my smiles. Days, weeks, and months, fled away, unmarked by the slightest anguish, till the villainous Duncaethal, like a devouring, desolating fiend, appeared, and blighted all my happy blissful prospects. A horrid, dreadful contrast has succeeded to my joys, and I shall at last resign my wretched life beneath the murderous knife of a cruel bandit! Oh, horror, horror! But let me not thus despair; there is an Omniscient Power, who rules all; in him I'll put my trust. Oh, thou all-seeing Providence! who before was most graciously pleased to rescue me from a wretched fate, again step forth and interpose thy all-powerful arm, to deliver me from a dreadful death! My father! my dear father! thou sleepest in peace, unconscious of thy wretched daughter's fate; soon now shall we meet in a better world, to live in realms of eternal bliss! Donald, beloved Donald, farewell! Long, long have I struggled with my cruel destiny, but now methinks the chilling hand of death is upon me, and the roscid sweat, trickling from my forehead, warns me of my premature exit from this transitory scene of woe, which will save Darthalgo's guilty soul from one more horrid crime. Donald, beloved Donald—!"

Her eyes now closed, a heavy stupor benumbed her faculties, and she sunk into a state of total insensibility, from which she at length awoke, raving in all the fever of delirium. Many times did she, in frantic accents, rave for liberty, and accusing Darthalgo of treachery, exclaimed—"But Heaven will avenge my wrongs, and strike the murderer with his hottest lightnings!"

Thus did she rave, till exhausted nature sunk into sleep, and when recollection again visited her, she beheld the terrific bandit hanging over her couch. When he found that she was sensible of his presence, he withdrew. Feeble and languid was the frame of Matilda, as she now endeavoured to recall the occurrences of the two or three last days; and, as remembrance struck upon her fancy, the torturing reality appeared in all its gloomy colours; then, closing her eyes, she wished again for that insensibility which happily deprived her of the sad conviction of her wretched condition.

CHAPTER II

Had I one grain of faith
In holy legends and religious tales,
I should conclude there was an arm above
That fought against me.

Rowe.

DONALD, ON THE MORNING he had left his mother, remained in his dungeon undisturbed for several hours; but at last his gaoler appeared, to whom he remarked that his visit was rather more than usually late.

Dargo morosely replied—"Perhaps it is, but I have other affairs to mind besides attending you; and then there's the other; but it seems he wished to save me further trouble—he thought to escape; but I have clipp'd his wings. For him to escape from me, quotha!"

Donald, fearing that their nightly rambles had been discovered, with some degree of tremor, said—"What do you mean?"

"Mean, quotha! why that the hungry elf, in the other dungeon, thought to give me the slip. I caught him in the very fact of trying to raise a trap door; but a padlock, which I have placed upon it, will prevent him for the future; he must be a cunning fellow, indeed, that escapes from confinement, when Dargo is his keeper."

The feelings of Donald during this recital, may be better imagined than described; and he, every moment, expected his wary gaoler would try the security of the friendly door, but, with all his self-boasted precaution, it seems it escaped his notice, for he shortly after left the dungeon. Donald mourned the fate of his faithful servant, whom he concluded would no more be able to leave his dungeon, and, perhaps, at last might perish by the hand of his remorseless keeper. He determined to visit alone his mother once again, when he thought he might venture unseen. The day seemed to drag heavily on, and when night at length arrived, long before the hour he intended to venture forth, a confused sound of voices, murmuring through the passage leading to his cell, struck upon his astonished ear; he had not ceased wondering at this unusual noise, ere his door was burst open, and Duncaethal, with his eyes darting fury, in a voice broken by passion, said—"What then, thou art safe? I thought thou too hadst escaped like the fugitive Matilda!"

"What!" said Donald, "has she escaped? Great Heaven, I thank thee! I now indeed rejoice!"

"Indeed!" returned Duncaethal; 'but thy triumph shall be short; for when I return from the pursuit I shall make to recover her, which if I fail in; thy life shall recompense my vengeance for her loss!" He now withdrew, leaving Dargo to secure the door.

The noise which at different times he heard in the subterraneous parts of the castle, made him deem it unsafe to put his resolution in practice. Not for himself did he fear, but for his revered parent; for should Duncaethal discover, by any means, their consanguinity, he would, most assuredly, exterminate them both. After deliberately weighing the hazard which he must run, he wisely concluded to remain in his cell.

Venella, on the evening of her mistress's strange disappearance, entered the room, to inquire whether she intended to take her evening's repast, but finding it vacant, proceeded to the bed-chamber, when finding her not there, she could scarcely believe her senses; and, after waiting a considerable time without her appearing, at last conjectured that she had escaped. She dreaded alarming the inhabitants of the castle, till she found it would be useless to remain longer silent, and running down stairs, exclaimed—"My lady is gone! She's gone, she's gone!"

"Gone!" said Dargo, "where to?"

"Why," said Venella, "I know not indeed, but she's not in her apartment."

He ran up stairs, and searching the apartments, found them in their usual state, but entirely evacuated. "Yes," says he, "she's surely escaped, but by what means I cannot conjecture." Then hastening to his master, who had not left his room since he had been conveyed senseless from the apartment of Matilda, he acquainted him with the event.

Duncaethal in a moment forgot his illness, and the remorse which at first preyed upon his conscience, in his anxiety to recover his victim. "What, has she escaped, and is her minion Donald a companion in her flight?" eagerly inquired he.

"My lord, he was safe at noon," said Dargo.

"Follow me," said his master; "I will myself see if he is secure!"

Being satisfied as to that, he proceeded to search every apartment in the castle, followed by a train of attendants; but their efforts were fruitless. He then ordered his horses, exclaiming—"Ere I will now lose, I will pursue her to the extremity of the globe!"

He ordered a party to scour the mazes of the forest, where, if they found her not, to meet him on an appointed spot; then bidding Dargo prepare to go with him, he retired to deliberate how or by what manner she had effected her escape; for at the time of her flight, his minister, the villainous Dargo, had the keys of the castle in his own possession; and after numberless conjectures, which only served to puzzle him still more, he could only suppose that she must have been aided by some one of his domestics, as it was evident it was somebody well acquainted with the different entrances of the castle; "which," thought he, "if I could detect him, he should dearly repent it: but I wrong my trusty servants by such suppositions. She's gone, but how? 'Tis fate that seems to snatch her from me! Fool that I was, not to seize upon my happiness when it offered! Fool that I was, to let an idle vision overthrow my purpose! But if my search proves abortive, I will revenge myself by the death of Donald; to-morrow shall he breathe his last!"

He now mounted his horse, and followed by Dargo, hastened to the place where he appointed to meet his attendants, who had not been able to procure the least trace of the fugitive Matilda.

Foaming with disappointed rage, he returned to the castle, with the full intent of fulfilling his horrid purpose. At night he repaired to the cell of his intended victim, and throwing open the door, beheld his prisoner in a tranquil slumber. "Ah!" said he, "does sleep then visit the eyes of my captive on this bed of straw, while I in vain do court its influence upon my downy couch? 'Tis even so; but he now shall close his eyes." Then, in a loud voice, he cried—"Donald, awake, and look upon thy death!"

He started, and beheld the glittering poniard up-raised, ready to pierce his heart; by a natural impulse he swiftly arose from his recumbent position, and suddenly caught the arm of his foe, which he held with a sinewy grasp; then each tugging with the other, breast to breast, the conflict long was doubtful, for fierce as lions did they encounter, each striving to gain the superiority of the other, but neither yet the conqueror or the vanquished. The natural hope for life stimulated Donald, and exerting his utmost strength into one great effort, pressed forcibly on his enemy, who must inevitably have fallen beneath the shock, had not Donald's foot struck against the iron ring on the floor, which caused him to stagger. The other instantly availed himself of this, and rallying his almost exhausted strength, by a sudden exertion overthrew him. Donald now sunk, and his exulting foe raised his arm to give the fatal blow, when a person rushed like lightning between them, and, in a voice of thunder, cried—"Duncaethal, hold!" who instantly exclaimed—"Who art thou?"

"Thine enemy!" said the other; "thy bitter enemy, the bandit Darthalgo!" at the same time aiming a dagger at his breast, which in the hurry failed, and only pierced his uplifted arm.

Duncaethal, with horror and surprise, fell senseless to the earth, in all appearance dead; when the bandit, beckoning to Donald, cried—"Follow me, youth!"

He instantly obeyed, and in a short time found himself in a cavern—the very cavern into which the night before the deceived Matilda had been decoyed by this wily bandit. They now ascended the steps which conducted them to the passage that terminated upon the edge of the forest, where was waiting several of the bravo's comrades, who motioning to Donald to mount behind one of them, and then mounting himself upon his own horse, when clapping spurs to their nimble-footed steeds, they made for their rendezvous.

They had proceeded a considerable distance from the castle, when Donald inquired whither they were conducting him?

Darthalgo answered—"To safety! but if sir Donald doubts our honour, why he is at liberty to go wherever he thinks fit; only, at the same time, I must inform him, if he chooses to go with us, we will conduct him to the presence of Matilda."

"Gracious Heaven!" ejaculated he, "is it possible? Can she be indebted to you for her escape?"

"If there is any obligation," returned the bandit, "she certainly owes it to us; but, sir, I had motives for acting as I have done, which shall be explained to you when we arrive at our place of destination. Comrades, let us on!"

They again proceeded, till halting at the spot where Matilda had been blindfolded, they used the same ceremony with Donald, who, submitting, was conducted through the secret entrance, when the bandage being taken from his eyes, he found himself in the midst of the banditti, who sat regaling themselves over some flasks of wine.

They desired him to be seated, and partake of their jollity; he thought refusal might give offence—he complied. Darthalgo, saying that he would acquaint Matilda with his arrival, withdrew, and immediately seeking out the old woman, inquired how the fair captive fared?

"Dying!" said she; "a high fever has caused her to be delirious ever since you last saw her."

He now proceeded to her chamber, where he earnestly contemplated the dreadful ravages which decaying illness had caused in her once beautiful countenance. Her lovely form was now emaciated, while a hectic glow, which suffused her cheek, bespoke approaching dissolution.

A fiend-like smile passed across the features of the exulting wretch, as he exclaimed—"Oh, vengeance, how sweet thou art to injured souls! This beautiful ruin, this havoc of love, is a grateful cordial to my long-thirsting heart! Fain would I exterminate the hated name of Bosmora! But where is my other victim, that minion Donald, the bane of my peace? Let him come, and by the exquisite torture of his feelings, gladden mine!"

At this moment Matilda opened her eyes, when the bravo left the room, and in a few minutes returned, leading in Donald, who rushing to the side of the couch, started back, for he could scarcely recognize the once blooming heiress of Bosmora, in the sad object which now met his anguished sight.

She at this moment cast her eyes towards the spot on which he stood, when a loud shriek bespoke her remembrance of him, and, in almost inarticulate accents, she uttered—"What, Donald, art thou then here, and has the wily wretch caught thee in his toils?"

"Alas! what dost thou mean, my beloved?" said he; "we have escaped from the power of Duncaethal."

"Alas, yes!" returned she, "we have indeed exchanged his chains for those of a worse villain—the villain Darthalgo! that cruel fiend, who, under the mask of friendship and protection, beguiles his unsuspecting victims to certain ruin."

A cold shiver ran through the frame of Donald, as he turned to examine the bravo, who stood in a distant part of the room, the fierce expression of whose dark eye, where gratified revenge seemed to glisten, convinced him of the dreadful truth, as he uttered—"Is it possible?"

"It is!" said the wretch, advancing. "Didst thou think, weak youth, that I rescued thee from the power of Duncaethal, actuated by motives of fnendship? No! I had more powerful reasons for my conduct—love, jealousy, and revenge!"

"Love!" said Donald.

"Yes, love!" reiterated the bandit; "love, disappointed love! Is it then a wonder that I should feel keen jealousy for my hated, damned rival? and my great revenge can only be appeased by the destruction of you both! Thou, boy, shouldst have perished beneath the dagger of Duncaethal, had it not been for the desire of gratifying my great revenge; for by thy death it would only have been half complete, and I should have lost the joyful rapture I feel in restoring thee to the sight of Matilda, and doubling both your pangs by separation!"

He now shrilly sounded the whistle, which he wore at his breast, when two ruffians made their appearance, whom he motioned to secure Donald; they obeyed, and rushed upon the defenceless youth. The heart-rending shrieks of Matilda made him repel them by force, and long he struggled vainly, like a lion in the hunters' toils; but being unarmed, and finding every effort fruitless, was at last compelled to submit. The ruffians enfettered and conveyed him to a dungeon, where he was left in all the bitter anguish of disappointment, and dread for the fate of his hapless Matilda. He now endeavoured to recall to his memory whether he had ever before seen this new and formidable foe; he thought that the sound of his voice was familiar to his ear, but, after fruitless pondering, he could not recollect that he ever saw any one that in the least bore any resemblance to the cruel, bloody Darthalgo!

"My beloved!" mentally said he, "hast thou escaped the power of the fierce Duncaethal, only to fall a victim to a remorseless bandit, sanguinary as mysterious?"

He now revolved in his mind by what miracle he entered his cell at that critical juncture. "Ah! he, no doubt, contrived to extricate me from Duncaethal's power, that I might the more easily fall in the gin laid to entrap my unwary steps! Oh, my mother! my revered parent! who now shall save thee? Alas! my parent, and my heart's beloved, are both in the power of villains, capable of the vilest measures! The chaste, the beautiful heiress of Bosmora will fall a wretched victim to the unlawful desires of a murderous bravo!" He was frantic at the idea, and smote his head with the enfrenzied action of a maniac.

In the intermediate time, Matilda's fever returned with redoubled force, and her loud ravings echoed through the decaying arched vaults of the old abbey, till the banditti, fearful that her shrieks might attract the notice of passengers, at length bound a handkerchief across her mouth, when the suppressed respiration deadened all her faculties, and she lay scarcely breathing, till Darthalgo every minute expected death would deprive him of his victim, ere he had completed his dire revenge; but in a few days her disorder took a favourable turn, and restored, with her own anguish, the hopes of the cruel, merciless bravo. Earnestly did she wish for the moment of her dissolution, to release her from her endless sorrows; but the awful minister of death shrunk from the eager grasp of the truly wretched, to visit the happy and the affluent, and our heroine was yet reserved to taste still more misery.

CHAPTER III

Techy and wayward was thy infancy;
Thy prime of manhood daring, bold, and stubborn;
Thy age confirm'd, most subtle, proud, and bloody.

Shakespeare.

WHEN DUNCAETHAL SUNK TO THE EARTH, apparently dead, it was not from the effect of the wound he had received, but from the sudden sound and terror of the words which so unexpectedly struck upon his ear—"I am thine enemy! The bravo Darthalgo!"

He had most potent reasons for remembering the name of this mysterious robber, for the explanation of which we must turn back to his early days. His parents were noble, and of an ancient race, but not wealthy; they were remarked for their virtues, which added lustre to the name they bore. By a study to render each other happy, their days glided in happiness, when their bliss was augmented by the birth of a son, the subject of these memoirs; dearly did they love him, and sought to rear him in those virtues which characterized themselves; but vain and abortive were their anxious and maternal cares; for in his early youth he betrayed a predilection for vice, with a disposition morose, ungovernable, and ferocious; and ere he had arrived to manhood, committed actions so very atrocious, that induced his parents to send him on his travels to a distant land, hoping that time and absence might effect more than reproofs or admonitions.

Italy was fixed upon for the place of his destination; and after fixing upon a good venerable priest as his mentor, to guide him in the path of honour, he set forth for that land of harmony and pleasure. There, unrestrained by the presence of his parents, and regardless of the exhortations which the good father never failed to use, he plunged into every species of extravagance and libertinism that could tend to ruin his future health and character—gaming with all the dissipated youths into whose company he fell, until he had contracted debts to a larger amount than what he possibly could discharge.

At this period, luckily, a summons arrived from his father, commanding his return, as he felt himself fast approaching to his end. This served him for a sufficient plea to his companions for his departure, whom he satisfied by promises of a speedy return, with a fresh supply of cash. "For," added he, "should my father die, which probably he will, I will make myself full amends for his niggard allowance during his life."

His profligate companions highly applauded his intentions, and wished him a speedy succession to the estates of his father. Then, bidding farewell to Venice, he embarked, and prosperous gales soon wafted him to the shores of Caledonia; but ere his arrival, his father had fallen a victim to his disorder, a malignant fever; and his mother, who, regardless of herself, had attended him during his illness, caught the infection, and shortly after followed him to the tomb. Their loss was not deeply regretted by their unfeeling son, for he never made a return of that tenderness which they so strongly evinced for him.

Now free from controul, he collected the greatest part of his patrimony, with an intention of returning to those scenes of debauchery that he had but just quitted; but, on the very eve of his departure, he learned the death of Alexander. This to him was joyful news—"For," thought he, "if the old baron should have no more children, and it is unlikely that he should marry again, I must, of course, succeed to the honours and dignity of Duncaethal;" for, by his mother's side, he was the next relation, and to whose children, in default of the baron's male issue, the honours of the family were to devolve.

His wishes were propitious, and the subsequent demise of the baron crowned his sanguine hopes. He now repaired to the castle of Duncaethal, to take possession of the wealthy inheritance, and invest himself with the titles and dignities which now became his, when he became deeply enamoured of the beauty of Agnes; and despairing of her ever consenting to gratify his unlawful desires, he disclosed his secret passion to his minister Dargo, a knave who attended him, and assisted his libertinism when in Venice; they both concerted a diabolical scheme to obtain her, which was executed in the manner already known.

The first journey he made after her confinement, exhausted his well-stocked purse; and, nearly at the period of Donald's birth, he returned once more to Duncaethal. But the unvaried life of a gloomy castle suited not a mind that had been foremost in scenes of gaiety and pleasure. He panted for the joys of carnivals, and the riotous scenes of gaming-houses; and entrusting the conduct of his affairs to the vigilance of Dargo, he once more set forward to the shores of Italy, and again plunged into every species of dissipation.

In the many of his acquaintance, he contracted an intimacy with a celebrated courtezan, who enslaved his heart, even beyond the power of freedom; her house was the resort of a set of the vilest wretches, for the black purpose of gaming, and often enticed the unwary to their ruin. Duncaethal fell a victim to their artifices; and when they had fleeced him of his fortune, he joined the desperate gang, who initiated him in their villainous arts, for the purpose of betraying other dupes, as he himself had been betrayed.

His rank gave him frequent opportunities of inveigling unsuspecting youths, upon whose credulity he and his associates enriched themselves. One of these deluded victims he pretended to profess a particular regard and friendship for; this youth was the nephew of a rich old signor, upon whose benevolence he was a dependant, and to whose liberality he was indebted for the sums which he daily squandered, till at length wearied out by repeated applications, the old signor refused all further supplies, and severely rebuked his nephew for his extravagance. The youth, being greatly embarrassed, applied to Duncaethal for the loan of a small sum, which was granted, in the hopes of securing him for his prey.

Valando, in a burst of gratitude, seized Duncaethal by the hand, and said— "Oh, my friend, 'tis not for myself I would become your debtor! No! but I have another cause—my repeated losses has deprived me of the means of procuring sustenance for my beloved wife!"

"Wife!" reiterated Duncaethal.

"Yes!" returned Valando; "I have married a lovely girl, a peasant, unknown to my uncle, or the world; but your goodness has merited my utmost confidence. Come this way, and you shall hear the history of my Paulina." Then, taking Duncaethal by the arm, and leading him to a retired part of the grove in which they were walking, thus began—

"One evening, as I was rambling near the vineyards, east of the city, a neat white cottage attracted my attention; the flowers which adorned a garden, laid out with excellent taste, convinced me it was the dwelling of some one superior to a common peasant; I leaned over the little gate, and was viewing it with attention, till the lovely mistress of this fairy mansion made her appearance, and was approaching down the walk, which terminated in the place where I stood rapturously gazing on her; but, raising her eyes, a slight exclamation of surprise escaped her, and she swiftly retraced her steps back to the house. I followed, and in a gentle manner apologized for thus surprising her; she curtsied, and modestly requested I would leave her; adding—'Signor, I every moment expect the return of my father, and, should he see you here, I know not what might be the consequence, as he has always charged me to avoid the sight of strangers.' I sought to obey her, but her enchanting simplicity rivetted me to the spot, when, for the purpose of prolonging my stay, I asked her who was her father? 'Delphine Roviria,' replied she. 'And what is your appellation, sweet maid?' 'Paulina, signor,' again answered she. 'Paulina!' I shall never forget it, thought I. At that moment I rivetted my eyes on her lovely countenance—her's eloquently met mine; love instantly took possession of my heart, and never since that period has its ardour abated.

"'Where is your father, sweet Paulina?' She innocently answered—'He is gone to attend our little vineyard in the valley, but I momentarily expect his return; pray begone, signor.' I was on the point of retiring, when a thought entered my mind of again seeing her, and I earnestly requested another interview; she, blushing, refused me; but her countenance betrayed that it was more proceeding from the idea of shame, in being thought too forward, than from any inclination to deny me. I urged my request with redoubled ardour, and obtained from the beautiful girl a half-reluctant consent. I now took my leave, and made my way to the city, but Paulina still remained before my sight, in all the charms of unsophisticated innocence.

"Earnestly did I long for the time of the appointed interview, not that I had resolved upon any plan in regard to her, and therefore ought to have shunned, not have sought her acquaintance. I was not villain sufficient to think of seducing the innocence of this unsuspecting child of nature, and marry her I could not; as my uncle, on whom I solely depended, I was well assured, would never forgive a step so seemingly rash. What infatuation then could possess me to further our intimacy? But to be brief—I repeated my visits several times to the cottage, and at last, in an unguarded moment, triumphed over the virtue of the hapless Paulina. I then avoided her; not that my passion was abated; no! Heaven is my witness, it was not! but I dreaded the reproach of her mild blue eyes, which affected me much more than words, as they silently conveyed the keenest signs of melancholy and despair. She at last appeared to be in a situation which forbad all further concealment; and, urged by my love, I sought her father, when throwing myself at his feet, confessed the dishonourable act, but offered to make what reparation was in my power, by immediately uniting myself to his injured daughter.

"He was at first struck dumb with amazement, for he had not in the least suspected our intercourse; but recovering the use of speech, he vowed vengeance on my head, and bitterly reproached his child for her clandestine proceeding; till at last, passion getting the better, in a paroxysm of rage burst a blood-vessel, and in a few hours expired.

"The miserable Paulina now became frantic, and, in despairing heart-rending accents, besought his forgiveness, which he bestowed, in accents almost inarticulate, ere death closed his eyes for ever. Paulina would not be removed from the inanimate corpse, but continued—'Oh, my parent, hear your wretched child! oh, bitterly do I repent deceiving you, but you have forgiven me! Yes, with your dying breath you have sealed my pardon—miserable else indeed must my lot have been!' Thus, in frantic accents, she continued, till I was at last obliged to have her removed by force; and as soon as her perturbed spirits subsided, soon as serenity once more visited the fair form of my beloved, I united myself to her by the most sacred bonds.

"She still resides in the cottage, which she cannot be prevailed upon to quit, and every day do I expect that she will become a mother; but to-morrow you shall see her, and she shall thank you for your present friendly aid, as my late extravagance and losses at the house of the courtezan Viola, have incapacitated me from supplying her with money, which her present wants demand."

Duncaethal now parted from Valando, promising to meet him at an appointed spot the next day, for the purpose of visiting Paulina. When the time arrived, they proceeded together to the humble residence, where the fair inhabitant welcomed Valando with all the joy demonstrative of a pure affection; he then introduced his friend, and explained to her his obligations to him. Her manner of acknowledgment sealed her destruction, for he inwardly resolved to betray Valando, and possess the beautiful person of the amiable Paulina.

He was already grown weary of the artful Viola, and this simple unsuspecting girl gave new ardour, and a fresh scope to his long dormant machinations. He had resided in Venice for several years, hearing occasionally from Dargo, and sometimes obtaining a supply to his finances; but this was only on particular occasions, for he generally found dupes sufficient to support his unbounded extravagance. He hoped to bear away the lovely Paulina, to enliven the dreary residence of Duncaethal, to which he was on the point of returning, and commenced his horrid plans in the following manner:—By his orders, Valando was seized for the debt, and conveyed to prison; then, in a few days, he repaired to the cottage of Paulina, when he gave her to understand she was basely deceived by Valando, who was on the point of marrying another lady of great fortune; and, after expressing pity for her helpless situation, offered to render her every assistance in his power.

She regarded not his proffered help, but said—"I will see you, my lord, to-morrow."

He took his leave, hoping to bear her away from her home at the next interview; and, lest his plans should be frustrated by the wretched husband, he wrote and informed the old signor of his degrading marriage, well knowing he would not then assist him in regaining his liberty. Every thing succeeded to the villain's wish, and the next night, with a heart triumphing in the success of his deep-laid scheme, he sought the dwelling of his victim; when all around seemed silent, he opened the door—no voice greeted him on his entrance. The moon, glimmering through the humble lattice, fell full upon the face of the wretched

Paulina, stretched lifeless upon a couch—having, by poison, put a period to her existence. The wretch retreated as his eye viewed the desolation he had caused, and in all the agonies of guilt sought his abode, where remorse, for the first time, touched his guilty soul.

On the evening preceding this, Paulina had, on the departure of Duncaethal, composed a billet, which she had conveyed to the wretched Valando, who had left orders where any letters, at any time, might be forwarded to him, as, by the law then existing, he might receive, but could not send any one, without their being first inspected by his gaoler; he therefore did not dare write to his hapless wife, for fear of discovering his connexions, but wrote, with great penitence, to his uncle; when the answer he received simply contained these words—"Release yourself with the dowry of Paulina!"

He now found that Duncaethal was completely a villain; concealment was therefore no longer necessary, and to ease the anxiety of his dearly-beloved wife, he took up a pen to explain the reasons of his absence, when, at that instant, the billet from Paulina was put into his hands; tremblingly he tore it open, and read the following words:—

"Valando, I do not accuse thee of cruelty, and yet I think the sorrows which our fatal connexion has cost me ought to have merited your love. Oh, my dear father, bitterly do I feel the effects of my disobedience! The signor whom you brought here the other day, has acquainted me with your desertion, and your intended marriage with another, which your non-appearance corroborates. I shall not attempt to prove my legality to the rights of a wife, but will leave you to the full enjoyment of the happiness which a perjured heart will allow, while I seek for peace in the silent grave. The fatal potion is now in my hand! I lift it to my lips! Farewell! In drinking this oblivious draught, I free you from those galling fetters which bind the husband and the father! Sometimes think on me, and always remember that your future bride will not love you with a more pure undisguised affection, than her, whose heart, when you peruse this, will have ceased to beat! My life is near a close! Farewell, Valando!—a name still dear but cruel; and my last breath shall pronounce Valando! oh, Valando!"

The wretched youth was almost petrified with horror at the perusal of this, and he franticly exclaimed—"Oh that I could but fly to save her! I would give my life for one hour's freedom!"

The gaoler now entered, whom he, on his knees, besought, in piteous sounds, to permit him to visit his wretched wife, pledging his honour to return. The unfeeling Cerberus was deaf to entreaties—accustomed to scenes of horror, his heart was inflexible; when, armed by desperation, he plunged a stiletto, which he had concealed, into his side, and instantly fled. Swift as lightning he sought the once happy peaceful cot. It was just after the departure of the vile Duncaethal, and he beheld the woeful scene, which had already met the eye of the author of this horrid catastrophe.

The billet had been entrusted to a village girl, who, not thinking it of any import, retained it till noon the following day. Though Paulina had procured her messenger after swallowing the fatal draught, yet so well did she conceal her pangs, that not the least suspicion of any rash attempt was ever dreamt of; and long ere it reached her wretched husband, the affectionate and faithful Paulina was no more! Valando called loudly upon her name, and his piteous moans attracted to the spot some of the vintagers, who were returning from their daily toil; when, imagining they were in pursuit of him for the murder of his gaoler, he fled, and never afterwards returned to Venice. Large rewards were offered for his apprehension, but in vain; and some time after Duncaethal received a billet, containing the following words:—

"Base wretch! I have seen the murdered Paulina, whose blood calls aloud for vengeance on thy destroying head: and if I dared to appear in the city, thy life should answer for thy perfidy; but as it is, I am hunted from society, to herd with outlaws; therefore dread to meet me, for thy arts have made me familiar with scenes of blood! If thou shouldst hear the name of Valando, may it strike thy conscience! but if ever thou hearest the name I have now assumed, expect my dagger to strike thy guilty treacherous heart.   The Bravo Darthalgo."

Duncaethal thought it prudent, for his safety, to hasten his departure, and in a few days he embarked, to return to his native clime; but he nearly met the reward of his crimes in a watery grave. A dreadful tempest drove the vessel on the isle of Orkney, and the seamen being unable to combat with the dreadful storm, it split upon a rock, and only himself and one mariner escaped upon a part of the wreck, the strong tide washing them overboard, and drove them upon the neighbouring shores, near to the castle of Monteith; they were both conveyed to this hospitable mansion, where, by great attention, they were restored to life. Duncaethal here, for the first time, beheld Margaret; her person enslaved his inconstant heart, and her fortune was sufficient to gratify his avarice. He offered her his hand in marriage, and when he quitted Monteith, bore her away as the lady Duncaethal.

They soon after visited Bosmora, where the wavering baron beheld the peerless Matilda; he burned to possess her, and his love for variety caused him earnestly to wish he had first seen Bosmora's beautiful heiress. The subsequent death of Margaret released him from his galling chains of bondage, and he was again free to offer himself to the beautiful Matilda. He never supposed a refusal, and when his offers were rejected, it aroused the revenge of his vindictive malevolent heart, and he resolved to stop at nothing till he had gratified his passion.

On the evening when he thought to stain his hands in the blood of the youthful Donald, when the mysterious bandit interposing, and uttering the name of Darthalgo, struck terror to his soul, and aroused all his long-hushed fears; for he never supposed in the least that the bravo would pursue him for revenge even to his very castle; when he a little recovered from his surprise and agitation, with his arm still bleeding, he sought Dargo, to whom he unfolded the manner of the youth's escape.

"Ah!" said he, after musing a moment, "then the man you have this night seen is, no doubt, a member of the desperate banditti, which infest the old abbey ruins, some miles distant, in the forest."

"Indeed!" said his master; "art thou sure that a band of robbers inhabit there?"

Dargo answered—"Report says so, and our sovereign has several times offered rewards for their apprehension; but nobody ever yet had the courage to effect it."

"Indeed!" said Duncaethal; "a thought strikes me! Muster our soldiers; we will proceed against this banditti, when, perhaps, we may secure our victim, and at the same time I shall be able to ingratiate myself in the favour of our king."

He had his wounded arm bound up, and, followed by Dargo, descended to the lower apartments of the castle, to discover, if possible, the means which the bravo had made use of to gain entrance. They proceeded to the cell in which Donald had been confined, where they at last perceived the entrance through which Darthalgo had conducted him; it was fastened on the outside, but being by Duncaethal's order broke open, they continued their search through the subterranean, and arrived at last to the cavern, which, unknown to them, communicated with the castle, and at a distance opened to the forest.

The mystery now was developed; and having the door properly secured on the inside, to prevent future intrusion, he gave notice to summon his clan, and bade them make preparation for a march in two days, for the purpose of attacking the banditti.

Chapter IV

Revenge, impatience, all that mads the soul,
All that despair and frenzy's flame inspires,
Shown by the tapers, in his eyes did roll,
Hot meteors they amid the lesser fires.

Richard Plantagenet.

ATILDA WAS SCARCELY RESTORED to a state of convalescence, when Donald was conducted to her apartment by Darthalgo, who said— "There, youth, take thy last farewell; for, by all my wrongs, she shall die, and ere to-morrow she shall breathe her last!"

"Monster!" said Donald, "wouldst thou dare to imbrue thy hands in the innocent blood of that lovely maid?"

"I dare, and will!" said the sanguinary wretch.

At this moment the old woman rushed in breathless, and, fast as her fears would permit, she cried out—"The abbey is attacked! Haste, Darthalgo, and head our band!"

He instantly left the chamber, followed by the trembling hag, when Donald, seizing a sword, which the bandit in his haste had let fall, took the hand of Matilda, and said—"Come, my love, now is our only time; Heaven favours our escape. I know the way to the caverns; let us seek out the private entrance of this den of horrors, and make a bold effort for freedom."

He bore the trembling girl in one arm, and with his sword explored his way to the subterranean, which he found was totally deserted by the band, who were defending themselves in an outer part of the ruin. With anxious eye he sought the concealed entrance, but in vain; and the sound of voices indicated the approach of some one, but whether friend or foe they knew not, and he expected each moment to be surprised. Desperation seized him as he swiftly hurried Matilda into a large natural cavity of the subterranean.

Soldiers now entered, bearing lighted torches, and discovered their hiding-place, and seizing upon Donald, who defended himself with great magnanimity, till he was disarmed, conducted him and the wretched Matilda to the chamber they had so lately quitted, where, to their great surprise, they beheld Duncaethal, giving orders for the disposal of the bravoes, who lay bound beside him.

When he beheld our poor hero and heroine, he exultingly and tauntingly said—"Now, my runaways, have I once again, by fortune's kindness, got you into my power, now dearly will I revenge myself!"

A soldier of his clan entered the room at that instant, and said—"My lord, a force, superior to our's, advances swiftly towards the ruin, for what purpose I know not."

Duncaethal stepped towards the window, and said—"If I can aright distinguish, they are the king's troops, coming, I suppose, to subdue this daring band; but we have already obtained the honour of victory."

They now entered, and Duncaethal was proceeding to harangue the commanding officer on the important service, when the other cried—"Seize him!" and in a moment he was surrounded and made prisoner, with the banditti already subdued.

"What means this outrage and violence of my person?" demanded Duncaethal; when a voice exclaimed—"Thou treacherous miscreant, where is my daughter?"

"Here! here!" shrieked the joyful Matilda, and in a moment fell senseless in the arms of her father, who, kissing her pallid cheek, by his fond embrace restored her senses: nor was Donald forgotten. Bosmora, turning to him, said—"Thou much-injured youth, receive from my hand this sword, and head the troops which shall convey that tyrant to a dungeon, where he must remain, till, by a proper trial, he is sentenced to a punishment adequate to his crimes."

"Ah! who dares accuse me of crimes which authorize this vile treatment?" said the fallen chieftain, while fear shook his guilty frame.

"Agnes, the lady of Duncaethal!—Well mayst thou start, thou vile usurper of the rights which, by thy villainy, thou hast dared to possess! Bow, proud wretch, to the lawful heir!—Donald, the son of Alexander, and Agnes, thy wretched captive, who for more than twenty years has been held a prisoner in her own domains. Matilda, my dearest child, greet your future husband—once the humble peasant, but now the noble baron Duncaethal! And you, the misled clan of this vile usurper, I promise a free pardon to all who shall acknowledge this youth, who is the lawful son of your late lord Alexander, for your laird."

They in a moment fell on their knees, and with one voice, unanimous, they loudly greeted their young laird, and besought him to forgive their late behaviour, which proceeded from the fidelity of their supposed laird, whom they now reviled.

"Hold!" said the villain, "do not suffer yourselves to be deceived; do not let a tale like this delude your senses: Agnes never gave birth to a son."

"'Tis false, villain!" said the baron Bosmora; "Donald was born in the very prison she was released from this day, and was conveyed secretly, by the humanity of old Peter, the steward, to the cottage of Allen: and what could it avail thee, even if she had not borne a child? As wife of Alexander (and the holy priest who joined their hands still lives to prove their legal union), she is mistress of the domains, long as she exists; of this thou canst not be ignorant, or else thou wouldst not so carefully have concealed her from the world: but your villainies are laid open—we have traced you through all your wicked schemes of guilt—and thy minister Dargo, who is seized, has confessed the manifold crimes of which thou art guilty. But why do we thus delay, by parleying with this monster? Donald, let us haste, and glad thy fond parent by our presence."

He was on the point of following Bosmora, when he, for the first time, bethought himself that he had not among the prisoners beheld Darthalgo. He briefly explained the conduct of this mysterious bandit to the baron, who immediately ordered a strict search to be made throughout the ruin; but it proved fruitless, and they were obliged to depart, with the conviction of his having effected his escape.

Matilda was seated on a horse, between the one her father and that on which Donald rode, when, addressing the former, she said—"My dear father, what wondrous act of Providence has restored thee to me at a moment so critical, when I have long lamented thee as dead? Do, my dear parent, explain this mystery, which has caused thy daughter so many hours of sorrow."

Donald requested the same, when the baron proceeded as follows—"On the fatal night when the castle of Bosmora was in the most treacherous manner subdued, I was left by my enemy for dead; and as soon as the place was deserted by the conquerors, the remaining few of my faithful servants, together with old Allen, came to remove the corses of those brave, zealous, and trusty men, who fell in the conflict. Among the rest whom they examined, to see if life yet remained, was myself; a slight pulsation convinced the affectionate Andrew that the vital spark was not yet extinguished; he called to the good old Allen, who hastened to his assistance, and together they conveyed me to the cottage of the latter, when old Jannet, by attentive and unremitting care, restored me to life. Several days passed ere I was able to quit my bed, and then I learnt the dreadful tidings of thy loss, my child. With a heart almost broken, I sent Andrew to a neighbouring baron, with my solicitations for his aid of troops to recover thee, which was immediately granted; and mustering up my remaining clan, we marched for the purpose of, jointly with our forces, attacking Duncaethal, where I had no doubt but you was held a prisoner. When we arrived at the walls of the castle, without demanding an audience, I ordered the soldiers to burst open the gates, and then entering, in the hall I was met by Dargo, who informed me that you had escaped, and that his lord at that time was absent. I, imagining it was only a stratagem to deceive me, ordered the rascal to be secured, and commenced a strict search, even in that part of the castle I knew long had been uninhabited. There it was my good fortune to find the poor imprisoned Agnes; she recognized me instantly, and I learned from her the villainous conduct which had been practiced against you, my son—and she added that you was confined in one of the subterraneous dungeons. Procuring the keys from the villainous Dargo, whom we forced, at the peril of his life, to conduct us, we examined each of them; in one I discovered poor Robert, who was overjoyed at beholding me and Venella; and the good old Gertrude informed me that you both had really escaped, and that you were among banditti, whom her master had gone against, for the purpose of subduing, and once more getting you in his power. While she was speaking, Agnes entered the room, when the old woman was terrified out of her wits, supposing it was her ghost, till your mother affectionately convinced her to the contrary. I left Agnes in her care, and gave orders to proceed instantly towards the ruin, to which we were conducted by a peasant, where the search has answered to our utmost wish. The base usurper shall be confined in the dungeon from which you are so lately liberated, until a jury of barons can sit in judgment, and condemn him to that sentence which his various and manifold crimes may deserve. But, my dearest Matilda, hast thou, at any time, ever before seen that fearful bandit?"

"Never, my dear father," said she; "the first time he ever met my sight was on the dreadful night I thought you had perished; he has often expressed hatred for our very existence, for what cause I know not, and his malice is extended equally to Donald as to myself."

"Indeed!" said the baron; "'tis strange, but we must leave the discovery to that Providence, who, by his great interference in this last wonderful discovery, has convinced us that the day of retribution must at last arrive."

They now came within view of the high turrets of Duncaethal, and Donald was soon clasped in the arms of his affectionate mother. "Oh, my son!" said she, "Heaven has heard my prayers! Oh, never let despair enter thy heart! After so many years, thou art at last restored, with my long-lost liberty!"

She now took the hand of Matilda, saying—"Thy father, maiden, has informed me of your mutual loves; take her, my son; she adds lustre to the noble name of Duncaethal! Heaven will repay you both for your many sufferings, by numberless days of conjugal bliss and domestic happiness!"

They now were joined by Robert and Venella, who, with warm congratulations and tears of joy, welcomed the return of Donald and Matilda. The joyous shouts of the clan, late their enemies, now the most loyal and zealous defenders of their rights, rent the air, while with bursts of acclamations they made the vaulted roof and arched halls resound the name of their new laird Duncaethal; and in flowing goblets they quaffed to the health of his destined bride. The neighbouring peasantry caught the glad tidings, when, forgetting all their toils, they thronged in the court-yard to behold the happy sight, till warmed by wine, and roused by the sweet brisk enlivening pipe, they sought each his favourite lass, and led forth the festive dance.

The late gloomy castle, so long a stranger to the sound of mirth, was now converted into a universal scene of Joy; every heart beat with rapture in the light bosoms of its inhabitants, save alone in the guilty breast of the usurper, who was manacled, and thrown into the dungeon, where he so malignantly sought the life of Donald. Dargo too was now a prisoner, in the very cell so lately occupied by Robert. Thus, in a short time, what a strange reverse of fortune was experienced by both lord and servant! The latter seemed to bear his fate by sullen insensibility; not so in the guilty tyrant's breast. Conscience! that never-erring monitor, told him he deserved not mercy here, nor could he hope for forgiveness hereafter! The shades of Paulina, Margaret, and all who through his damned machinations fell, seemed to flit before his tortured sight within the gloomy cell, till, in bitterness of soul, he cursed the hour which gave him birth; and had he possessed the means, of which he was carefully deprived, he would, by horrid suicide, have ended the career of his wretched, miserable, and guilty life.

Chapter V

When rugged March o'errules the growing year,
Have we not seen the morn, with treach'rous ray,
Shine out awhile, then instant disappear,
And leave to damp and gloom the future day?
So dawn'd my fate, and so deceiv'd my heart,
Nor wean'd me from my hopes, but cruel tore,
In one unlook'd for moment, bade me part
From all my comforts, to return no more.

Richard Plantagenet's Tale.

DAYS PASSED AWAY IN HAPPINESS to our heroine, and the most blissful prospects to Donald, till the day preceding the trial of Duncaethal, when, on his going to Venella, to inquire for her mistress, he found they were both absent, and, after many efforts to find her, he sought Bosmora, and recounted his fears. A strict search was then set on foot, which not availing, they were at last forced to conclude that, by some unknown means, she was spirited away from the castle.

Who could be the perpetrator of this daring outrage was the next subject of debate. "Ah!" said Donald, "'tis, doubtless, the villain Darthalgo! Fool that I was, to reckon on happiness, while that fiend had escaped from our power."

"Patience, my son!—patience!" cried the baron.

"Oh, my gracious lord!" returned Donald, "have I not the cup of happiness again snatcht from my lips, when I was on the point of quaffing the nectareous draught, the beverage of bliss, which gods might envy me the taste? Order my horses; instantly will I pursue my search."

"Alas! whither?" said the sorrowing Bosmora.

"No matter! The abbey ruins; and if she is not there, why fortune must be my guide; for never will I return without my dearest, best-beloved Matilda!"

His frantic accents of grief attracted the attention of his mother, who, feelingly alive to the happiness of her long-lost son, inquired the cause of his sorrow.

"Alas! my dear mother," sad he, "our sweet Matilda is gone!"

"Gone! Where?" asked she.

"Alas! I know not; but I suppose the wretch Darthalgo, I fear, has once more got her in his power! Where is Robert? I will leave the castle this night in quest of her. She cannot be conveyed to a great distance as yet, for she was here at noon."

Robert now attended, and in a few minutes they bade adieu to Duncae-thal; and, applying the spurs to their light-footed steeds, posted towards the ruined abbey. The shrill sound of the bleak wind whistling through the trees, gave notice of an approaching storm, and in a few minutes large drops of rain fell upon their armour. Robert exclaimed—"Sir, do let us seek some covert, to shield us from the tempest, for I fear it will be terrible!" At that instant a loud crash shook the earth to its foundation, while the vivid lightning gave a partial light to our wanderers.

Donald dismounted, and ordered his 'squire to do the same, as it was become dangerous to keep longer on their horses, whose feet every moment slipped, owing to the wetness of the grass. They gently led them by the reins, while with anxious eyes they sought for some hospitable cottage, whose brisk blazing hearth might dry their garments, and warm their chilled limbs, which already began to stiffen with cold; however, no such friendly habitation ap-peared, and as they feared they had missed their way, they proposed to stand still till the light of day should gladden their sight. Long had they not remained in this situation, before a glimmering light, through the trees, gave a renewal to their hopes; they set forward, but finding they gained not upon it, Robert, by his master's orders, loudly shouted, when the light, which before seemed to recede, became stationary, and a few moments brought them within view of the figure who bore it.

By his dress he appeared a hermit. His long beard almost reached to his waist, and the large rosary of beads, which was suspended by a cord from his girdle, add to which the placidity of his countenance, convinced Donald that he was right in his conjecture, and addressing him by the name of holy father, he said—"We are poor benighted travellers, who have missed our way; can you direct us to any dwelling where we may obtain shelter till the day's approach?"

He answered—"Strangers, I know of none which you can reach in haste, but if you will follow me to my humble cell, you shall be welcome to all it af-fords, and it will at least shelter you from the inclemency of the storm."

"Ten thousand thanks, father!" said Donald. "Come on, Robert, and lead the horses."

The drenched 'squire speedily obeyed this welcome command, uttering to himself—"If ever there was an angel with a long beard, this is he! Methinks I hear the faggot crackling on the hearth, with a cold pasty and a flaggon of wine on the table, which I have often heard these holy men like as well as their neighbours; perhaps a good couch too, to rest a body's bones on, after we have satisfied our appetites. 'Tis very hard my master could not keep Lady Matilda when he had her; and as for our going to the ruins, why 'tis all nonsense. Darthalgo knows better than to go where he is sure to be searched for; but, however, as I told Dargo, we poor servants must do as we are bid, so I must e'en jog on with him in this wild-goose chase."

He was interrupted from this soliloquy, by his master loudly calling him to come on.

"Oh, my dear lord, I cannot make the steeds walk any faster; they have not half the appetite I have, or else they would feel for a fellow-sufferer; but they keep slipping down every minute, and don't seem to mind anything but the fear of breaking their legs. How much further is it, holy stranger?"

"We are within sight of it," said the hermit.

"Oh, St. Andrew be praised! Is that the little chimney that smokes so merrily?"

"It is," said the conductor, the lightning now, at intervals, being so vivid, that they could plainly discern the dwelling of this venerable anchorite. "So, please you, sir knight," added he, "you must fasten your horses to one of these trees, as I have no accommodation for them, though I will do my best for you."

They did as he desired, and following his steps, soon found themselves in a spacious cave, in which stood an antique oaken table, with some fruit, the remains of what had composed his repast; to these he added a fresh supply; and going to a kind of recess, brought forth a flaggon of wine, saying—"You see, son, though I live as it were from the world, I am not without some of the good things thereof. Come, be seated, and eat and drink heartily."

"Aye, that we will," said Robert. "Oh, how comfortable it is, after one thought of passing the night under an old tree, to find one's self by a blazing fire, with a cup of good wine to cheer one's spirits! Egad, I think I will turn hermit myself if they always live so merrily! But do hermits, father, ever marry? For, notwithstanding every other comfort, I should, I think, like to solace myself with a wife."

"Silence, Robert!" said his master; then addressing the friendly anchorite, he said—"Venerable father, have you long inhabited this retreat?"

"Some years, my son," answered he; "but if you are not inclined to sleep, to beguile time, I will recount to you the sad events of my life, which caused me to abjure the world, and seek retirement in this humble cell."

Donald expressed the gratification it would give him, and said that he was all attention, when the other began—"First, 'tis necessary to give you some account of my family, ere I proceed to relate my own unfortunate history. My father, whose real name I shall conceal under that of Flodiardo, was a noble Venetian; he was his parents' only child, who, by too much indulgence, spoilt his temper, which was naturally good; but, by such ill-timed lenity, made his disposition, as he advanced in life, rather ungovernable; and at his parents' death, being possessed of a handsome fortune, he fell into the destructive company of the libertine youths of the city which gave him birth. A courtesan squandered his substance, to which he greatly contributed by gaming. He had attained his twenty-fifth year, when one evening, as he was walking in a grove near to the suburbs of the city, the loud cries of a female sounded in his ear, and, ever ready to lend assistance to the distressed, he fled towards the spot from whence the cries proceeded, where he beheld a lovely young girl in vain endeavouring to extricate herself from the arms of a man, who, with brutal force, dragged her towards a horse, seemingly for the purpose of bearing her away. My father rushed directly to him, and commanded him to desist, when, drawing a stiletto, the stranger wounded him in the arm, and swiftly mounting the steed, fled precipitately towards the city. The lady he had so fortunately rescued, perceiving the blood flow from the wound he had received, expressed her sorrow for the accident, and lending her arm, endeavoured to assist him in reaching the dwelling of her father, which, she said, was not above half a mile distant; he accepted of her offer, and they slowly proceeded through the windings of the grove. At length they came within sight of an elegant residence, which, she said, belonged to signor Rivolti, her father, and, stepping forward, she rapped at the gate, which was opened by a female servant. She conducted Flodiardo to a room, the elegant simplicity of which bespoke the dignity of the inhabitants.

"At that moment the owner of the mansion made his appearance, when, on seeing his daughter's companion, he exclaimed—'Rosalie, my child! where is Vallentia?'—'Ah, my dear father!' said she, 'Vallentia is a wretch! and it is owing to this stranger's interposition that I did not fall a victim to his villainy. See, my dear father, my brave deliverer is wounded in my defence!'—'Good Heavens, signor, you bleed!' said he. 'Here, Alberti, instantly fetch a surgeon.'—'You need not,' said Flodiardo; 'it is only trifling. Suffer your servant to bind it up, and I will have it dressed when I reach the city.'

"Rosalie now left the apartment, to summon an ancient domestic, who, she said, understood something of surgery: when he appeared, with a look of skill he said it must not be disturbed by motion, and declared that it demanded immediate rest. Signor Rivolti insisted upon his not leaving the house till he was recovered, and offered to dispatch a messenger to acquaint his friends of what had transpired. 'It is unnecessary,' said my father, 'for it is what often occurs,

and will cause no alarm in my being absent for the night.' In fact, Flodiardo
was rejoiced at this invitation, for the fair Rosalie had made a deep impression
upon his heart, and virtuous love, for the first time, reigned in his breast tri-
umphant. 'May I presume to ask,' said he, addressing himself to Rivolti, 'who
that ruffian is, from whose violence I had the good fortune to rescue the fair
Rosalie?'—'Alas, it is a grief to me to say!—but I had intended Vallentia for the
husband of my daughter, and by his vile conduct, the son of my friend has not
only rendered himself hateful to her, but has forfeited my esteem for ever. I
will recount to you the circumstances which led to this proposed union:—The
father of Vallentia and myself were schoolfellows and soldiers together; we both
married nearly at the same period, and this young man was born in the same
year with my son. We often, previous to their birth, said, should the children
prove of different sexes, we would betroth them to each other: we, however,
were disappointed in our intentions by their both proving males; but in two
years after my Rosalie was born, and we hoped at a future day to see our families
united by her marriage with Vallentia. Rosalie, as she advanced in life, improved
in beauty and accomplishments; but ere she had attained her fifteenth year,
both the parents of Vallentia were carried off by a fever, first expressing their
wishes that he should take in marriage my daughter, which he faithfully promised. He now visited our residence at Venice, as my future son, and I thought he
loved my child with a passion beyond the power of fortune to diminish; but his
conduct to-night has proved the base motives of his selfish heart. A few months
since I lost the principal part of my fortune by fire, which destroyed bills to a
large amount; and since that time I have, with the residue of my wealth, procured this dwelling, with an intention of ending my days in it; as, by economy,
I have still sufficient to support me with credit, though not with the splendour
I was wont to enjoy. Vallentia still continued his visits, and now it appears he
wished to obtain her as a mistress, who it had long been his pride to seek as his
wife. Oh, stranger! I know not how to requite you for preserving her virtue,
and restoring her to me! For had Vallentia succeeded in his diabolical schemes,
the shame of Rosalie would too surely have broken the heart of her wretched father.'—'Did Rosalie love Vallentia?' eagerly inquired Flodiardo.—'Alas! I
think so, signor; but she has been from childhood accustomed to regard him
as her destined husband, and she never expressed the least repugnance for him,
though certainly I sometimes thought she treated him more as a brother than
a lover.' The heart of Flodiardo leapt with joy at the conclusion of this speech;
and, during the few days he remained with them, he ingratiated himself so far
into the favour of both child and parent, that he was the declared and accepted
lover of Rosalie.

"Sometime after, when business had required his presence at Venice, previous to his return to the villa, which he intended to do in the evening, a messenger arrived, informing him that signor Rivolti was taken suddenly and dangerously ill, and was scarcely expected to survive till his arrival; he instantly followed the messenger, mounted on a swift horse, and speedily reached the residence, where he beheld his loved Rosalie weeping beside the couch of her dying parent. His disorder was a sudden fit of apoplexy, which deprived him of speech; but taking the hand of Flodiardo and that of his daughter, he joined them together in his; then, murmuring a blessing on them, expired. I will not dwell upon this, but let it suffice to say, that, soon as decency permitted, my father made Rosalie his wife; he took her to a grand chateau which he possessed in Venice, where, in due time, she gave birth to the unfortunate being who now addresses you. My father, whom the novelty of marriage had made domestic, for the first two years was scarcely ever from her side; but at length growing palled with the chaste beauties of my mother, his inconstant heart sought for variety in the arms of courtezans. Often did poor Rosalie drop tears of anguish on my infant face, as she saw my inheritance wasted by gamblers and sharpers. She expostulated with my father, but he was deaf to her apprehensions, and laughed at her fears: however, one fatal night, when wine had got master of his senses, and fortune declared against him, he betted deeply—the dice betrayed him—he grew desperate, and staked the whole of his property on one fatal cast—it was decided against him, and he arose from the board a beggar. 'Twas now he sought my mother, and from her pious resignation learned to bear his lot with some degree of fortitude. The villa still was her's, and there they sought for tranquility; but, alas! my father was not formed for happiness. One fatal night, returning from the city, he slowly entered the apartment level with the garden, and was making his intention of surprising his wife by his quick return, when, passing a door which led to another room, he beheld my mother in the close embrace of a man of noble appearance; he stole behind the couch on which they both sat, when he saw his wife kiss the stranger, and exclaim—'Flodiardo is in the city, beloved Orsino!' 'Thou liest, base strumpet!' said he; 'he is here to reward thy perfidy!' Thus saying, he plunged his stiletto to the heart of my mother, who sunk weltering in her blood.

"'Oh God! my sister!' said the stranger; 'look up and speak to me, my sweet Rosalie!' My father uttered not a word, being struck dumb with horror; for he now conjectured this must be the brother of his murdered wife, who had been absent many years. In frantic accents he called upon her to forgive him—'Oh, slaughtered saint, look up one moment, or I will follow you.' Alas! she was already dead! My father, in despair, took the stiletto, still reeking with my mother's blood, and plunged it deep into his breast, ere he could be prevented by the horror-struck Orsino. He kissed the pale cheek of Rosalie, and told my uncle he left a wretched orphan to his care, who now had no claims of kindred to any but himself. My uncle promised to protect me, and my father soon bade adieu to this world for ever. I was at this period about four years of age, and my foster-parent took me with him to Venice, where he bestowed on me every accomplishment which money could procure. When I had attained my eighteenth year, a very distant relation of my uncle's died, and as he was next in ties of blood, left him an immense fortune, providing that he would forsake the name of Rivolti, for the one which his family bore—of course he consented; at the same time adopting me as his son, with the promise that I should become heir to all he possessed. His unlimited indulgence was my ruin; I followed the footsteps of my father, and was often made the egregious dupe of the fraudulent and designing. At length my unbounded extravagance called forth the serious anger of my relative, who refused to advance me a sous beyond the sum stipulated for my allowance, which was rather liberal; this I soon squandered; and, to complete my disgrace, I married a young woman considerably beneath the rank I bore; but she was beautiful and amiable, and proved truly affectionate; yet I knew my uncle would never be reconciled, so I intended to keep it from him for ever as a secret, when a villain, to whom I confided it, betrayed me, and by his diabolical machinations, caused my innocent unsuspecting wife to end her miserable existence by horrid suicide. A letter, which she had written to me previous to her perpetrating this rash deed, made me frantic, and, in hopes of again beholding her, I plunged my stiletto into the breast of one who detained me from her side: but, alas! I was too late—she had been dead some hours. Her billet had informed me of the base contriver of this dreadful tragedy, and had I dared to venture in the city, his life should have paid the price of his perfidy; but my crime had doomed me to proscription; and, growing desperate from grief, I joined a band of lawless ruffians which infested the neighbouring forest, and subsisted by plunder, when abandoning my own name, I assumed that of the bandit Darthalgo!"

Donald, who till now had listened with the greatest attention, started at the mention of that dread name—"Yet," said he, mentally, "there probably might be two of one name." Robert sat trembling; he had never seen the bravo, and concluded that this was he, in the disguise of a hermit. They neither of them uttered a syllable, but the agitation they both evinced proved to the stranger they had heard the name before.

"What's the meaning of this surprise?" said he to Donald; "have you ever heard of Darthalgo?"

"Oh, yes!" returned he; "this night were we in search of a bravo of that name, but you are not he. Will you favour me by continuing your history?"

"I will," said the astonished stranger. "I wrote to the wretch who was the contriver of my miseries, and threatened vengeance, should we ever meet, upon his wicked head. Upon this information he quitted Venice, to return to his native land, and I have never since beheld him, though I sought these shores for that purpose. The time when I commenced robber was during the period I was frantic with sorrow; but no sooner did reason regain its seat, than honour represented unto me the horrid calling of a bandit, and I was determined to abandon it. One day I made a proposal to our band, to divide what money there was in the hoard, and separate; this met with the approbation of the majority; when, on receiving my share, I embarked for this country, with the intention of wreaking my vengeance on the destroyer of Paulina; but several miles distant from this, during a storm, the vessel was wrecked, and I alone of all the numerous crew on board was the only one who survived. The little wealth which I possessed luckily was about me. Long did I wander about the neighbouring shores, undetermined how to proceed or act, when chance brought me to this hermitage; here I found the unburied body of the former inhabitant, who seemed to have departed from this world several days; I dug up the earth with an iron instrument which I found in the cavern, and laid him decently under the green sod, at the back of the cell. In the recess I found some fruits, with which I satiated my hunger, and sinking upon yon couch of rushes, I fell into a profound sleep, during which I beheld a vision, that made me determine to take up my abode here. Methought the spirit of Paulina appeared to me, and said—'Valando! seek not revenge; leave to thy great Creator the disposal of thy enemy; but by devoting the remainder of thy sinful life to religion, in seclusion from the world and all its follies, seek to purify thy soul from all the foul crimes thou hast committed—so shall we meet again in those bright realms and regions of peace, where deceit and hypocrisy never again can part us.' I started and awoke from my sleep, resolving to obey the heavenly vision, which, under the form of the spirit of my departed wife, thus converted me. I attired myself in the habit belonging to my predecessor, and have by penance endeavoured to atone for my mispent life. You are the first that have entered this lowly dwelling since I have possessed it, except a poor hind, who sometimes purchases for me a few necessaries which nature requires; and it was by going to seek for whatever the storm might cast upon the neighbouring shore, that I this night have had the pleasure of shielding you from its inclemency. And now, my son, if it be not inconsistent with prudence, I prithee unfold to me what thou knowst of Darthalgo?"

"I will, venerable father," said Donald, "and will be equally candid as your-self." He then recounted all the knowledge he possessed of that mysterious ban-dit, which greatly excited the wonder of the hermit, who could not give the least clue respecting the sameness of names. Daylight now began to appear, and the tempestuous night was succeeded by a serene morning; the sun darted its bright rays into the cell. Robert, who had fallen into a sound sleep, was roused by his master, who sent him forth to search for their horses, which he found quietly grazing beneath a clump of trees, where he had fastened them; he led them towards the cell, where both mounting, after thanking the venerable anchorite for his hospitality, who at parting bestowed on them his benison, they depart-ed, and with some difficulty gaining the right road to the ruins of the abbey, proceeded onwards.

Chapter VI

The cloud-capt towers, the gorgeous palaces,
The solemn temples, the great globe itself,
Yea, all which it inherit, shall dissolve,
And, like the baseless fabric of a vision,
Leave not a wreck behind!

Shakespeare.

WELL," SAID THE LOQUACIOUS 'SQUIRE, the first who broke silence, "who would suppose, my lord, to look at the hermit, that he had ever been a bravo? When he called himself Darthalgo I shook in my skin, for I have never seen this famous robber, and I expected every moment that he would eat us both alive."

"Nay," said Donald, "I think he had most reason to fear that you would eat him, for you paid a great deal of respect to his wine and provisions."

"Why as to that, my lord, I like good eating and good drinking, more especially after a storm; for I think, with submission, when one has been well drenched without, we should also be well drenched within."

"A very sound reason indeed," said Donald; "but come, Robert, spur on your horse, and let us press forward."

"Certainly, my lord, I will; but if I might be allowed to speak the sentiments of my mind, I think it is but a wild-goose kind of a chace, as a body may say."

"What do you mean?" said his master.

"Mean, my lord! Why, my lord, I hardly know what I mean. But do you think it very likely that Darthalgo would be fool enough to take my lady to the very place where they were all routed out from but the other day, as a body may say? No! no! I plainly foresee, my lord, that we shall have our trouble for our pains, and very likely we may only be wandering further from lady Matilda and poor Venella, when we ought to rescue them from the power of demi-devils, who, perhaps, ere this have found out a fresh haunt."

"Pshaw! nonsense, Robert; I have reasons, at any rate, for going to the ruin; for I believe there still remains the old hag, whom Bosmora gave liberty to go where she pleased. Now we can inquire of her, if, since the day the rest were subdued, she has ever seen Darthalgo, and by that means judge if it was really him who carried off my dear Matilda."

"And pray, my lord," said Robert, "with all possible deference, do you suppose she would tell you, even if she knew? No, no! I plainly foresee, my lord, she would not let you into the secret; no, she's not fool enough for that."

"Well," said Donald, "however, I am determined, at all events, to proceed; and if you are afraid to accompany me, you are at liberty to return."

"Return!" said Robert; "I return! Well, I never suspected, my lord, you could have uttered such cruel words;" and, with his eyes almost filled with tears, he added, "I am sure I never foresaw that indeed."

"Well, well, my good fellow, I did not mean to offend you," said Donald; "but I am so heart-rent by this second loss of my beloved, that I believe my temper is grown irritable. Robert, I ask pardon for those words spoken in my wrath."

"Oh, that is quite enough!" said the other. "When a lord asks pardon of his 'squire, I foresee that would content any body as well as myself: and look, my lord, yonder is a high turret; does that belong to the abbey ruin?"

"It does," replied Donald; "Heaven grant that within its walls I may find my beloved Matilda!"

"I hope we may, my lord," answered Robert; "I prayed to St. Andrew to direct us when I was getting the horses ready: and now, my lord, which is the nearest way, for both these roads seem to terminate near its walls, as far as I can guess? Ah, I sadly wanted to accompany my lord the baron, but he would not let me, because I was somewhat debilitated by the long confinement I endured in the dungeon. Which, my lord, is the right road?—do you know?"

"Why," said Donald, "near as I can guess, this branching off to the left."

"Well then, my lord, we shall soon be there. Oh, if we do but find the lady Matilda, how the baron will rejoice, and how glad the lady your mother will be, my lord! and how pleased Venella will be at seeing me! But look, my lord, what black clouds! As sure as I live, there is another storm coming on; let us hasten, and reach the ruin ere it commences. What an unlucky 'squire am I, that there should be one tempest following another in this manner!"

"Fear not," said Donald; "we shall reach the abbey in a few minutes." He applied his spurs to his proud courser, when, after riding about a quarter of an hour, he stopped, exclaiming, "We must certainly have come the wrong way!"

"There now!" said Robert; "my mind misgave me when you took this road, for I plainly foresaw we should be caught in the shower; the rain begins to patter on my head already. Oh that I could see another angel, in the shape of a hermit, for I have not yet broke my fast!"

"Prythee cease prating," said Donald, "and ascend that tree, and see if by that means you can discover anything of the ruin, that we may be able to tell the nearest direction to proceed in."

"I will, my lord, but really I am a poor climber of a tree; for once, when I was a boy, I fell backwards from the top of an elm, and ever since I have had a sort of antipathy to exaltation; but however, my lord, to oblige you I will do my best, and I plainly foresee that it will be the worst imaginable." He had scarcely spoke, when taking hold of a weak branch, it broke; and the unfortunate Robert, without the least foreknowledge, was precipitated into a ditch. "There!" said he, with a rueful countenance, "I knew I should never reach the top." He clambered up the side of the bank, by the assistance of his master, not much worse for his fall, except being covered over with mud, and then, in a peevish tone, continued—"What would Venella say if she saw me now?"

"Prythee cease prating," said the impatient Donald, "and I will see if I cannot succeed better than yourself."

"Then, my lord, do take a fool's advice, and do not get up that same tree. What a blockhead was I, when I foresaw that I should fall, to choose that whose branches hung over a ditch! had I but gone on the other side, I might have tumbled on the soft grass, and avoided being in this confounded pickle."

Ere Robert had finished these wise observations, Donald's agile limbs had reached the highest branch, when quickly descending, he exclaimed—"Let us take the cross path! We cannot be far from the spot; for, as well as I can distinguish through the thick mist, it lies to the right. Come, bustle, Robert, bustle!"

"Indeed, sir, I wish I could bustle this mud off my clothes; but as that seems impossible, why I must e'en remain in my present trim. Heigho! I wish our journey may prove successful, and then I will so eat and drink when I get back to Duncaethal, I should not wonder if I got tipsey."

"Nor I either," said Donald, laughing, in spite of his misfortune.

"Well now, my lord," said Robert, "I am quite ready to set forward, and I hope this road may prove the proper one, though, under favour, sir, I think we are the first that ever travelled this way on horseback; for if a man be not as short as a dwarf, he will certainly get his head taken off by the boughs of the trees, they grow so near the ground. Now, my lord, my advice is, that we dismount and lead our poor steeds."

Donald acquiesced in this plan of the honest 'squire's, for it began to be so very foggy, that they could scarcely see a yard before them; and often as the branches of the trees came in contact with the head of Robert, he would cry—"Well, I plainly foresee I shall never return alive to Duncaethal! Do, my dear lord, let us rest till this mist disperses; who knows but we are going wrong all this time."

A large projecting limb of an aged tree at this moment knocking the helmet from off the head of Donald, made him determine to adopt the advice of his 'squire, and seating themselves at the root of a large oak, they waited for several hours the dispersion of the heavy fog which filled the atmosphere. At last Donald, suspecting the near approach of night, was determined at all events to proceed; and after a great deal of difficulty, and some danger, they found themselves in a beaten road, which he recognized to be the same he had travelled on the night he left the abbey with Bosmora. The mist now was, in a great measure, dissipated, and was succeeded by the sober grey of evening; they pressed forward, but night overtook them by their arrival at the tumbling gates of the abbey. Robert, taking the arm of Donald, pointed to a window, where they perceived a light, borne in the hand of a figure, but whether male or female they could not distinguish, owing to the old dusky windows, whose heavy frames and painted lattices were covered with the accumulated dust of many rolling years.

"'Tis well!" said he; "there are yet inhabitants remaining."

"Ah, my lord, too many for us, I fear!" said Robert.

"Hush!" said Donald; "follow me—we must work by stratagem here; I wish to obtain entrance without alarming any one. Fasten our steeds to this stump, and let us proceed in silence."

Robert obeyed, and Donald, making his way to the entrance, applied his hand to the fastening, which yielded to the touch; then proceeding together, they found themselves in the ancient halls.

"Oh, my lord, look there at that white figure!" said Robert.

"Where?" said his attentive master.

"Why there, my lord!—as I live it's coming towards us! Oh, it's a ghost, my lord, it's a ghost!"

At this moment the object of Robert's terror sent forth a dismal moan, which convinced his master that it was no other than a harmless owl, which they had disturbed in its nocturnal ramble. He whispered to the simple 'squire—"Be more careful, Robert; you vociferated so loud at the sight of this poor bird, which your fears transformed into a ghost, that it might have subjected us to a discovery."

"I beg your pardon, my lord," returned he, "but I hate the sight of ghosts; and where is any one so likely to meet them as in an old abbey, where hundreds of monks and friars have been buried? Who knows but they may haunt this place? and though I have all possible respect for priests, yet I can't say I should so very much like to meet one after he was dead. 'Tis dreadful dark, sir! do you know where we are going, sir?"

"Why," said Donald, "as near as I can remember, the caverns lie off to the right, so follow me, and draw your sword, which will serve to explore the way, and we shall be ready in case of a surprise. Come on! By the glimmering of the moon," which now began to shine forth, "I can perceive a door, that I think belongs to the room in which Matilda was confined when the abbey was attacked." He pushed it open, and on a table they beheld a lamp burning; Donald concluded it must have been left there by some one, who would, no doubt, soon return for it, and he resolved to lie perdue behind the ruins of a kind of altar, to wait for their appearance. Robert retired with him, and after waiting about ten minutes, a door, at the extremity of the place, was opened, and, with a small basket on her arm, the old hag made her appearance. The 'squire was on the point of rushing from his hiding-place, to seize her, but was restrained by his master, who wished to gain that knowledge by stratagem he feared he could not effect by force. Soon as she had taken up the lamp, motioning to Robert to do the same, they followed her through the door-way by which they had entered. She proceeded straight to the hall, till, seemingly through fatigue, she seated herself at the foot of a kind of throne, which had once borne the dignitary of the house, arrayed in the abacot and purple, on the festival of their patron saint, but was now fast sinking to that oblivion which had long been the lot of its possessors. After resting about two or three minutes, the old beldam got up, mumbling something to herself, and seemed as though she had forgot some article or other; for, leaving the basket on the place where she had just been seated, she retraced her steps back again. Robert now proposed stealing from behind the buttress, where they lay concealed, and helping themselves to its contents, but was reprimanded by Donald, who said—"Would you, for the gratification of your appetite, lose the knowledge of where lady Matilda is concealed? for I have no doubt but she is going to convey those provisions to her, and I am resolved to follow and watch her motions. Hush! she comes."

The old hag returned, bearing in her hand a stone vessel, which they concluded contained water for her captives, when, reaching the basket, she slipped behind the throne, and, opening a secret entrance, disappeared; they quickly followed, and observed her almost at the bottom of a flight of steps; they lost no time in pursuing as quick as they possibly could, without her hearing the sound of their feet. A dark subterranean appeared, through which she advanced, and applying a key to one of the cell-doors, entered, ironically saying—"Well, my fine madams, have you found your appetites? Can your dainty stomachs relish any thing? Here is some good black bread and water as—"

Donald's heart leaped with Joy at this address, and his rapture was un-bounded at hearing Matilda interrupt her, by saying—"Do you call yourself a woman, that you can have the cruelty to assist a villain like Darthalgo, in the persecution of those who never injured you?" The old hag was about to reply, when Donald, followed by Robert, rushed in and secured her.

Matilda, at the unexpected sight of her beloved, gave a loud shriek, and sunk in a swoon upon her wretched couch, while Venella, who before was sit-ting in a corner, clung round the neck of the 'squire, exclaiming—"Oh, my dear, dear Robert, take us out of this nasty place directly, for I shall die if I stay in it a moment longer. But, lack-a-day, look at my lady!" She took up the stone jug brought by the old woman, and rushing towards Donald, who was in vain endeavouring to recover her, when sprinkling some water on her face, and forcing a little in her mouth, it had the desired effect; and opening her eyes, she perceived what she at first took for a vision was real. She expressed her happi-ness by tears of joy.

Robert, who had bound the old woman, asked how he should proceed; then turning to the captive, politely said—"Shall we leave you here a prisoner, where you have so lately officiated as gaoler?"

She replied only by horrid curses and imprecations, and earnestly wished they might be taken by Darthalgo and his party ere they left the place. This was a hint sufficient to hasten their departure; for instantly quitting the ruin, leaving behind the old beldam, and mounting Matilda and Venella behind them, with all possi-ble speed made towards Duncaethal, whose lofty turrets met their anxious sight just as the morn began to dawn, and pressing forward their wearied steeds, shortly reached its walls. Robert dismounted, and knocked loudly at the gate.

Old Andrew, whom the baron had brought with his clan, answered the summons, and demanded—"Who's there?"

"Open, open!—'tis I, Robert! Where is the baron? We have brought back the Lady Matilda."

"Indeed! Marry that is rare news! And is my young lord come too? are they both well?"

"Come, Andrew, you talk so, we shall never get in—make haste and draw back the bolts—my lady is almost fainting!"

"Oh, marry," said he, as the gate flew wide open, "then enter I pray you!"

"Ah, that will I!" said the other. "I little thought one night, as I was groping about this castle to try if I could escape, I should ever be so glad to come into it again when I had once got away; that is, when I was visited by my good friend Dargo, who used to supply me with food and drink, sparingly enough, the saints bear witness, for which I will make ample amends this day."

"La, Robert," said Venella, "how you chatter! why don't you lead me in? Don't you see how tired I am?" said she, exalting her voice.

"Tired!" said the other; "I should like to know if your tongue is ever tired? No, no, I warrant it never is."

"Silence!" said she, "here is my lady; see how nicely my lord leads her over the bridge by the arm, while I was obliged to walk by myself."

"Ah," said Andrew, "my dear young lady is welcome back; and give me leave, my lord, to congratulate your return; and proud am I in the honour of admitting you into your own castle, the rights of which you are to be invested with tomorrow. But let me haste to acquaint the baron with your arrival, and send word to the lady Agnes, who has been almost distracted lest any evil should have befel you. Come in, my dear young lord Alexander, heir of Duncaethal!"

The old man, with tears of joy streaming down his cheeks, conducted the youthful pair into the hall, then hasted fast as possible to acquaint the baron, who had but Just retired to rest, for the first time since the departure of Donald, when, worn with watching, sleep overtook him, and he was unconscious of the entrance of the good old steward, who, not wishing to disturb his repose, was on the point of retiring, when hearing his master exclaim— "My daughter! oh, my daughter!" the old man, thinking he was awake, drew back the curtain, and said— "She is arrived, my lord!"

The baron started from his unquiet slumber, and, seeing Andrew, inquired what news of lord Alexander and Matilda?

"They are both returned, my lord!"

"Indeed!" said the baron.

"Yes, my lord; they are both in the hall."

The baron, dropping on his knee, said— "Gracious Heaven, accept my thanks! Come, Andrew, assist me to dress," then hasting down stairs, he found them with Agnes, who had heard of their arrival from Gertrude. She saw them from her window enter the court-yard, and ran directly to her lady, the bonny Agnes, as she called her, with the joyful tidings. They both were alternately pressed to the bosoms of their parents; and after the first flood of joy was past, Bosmora said— "My son, the castle is full of company; numbers of the greatest nobles in Scotland are assembled, to be present at the trial of the usurper, and to-morrow it will take place: yesterday, you know, was the time appointed, but it was obliged to be postponed on account of your absence. Now will you stand forward to crush your deadly foe, and at once revenge the injuries of yourself, your mother, and your elected wife. But say, my child, was you in the power of Darthalgo, that mysterious bandit, who seeks to revenge an injury ignorantly given by us, yet he affirms it was given? Was he the ravisher, my child?"

"He was, my dearest father, and I will relate to you the whole proceeding."

"Had not you better rest first?" said Agnes; "and you too, my son? Let us defer it till you have recruited your exhausted strength."

They acquiesced in this necessary arrangement; and after the repose of several hours, they met in the apartment of Bosmora, where Matilda related the event, as recorded in the next chapter.

Chapter VII

Oh! I have a pass'd a miserable night!
So full of ugly sights, of ghastly dreams—
I would not spend another such a night,
Though 'twere to buy a world of happy days!
So full of dismal terror was the time!

Shakespeare.

ON THE AFTERNOON WHICH MATILDA had been forced from Duncae-thal, she had, attended by her maid Venella, strolled to the outskirts of the adjacent forest, the day being remarkably fine. "How beautiful is the surrounding scene!" exclaimed she; "the peasantry appear so clean and healthy, and look so cheerful, while, as they attend to their different occupations, they beguile time, and lighten their labour by merry songs or mirth-inspiring jests. Oh, how much they are to be envied, for they certainly are the happiest race of mortals existing!"

"What!" said Venella, whose ideas of happiness consisted only in riches; "what, madam, a parcel of shepherds the happiest folks? Oh, no! With all possible deference to your ladyship, I think that you are the happiest person in the whole versal world."

"I!" said Matilda: "by what means," blushing at her maid's allusion, "am I so happy?"

"By what means, madam! why are you not the rich heiress of Bosmora? Is not your enemy a prisoner in the castle? Will you not have the pleasure of seeing him condemned to death, and not the most gentle one, I am sure, if he gets half what he deserves? And is not sir Donald free? I beg pardon, my lady, I mean my lord Alexander. Does he not go down on his knees every day, to pray for the arrival of that period when he may claim you as his lady? Then will not his rich domains be added to your's? Ah, madam, how often have I heard you say that you would sooner die than be the wife of Duncaethal! Ah! little did you then know that sir Donald's real name was Duncaethal, or else I think, my lady, you would have spared your vows on that head!"

"You are too free, Venella," said her mistress.

115

"Oh, I beg pardon, my lady! but you know you asked me by what means you was so happy, and I was only explaining, my lady, what I thought made you so, my lady."

They had now wandered a considerable distance from the castle, and were just going to return, when a piteous moan, seemingly close to them, caused them to look round, and they beheld a person, in the habit of a pilgrim, under a tree, seemingly in acute pain. Matilda, ever ready to assist the distressed, hastily advanced, and, in a voice of commiseration, asked if she could do anything to serve him?

"Sweet lady, if you will help to raise me up, I should be obliged to you, for I am faint and weary." She stooped for that purpose, when being raised from the earth, he, in a tremulous voice, said— "Alas, alas, I am very feeble! Gentle lady, would you so far extend your charity, as to allow your attendant to lead me to the hollow of the glen? There is a cave which I inhabit, and from which I have wandered so far, I cannot get back in my present state without assistance, and night is coming on; therefore, dear lady—"

"I will attend you, father, but do not exhaust yourself with talking. Venella, take hold of the stranger's other arm. So, father, take your time— we will assist you."

In this manner they slowly walked forward, till stopping, as if to rest, the old man pointed to a thicket, saying— "There, charitable lady, there is my humble dwelling."

"So, so, we shall be there anon."

They reached the spot, when once more stooping, he said— "Oh, I shall sink!" and seemed falling to the ground. Matilda placed her arms round his body, and endeavoured to support him, when, thrusting his hand into his bosom, he drew forth a whistle, which he applied to his mouth, and blew a shrill sound. Two men rushed from the thicket, forcibly seized Matilda and her attendant, while the hypocrite, casting off his disguise, discovered to her maddened sight the countenance of Darthalgo. With a loud shriek she sunk upon her knees, imploring him to save her.

"What," said he, "is the proud Matilda once more before me? Ha! ha! Bring forth the horses, Hugh, and let this fair captive again be conducted to our retreat."

Venella now loudly screamed—"Help! help!" upon which the ruffian gagged her mouth, and confined her hands, the fingers of which she had several times applied to his cheek, and, by the red stream that followed, gave evident proof of her powerful nails Though she had used him thus scurvily, he told her, if she would be quiet, he would unbind and suffer her to travel comfortably;

she bowed her head in assent, inwardly resolving she would call again for help, should she see the least chance of assistance. He set her mouth at liberty, and placing her before him, in the same manner his comrade did Matilda, they set forward, preceded by Darthalgo. They passed the glen, and kept in a circuitous rout through the forest, and, after a few hours riding, Matilda once again beheld the hated ruin. They did not, as before, convey her through the cavern, but rode boldly to the gate, which was opened by the old woman.

"Ah!" said she, "welcome! What have you brought the fine madam back again?"

"Aye," said Hugh, "we have brought two ladies."

"Two!" said she, eyeing Venella, who could scarcely refrain serving the old hag's face as she had the ruffian's, "who is this other? Do you suppose, Darthalgo, I can take care of two?— No, not I. You must stay and attend to them yourself."

"Well," said Venella, who, in spite of the perilous situation, could not restrain her natural flippancy, "and pray who wants you to take care of us? we had much rather go about our business, I assure you. Who do you suppose wishes to be attended by an old weather-beaten beldam like yourself? If I was to meet you in the forest, I should take you for a witch, and expect to see you mount a broomstick, and fly away."

"I'll take pretty good care that you don't fly away upon—— " growled the other. "Marry come up! weather-beaten indeed!"

"Silence!" said the bandit; "is the apartment of lady Matilda prepared for her reception?"

"It is," answered she; "there is a stone vessel of water, a basket of food, and a clean truss of straw to rest her dainty joints upon."

"Straw!" said Venella, "indeed my lady can't sleep upon straw, nor I either."

"Then her ladyship may stand, and you too," muttered the old hag.

They were now conducted through the secret entrance behind the altar, upon which the hopes of Matilda yielded to despair, and the pellucid drops chased each other down her cheeks, as Darthalgo thus scornfully addressed her—"Madam, you see I am provided against a surprise, should any one come in quest of you. To your care," addressing the old woman, "I commit her; and should any one come to search for her, conduct them through the abbey; fear not the most rigid scrutiny, for I defy any one, but our band, to discover the entrance of this dungeon, the future residence of Matilda." He now closed the door of this horrid prison, from which she never could have been released, had not Donald luckily followed old Peg, when conveying them provisions.

Darthalgo, after seeing his victims properly secured, returned to the hall, where being joined by his two myrmidons, said— "Come, let us leave the abbey for a short time, as I have no doubt but the love-sick Donald, or Bosmora, will come in search of our captive; therefore we will be absent, while Peg will conduct them through the ruins, when they will conclude it to be deserted by all but herself, and then depart." The storm now began to rage with great fury, but it deterred not the villains from quitting the abbey; and while Donald was listening to the tale of the hermit, they were proceeding to a new haunt, which was inhabited by Morven, chief of the band.

Bitterly did Venella weep when she found herself left in the gloomy cell. "Ah, my dear lady, how differently did we rest last night! Then you had a handsome couch, covered with velvet, and I a nice soft mattress by your side. Ah, but a few hours since I said you was the happiest person in the world, and now you are in a miserable dungeon! Oh dear, I wish we had never ventured out of the castle! Oh dear, who would ever have thought it! But do you think, my lady, they will kill us?"

"Alas! I know not," said Matilda; "perhaps, at least, they may me, for that mysterious bravo seems to bear me the most inveterate malice."

"Ah, my lady, what have you ever done to offend him? If I was in your place, I would ask his pardon, and see if that could induce him to release us."

"Alas! he is deaf to all entreaties," said Matilda, "and my begging pardon would avail nothing; indeed I never did any thing to offend him: often has he terrified me by presenting a poniard to my breast, but some powerful motives has restrained him from becoming my destroyer, though Heaven only knows how long he may be now before he does indeed put a period to my existence. I hope the moment is not far distant, for rather would I perish beneath his dagger, than linger out a miserable existence, while memory would continually torture me with what I might have been, and what I am."

The tears quick chased each other down her cheeks as she concluded these reflections, and, hiding her face in her robe, she fell into a reverie, when all the torturing horrors of her fate passed in rapid succession, till frenzy almost took possession of her brain, and, bitterly weeping, she prayed for instant dissolution. In this manner did the night pass on in silence, save that time they were alarmed by the loud peals of thunder, which shook the ruins to the foundation, and, in awful sounds, re-echoed through the vaults of the subterranean, and they every moment expected to be buried beneath the ruins. The day dragged heavily as the night, when at last hearing a key applied to the door of their prison, they expected the appearance of the bandit; how great then was the surprise of Matilda, in beholding her much-loved Donald, who, by his magnanimity, once more restored her to the arms of her affectionate father!

When Matilda had concluded the recital of her sorrows, the baron again clasped her to his heart, and bade her prepare herself for the banquet, where she was expected by the numerous lords and ladies, who had assembled to congratulate her on her deliverance, and Donald on his newly-acquired dignity. She retired, and, after some time devoted to her toilet, arrayed herself in a plain white robe; she was then led into the banqueting room by the joyful Agnes, who in the other hand conducted Donald, and proceeding forward in an introductory manner, said—"Noble lords and ladies, my son Alexander and the lady Matilda!"

Earl Malcolm, of Rosse, now stepped forwards, and, after congratulating him, said—"I too have been an innocent enemy of your's, my lord, by corroborating the report of your cowardice, made by the villainous Duncaethal, who, by his diabolical stratagem, caused me to suppose you had failed to meet him; and were he not situated as he is, with his sword should he answer for the stain cast upon my honour, which no man before ever presumed to trifle with."

Donald, whom for the future we shall distinguish by his proper tide, answered—"That he felt fully assured, that had he even suspected the least idea of its being a device to sully his fame, he would have been the last to join in the plot."

These conversations were interrupted by the sounding of a harp, and an aged minstrel accompanying it with a song, expressive of the happy occasion on which the assembly had met. After several hours spent in festivity, they all retired to their respective couches, while the servants prepared the hall for the trial, which was to take place on the following morning, when the base usurper was to be stripped of his ill-acquired dignity, and receive the reward due to a villain.

Chapter VIII

Oh! had I dwelt in the bright beam of my fame, then
had my years come on with joy! But I fall in youth!
My father shall blush in his hall!
Who on his staff is this? Who is this, whose head is
white with age? whose eyes are red with tears? Who
quakes at every step? It is her father!

Ossian.

THE PLACE OF TRIAL WAS CROWDED at an early hour, which exhibited an assemblage of the most noble families in Scotland. Bosmora sat as the principal of these impartial judges, for the culprit's numerous crimes would admit of no palliation; yet was he allowed a fair hearing and defence. A signal being given, the door was thrown open, and the once imperious Duncaethal entered that hall, a captive, where he had long reigned the lord. Silence being commanded, the baron arose, and addressed the degraded chief in the following words, while he stood with an unaltered countenance—"Philip, or, as thou hast long called thyself, lord Duncaethal, bitter indeed is it to me to see a noble of Scotland arraigned for so heinous a crime as your's; can you hope for mercy, after basely wronging both the widow and the orphan? What punishment inflicted on you can atone for the lady Agnes of Duncaethal's many years of sorrow and captivity?"

"I ask no mercy!" said the haughty Philip; "but if Donald is indeed so brave, as he would fain have it believed, why did he appeal to the arbitration of those noble barons? why not rather justify his claims by his sword? Nor can you, my lord, say I have intentionally wronged the orphan, being ignorant of his existence."

"Thou hast wronged him," said the baron, "in the unknown Donald, by diabolical machinations and stratagems, disgraceful for a noble to use; but sanguinary and inhuman has always been your conduct. Thinkst thou the youthful lord would again meet him in the field, on equal terms, who had, by so base a fraud, stained his honour as a knight? Nor is it proper the usurper of his father's house should, black with crimes, have equal chance with the virtuous son of the brave Duncaethal."

Alexander now arose, and, bowing, requested permission to be heard, which being granted, he addressed the assembly as follows:— "My lords, if it be consistent with the laws, restore to Philip his sword, and I, by force of arms, will prove my rights; my cause is just, so fear not I the victory; nor can there be a more honourable method of revenging my own and my mother's wrongs."

The eyes of Philip flashed with gratification at the thought of his offer being accepted; not so much did he cherish the idea of conquering, as by an honourable end he should escape the degrading sentence he had no doubt would else be passed upon him.

Bosmora, in the meantime, thus addressed his accepted son—"I have no doubt the taunt of cowardice, conveyed in the speech of that wily wretch, hath induced you to rush into the danger that is proposed, with a view of clearing the stain from your honour; I wish not to check your bravery, and if those noble lords thereby are content, you have my consent."

The majority acquiescing, Alexander was on the point of leaving, to arm himself for the occasion, and Philip, the usurper, accompanied by a guard, was about to retire for the same purpose, when Matilda, who sat next to Agnes, unable any longer to restrain her concern, burst into a flood of tears, while a blush of crimson suffused her cheek at the weakness she had thus evinced.

Her lover sunk at her feet, saying—"My beloved Matilda, shake off this depression; shall I not in this combat revenge your wrongs also, and prove myself worthy of being Bosmora's son, when there cannot be the least doubt remain of my courage, even in the breast of my enemy, by accepting his challenge?"

"Why then," a voice loudly exclaimed, "would Alexander stain his dignity by combating with a murderer?"

"Ah!" said the usurper, while the paleness of death succeeded his late exultation, "who dares to accuse me of a crime like that?"

"I!" said a tall figure, rushing forward, and casting off a long cloak by which he was concealed; "I, the bandit Darthalgo!"

Matilda gave a loud shriek when she beheld him, and cried—"My father, 'tis he! 'tis he!"

"Ah!" said Bosmora, "seize him!"

The guard advanced, when waving his arm with dignity, he exclaimed—"I will follow you, when the purpose is answered for which I came hither. My lord Bosmora, thinkst thou, if I feared you, I should thus voluntarily appear before you when surrounded by soldiers?—No! But I come to criminate that murderer!"

"Ah, again!" said Philip, trembling. "Who art thou?—not Valando?"

"Dost thou not know me? I am not indeed Valando, but one still more injured than that unfortunate Venetian!"

"I know you not," said Philip, in trembling accents; "but produce the proof of your injuries."

"I will!" said the bandit. "Here, look in this sun-burnt visage—are there no traces left of your victim? Then come nearer!" said he, drawing close to the usurper: "what, you dare not! then I will advance to you, and whisper in your ear the name of—" Then, drawing near, a poniard at that moment pierced the heart of the guilty Philip, and ere the horror-struck assembly could prevent it, plunged it deeply in his own, at the same instant exclaiming—"Revenge sweetens the pangs of death! Look on me, Alexander, and triumph in my fall! and you, proud Matilda, behold the victim of your beauty!"

She tore off her false hair and counterfeit beard, that had half covered her face; they both rushed towards her, for in the mysterious bandit they beheld the once-lovely *Margaret of Monteith*. The struggles of dissolution convulsed her frame as she continued to address Matilda, whose tears fast trickled down her cheeks, for all her past sufferings were forgotten, in the surprise and pity she felt at beholding this martyr to her ungovernable passions. "Can you forgive me," said the dying Margaret, "for all the sorrows which I have caused you? for, oh, Matilda, you have caused the fatal pangs you now behold! I was made a sacrifice to your superior charms, by that fallen wretch, whose guilty soul has only set forth a few moments before mine, to account for his manifold crimes! Did I, did I not deal the blow? Oh, sweet revenge! how grateful art thou to my—Ah! what horrid fiend is that? Art thou impatient to conduct me to those shades of woe, the just reward of deeds so foul as mine? Duncaethal, we shall meet again! I thought to revenge myself by thy death also, Matilda; but, wretch as I am, my arm was palsied at the idea of murder till this fatal moment! Now have I stained my soul with the blood of Philip!—yet can *that* be called murder? Did he not suppose he had done the same by me? I should have left his punishment to the retributive hand of Heaven, but 'tis now too late; repentant pangs and dire remorse is all in vain! Farewell! Pray for the guilty Margaret! Oh!—oh!—oh!"

A lengthened groan bespoke the final exit of this once beautiful creature, who, beneath the rough disguise of a bandit, had long been the scourge of the innocent Matilda, and the unoffending youth who had excited her deadly hatred by refusing her proffered love. Not the least whisper in the assembly had interrupted this awful tragedy, till Bosmora, now somewhat recovered from the amazement which had enchained every faculty, led his weeping daughter from the spot, and ordered a courier to proceed immediately to the castle of Monteith, and request the speedy presence of the earl.

The remains of the unhappy Margaret, together with the guilty Philip, were laid in state, with all the mournful magnificence due to their exalted rank; for the generous Alexander forgot his wrongs, and pursued not hatred beyond the grave, but bowed himself to that Omnipotent Power, who had taught him vice could only flourish for a time, and must at length sink before the virtues of the innocent. Bosmora would have demanded of Dargo, whom he had no doubt could have given, some clue to this wonderful event, but he had the preceding day left the castle with the banditti, who were sent to meet the punishment due to their infamy.

Alexander, on the following day, accompanied by Matilda, sought the apartment where lay the bodies of Margaret and Philip. He approached the bier of the former, and while he contemplated her inanimate countenance, he thus apostrophized—"Are then those eyes for ever closed! those that could once assume the melting tenderness of love, but, being thwarted, flashed forth sparks of ireful vengeance! and will that voice, which thou couldst sink to whispering melody, or raise to the rough-sounding accents of a remorseless bandit, never again will it charm by harmony or terrify by threats—threats which thou hast too well fulfilled! Thou hast indeed oft rended my heart-strings, and in the person of Matilda—"

"What means my lord?" said the latter, who had listened with an attentive ear to his incomprehensible words.

"Oh, my beloved," said he, "that bitter foe, whose sad remains we now behold, vowed dire vengeance on thy innocent head, the evening the festival of thy birth was celebrated at Bosmora."

"I pray you, my lord, explain yourself; I have long had an earnest desire to learn what passed during your interview with lady Margaret in her bedchamber."

He started; he knew not that she was acquainted with the circumstance, but on this discovery being made, fearful lest the smallest suspicion should yet remain on her mind, he took her arm, led her to another room, and unfolded the whole affair.

In a day or two the venerable Earl of Monteith arrived, to whom Bosmora, with all the delicacy possible, imparted the late wonderful transaction. The old man clasped his hands in agony, while the drops of bitter anguish stole in torrents down his furrowed cheeks, as, in heart-broken accents, he said—"Lead me to her! let me behold her hapless remains! Great indeed have been her injuries to you, my lord, but you are a father, and can feel with me! Oh, my child!—a robber's disguise!—the heiress of Monteith! Horrid indeed must have been the prelude to this fatal tragedy! Alas, my daughter! Bosmora, I beseech you let me see her!"

"Check these passions, my Lord, and I will instantly conduct you to the apartment," said the baron, while the sight of the old man's tears excited the commiseration and sympathy of his feeling heart, and he was obliged to summon all his fortitude to prevent weeping in unison.

When they entered the room, the sable draperies and funeral ornaments, which by the baron's orders it had been decorated with, caused the venerable Earl to tremble, and supporting himself upon the arm of his conductor, with tottering steps he approached the bier. He started; scarcely could he recognize a single feature, so much was she altered since the time in which he last beheld her. "What!" said he, "is this Margaret, my child—she who was so justly extolled for her great beauty? Can this weather-brown'd visage have taken place of the lily, which once intermixed with the damask tint, that used to charm the eye of every beholder, and was the pride and glory of her old father? Oh, my child, my child!—my beloved, my sweet, my beautiful daughter!—little did thy wretched parent think, when thou didst beguile him with thy infantile prattle, that he should one day see thee engored with blood drawn from thy heart, or sure his own had broke! Let me once again press upon those lips a father's kiss! Happily thy mother is no more, and I shall not long remain to bear this load of sorrow and disgrace which so heavily oppresses me!" He placed one hand upon his breast, and again stooping to the corse of his daughter, he staggered back into the arms of Bosmora; the cordage of his heart was rent asunder, and, without a sigh or groan, he expired.

The terrified baron called loudly for assistance, and the room was presently filled with domestics, who, on seeing the situation of their master, supposed the old earl had only fainted, and bearing him to a couch, some flew for cordials, till Bosmora, in a voice of grief, informed them it was quite useless, for his spirit was for ever fled. Many of the company now assembled unfeignedly mourned his death, for they had known him to be a man of most excellent qualities, and his only failing had been too great an indulgence of his daughter, whom he had loved even to a fault. Time had almost meliorated his sorrow for her supposed death, when this awful renewal of his grief, added to the ignominy she had brought upon their illustrious and hitherto unsullied name, proved too great for his exhausted nature to endure, and he sunk beneath the oppressive burden, never more to rise.

"Peace to his departed soul!" said the surrounding spectators.

After some time spent in making necessary arrangements for the funeral solemnity, which shortly after took place, the remains of both the father and daughter were conveyed to Monteith, where all the remembrance of her crimes were buried in the tomb of Margaret.

CHAPTER IX

There's not a wretch, that lives on common charity,
But's happier far than me: For I have known
The luscious sweets of plenty; every night
Have slept with soft content about my head,
And never wak'd but to a joyful morning:
Yet now must fall, like a full ear of corn,
Whose blossom 'scap'd, yet's wither'd in the ripening.

Otway.

MARGARET OF MONTEITH, when she consented to be the bride of Duncaethal, was not inclined so to do from any affectionate motive, but to gratify her ambition, in being united to one of the most powerful nobles in Scotland; and she ardently panted to launch forth into all the unrestrained liberties of a wedded beauty. The masque, the tournament, and revels, delighted her imagination; and though she had never felt the soft interchange of mutual love, yet was her unbounded pride won by the humble adoration of Duncaethal, who seemed to exist only by her smiles, and expire with her frowns; though, to do him justice in this instance, he did not act the hypocrite, but did really feel for her all the passion of an enthusiastic admirer: but was it doomed to be lasting?—No. It was not in the nature of Philip to feel constancy.

That he was enraptured by her commanding dignity of deportment, and her regular symmetry of features, it is true; then her great fortune, added to his own, was sufficient to make him one of the wealthiest, as well as the most powerful barons of his nation: yet had her anxious father, desirous of placing her beyond the power of a husband's caprice, settled this immense fortune upon her, by way of jointure, except a very handsome sum paid down upon her marriage, as her dowry; and in default of an heir, she was at liberty to bequeath it to whom she might think fit. This arrangement did not altogether meet with the approbation of her lord, but he hoped, by indulgence, he should so far be able to win upon her nature, as to induce her to resign her power unto himself; but he was mistaken; for the discerning and political Margaret was fully aware, as she each day witnessed his wavering disposition, that by resigning to

125

him unlimited sway over her fortune, she should lose the superiority which she possessed over himself.

Being convinced of the propriety of this determination, she still retained the first in gaiety and splendour; and one day, when he reproached her for wasting his substance, she tartly replied—"I think, my lord Duncaethal, my father's liberality to you on our marriage is not yet expended; and when it is, I have a resource, which, like that of Croesus, cannot be exhausted by all the extravagance that your lordship is pleased to complain of."

"Then why not, beloved Margaret," said he, "invest me with that power? It is not well that the baron should look up to his lady for a supply. Would it not have been more proper if your father had entrusted me? Surely I should have proved a better guardian of your fortune than you can possibly be."

"Oh pray, my dear lord, don't alarm yourself," said she, ironically; "I don't wish to give you so much trouble; I can take care of it myself: and give me leave to observe, my lord Duncaethal, that if you disapproved the arrangements made by the baron of Monteith, you should have rejected them, ere the priest had bound us in those trammels, which, I think, from your late conduct, do not promise to be very agreeable to either party. In the meantime, my lord, rest assured that I shall never yield to your covetous nature the unrestrained liberty of disposing of my fortune to those who, by their conduct, may most merit my esteem. Not any mortal living shall ever possess the least command over me during my existence! No, never will I give I the reins out of my own hands; and were I even weak enough to I settle it on you, in case of my decease, your lordship could not be much the gainer; for, according to the regular course of nature, there is all likelihood of your first bidding adieu to this transitory life; but, perhaps, your lordship could remedy that, by removing me, as you have already done the hapless *Paulina!*"

"Ah! what mean you?" said the conscience-struck wretch. "Madam, beware, beware what you say! I murdered not Paulina! What Paulina do you mean?" endeavouring to recover himself; "who do you mean, madam?"

"I shall leave that to your superior judgment, my lord;" and, curtseying sarcastically, withdrew, leaving Duncaethal overwhelmed with surprise and confusion.

Margaret had come at the knowledge of this black affair in the following manner—by going to a cabinet, to procure something for which she had an occasion, belonging to her lord, when observing a small desk of curious workmanship, having the key left in it, prompted by her curiosity she opened it, for the purpose of examining it more minutely; in one of the drawers she discovered a packet of letters, which, being written in the hand of a female, she was tempted to peruse the contents. They were from Viola, the Venetian courtesan, and addressed to Duncaethal; five of which contained all the seeming fervency of an ardent affection. She was proceeding to unfold the sixth, when the billet of the unhappy Valando met her eye; horror ran through her veins as she perused the dreadful words—"I have seen the murdered Paulina, whose blood calls for vengeance!"

"Oh God!" uttered she, "have I wedded a murderer?" She, quick as her agitation would permit, replaced the drawers, immediately left the apartment, and retiring to her own, ruminated upon this extraordinary and unexpected discovery. How he could think of retaining a paper of so much danger, was to her a source of the greatest astonishment. In fact, Duncaethal knew not of its being in his possession, for when he received it, it was at a time he was engaged with company, and, after hastily glancing over the contents, he put it in his desk; and fearful lest by any chance it should be seen, he unfolded a letter of Viola's, and enclosed it. This circumstance entirely forsook his memory, so great was his confusion at the time; for shortly after, wishing to peruse it again, he felt for it in his pocket, when missing it, he felt much alarmed, and concluded it to be lost. Upon his departure from Venice he forgot it altogether; and little did he suppose when he was shipwrecked near Monteith, when every thing valuable was lost, save only a pocket-book, containing letters and other papers, which were preserved by being about his person, and among the rest this witness of his infamy; therefore it was to him a matter of the greatest astonishment how she could possibly gain a knowledge of this horrid circumstance.

Margaret would never have betrayed it, had not an incident occurred, which converted the cool indifference she felt for her lord into the deadliest hatred. She had long beheld his neglect towards herself with no little indignation; and one evening, returning somewhat unexpectedly from a walk, she heard voices whispering in the apartment of Duncaethal; and, applying her eye to a crevice in the door, she discovered her own maid, a pretty brunette of seventeen, familiarly seated upon the knee of her inconstant lord. In the greatest mortification she retired, and meditated how she should revenge this wounding insult. After revolving in her mind various modes of vengeance, she concluded it would be wisest to dissemble her knowledge of his incontinency, and come to the determination of dismissing her attendant immediately, who, when she came to assist in undressing that night, she informed that she might return to Monteith, as she had no further occasion for her services.

Guilt flew in her face, and, stammering, she said—"She hoped no part of her conduct had been construed into offence?"

"No matter!" said the indignant Margaret, "'tis my desire!" and was accordingly complied with.

This obstacle removed, she began to adopt measures of retaliation, which seemed to her the most feasible method of revenge; for she could not forgive such a slight of her resplendent beauty, which she most certainly possessed.

A young gallant knight, with other visitors, was then at the castle, who, presuming upon his address, which was somewhat winning, made repeated advances, which by her were met with all possible encouragement; they frequently had private interviews, and their illicit connexion was suspected by every one but him whom it most concerned. This once begun, vice succeeded vice; and Margaret always consoled for her lord's neglect in the arms of another, which gratified at once her unchaste desires, and her great revenge.

She now, in company with her lord, visited Bosmora, on the celebration of Matilda's birth-day, where the youthful Donald excited her warmest admiration; and when she found he did not, or would not understand the advances made to him, she ascribed it to his fear of giving offence; and resolving to procure an interview with him, she mixed a strong soporific in the drink of her detested husband. Thus making herself secure, she conducted the object of her passions even to her very chamber, where, for the first time in her life, she experienced a refusal, which aroused all the malevolence of her nature; for, supposing Donald's coolness towards her to proceed from his affection for Matilda, she vowed vengeance on her innocent head; and, uttering dreadful threats, the interview intended for love terminated in hate.

Upon their return to Duncaethal, the alteration of her lord's behaviour struck her forcibly. He became attentive, and seemingly affectionate, which gained imperceptibly upon her heart, not naturally hard; for had her headstrong disposition been duly checked in its earliest appearance, she might, by the virtues of her mind, have added lustre to the dazzling beauties of her person. This altered conduct of Duncaethal's was only an artifice to win her to his purpose; and it too well succeeded; for, in an unlucky moment, being thrown off her guard by his pretended affection, she signed an article, by which she bequeathed to him, at her decease, the whole of her jointure. This was what he wanted, and her fate was now decided. He had cast his eyes on the fair Matilda, and waited but the signing of this deed, by his devoted victim, ere he removed her, in a way that should not impede his intended offers to the heiress of Bosmora. Two days after, a certain drug was procured by Dargo, which, being infused into her wine, caused her to rave in the fever of delirium. Her confessor, from the neighbouring convent, for a rich reward presented him by Duncaethal, who too well knew the force of a bribe, administered a draught, which caused the appearance of death, and giving out she had fallen a victim to pestilential disease, prevented the approach of servants, and avoided her being laid in state, which would have discovered the fraud, and defeated the diabolical schemes of the villainous Duncaethal. No one, except Gertrude, was permitted to enter the apartment, who, being old and almost blind, was not feared by this triumvirate of wretches. A coffin, with a sufficient quantity of weight in it, was conveyed to the tomb of Monteith, with all the mockery of woe and solemnity of religion.

After the departure of his master, Dargo visited the apartments in the east wing of the castle, whither they had conveyed the wretched woman during her counterfeit death, from which she had not yet recovered. Placing a lamp on the table, he retired, and shortly after she awoke, and looking round her in great amazement, she suspected the deceit which had been made use of; then, raving with all the frenzy of a maniac, she struck her head violently against the wall of her prison, wishing indeed to end her being, rather than drag on a miserable existence, deprived of the blessing of liberty. Her loud screams alarmed the villain Dargo, who now proceeded to gag her mouth, lest she should be heard by any of the servants; this was almost an unnecessary precaution, for her place of confinement was situated at the very extremity of the inhabited part of the castle.

Duncaethal soon returned, exulting in the success of his diabolical scheme, and repairing to her to prison, where Dargo, after allowing her to take refreshments, had left her in a state incapable of speaking, or even using her hands, she started from her seat at the sight of her deceitful tyrant, and endeavouring to speak, which being unable to effect, the wretch laughed at her defeated efforts, and, in a voice of derision, said—"Is this Monteith's heiress, that vain beauty, who was wont to reign paramount in the gay throng of visitors which infested my castle and devoured my substance? Pity 'tis she cannot express herself with the same fluency of eloquence she was used. I prithee, good Dargo, unbind her mouth, for I think she will make no ill use of this indulgence; if she should, we can easily silence her again."

The ruffian now ungagged her mouth, when, disdaining the idea of a tear staining her cheek, or a sigh to ruffle her bosom, she, with a haughty dignity of manner, and commanding tone of voice, said—"Insulting, barbarous wretch! dearly wilt thou repent this treatment! for deeply will my noble father revenge my cause, when he learns the base conduct practiced against his child!"

"Thou weak woman," returned he, "canst thou for a moment suppose I have not taken means to prevent his ever knowing it? Thou shallow defeated fair one, thy foolish sire is mourning over the tomb, which he is led to think contains thy remains."

"Then," exclaimed Margaret, clasping her hands in frantic grief, "I am for ever lost!"

"Thou art," returned he, "while I enjoy that fortune, which gratified vanity, not love, caused you to bequeath me in case of your death. Short-sighted woman, know that when you signed your hand to that instrument, you signed the deed for your own death."

"Wretch!" returned she, "waited you but for that to complete your horrid purpose?"

"I did," answered he; "nor is that all—another possesses that love once your's! The fair Matilda, Bosmora's heiress, is to reign sole mistress of this castle and of my heart." He now left the room, first telling her violence would be of no use, unless to be again punished by a bandage across her mouth, which, on the slightest noise or intimation, should be replaced by Dargo, who would be in the adjoining apartment.

She profited by the hint and remained silent, except muttering bitter threats of vengeance against the innocent Matilda, should she by any chance ever be liberated. "Oh!" said she, "what would I give for my freedom, to be able to repay my wrongs in the blood of my rival—my double rival, both with him I loved, and with him whom I hate! Oh for revenge!—revenge!—revenge!"

A lucky thought now struck her—and when Dargo again visited her, she, throwing all the softness she could so well assume into her voice and manner, besought his pity. He was deaf to her entreaties, till she thus proceeded—"Dargo, in a secret repository of my own apartment, I have concealed a thousand angels, and a diamond ring of immense value; help me to escape, and half of the money, together with the ring, shall be your's."

The wretch listened to this proposal with some attention, and saying—"But when my lord shall know of your flight, my life will pay the forfeit, lady; I cannot consent to release you, unless you take a solemn oath never to discover yourself to him by word or action, directly or indirectly, so long as you shall live."

"I consent," said the delighted Margaret, "and do here most solemnly swear that I will never make known my existence, but quit Scotland for ever, and end my days in some religious house in a foreign land."

"I then will aid your escape: I shall easily persuade my lord you are dead, as he this night desired me not to return to his presence till I had taken your life—Yes, he commanded me to murder you! But how shall I procure the reward if it be in a secret repository, lady?—how can I find it unless you direct me?"

"Oh, fear not!" said the discerning Margaret, who was aware of the crafty wretch she had to deal with; "you shall, when all in the castle are wrapt in sleep, conduct me to the room, for no one but myself can discover the secret spot where it is concealed."

He was obliged to consent to this measure, and telling her he would soon return, withdrew to acquaint Duncaethal that she was no more. He had ordered him to dispatch her, for he was ever in dread of discovery, as guilt ever is suspicious; and he long ere this had ended poor Agnes, but her quiet resignation to her unhappy lot lulled his suspicions. Add to this, Dargo could not, when company arrived to celebrate his nuptials with Matilda, which he was resolved should take place, as he felt assured he should possess her; and thus determined, he concluded to end the unhappy life of Margaret.

When Dargo entered the room, he eagerly inquired—"Well, is it done? is she dead?"

"She is, my lord, and buried," answered the other.

"Buried!" said the baron, "where?"

"Why, my lord, I did not think it proper to murder her in that apartment she was in, as I could not there conceal the body; so I betrayed her into the subterranean, by the pretence of assisting her to escape—there, my lord, I plunged my poniard to heart; she now lies beneath the flooring of the bottom dungeon: shall I conduct you, my lord, to the spot, for I have so concealed it from the eye, that no one can discover it but myself?"

"No, no, my kind fellow!" said the wretch; "she is at peace, and I care not to behold her grave!" A demoniac smile passed his features as he put a well-filled purse into the hands of this miscreant, who, in hopes of possessing the five hundred angels of Margaret, had thus deceived his villainous master.

When all was still, he again repaired to her prison, where, first making her swear not to alarm the inhabitants of the castle, conducted her through the corridor to her own apartment, and standing at the door, waited for her return with the prize which was to be his, that in value exceeded all that had been ever presented him by his master.

She shortly appeared, and, shewing him the glittering ring, said—"Dargo, art thou deceiving me, or wilt thou conduct me from the castle?"

"I will, lady," replied he.

"Well then," said the politic Margaret, "give me thy dagger, and when thou hast brought me without the walls, thou shalt receive thy reward."

Content with this arrangement, he led her from the castle, when, finding herself enlarged, she gave him the promised prize, retaining, by his consent, the dagger. With a bounding heart she proceeded onwards, while Dargo stole to his bed, well satisfied with this night's enterprize.

Chapter X

Like to the Pontick sea,
Whose icy current and compulsive course
Ne'er feels retiring ebb, but keeps due on,
To the Propontick, and the Hellespont;
Even so my bloody thoughts, with violent pace,
Shall ne'er look back, ne'er ebb to humble love,
'Till that a capable and wide revenge
Swallow them up—Now, by yon marble heav'n,
In the due rev'rence of a sacred vow,
I here engage my words—

Shakespeare.

MARGARET, ELATE WITH HER LIBERTY, walked with tolerable brisk pace. She had about her person jewels to a large amount, and fifteen hundred angels, in addition to the sum which Dargo supposed her to have; for she did not think it proper to make him acquainted with all she possessed, lest he should extort from her a greater reward than what she proposed. This treasure had been presented to her by her father, unknown to Duncaethal, who, during her confinement had searched the little cabinet for her jewellery; yet some of the richest remained in the secret drawer, which escaped his notice, not supposing it contained such a concealment.

A pelting storm overtook her in the forest, through which, without knowing whither to bend her steps, she was quickly hurrying, and, under the wide-spreading branches of an aged oak, the once proud heiress of Monteith sought shelter from its fury. Here it was that, kneeling, she again vowed destruction on the authors of her degradation. "Yes," said she, "I am dead to the world! I will cast off my woman's attire, and with it all the puerile fears and timid delicacy of my sex! I have sworn never to discover myself to Duncaethal or any one—I never will; but, in the disguise of another, I will sting him to the heart! I will be his bane!—his curse! Matilda, Donald, beware! Dreadful is my fate, dreadful shall be my vengeance!—direful, deadly, and horrid!"

Her fiend-like passions distorted her countenance as sternly she again pursued her way. Daylight appeared as she gained the outskirts of the forest, and perceiving a neat white cottage, she thought of taking some rest ere she fixed upon any plan relative to her future proceedings. On reaching the door, she gave a gentle tap, and it was instantly opened by an old woman, who asked what she wanted, at the same time expressing surprise at her rather strange appearance. Margaret silenced all further inquiries by the timely application of a piece of gold, and asking if she might rest herself, as she felt greatly fatigued.

"Your ladyship shall have my humble couch, in welcome," said the old woman; "there is no one at home but myself."

Margaret being conducted to the apartment, threw herself upon the bed, where she forgot her cares in a sound refreshing sleep. When she awoke, the first thing that met her sight was a mean suit of male attire, hanging against the wall, at the foot of the bed; calling the old woman, she asked to whom it belonged?

"To my son," answered she, "who had not long been gone to work, in the wood, when your ladyship came."

"Will you sell it?" asked Margaret.

"Sell it, lady! gramercy, what use will it be to you?"

Margaret told the old woman that she fled from the pursuit of one who sought her life, and she wished to disguise herself; then putting in her hand a couple of pieces of gold, six times more than they were worth, she asked no further questions. She left her to array herself in them, which she quickly did, and cutting off her fine long hair, she put on a highland cap, as worn by the peasants, and concealing her wealth in her clothes, she set forth from the cottage, with many blessings from the old woman, who said she made a bonnyer lad than her son Michael.

After walking a great distance, she perceived a quantity of berries which grew around, and plucking some, pressed out the brownish liquid that they yielded—with this she disguised the snowy delicacy of her skin. She was on the point of pursuing her journey, when the voices of men attracted her ear, and stepping behind a tree, overheard one of them say—"I tell you, comrade, the trade is a very good one; who do you think would work, when he can be so well paid for doing nothing, as a body may say? Think you I would stick at any thing for money? No, not I, i'faith! though our chief, Morven, being unluckily wounded, and lies here hard by, we live in a state of idleness, as a body may say."

A thought entered the prolific brain of Margaret, and advancing, said—"Which of you will conduct me to Morven, the noble chief of your band?"

"Ah!" returned they, "who art thou that dares thus undauntedly address us? Know you who we are?"

"I do," said she; "are you not a brave set of men, who live by taking from others what they can very well spare?"

"We are," answered they; "and now, youth, who art thou?"

"One who fain would be of your noble calling," said she: "but come, conduct me to your chief."

"Come on then," said they.

They led her to a kind of hovel, where, on a bed, lay the wounded Morven, attended by an elderly-looking woman, who was administering to him medicine, unconscious of his real way of life, or even caring, so long as she was well paid for her trouble. He was wounded in an attack, with the other two, who, being overpowered by superior numbers, fled, and left their chief for dead; but, on returning to the spot after the victors had departed, they found he still breathed, and, conveying him to this cottage, said he was their master, who had been wounded by a robber in the wood, it being at too great a distance to think of conveying him to the abbey. Whether the cottagers believed this or not is uncertain, but they did not think fit to express any doubts, as they were well rewarded.

When Margaret entered the room, she expressed a desire of speaking in private. Morven, desiring all to withdraw, then requested the purport of this interview; to this Margaret answered—"I am a nobleman, that has been basely wronged by the united houses of Duncaethal and Bosmora; I loved the beauteous daughter of the latter, but my offers were scorned for a mean youth—a peasant boy: let me be admitted into your band, by which means I can get her into my power, and I'll reward you amply."

"My lord, you shall have our assistance; but why wish to join our band, for we will follow your directions?"

"Because," returned she, "in disguise I can act unknown; as the heir of—but no matter who I am—here's a hundred angels to divide amongst the noble fellows who shall assist me," putting into his hand a purse for himself.

"Marry, my lord, your argument is very powerful, and you shall have all the aid our band can afford; and, as I am incapable of attending at the abbey, the rendezvous of our band, you shall act as chief, and by my orders they will obey you as myself."

"Revenge will then be mine!" said she.

"It will, my lord," returned the other; "but I beg pardon, what should you like to be called, as it is necessary you should be distinguished by some appellation?"

After pausing a moment, she recollected the Venetian letter, and she said—"My name shall be Darthalgo!"

"Very well, my lord," answered the chief, "it shall be that. Would you please to retire for a moment, while I commune with my men?"

She complied, and summoning to his presence the two robbers, he thus begun—"My boys, here's a lucky day's work! here are an hundred angels to be divided among the band." He then gave them instructions how they were to act towards the stranger, who he said was a powerful baron, who had promised to reward them well, if they assisted him in the purpose for which he had assumed this disguise.

They readily agreed to all their chief proposed; then, setting forth for the abbey, promised to return the next day to see how he fared. Upon their arrival at the rendezvous, she was introduced to the rest of the band, and then conducted to a room full of arms of every description. After selecting a dress, which she thought the most terrific, she arrayed herself in it, together with bushy hair, and a large beard, which she discovered among the various disguises made use of by the band on particular occasions; she added a black patch on the right side of her forehead. Thus metamorphosed, who could recognize the once-lovely heiress of Monteith? She soon became acquainted with the manners of the banditti, but never accompanied them on any of their excursions for plunder; neither would she allow them to be a spy upon her actions.

In this manner, week after week passed on, without any opportunity occurring by which she might ensnare Matilda, until the fatal night in which the castle was attacked, when, scouting round in company with one of the robbers, she beheld the motions of Duncaethal, and giving directions to her companion, rushed in at the private door, which had been thrown open by the terrified domestics, and being well acquainted with the interior, made for the apartment of Matilda, where finding her in a state of insensibility, caught her in her arms, and, snatching up a half-extinguished torch, hurried down among the subterraneans, whence she hoped, as soon as animation should revisit her, during the confusion to convey her safely away. Matilda's scruples, however, prevented her; and with bitter execrations, on account of her views being thwarted, she left the castle, and, seeking her companion, mounted her horse and rode away.

She now turned her thoughts towards Duncaethal, whither she felt assured Matilda would be conveyed, and reconnoitering the spot, a loud noise caused them to start; and having left their horses in the forest, they sought to conceal themselves in what appeared to be a natural cavity of the earth, but was, in fact, the passage leading to the door of the subterranean, which, by the quantity of rubbish that appeared, seemed as if it had not been made use of many years. Thus, by mere chance, she discovered the passage by which she so often afterwards made her secret and nocturnal visits to our poor heroine, and learned the confinement of Donald, by overhearing a conversation between Dargo and his lord, relative to their future proceedings towards that unhappy youth.

In her different visits she covered herself with a long white robe, stained on the breast with blood, in case she was ever seen by any of the inhabitants, they would suppose her to be a ghost; this she always cast off and left behind the picture (the device of which she had discovered when she inhabited the apartment) whenever she visited Matilda. On the evening she had quitted Matilda, at hearing the voice of Duncaethal, she plucked the beard from her face, and quickly putting on the robe, appeared to her guilty lord as the spirit of his murdered wife! The event answered equal to her wish, and she had the pleasure of seeing Duncaethal writhing in the agonies of conscience stained with blood, as he sunk prostrate to the earth; then repairing to the trap, which she had discovered one night in her researches, she rejoined her companions, whom she told that she had not succeeded with Matilda according to expectation, and that they must return another night; then presented them with a well-filled purse, which not only prevented them from murmuring, but won their hearts. Thus did Margaret, by timely bribery, gain the esteem of the ruffians, who thought her a worthy generous nobleman, and would, if required, have sacrificed their lives in her defence.

At last, by various stratagems, she ensnared the person of Matilda, whose blood, though she had at first resolved, she now hesitated to shed; for though the inmate of a banditis' cave, yet did she start at murder, and what she oft intended to perform, her hand would shrink from. Often did she say to herself—"Margaret, thy wavering spirit shames thee! Can thy miseries be washed away but by blood? Impossible!—therefore she must die!" And one night, being rather more than usually determined, she went to the cell of Donald, and bidding him follow, resolved before his face to end the life of her victim. Her dagger was raised for that purpose, when the old woman rushed in with intelligence of the abbey being attacked; in this dilemma she knew not how to proceed; she dared not to meet the presence of Duncaethal, who she rightly conjectured had come for the purpose of recovering his prisoners, when she recollected the secret entrance behind the altar, where she concealed herself, and was shortly joined by two of the band, who, finding the day against them, sought here for refuge.

After the abbey was evacuated by all but the old hag, whom Bosmora suffered to remain, they ventured to steal from their hiding-place. These two ruffians, who often had assassinated in the dark, had not the courage to stand the issue of the battle, but had fled after the first onset, under the idea that they were attacked by royal troops. The politic Margaret knew better than to undeceive them, for she feared, when they should know it was through her the band was routed, they would refuse again to assist her, and perhaps by her life revenge themselves for the injury.

"Fool that I was," thought she, "so often as I've had it in my power, not to revenge myself for all the sufferings caused me by her life, and that of the upstart Donald; but she shall not yet escape my vengeance!"

She now, in concert with the two robbers, in disguise, wandered round Duncaethal, till that day when they seized poor Matilda and her maid Venella; the latter Margaret would willingly have dispensed with, but was obliged to retain her, lest she should be the means of discovering the perpetrator of this action. She concluded that they would not suspect her when once they found the abbey vacant, which, by her instructions to the old woman, they would, no doubt, suppose it to be.

Judge then her disappointment and rage, when, on repairing to the ruin, she found Matilda had again escaped her! With many useless exclamations of regret, they retraced their way to the cave which Morven had fixed upon for their future residence. Unluckily, during their absence, he had been informed by a wood-cutter, with whom he fell in conversation, who were the real besiegers of the abbey. "Ah! ah!" continued the man, ignorant of who he was addressing, "the rogues will all swing for it, I warrant them! Do you know that one of them conveyed away the heiress of Bosmora? By saint Andrew, he had a liquorish tooth! Don't you think so?"

"Pray how do you know all this?" said the other.

"Know, quotha! why because some of the guards passed by my cottage, who had the rogues in custody, and were conducting them to the punishment they deserve."

Morven walked away, and soon as his two comrades returned, accompanied by Darthalgo, he regarded not the latter by any pleasant looks. Margaret's suspicions were aroused, and, pretending fatigue, retired to an outer cave; but instead of resting on the couch, she listened through a chink of the door, and overheard their conversation, the subject of which was revenge for the loss of their companions, by her death.

She, unperceived, left the cave, and taking a horse that was near, mounted it, and swiftly pursued her way to Duncaethal, covering herself with a long plaid cloak to conceal her strange habit. Upon her approach to the castle, she alighted at the door of a cottage, and asked for a little water, which being granted, she inquired if lord Duncaethal was married yet to the heiress of Bosmora?

"Not yet," said the cottager, 'but he will when the trial is over."

"Trial!—what trial?"

"Why didn't you know, stranger, that the tyrant lord who wedded the heiress of Monteith was a usurper?"

"A usurper!" said the astonished Margaret.

"Yes, stranger, a usurper; and a youth, called Donald, is proved to be the lawful heir of Duncaethal."

"Indeed!"

"Yes, stranger, it is true; and at this very moment they are trying the usurping lord for unlawful possession," added the cottager.

Margaret, thanking her informer for his politeness, quitted the door, and, after a moment's pause, she said—"And is vengeance at last snatched from me? He once escaped a blow aimed by my hand, but he shall not escape another! I must perish in the attempt; but my long-cherished revenge, at least on him, shall sweeten my fall." She now rushed amongst the throng into the hall, and fell by her own hand, after dealing retribution on the guilty Philip. She fell in the pride of her days, a dreadful example of the bitter effects of an ungoverned temper and unrestrained passion. Peace to her sad remains! "We war not with the dead!"

Alexander, in a few weeks, received the hand of his beloved Matilda. The gloomy halls of Duncaethal were again filled with aged bards; the gates were again open to hospitality; the wretched never went unrelieved from the portal; while meek-eyed benevolence, and genuine charity, presided in the person of Matilda.

Lady Agnes and the baron lived to witness the continuing glory of their families, in the persons of a grandson and daughter. The former inherited all his father's virtues; the latter, all her mother's beauty, chastity, and goodness. Old Allen and Jannet finished their days beneath his roof, while Venella and Robert, who were shortly united, dwelt in happiness and prosperity; the latter often indulging in his natural propensity of feasting and drinking in the halls of his lord.

Thus did Alexander, happy himself, by the happiness which he caused to others, sink gently into the vale of years. While surrounded by his lovely offspring, he sat in his hall, and listened to the song of minstrelsy, as touching the golden strings of the harp, they recalled to his mind—-

"The time which has rolled away;
The deeds of the days of other years."

FINIS.

Barozzi,
or
The Venetian Sorceress

A Romance of the Sixteenth Century

In Two Volumes

Volume I

CHAPTER I

The Assassins

"SPARE HER! oh, spare her! I implore thee!" in frantic accents cried the aged Ferrand. "Accursed villains! wouldst thou imbrue thy hands in the blood of innocence? What is our crime? Who is your employer? Horrible assassins! for such indeed you are, or why do I behold your stiletto raised against the pure bosom of Rosalina? If 'tis only plunder which induces you to this rashness, take our property, fire our cottage, or raze it to the ground; but spare, oh, spare my child!"

"Thy pleading is in vain, old man!" exclaimed one of the ruffians, whose manner bespoke him the superior; "'tis the life of Rosalina we seek; she has offended by a crime so great, that it can only be expiated by her death."

"Her death!" said the wretched parent. "Oh, Heavenly Powers! has Ferrand St. Almo watched his child with parental fondness, reared her in the pale of rigid duty, and taught her the practice of every virtue, to hear it said she merits death! Oh, thou miscreant, 'tis false! Her life has ever been pure and unsullied; free from stain as frozen snows upon the Alpine cliffs—See! she revives! Oh, give her to my arms, and you shall receive an old man's blessing. My Rosalina—"

He rushed to clasp her in his embrace, but was restrained by the bravo that had before addressed him, who, putting forth his arm, said, "Hold, Ferrand! I will make one proposal. Your daughter is recovering from the swoon into which she was thrown by our first appearance; if you will freely consent to part with her, and consign her to my charge, I promise faithfully to spare her life; but should you dare to resist, she shall sink beneath the dagger of my comrade Darano, who waits only for my voice to execute our orders."

"Cold-blooded villain!" exclaimed Ferrand, gazing frantically on his daughter, who till now had remained senseless in the arms of the last-mentioned ruffian, "thinkst thou I will trust to thy word—part with my child, and give her to thee, an assassin! No! sooner will we both perish!"

"Then be it so," cried the other: "Comrade, you know your duty; drag hence the girl; and thou, old man, at thy peril beware; for if thou darest to follow, or by the slightest noise give alarm, that moment shall be your last."

He now motioned Darano to the door, who instantly proceeded, bearing in his arms the almost-inanimate form of the lovely peasant, who, by this

1

movement felt aroused from her stupor, with strength till then unknown, and a heart-rending shriek, extricated herself from the ruffian's grasp, and rushed into the embrace of her aged father, who strove in vain to secure the precious prize which he had now regained to lose for ever.

"Part them!" cried the enraged Roldon. "Ferrand, quit thy hold, or this moment is thy last!"

"Murderer, fulfil thy threat," returned St. Almo, "and let me perish in the embrace of my child!"

"Take then thy desire, obstinate old dotard!" cried the ruffian, and instantly plunged a poniard into the breast of the miserable father, who, sinking to the ground, murmured the name of his Rosalina, and expired.

The latter stood in mute despair; no tear moistened her cheek, no sigh convulsed her bosom; but with her starting eyes fixed upon the bleeding corse of her martyred parent, she seemed dead to the sense of every object except the dreadful one upon which she gazed.

To have beheld this scene would have rent a heart of stone; even something like pity shot across that of Roldon, and (for the first time in his life) he felt a degree of horror at the sight of the ensanguined stream which flowed with purple tide upon the floor of the humble dwelling; but instantly recovering himself from what he thought pusillanimous, once more bade Darano drag forth his victim, who instantly complied, and Rosalina, without resistance, and seemingly unconscious of their proceeding, suffered herself to be borne from the spot, with her eyes fixed on the ground, as if the body of her slaughtered father still met her distracted sight.

Roldon then advanced towards a tree, to which their horses were fastened, and unloosing them, with the assistance of Darano, they raised their senseless victim upon the ablest, and quickly mounting themselves, set off with all possible speed through the forest.

They had not rode more than a league, ere the clouds became suddenly overcast with darkness; the hollow blast in dismal sounds howled among the trees; no ray of light was visible, save at intervals the red lightning's vivid flash, which was followed in quick succession by heavy peals of thunder, that rolled dreadfully along the concave of the heavens, attended by such swelling torrents of rain, that it appeared as if the world was going to suffer a universal deluge.

The ruffians grew alarmed, and the guilt-struck Roldon, in a tone of tremulous weakness, declared he had never witnessed any tempest half so dreadful—"'Tis as if the threatened day of judgement had arrived!" said he, tremblingly.

"True," replied the hardened Darano, "and that is a sad job for him who has the blood of Ferrand still reeking on his dagger's point."

"Silence, villain!" cried Roldon, approaching in a threatening posture; "dare you moralize—you, the most confirmed bravo in all Italy!"

"Put up thy weapon," said the other, coolly; "thinkst thou I was moralizing? not I indeed; I know better than that truly; 'tis not a tempest can intimidate Darano, or frighten him into morality; no, no, all my fear is, that we shall not be able to pass the mountains, and ford the river, which must of course have o'erswelled its limits by this drenching rain. What then will become of us? It is utterly impossible we can proceed with our charge by daylight; and now, Rol, as our noble employer desired us to stab the lady, why did you prefer killing the old man?—Ah, I perceive your motive of morality; it is only extended to youth and beauty; for certainly this little insensible I have in my arms is a feast for an emperor. Ah, Roldon, you have a most excellent taste."

"Silence, fool!" cried his enraged comrade; "'twas indeed that beauty of which thou speakest that induced me to spare her, but not from the idea which you suspect—no, no; 'twas from other motives; for I thought at the sight of her, our lord might not only be pleased at our saving her, but even treble our reward. You remember how much he gave to us for procuring the fisherman's little daughter, who was no more in comparison to this beauty than port is to Burgundy."

"Oh, I understand you perfectly," answered Darano; "it was a most excellent thought of yours truly; but I cannot possibly conceive what great dislike our lord can have to a peasant girl, who can never have done him any injury."

"He has his reasons," returned the other, "or he would never have sent us this long journey; but of that enough. Let us consider how we shall cross the mountains before daylight; for should we be seen, the sight of that girl, whose clothes are stained with blood, doubtless will create suspicion, and of course betray us." He checked his horse, and exclaimed, "What shall we do, Darano?"

"Do!" said the other, "why, suppose we—"

At that instant a loud halloo sounded on the left, which in a moment was answered by a voice on the right.

"We are undone," said Roldon; "how shall we proceed?"

"Why, do you dismount," answered Darano, "and lead my horse and your own to yon clump of trees, which the lightning enables us to discern; there let us couch till those unwelcome intruders have departed."

"I like your counsel well," returned the other, dismounting as he spoke; "but be careful and hold the girl fast; for it is so very slippery, our horses can scarcely keep their foothold; and should we lose a prize so dearly earned, it will be devilish hard."

"It will indeed," replied his comrade, "therefore proceed with caution, but with as much haste as the dangerous state of the ground will permit."

They had not moved far, ere voices again broke the solemn silence which succeeded each dismal clap of thunder. Torches now gleamed in different directions through the forest's maze. Darano alighted, and wrapping Rosalina in a large roquelaure, which he took off himself, they sat down, hoping to escape unnoticed by the persons they had heard.

Ere they had remained long in this situation, a rustling amidst the trees, and sound of footsteps, proved their wishes abortive.

Roldon started up, and drawing forth his stiletto, exclaimed, "Speak! Who art thou that thus intrudes upon our shelter? If with a design of plunder, you are deceived, for we have not much to lose."

"I am no robber," said the unknown, still approaching; "I am the friend to all men. Having been till a late hour hunting in the forest, my horse stumbled, and threw me with great violence to the earth, and it grew quite dark ere I was sufficiently recovered from the fall so as to be able to explore my way, which I have now entirely lost; but my people, I suppose, are now in quest of me, for within the last few minutes I have several times heard the sound of voices."

"So have we too," said the other; "but as we are no part of your retinue, and rather suspicious of injury, must desire you to be gone."

"Well," replied the youthful hunter, "you are the most uncourteous persons to a benighted stranger I ever heard of."

"Perhaps we are, signor; but take our advice, or else it may prove worse."

The stranger was about to depart, when a loud shriek arrested his attention. "What is that?" interrogated he.

At the same moment Rosalina, who had been laid a few paces distant, amongst the trees, rushed forth, and casting herself prostrate at his feet, in a heart-rending voice, cried, "Save me! oh, save me!"

A vivid flash of lightning which shot across the atmosphere enabled him to discern the form and features of the lovely suppliant, whose appearance struck him both with horror and surprise. She had on a loose white linen robe, bespotted with blood; while her long chestnut ringlets spread on her shoulders, disheveled and dripping with the storm, which had fallen upon her defenceless head; her delicate white hands were upraised, in the attitude of earnest supplication, while her starting eyes spoke volumes of eloquence to the soul of the astounded Rosalva.

Darano sprung forward to seize her, when the sound of hallooing, close to the spot, accompanied by the glare of numerous torches, caused the ruffians to think more of their safety in escaping by flight, than making any resistance. Instantly throwing the reins across the necks of their horses, they vaulted into their saddles, and with all the speed the situation of the place would allow, were out of sight in a moment, and almost without the knowledge of Rosalva, who thought of nothing but the fair peasant, whom he had caught safely in his arms.

His people now came up, who expressed their great joy in finding him unhurt, and by their looks seemed astonished at the sight of his companion, of whom he inquired the means by which she had fallen into the hands of those whom the arrival of his attendants had put to flight?

Rosalina cast her eyes upon her dress; the ensanguined robe caused the dreadful circumstance to visit her recollection; and with the words, "Oh my father!" bursting from her lips, she sunk insensible into the arms of her deliverer, who from this exclamation, which was corroborated by her appearance, concluded that her parent had been murdered by those ruffians, and that she was most truly wretched. He instantly bade his servants prepare a kind of litter, and carefully convey her to the castle, which stood at some distance from the borders of the forest.

CHAPTER II
The Assignation

ROSALVA BAROZZI was descended from the noble Venetian family of that name. He was wild and impetuous. The ill-judged fondness which his father had ever evinced, spoiled a disposition naturally excellent. He had been indulged in his boyhood even to a fault, the consequence of which was, that all his actions were precipitate and unruly. He always followed the bent of his inclinations, without reflecting even for a moment whether such desires were proper or improper. His graceful form and comely countenance rendered him the universal favourite of the fair signoras who frequented the Piazzo di St. Marco, the Ridotto, and other places of public entertainment.

'Twas on the last evening of the carnival, when having left the Pallazzo di Barozzi, (heated with wine, and ready to engage in any enterprize, howsoever dangerous), that he perceived, in earnest conversation, at the corner of St. Lorenza, two men, seemingly strangers, at least to him; they walked to and fro for some time, at a tolerable pace, afterwards made a stand; then one of them, energetically raising his hand, claimed the attention of the other, who seemed to listen eagerly to what he advanced. They now turned back, and were proceeding towards the place from whence Rosalva first beheld them, who, with his usual impetuosity, resolved if possible to become a sharer in the secret. Sliding into the opening of the building, he slipped behind one of the pillars, and one which he knew they might probably pass. His conjecture was right, for they paused for a few moments exactly against it; when he that had before seemed to be the principal speaker, thus addressed himself to his companion—"I tell you there is no danger, Pisano; is it not the last day of the carnival?—will not every body be engaged by their own pleasures, without attending to those of others? By the mass! I think the lady has a good taste certainly. Flodiardo is as comely a youth as signora need wish to look on."

"Ah that he is," said the other; "but how is it to be ordered?"

"Why you, Pisano, can engage a gondola to be at the foot of the Rialto; you can manage to row, which will prevent the possibility of discovery, so you must pay a satisfactory sum to the gondolier, and take Flodiardo down the river yourself."

"Well, but how am I to know the signor when I see him, if he is masqued?" inquired the other.

"Know him!" said the first, at the same time moving onwards, (and Rosalva cautiously following to listen, at the hazard of exposing himself, so anxious was he to come to the bottom of this strange adventure), "why he is to stand there ready, and be habited in blue. You are to ask him the way to St. Euphemia's, as if you were a stranger; and if he, instead of informing you, answers Olivia, you may be certain that you are right."

"Well, and the exact time is to be—"

"The hour of vespers," answered the first. "Now haste, and leave me to settle the other affair, for the execution of which I think I merit two-thirds of the reward."

"Not you, indeed," retorted Pisano; "I had as soon engage in one as the other; therefore half the reward, or I declare off."

"Well, well, then you shall have it," grumbled his comrade, "though mine is by far the most dangerous."

"Not at all. Should you be pursued, you may easily seek refuge in some holy house."

"You need not tell me how to act, Pisano," answered the first, pettishly.

"Well, well, good-bye! I'll haste to prepare the gondola."

They separated, and Rosalva, who, to avoid being seen, had stepped behind a buttress, on their parting came forward, and mentally exclaimed, "Here's a pretty business! an intrigue and assassination! Now would I wager my life a woman is at the bottom of both. Olivia! 'Gad! a good thought! Bravo, Rosalva! I will pass myself on this sham gondolier for this favoured Flodiardo. Hold! would it not be more praiseworthy to prevent the murder? But that's impossible; I know not when it is to be perpetrated, or even where. I am alone, the people all amusing themselves in St. Mark's Place, and I dare say would not break in upon the pleasures to pursue the bravo, even though I could point him out; therefore I will certainly be a principal in the intrigue, which is the most pleasant, as well as the most profitable part of the ceremony."

Thus resolved, the volatile Rosalva went to procure a habit, such as was described, and repairing to the appointed spot, walked backwards and forwards to amuse himself, as it wanted near an hour to the proposed time.

Perhaps our readers may think he was cold and insensible to the danger in which he knew a fellow-creature to be placed, and did not act as became him; but had he raised the officers of justice in pursuit of the ruffian, his own life hereafter might have been in imminent danger; add to which, occurrences of this kind so frequently happen in Venice, that they are nothing thought of.

A difficulty now presented itself which had not before struck him, namely, that Flodiardo might arrive before the gondolier; but as this could not be guarded against, he was resolved to risk the issue of a rencounter. However, fortune seemed to favour him, for he saw no sign of his rival, and beheld the man approach with the gondola, who, on landing, inquired the way to St. Euphemia, as had been agreed upon, to whom he gave the expected answer, and was instantly conducted to the vessel.

Rosalva hugged himself in the idea of his good fortune, and anxiously longed to behold the fair lady incognita, with whom his meeting would probably be attended by some danger, should he be discovered by the signor whom he personated; but as he had now ventured beyond the power of receding, he was determined heroically to encounter the event.

The boat swiftly glided along, and in the space of time, which he conjectured to be an hour and a half, they landed on the banks of the Brenta, when Pisano making fast the gondola, bade Rosalva follow him; he willingly complied, and stopped not until they came to a gate, situated in the back part of a garden, apparently belonging to some nobleman. His conductor applied a key to the lock; they entered, and Rosalva felt himself caught hold on by a female, whom he concluded to be the confidant of his destined mistress, by the following salutation—

"Oh, signor, how glad am I that you are come! My lady, the marchioness, has almost fretted herself to death, lest any accident might have happened to detain you, and that probably we might not be able to reach Padua before morning. She has collected all her money and jewels, and intends journeying towards Paris. But why need I tell you what my lady's letters doubtless have already acquainted you with? Come, signor, for she is impatient to behold you."

The confidant led him forward through the garden, to the mortification of Rosalva, who now found that he was to elope with the lady, an office which he had not the least desire to engage in; but endeavouring to conceal his confusion, he followed the base conniver of her mistress's infamy to an elegant saloon, where, pausing and pointing towards a door, she told him he would find the signora in the next apartment; then retired, leaving Rosalva in a state of perplexity, and for a moment undecided how to act; but summoning all his confidence, he entered the room, where, seated on a couch of pink taffeta, he beheld a lady, who, though not very young, had yet charms sufficiently attractive to have given his heart full content, if the terms of elopement did not purpose too much permanency for his volatile disposition.

On his entrance she held out her hand, and said, "Flodiardo, I am uneasy till we are on our journey; partake of some refreshment, and then we will proceed to the carriage, which I have ordered to be ready within half an hour after your arrival."

"Rosalva felt confounded, but approaching to the table, where stood the only taper which gave light to the room, he took it up, as if to examine something minutely which he had beheld lying on the ground, when purposely stumbling, extinguished the flame.

She had not the least suspicion of his design, but said, in a tender tone of voice, "Are you hurt, Flodiardo? I will ring for attendants, and a fresh taper."

"Beloved marchioness!" said he, in a low key, "there needs no other lights in the place where Olivia's eyes shed their dazzling radiance."

"Flatterer!" said she, as she yielded her cheek to the delighted Rosalva, who, under the cover of darkness, had removed his mask, and embraced her; she repelled him faintly; and speaking to her only in whispers, while he left her no doubt that her beloved Flodiardo was before her, he triumphed at once over her virtue and her honor.

Swift as lighting reflection followed; the critical situation in which he stood now struck him with tenfold force, and all his thoughts were how to extricate himself from the danger he might well apprehend. "My best beloved!" said he, "surely now the carriage should be in readiness; we must start directly, if Padua is to be reached by daylight."

"Flodiardo!" said the bewitched Olivia, "thou love of my heart, and darling of my soul! we part, I hope, no more! My travelling habit will be on in a few minutes, and all is ready."

"Then hasten, my love," returned he, "and I will again put on my mask, lest we incur a discovery."

"Do so, Flodiardo," said she, and ringing the bell, the same female who had been his conductress made her appearance, with a taper in her hand, and seemingly arrayed for a journey. "Is all in readiness?" inquired Olivia.

"It is, signora," replied the other. "The servants suppose my lord has sent the carriage for you, therefore hasten, my lady."

The attendant withdrew, and was immediately after followed by Olivia, who, suddenly stopping, put into the hand of Rosalva a casket of rich jewels, saying, "There, dear Flodiardo, there is all I can procure, besides this purse of gold. Take them, with all my heart, for they both are yours."

He, with a well-assumed gratitude, kissed her hand, and leading her to the carriage, seated himself by her side, and, together with the attendant, the vehicle drove off at full speed.

Our adventurer, to avoid discovery, pretended sleep; it was a rude artifice, but the only one which could be effective. At dawn of day they arrived in Padua, and stopping at an inn to change horses and refresh, Olivia requested him to unmask, saying there was no dread of danger now.

"I think there is not," replied he, exultingly, "and therefore, my dear kind marchioness, the humblest of your slaves obeys the commands of his most sovereign mistress;" then pulling of his mask, and sarcastically smiling, he discovered to the confounded fair one the face of a total stranger.

"Oh, holy Virgin! I am betrayed!" said she, rising.

"Not unless you are weak enough to expose your own secret," said Rosalva, preventing her from quitting the room. "Here are your jewels, signora; take them, for I wish not to be master of either them or your heart, which you so kindly presented me with. Adieu! divine marchioness! and know that last night, instead of the beloved Flodiardo, you claspt in your embrace the fortunate Rosalva Barozzi."

He now, coolly bowing, left the room, while the guilty, indignant lady, vowing dreadful revenge, dismissed her carriage, and returned in a brucello to Venice, from thence to her own seat, the palace of Loredo.

In the meantime, Rosalva, exulting in his policy and successful address, had reached his residence, and thoroughly fatigued with his journey, threw himself on a couch, and shortly after sunk into profound sleep, little dreaming how dearly he was to pay for the frolic in which he had indulged, and had conducted, as he flattered himself, with adroitness and success.

Chapter III
The Death-Bed

WHEN ROSALVA HAD ENTERED the Palazzo, he had seen no one but Henri his valet, who bowed obsequiously, and beginning to address him, was instantly silenced, by his master telling him he wanted repose, and none of his impertinent loquaciousness. This hint was sufficient for poor Henri, who, knowing the consequences of forcing his conversation when it was not required, left his master to enjoy his rest uninterrupted.

Rosalva slept till a late hour, when wishing to dress for dinner, he summoned his attendant by loudly sounding the bell.

Henri quickly appeared, and lowly bowing, said, "Please your excellenza, my lord the count says he will esteem it a favour if, when you have any more commands, not to ring the bell quite so loud."

"Ah," cried Rosalva, laughing, "does his head ache after the carnival?"

"No, my lord, I don't think his excellenza's head aches, but I dare say that of the noble Florentine does, who was last night assassinated at the back of our garden, and who now lies in the room at the left of the gallery."

"Assassinated!" cried Rosalva, as the mysterious conversation he had overheard rushed forcibly on his memory. "Who is he!—What's his name?"

"I think it is the marquis of Loredo," replied the obsequious valet.

"Loredo! I have met him at the ridotto; but how came he here?" interrogated the master.

"That your excellenza shall hear. Petro went to fasten the back gate of the garden, when he heard on the other side of the wall a loud scuffle, and the words 'Villainous assassin!' This was followed by a deep groan, as if the attacked was overcome, and directly after he heard footsteps swiftly pass by the high wall, near which he was standing. The groan, though faintly, was still repeated. So Petro came hastily in, and told our Erasmus, who quickly informed his excellenza, and, to the honour of my lord it be spoken, he instantly sent us all to the assistance of the wounded man, who was not quite dead, signor, though very near it. He bled profusely, and seemed senseless. Well, to make short of my story, he was put to bed, and medical assistance procured, but he never spoke until some time after your return, my lord."

11

"Indeed! and why did you not tell me all this, babbler, when I first arrived?"

"Why, I was about to let your excellenza know it, but, if you remember, you said you wanted sleep, and none of my prate."

"Well, well," said Rosalva, "and since the marquis has recovered his use of speech, does he say whom he suspects to be the perpetrator?"

"No, my lord; he seems not so much disturbed in that respect as he is about his lady the marchioness, who, he says, will be distracted at his absence; so his excellenza the count bade him make himself easy on that head, for he would dispatch one of his domestics immediately, if he wished for her attendance.—' 'Tis some distance,' said the wounded stranger.—'No matter,' replied his honourable excellenza, 'he shall have the fleetest horse in my possession.'"

"Well, well, to the point," said Rosalva, eagerly, "Where was he to go when he had the horse?"

"Why, my lord, Erasmus is gone in a brucello, for it is upon the banks of the Brenta."

"The Brenta!" cried Rosalva, in surprise. "'Tis the same! What did he call the lady?"

"Did I not tell your excellenza?" said Henri, surprised at the hurried manner of his lord. "She is the marchioness of Loredo."

"Well, but did not he mention her name?—Did he not speak of her as Oriana, Victoria, or Paulina, or any other?"

"Oh, I remember," said Henri, "he kissed a picture which hung round his neck, and called it his adored Olivia."

"Gracious Powers, 'tis she!" exclaimed Rosalva. "Oh, Circe! how ill deserving such affection, to repay that generous breast by directing the assassin's hand to the heart which inhabits it!"

"Why does your excellenza think she was the person who hired the bravo to murder the marquis?" inquired the astonished Henri.

His master now inwardly cursed his precipitancy and unguarded manner, which, as usual, had betrayed him to the suspicions of his valet, whom he instantly seized by the throat, and holding his poniard over him, vowed that moment should be his last if he did not solemnly swear by the Virgin never to disclose a single syllable of what he had so inadvertently uttered.

This the poor terrified fellow made no hesitation in complying with, and was glad to get so cheaply off, well knowing his master was a dangerous being to deal with when enraged; and for the rest of the day, as much as possible, avoided his presence, his usual mode of proceeding upon like occasions.

Rosalva impatiently waited the return of Erasmus, wondering how the marchioness would act on hearing fate had conducted her lord beneath the roof of the very man she had so much cause to fear. He was aroused from his various conjectures by a loud noise issuing from the chamber appropriated to the use of the wounded stranger; he arose from his seat, and repairing thither, inquired the cause, and was informed the marquis was in the agonies of death, anxiously waiting the arrival of his wife ere he might breathe his last. On hearing this, he entered the apartment, and beheld, laboring under the most excruciating torments, the affectionate husband of the meretricious wretch with whom he had passed the preceding night. A sensation of pity, mixed with indignation against the perfidious instigator of those dreadful pangs, filled the heart of Rosalva.

Henri entering, hastily announced the arrival of the marchioness.

A beam of pleasure flushed the pallid cheek of the much-injured Loredo, as he lifted up his hand, in token of desiring she might be immediately admitted.

He wondered within himself how she would act at beholding him in the presence of her dying husband. "No doubt," thought he, "conscious guilt will quite overpower her, and she will confess to her deluded lord the share she has had in this horrible transaction."

His supposition was erroneous. The haughty Olivia entered with an erect and steady step, and approaching the bed with well-assumed sorrow, seemed to stifle the grief which would have found vent in tears.

Rosalva was quitting the apartment, but ere he had closed the door, the murdered Loredo, in bestowing a blessing on his faithless wife, with a deep groan expired.

A loud shriek from Olivia summoned the domestics, who, conducting her to the saloon, proceeded to pay their last duties and offices of humanity to the departed marquis.

Rosalva, on beholding the pretended grief of Olivia, could scarcely command those feelings of indignation which were excited by her well-managed hypocrisy; and advancing towards her, when out of the hearing of any attendants, he satirically said, "Weep not, fair signora, nor dim the lustre of those bright eyes, which shed their lovely radiance on the beloved Flodiardo.

"Signor," said she, with an affectation of surprise, "I understand you not! What is't you mean?"

"Mean!" said he, wondering at her pretended ignorance to what he alluded, "mean, signora! Why sure you have not forgot that this morning at dawn we parted at Padua?"

"You are certainly deranged, or in a jesting mood," replied the unblushing marchioness; "but, pardon me, this is not a proper time for raillery."

"Indeed I was never less inclined in all my life," returned he with some warmth, "for mirth. I do not jest, and you are as well convinced of that as myself; and must add, I know not which most to detest, your monstrous atrocity, or your consummate assurance in denying it."

"Signor," replied Olivia, rising, "'tis time for me to quit your palazzo, when, forgetting the rights of hospitality, and the respect due to the widow of the marquis Loredo, you make me the subject of your ribaldry. Neither can I conceive the latent motive from whence proceeds this treatment, as this is the first time I have ever beheld you, and in all probability never should now, but for the melancholy event which has brought me here. But I shall order my attendants to convey home the body of their lord, and after returning my thanks to your noble father for his politeness and generosity, you will excuse me if I decline remaining longer beneath a roof where I have received such unmerited insult."

Thus saying, she stalked forth, leaving Rosalva almost petrified at her amazing confidence.

Chapter IV
The Adoption

NO GREAT LENGTH OF TIME had elapsed after this strange occurrence, ere Rosalva was one night attacked furiously by a bravo, but by his courage and skill he successfully repelled the assailant, who, however escaped, having wounded him severely in the arm.

Not doubting but he was indebted to the lady Olivia for this attempt upon his life, after deliberating maturely, he came to the determination of unfolding the whole affair to his father, which till now he had avoided, on account of the promise he had given to the depraved marchioness never to divulge the circumstance; but as he now believed she thirsted for his blood, he was justified in so doing.

When he had imparted to his fond parent the whole transaction, it rent his aged bosom, lest his son should fall a victim to the revengeful Olivia, and thought it would be the safest expedient for him to quit Venice, at least until she was departed for Florence, as was expected.

Rosalva, taking his favourite servant Henri and two others, bade adieu to his father, and set out upon his journey towards a castle, which was situated near Pyrano, inhabited by the marchioness La Rosa, sister to the lady his mother, who doted on her nephew almost to distraction, and who, on his arrival, gave an elegant and splendid féte in honour of the occasion.

Rosalva was fond of the chase, and having in one of his excursions been thrown from his horse, who ran away, and straying through the forest on foot, was, by this accident, the means of releasing the wretched Rosalina from her inhuman persecutors.

Rosalina being conveyed to the castle, and her situation explained to the marchioness, was put to bed, where her sufferings preyed upon her senses to such a degree, as brought on a raging fever. In delirium she would call upon her father—implore the ruffians to release him—then execrating their barbarity, in frantic accents would shriek aloud for vengeance on their heads.

Thus did she rave for many days, till at length, nature exhausted, sunk her into a deep sleep, which the physician pronounced the crisis of her disorder. Youth and a good constitution triumphed over the conflict of ravaging disease. Waking somewhat recovered, she gazed round, and for some time seemed busied in tracing the sad events which had brought her to a place she was totally unacquainted with; and her father's image flitting across her imagination, brought to her relief a friendly shower of tears that prevented a relapse. "Oh, signora," said she to the kind marchioness, who was anxiously watching her recovery, "I know not how to thank your kindness, nor know whether I ought to rejoice or grieve at the restoration of my senses, which now recall the knowledge of my wretchedness."

"Hush, child!" said her hostess; "thank our holy virgin for prolonging your existence, and permitting your escape with life from the ruffians in whose power you was discovered by my nephew."

"Is he your nephew, lady? Ah, I remember when I heard his voice as I awoke from insensibility, my first idea was—ah, this is my preserver from destruction! I then rushed and implored his protection—You know the rest. Ah, my dearest benefactress! life is sweet, even to the most wretched, or wherefore should I have sought it, after I had beheld my father weltering in his blood? Oh God! what had the pious Ferrand done to merit such a death—to perish beneath a murderer's steel—he who was all goodness—who would not have hurt a worm, or the smallest insect the Omnipotent had endowed with breath? Meek, gentle, and benevolent to all around him, what demon could be to such a soul an enemy? and yet he sunk weltering in his blood on the very spot even where for years his early matins had been raised in pure devotion to our holy Mother. Yes, there, where, with uplifted hands, I have often seen him implore Heaven's blessing and protection—there did I behold him murdered—my father, my protector, my all! for who has the wretched Rosalina now left to fly to for aid? My mother has long since joined her kindred angels, and now my last, my dearest, only friend, has followed! Oh, these tears must flow forever! I am without home, without parents, without support! Oh, miserable, forsaken girl!"

"Hush! My love," said the marchioness, "Can you want protection and support while beneath the roof of La Rosa?"

"Oh my beloved protectress!" replied the distracted girl, "pardon me, pardon the wretched Rosalina, whose griefs transport her beyond herself. I never can be sufficiently grateful to my generous benefactress, who has attended me in sickness; but who will hereafter receive me? If I return to my cottage, who shall cultivate our little vineyard, now my father is no more? Can I again behold the place where I saw my venerable parent perish?"

"Fear not, my child; you shall henceforth reside with me; your misfortunes have excited my pity, and your ingenuous simplicity won my esteem; and if Rosalina will accept the marchioness La Rosa's protection, she shall never want a friend or parent."

"Oh, dear marchesa," said the grateful girl, "let my tears thank you, for words are too poor, and my actions must prove my feelings, which cannot by any other method be expressed."

"Fear not," said the marchioness, tenderly pressing her hand; "and if you can sufficiently confide in my friendship, by unfolding to me your history from its earliest period, I shall esteem myself sufficiently repaid."

"Alas, lady! if the recital of the life of a simple girl like me, who has never been but beneath one roof since she can remember, will prove of any satisfaction, you may command it freely."

"Well, dear Rosalina," said the marchioness, "you shall not at present fatigue yourself by too much conversation; only answer me one question— do you think the villains whom my nephew saw were common robbers, who sought but for booty, or assassins, employed by some enemy to your father?"

"Alas, madam! I cannot tell; I do not think my father was of consequence enough to be dreaded by any one; hated I am sure he could not be, therefore I think they were marauders belonging to the banditti who have long infested the forest adjacent to our humble dwelling."

The marchioness, musing, said, "'Twas strange!" and imprinting a kiss on the cheek of Rosalina, with a renewal of her promised protection, left her to repose, and repairing to her nephew, communicated the welcome tidings of her being out of danger.

This was pleasing intelligence to Rosalva, who had thought of nothing else but Rosalina since the first moment he beheld her. This he ascribed to pity; and when feelings, which he knew not how to define, were mixed with his thoughts of her, he would exclaim, "The circumstances I first beheld her in were so strange, that she has a claim upon my protection." Then he would sigh so heavily when his aunt said her recovery was doubtful. Ah, Rosalva! the peasant girl Rosalina in one poor moment had aroused a sensation in that heart, which all the beauties of Venice could not effect even in years. Rosalva, the gay, the libertine Rosalva, for the first time in his life felt love in its pure state, uncorrupted, and free from all sensual desires.

In the space of a few days, the fair sufferer was enabled to leave her chamber. A loose robe, white, emblem of the purity of her heart, whose bosom it covered, was the dress of our heroine; while the languid smile, which, in spite of sorrow, she endeavoured to assume, added to her pale but beautiful countenance, and gave her the appearance of something more than mortal, as Rosalva thought, while he contemplated her with such adoration and respect as a sinner pays to the image of a favourite saint. He took her hand, and with unfeigned pleasure congratulated her upon her recovery.

"I thank you, my lord," said Rosalina, smiling gracefully. "But for your kind interference, I should ere this have been past all cure in this world. I know not how to repay your goodness, nor the dear marchesa's, your noble and benevolent aunt, who has sheltered beneath her hospitable roof an orphan, friendless and forlorn."

A tear unbidden started, but she checked it ere it fell. The drop settled beneath her fringed eyelash, and appeared as the orient pearl when it ornaments the superior diamond.

"If it would not renew the sorrows of Rosalina," said Rosalva, tenderly, "I would venture to inquire how you came into the hands of those ruffians from whom it was my happy lot to be the means of rescuing you?"

"My lord, you may command me," answered Rosalina; and as she spoke, a crimson blush tinged her cheek, for her eye met the earnest admiring gaze of her deliverer.

"No, not now, my sweet girl," enjoined the marchioness; "by too much discourse you will endanger and retard your recovery."

"Ah no, madam," said she; "thanks to your goodness, I am sufficiently well, and will, if you please, commence the promised recital of my history, which is not an eventful one, and contains but little to excite the interest of a stranger."

"You wrong yourself," cried Rosalva, "greatly; for every thing must excite interest that belongs to Rosalina."

She slightly inclined her head in return to this compliment, and began in the following manner—

"My father was by birth a Frenchman: misfortunes had driven him to seek refuge here in Italy, together with my mother, whom I cannot remember, for she died while I was in a state of infancy; and often have I heard my dear father grievously deplore her loss, in bitter tears of sorrow. I have reason to think he was descended from some family of distinction, and did not always move in the humble sphere in which I have been reared, for he possessed many elegant accomplishments generally unknown to vintagers. He was the tenderest of parents, and took upon himself the care of my tuition. The improvement I made from his instructions afforded him infinite pleasure, and he would listen with great attention while I read from his favourite authors, or played on the harp, (which was his delight), when he returned from the vineyard of an evening, while we enjoyed the pure air, which wafted through the window of our humble dwelling. Ah, madam, these were happy days! but, alas! they are fled, never again to return. No more shall he smile approbation as he listens to my song! No more will he rapturously trace in my countenance the resemblance of features to my departed mother, or praise my humble attempts when with a pencil I used to sketch views of my most favourite spots round our enchanting cottage!"

The tears from her lovely eyes now coursed each other swiftly down her pallid cheeks at the recollection of past felicity; but checking them with all the power she could assume, she thus continued—

"But to finish my short, though calamitous tale. 'Twas on the close of evening, when the rest of the vintagers had retired to rest, and we were on the point of doing the same, a loud knocking at the door alarmed us. I arose, irresolute whether to unclose it or not. But my dear, unsuspecting father, cried, 'Haste, Rosalina; perhaps some of our neighbours are ill, and want assistance.' I instantly complied, and unfastening the door, two ruffians rushed in; one of them caught hold of me, and drawing a poniard, appeared ready to plunge it in my bosom. The horror which I felt caused me immediately to swoon, from which, when I was somewhat recovered, oh, God! 'twas to behold the dreadful sight of my venerable father bleeding at my feet! Oh, what a heart of stone must be mine, that it did not at that instant burst! What followed I know not, for I was insensible until the arrival of the signor, whom Heaven was most graciously pleased to make the instrument of my delivery, and who must be better acquainted with succeeding circumstances than myself."

She now for a moment paused, then said, "My gracious benefactress! I have one request to make, which, if your exalted goodness would indulge me, I would hereafter, submitting with resignation to the decrees of Providence, endeavor to forget my sufferings, and strive to be all that you wish me."

With a voice full of sweetness, the marchioness answered, "Dear girl, I promise, should it be in my power, nothing shall be wanting to make you happy."

Rosalina then thanking her patroness, said, "My desire is, madam, that you will permit some one to conduct me to the cottage which I once inhabited, to learn if the last sad duties have been paid to the corse of my beloved father, and to drop the tear of filial duty on his grave; then I will return to your gracious protection, and for this indulgence will ever endeavor to prove most grateful."

"'Tis a request which shows the unfeigned piety of your heart, and I will, if you think proper, instantly attend you," cried Rosalva, starting up.

"Hold, nephew," said the marchioness; "you are so impetuous. Rosalina shall go, but with this necessary restriction. I think, my love, from what I can gather from the narration of your simple tale, that it is evident the villains were employed to seize upon your person; therefore it would be wisest to have the precaution not to drop a hint where you are to reside in the future; and on your return, to ward off a similar danger, you shall change your appellation to one which I will myself appoint."

"Ah, dear signora, how watchful you are for my safety! How do I merit such extraordinary kindness?"

"Why," answered Rosalva, taking the hand of his aunt, and pressing it to his lips, "you are in affliction; you are amiable, and want protection; and that was ever a claim sufficient to the friendship of the marchioness La Rosa."

"Ah, nephew," cried she, "you have learnt the art of flattery, and I shall chide you for using it to me."

"Nay, my dear aunt," replied the other, "I never use guile, but always speak the true sentiments of my heart."

"Well, Rosalina, my child, when you are able," resumed the marchioness, "you shall commence your journey; but I fear you are too weak to undertake it at present."

"Ah, madam, urge no delay, I beseech you," answered Rosalina; "I make no doubt but I shall be sufficiently recovered by to-morrow, under the care of the signor."

"What is the name of the place?—Can you direct my nephew to it?"

"Oh yes, madam; it is called the Valley of the Vintagers; there are but five or six cottages besides our own, which stands north of the forest."

"We are full seven leagues from it," said Rosalva. "Henri and Paulo shall attend us, and we will go round by the road, and so escape the danger of being lost in the intricacies of the wood."

This being agreed on by each of the party, they separated for the night, the marchioness pleased with self-gratification of being instrumental in the preservation of a fellow-creature—Rosalina at the idea of again beholding the sweet vale of her nativity—and Rosalva delighted with that of attending her.

CHAPTER V
The Grave

WHEN OUR HEROINE reached her chamber, she reflected with pleasure on her intended journey, mixed with painful sensations occasioned by her dear father's unhappy death. A sigh burst from the inmost recesses of her heart, succeeded by a torrent of tears, which gave some degree of ease to her laboring bosom, and offering up a fervent prayer to the Virgin for fortitude to support her afflictions, she sank into a refreshing slumber.

In the morning she was awakened by an attendant, who came to assist her in arraying herself in a travelling-dress prepared for the occasion, who informed her that Paulina (the name of a female domestic) was to attend on her journey.

This the delicate marchioness had previously concerted, to prevent the indecorum of Rosalina's being alone with her nephew, whose admiration for women she well knew, and was not surprised at the ardency of his looks towards one so lovely, who would have fired a heart not half so susceptible.

Rosalina was then in her sixteenth year; her person well proportioned, and of the middle size; a complexion which vied in beauty with the transparent lily; eyes fine and dark, whose languishing brilliancy gave lustre to a face expressive of every virtue which can adorn the sex; her long hair, which waved upon her taper neck and graceful shoulders, in all the luxuriance of nature, rendered her appearance more than commonly engaging.

The prudent marchioness resolved, on the first opportunity, to send Rosalva back to Venice, or place Rosalina in security at a neighbouring convent till his departure, thinking that by such method of separation it would check the growth of any passion which probably would be excited between persons of their susceptible age, and might hereafter only prove the source of unhappiness; but this intended arrangement she kept concealed, well knowing if she appeared to oppose the inclinations of her nephew, it would act as a stimulus, and inflame his wild, unchecked desires.

Rosalina, after bidding her adieu, stepped into the carriage, which was waiting, attended by Rosalva and Paulina. The two faithful domestics, Henri and Paulo, followed the vehicle on horseback, which rolled swiftly along; and after a few hours riding, she came in sight of the valley where she first drew her breath.

The neat white cottages appeared peeping forth from amidst the fruitful vines. The happy inhabitants were passing their harmless jests, and caroling their merry songs; thus lightening the fatigue of labour, as each in his own vineyard exerted his daily toil to prune and dress the grateful trees, whose ample produce rewarded well their pains. So passed their days, free from the noise of cities, or the bustling stir of the busy world; unmindful of the cares of kings or courts, with consciences undisturbed by guilt, they lived in harmony, innocence, and peace.

Rosalina looking beheld her own humble, and once happy dwelling; she pointed it out to Rosalva, but dared not trust her tongue to speak, lest her faltering voice should betray the sorrowful feelings she in vain struggled to conceal.

He directed the driver to proceed towards the gate of the garden, which separated it from the beaten road.

The carriage stopped, and as they alighted, two of the villagers, whose attention had been attracted by the sight of the equipage, came forward, for the purpose of informing them that the cottage was uninhabited; one of them recognized our heroine, and almost shouting with joy, cried, "'Tis Rosalina St. Almo! Run and tell your mother," said he to the youth who accompanied him.

Rosalina laid her hand on his arm, and looking in his face, exclaimed, "My father, Gerrard—is my father buried?"

The honest peasant, wiping a tear from his cheek, faltered out, "He is! But your grapes are flourishing—your furniture is safe. Here is the key of the cottage, which I have kept in my possession, hoping you would one day or other come to make your claim; and, the Virgin be praised, here you are! But how did you escape? for I suppose you was forced away."

"Alas! I was indeed," answered Rosalina.

"Ah, damigella, the morning after, as I was passing by the house, I thought I would step in and ask your good father for something for the relief of my poor child, who laid grievously ill, and you know he used to be a kind of doctor to us all. Well, when I knocked at the door, no one answered, which surprised me greatly; and after waiting a little, I ventured to lift up the latch, when I was struck almost senseless at what I beheld. But why should I repeat it?" said he, seeing Rosalina almost ready to sink with grief. "Well, we buried the body with decency, and all the respect we could shew, and concluding that one day you might return, we took care of your vineyard, and locked up your cottage. There, dear Rosa," said he, throwing open the door, "there is all as you left it."

"No!" mentally exclaimed Rosalina, "not all;" but she checked her feelings, and sinking into a chair, thanked the honest peasant as well as she was able.

She was aroused from the reverie in which she was a few moments plunged by the arrival of most of the vintagers, who came to welcome her return, (for the youth Gerrard had sent to acquaint his mother had spread throughout the whole valley the news of her arrival); but their joy was damped on her saying she was about to leave the place for ever.

She went into the chamber of her father, and desiring no one to interrupt her meditations, sunk on her knees, and poured forth her whole soul in fervent prayer to the great Disposer of all things; then resting for a few moments on the side of the couch where her beloved father once used to sleep, endeavoured to rouse to her relief sufficient fortitude to enable her to make proper arrangements.

On finding her feelings somewhat composed, she proceeded to unlock the drawers where her father used to deposit his most valuable property, as the place of greatest security, in which she discovered two purses of gold, and a small bundle of papers and letters. These she took, together with a ring, which was once worn by her father, and another, by which he had used to set great store. A pearl of immense size was in the centre, surrounded by a slender twist of hair, and without the hair a circular row of fine sapphires; and on the back of the gold setting, in large and distinct characters, were seen the letters, "F.B." This she placed on her finger; and opening the casement for air, she beheld in the garden a new-made grave, with a stone, on which were roughly cut the words—"Sacred to the memory of Ferrand St. Almo, who was barbarously murdered by assassins." She clasped her hands in agony, and raising her eyes to heaven, cried, "Yes! thou wert indeed barbarously murdered! Oh, gracious Powers! give me strength to support this sight! Oh my father!" A flood of tears now came to her relief, and sinking on a seat, she gave way to her sorrows.

She was aroused by a rap at the door, for Rosalva grew impatient; and fearing she might be ill, would not be restrained by honest Gerrard, who fain would have had him desist. He retreated on Rosalina's saying she would attend; and coming forth with a small parcel in her hand, said she should soon be ready for departure.

Amongst the villagers she distributed several articles by way of keepsakes, who all dropt a few tears at the idea of separation. She then, addressing Gerrard, and endeavouring to force a smile, said, "Till the vineyard, and keep the garden in order, and take to yourself the produce which they yield. Receive again the key of the cottage, and let your daughter who was lately married inhabit it with her husband. Here they may find a home for ever, provided I should not return; but if I should, I trust I shall find a roof to shelter me."

"To shelter thee, Rosa!" said honest Gerrard. "Ah, madimagella, why will you leave us at all? Could you not be happy here? Pardon me, signor," turning to Rosalva, "I doubt not signora Rosa's new protectors love her, (indeed who can do otherwise?) but they will not make her more happy than we, at least than what we would endeavor to do."

Rosalina felt half inclined to take the peasant at his word, but thought it would appear like ingratitude towards those who had relieved her from peril, and made such generous offers of protection; therefore thanking the honest vintager for his goodwill, she promised to return, should she ever want an asylum.

Watching for a fit opportunity, she slipped into the garden by a back way unobserved. She knelt, and dropt a tear upon the sod which covered the body of her father; then accompanying Rosalva to the carriage, stepped in; and, after bidding a long adieu to all her neighbours, departed from the place of her nativity amidst their wishes and prayers for her welfare.

Rosalina continued gazing upon the once happy cottage, and waving her handkerchief to the peasants, who followed her with their anxious eyes, until the carriage ascended the hills which divided the valley from the road, and obscured them from sight; when unable longer to smother her grief, she burst into a torrent of tears, and sunk into a corner of the carriage, to indulge in her sorrow. To Rosalva's endeavouring to sooth, and offer her consolation, she replied, "Alas, my lord! esteem me not insensible to your kindness, but allow me once more to dwell upon the scenes of my childhood; do not seek to prevent my tears; they give ease to a heart almost bursting with the various feelings which assail it; think not I am ungrateful in refusing your consoling advice, for I revere, though I cannot profit by it."

Rosalva desisted, and was silent till they had nearly reached the castle, when perceiving Rosalina dry her eyes, and appear as if she wished to assume a look of placidity on meeting the marchioness, he ventured an observation, to which she with seeming tranquility replied, and at length entered into conversation, to the great joy of Paulina, who all the time sat upon thorns, because she could neither speak herself, nor hear any one else.

Rosalva directed the attention of his fair companion to the beautiful scenery that surrounded them, which was truly sublime, and merited the attention it excited in the mind of Rosalina. On one side, an extensive forest, filled with tall trees, whose leafy branches resounded in gentle murmurs, by the freshening breeze which Æolus then was wafting all around; on the other, an extensive chain of mountains, the towering heads of which seemed lost in the fleeting clouds that passed in quick succession. In one place was seen the anxious shepherd, with eager eye, and palpitating heart, clambering on the rugged mountain's side, in pursuit of the fugitive chamois, while the wanton straggler, mocking his vain attempt, leapt upon the craggy point of a jutting rock, where human foot had never trod, and seemed to the beholder's eye poised in air, whence, if by giddy chance it had lost its balance, it must inevitably have been precipitated headlong into the loud roaring torrent, which sought its rapid course in the deep windings at the foot of the stupendous cliff. In another, the happy shepherdess, resting on her crook, watched the innocent gambols of the playful kids, that were frisking in sportive tricks round their gentle dams, gave to her the grateful delight of beholding thus her humble stores increase.

While Rosalina's thoughts were gradually engaged by this enchanting scene, the carriage moved swiftly on, till at length the Castle of La Rosa appeared in view.

The marchioness stood ready to receive her adopted child, whom she felt persuaded was of some noble, but unfortunate family in France; for it was unlikely that any one of low extraction should possess the qualifications that belong only to people of rank, and which had been communicated to her by her father's sole tuition. When Rosalina alighted, she received her at the portal, and kissing her cheek, bade her welcome to her future home, for which she returned her grateful acknowledgements. The marchioness then taking her hand, entered the saloon, followed by Rosalva, who recounted to his aunt their reception from the villagers. "Ah," thought she, when her nephew had ceased, "this girl must ever have been truly amiable, or those honest peasants would not have been so very desirous of her remaining with them;" and turning, said, "My child, henceforward I shall always ever esteem you as if really mine; you shall no longer be Rosalina St. Almo, but for the future be styled Rosa Falieri; and, nephew, I beseech you never to mention this necessary deception, even to our dearest friends at Venice, whom, by the bye, I intend visiting at the feast of the regatta."

"Enough, my dear aunt," replied he; "you may firmly rely on my prudence, and no indiscreet discovery on my part shall ever endanger the safety of Rosa Falieri."

Rosalina bowed in token of thankfulness; and lights being brought, she requested permission to retire, which was readily granted.

On her leaving the place, the marchioness said, "Rosalva, I have news for you. Here is a letter from Venice, in which your father requests your immediate attendance."

Had a thunderbolt fallen at his feet he could not have been more surprised. "How, madam," answered he, "return to Venice! Has my father forgot the danger under which I lie, from the dagger of the assassin?"

"No," returned she; "but he says all danger has ceased, for the marchioness Loredo has long since been gone to Florence, her paternal home; therefore, my dear nephew, 'tis fit you obey your father, who, I am sorry to say, adds that he is ill, and particularly wants to see you. I have given orders for the preparation necessary for your journey, and to-morrow you may set forward."

Rosalva now perceived there was no method of extricating himself without betraying his passion for the lovely peasant, which had hourly increased, beyond all power of resistance; and lest his aunt might discover it, made light of returning home; said he was glad all apprehensions for his safety had subsided, but was sorry his father was indisposed; begged the marchioness would attend the feast of the regatta, which was to be held in a few weeks, and retired in seeming good spirits, insomuch that he quite deceived the unwary marchioness, who now thought that he had only regarded Rosalina with an eye of pity for her misfortunes, and concluded with the resolution of suffering her accompanying her to Venice.

In the morning all was prepared for the departure of Rosalva, who, taking the hand of his aunt, and that of Rosalina, he joined them, at the same time saying, "My dear aunt, never let your friendship towards this poor orphan decline, until her conduct merits the withdrawing your protection; and do you, Rosalina, never forget to look on my relation as a parent. Adieu, sweet girl! Heaven bless you! and may fortune always prove as propitious as your innocence and loveliness deserve! Farewell, my dear aunt!" and brushing a tear from his cheek, as if ashamed of his weakness, departed, leaving the marchioness overwhelmed with surprise at his tender method of separation.

"Rosalva improves," said she; "he had not used to be so moral, nor did he ever before possess one serious thought or reflection."

Rosalina was truly sorry at his departure, for she felt gratitude towards him as her deliverer; but that all-powerful, unresisting passion, called love, had not yet entered her heart.

Weeks passed on, and she increased in favour with the marchioness more and more, who found in her the companion she had often wished to have in her solitude. She would play on the harp in the evening as they enjoyed the cooling zephyr, which wafted through a grove of pines, or read, while her benefactress was embroidering, (the favourite amusement of the latter). Thus one avocation succeeding another, she had no time to revert to her own sorrows; therefore, if she could not be termed happy, at least she was tranquil, and felt unfeigned reverence and love for the indulgent and benevolent marchioness La Rosa.

Chapter VI
The Mask

WHEN ROSALVA (after a safe journey) arrived in Venice, he was astonished at the altered appearance of his father, who was pale and emaciated, and no less changed in health than in tempter; for he was now grown imperious and pettish, even towards his son, whom he had treated with such great indulgence, that he could but ill bear this great change in his disposition. He would suffer no one near him but a favourite page, whom he had lately taken under his protection, and seemed sinking into a hypochondriac state, caring for no company or amusement but his own melancholy thoughts. He continued thus till the feast of the regatta, when mustering all his usual spirits, proposed to meet the concourse of people that were to be assembled for the purpose of the celebration of the birthday of his son. A grand fête was to be given at the Palazzo di Barozzi, in honour of the occasion, and half the nobles in Venice were expected to grace it with their presence. Amongst the rest came the marchioness La Rosa, and her lovely ward, for whose arrival he waited with the utmost impatience. "Beloved Rosa!" he would mentally exclaim, "thou resembles in purity and innocence of heart the lilies which ornamented the garden of thy cottage, and where thou stoodst confessed paramount, as the fairest of the fair! Accursed be he that would rob thee of thy virtue, or despoil the brightest jewel ever contained in so rich a casket! Yet, can I wed her? Impossible! My haughty father would never consent to such a measure; add to which, she is but a peasant, and our laws are such, that by espousing her I shall debase my own issue, for, alas! she is not a cittadina. Curse on all such rules which prevent me calling her wife! Well then, she shall not hear of my passion—I will not rob her of her peace—no; I will not be villain base enough to steal into her guileless bosom, and plant there a wound which neither time nor circumstance can ever cure."

Thus argued Rosalva, who, with all his faults, when he gave a moment to reflection, would never commit a premeditated wrong; generous friendship could glow around his heart, and the unfortunate had often felt the warm effects of his benevolence.

After this laudable resolution, he went forth to meet the object of his affections as collected as possible. After the usual salutations had passed between him and his aunt, he conducted them to a saloon, where was seated his father. "La marchesa La Rosa," said he, announcing her.

The marquis bowed, and expressed himself pleased at her attendance, "For," said he, "'tis so seldom that you can be prevailed upon to leave your retirement, that I think myself and son highly honoured by this mark of your politeness."

"I have a stranger to introduce to your notice," said Rosalva, leading forth our heroine; "this is Rosa Falieri, my aunt's ward."

The marquis fixed his eyes on her earnestly, as if some sudden recollection, not of the most pleasant kind, crossed his memory. "What is the lady's name?" asked he.

"Rosa Falieri," repeated Rosalva, somewhat astonished at the manner in which his father seemed to observe the lovely fair one.

The marquis slightly bowed to Rosa, who now shrunk from his earnest gaze, which he perceiving, turned the conversation; and entering upon various subjects, amongst others, mentioned the féte, and asked the marchioness what character she intended to support in the mask?

"I have not yet thought of it," said she, smiling; "but it is all in good time at present."

The marquis began to grow thoughtful, and appeared as if conversation was irksome to him, which the marchioness perceiving, made some plausible excuse for leaving the place, to the great joy of Rosa, who, for some reason which she could not define, felt uneasy and embarrassed in his presence.

Rosalva quickly followed, and addressing himself to the signora, said, "Dear aunt, tell me what dress you intend to wear in the mask, for I should like to be able to distinguish my friends."

"You shall know," answered she, "ere the time arrives, not only mine, but also that of Rosa, whom I am now going to consult upon the subject."

"Well, I will trust you," said he, and retired.

As the ladies sought their apartments, the marchioness said to Rosa, "What will you choose to represent at the ensuing mask? Will you personate Venus, or Pallas, or what?"

"Alas, dear madam! why should I presume to mix amongst the noble lords and ladies of Venice—I, a poor orphan, at best but a humble peasant? Ah, I would you had left me at the Castle of La Rosa, for methinks his excellenza looks upon me as an intruder. Did you not see how coldly he looked upon me?"

"You are," replied the other, "too diffident, my dear, of your own deserts; nor do I regard you as a peasant; a combination of circumstances convinces me that you are of superior extraction. That jewel on your finger plainly speaks that it was never originally the property of a plebian; no; and I feel assured, my child, that your birth is as exalted as your merit, therefore no more refusals in attending the mask."

"Well, I will in every thing obey you, my dear madam," said Rosa, raising the hand of the other, and pressing it gratefully to her lips; "but did you not observe the manner of his excellenza di Barozzi?"

"Yes," answered the marchioness; "but I did not think it cold, or devoid of that politeness which ever was the characteristic of the marquis." The truth was, she had observed the manner of her brother with astonishment, but did not wish to express her real opinion on the subject, and turning to another more pleasing, they discoursed near an hour, then separated for the night.

Rosa in vain courted sleep, for she still beheld in imagination the dark eye of her host earnestly fixed on her face. "Can he ever have known me?" she mentally exclaimed. "No, that's impossible! Away then with all idle, ungrateful thoughts. I ought to be happy in the protection of my beloved patroness, who confers her favours with so sweet a grace, that she appears the one obliged, and not the generous donor."

Thus did she soliloquize, until the rising beams of the morn, in golden rays, tinged the windows of her apartment, when nature growing weary, caused her to sink into the arms of generous sleep.

After some repose, she was aroused from slumber by the voice of Paulina, which convinced her it must be late. Starting from her couch, she asked if the marchioness had risen?

"She has breakfasted these two hours," answered the other.

"Then why did you not call me?" asked Rosa. "I am ashamed to be such a sluggard."

"I should have done it," replied Paulina, "but her excellenza the marchioness ordered me to come and see if you still slept, and if you did, to let you remain."

"She is all goodness," said Rosa.

"Ah, see what she has sent you," said the other, pointing to a sofa, where lay a splendid dress of green, ornamented with shells of silver; "my lady intends you shall represent Thetis, and be discovered near the cascade, which is to play to-night in the garden during the féte; it will be so grand, signora! and no one will be better dressed than yourself. Oh, how gay you will appear amidst all the coloured lamps!"

Rosa could have wished to have been in a character less conspicuous, but as it was the will of the marchioness, she was resolved not to let a single word of regret on the occasion escape her; and after she had breakfasted, repaired to the apartment of the latter to thank her for this mark of attention, which she did with all the warmth of one who had received the greatest favour.

"Ah, I am glad you are pleased, Rosa," said she, "for you are indebted to Rosalva for the character you are to sustain. The cascade is a contrivance of his own, and he wanted a Thetis, to render the scene more striking. When it is discovered, you have nothing to do than remain stationary until the curtain descends on the ceasing of the music, which is to be concealed behind the rocks."

"I shall use my best endeavours to sustain what is allotted me," said Rosa.

"I have no doubt of your good intentions in every thing," answered the marchioness, at the same time tenderly kissing her cheek, and recommending her to be ready in time.

After an early dinner, they separated, for the purpose of preparing for the occasion.

While Rosa arrayed herself in the splendid habit, youthful vanity whispered to her heart that it became her, and, for the first time in her life, she took pains at the toilet. Her hair was twisted round her head in small braids, in which was placed, with a great degree of taste, a broach of coral, while the lightness of her drapery, fitted to her sylph-like form, enabled her well to support the appearance of the imaginary deity she was to represent.

To the scene of festive mirth she went by a private entrance, and placing herself as directed by Rosalva, waited, with some degree of timidity, until she was discovered.

The melodious strains of bewitching harmony, from a well-selected band, announced the beginning of the fête. The dancing then commenced, and innumerable variegated lamps, hung in fanciful devices, gave light to the jocund group, who, with airy steps and lively gambols, gaily tripped beneath a sky of ethereal blue.

The marquis, seated by the side of the marchioness La Rosa, on an exalted seat, viewed this exhilarating scene, and seemed to have recovered his usual flow of spirits.

At an appointed signal the curtain of green drew up, and discovered a sight which attracted the attention of all beholders.

A cascade, with roaring sounds, was seen pouring into the sea, in which, seated on a car drawn by Tritons, appeared Neptune and Thetis. The lovely and interesting appearance of the latter soon caught the earnest gaze of all the Venetian youths then assembled, and the questions of "Who is she? Do you know her?" ran in whispers throughout the garden.

On the falling of the curtain, a young Florentine, wishing to be acquainted with her name, sought out Rosalva for the purpose of making inquiry. He soon discovered him by his dress, which was that of Apollo, to whom he laughingly said, "Would you deign to vouchsafe, divine god of poetry, to inform me who or what is that beautiful representative of Thetis?"

"Ah, what, then, you are caught, Angelo?" said Rosalva.

"Nay, do not trifle," said the other, "but tell me."

"Well then, she is the ward of my aunt, and her name is Rosa Falieri," answered Rosalva.

"Well, go on."

"Nay, I cannot tell you more, because I know not more myself," said he, and set off in pursuit of a Minerva, whom he perceived at a small distance, leaving the young noble but half satisfied with this information.

On his approach the lady had mixed with the crowd; and while he was endeavouring to regain a sight of her, he was surprised by Rosa's catching his arm, and in tremulous accents, entreating him to conduct her to the palazzo. "What has alarmed you, sweet girl?" said he; "you look pale and terrified."

She pointed to a woman in strange attire, saying, "'Tis she who has thus frightened me, by speaking something that has shocked me inexpressibly."

"Oh!" said Rosalva, smiling at her simplicity, "she is only supporting her character, which is that of Medea, a sorceress."

"I think she is indeed a sorceress," said Rosa, shuddering.

"Come," added he, "allow me to conduct you to my aunt."

He led her forward, and placed her by the marchioness, who congratulated her on the appearance which she had made in her character.

"Ah, dear marchesa, there is one in the garden who supports hers better than I did mine, and behold she approaches; let us retire, dear madam, for I am fearful of her—do pray let us retire."

"Silly girl," said the marchioness; "what! afraid of a mask!"

"Ah, madam, you know not what words of terrific import she has addressed to me," said Rosa.

By this time the strange-looking person drew near, and advancing towards the marquis, in a sepulchral kind of voice, cried, "Marquis, cross my hand, and I will acquaint your excellenza with your future fate."

"Be gone!" cried he, in a tone of pleasantry; "I do not wish to encourage diviners; be gone, or I shall commit you to the charge of the officers of the Inquisition."

He carried on this conversation with so much raillery, that a number of his guests were attracted to the spot, not only by his refusal to have his fate prognosticated, but also the earnest manner in which he was desired to look into the book which unfolded future events by the sorceress, whose appearance was so very strange, that, though only at a mask, she excited a degree of horror in all the beholders.

Her robe was of white, bordered with various mystic figures; round her head was entwined a serpent; her long, black, matted hair hung disgustingly on her shoulders; while her piercing dark eyes rolled beneath the raven locks which half concealed her face, and seemed to read the hearts of the surrounding spectators. In her right hand she held a wand, and in her left a book, which she called the Mystery of Fate, and into which she frequently invited them to look.

Barozzi grew somewhat peevish at her frequent urgent requests, and at last, rather sharply, bade her trouble him no more.

"Nay, then, if my lord will not hear me," said she, "I must be gone; but hereafter, perhaps, you may repent for not listening to what I could unfold." She waved her wand and retired, followed by many, and amongst the rest Rosalva, whom she beckoned to a distant part of the garden; and when she thought they were unobserved, said in whispers, "Rosalva loves!"

"Whom?" said he, laughing.

"Rosalina St. Almo."

He started—"You are then acquainted with her real appellation?"

"That I am," she replied; "for nothing is unknown to the sorceress Magdalena!"

"Then tell me," said he, struck by her mysterious manner, "why was you so very importunate to the marquis?"

"To tell him that I know him," answered she.

"Of course you do, or you would not have been present at this entertainment, given by way of celebration of my birth."

"I came not on that account," returned she.

"For what purpose then do you come?"

"To warn innocence of danger, and to save from destruction."

"Ah! who is in danger?" inquired the eager youth.

"Rosalina St. Almo!" answered she.

"Ah! From whom?"

She waved her hand, as if forbidding him to inquire.

"Nay, if you are indeed what you pretend, which I feel, from what you have already said, half inclined to believe, leave me not unsatisfied. Tell me, I conjure you, tell me who is the person from whom she is in danger? for my dagger shall drink the blood of that villain, who, by his cursed arts, would dare to harm the angelic Rosalina!"

"Your dagger will never reach the heart of that wretch who basely seeks her life," said she.

"But it shall, I swear by all the—"

"Hold!" commanded she. "Swear not. Fate forbids the deed."

"Wherefore? What prevents me?"

"Because," continued she, laying her hand upon his arm, and fixing her eyes earnestly upon his, "that villain is the marquis di Barozzi, your father."

On pronouncing this, she vanished amongst the trees, while the petrified youth, unequal to the task of following, sunk upon a seat overpowered with horror at the tenor of her departing words.

He was quickly aroused by the approach of Angelo Monturino, the nobleman who had interrogated him respecting Rosalina, who, coming briskly up, said, "Well, has the sorceress told you any good things in regard to your future life? I saw her leave you, so I came to ask you what you think of her predictions; but good Heavens!" added he, on beholding the ill-concealed agitation of Rosalva, "what is the matter? Surely you are not weak enough to suffer the pretended prognostic of a mask to affect you?"

"Nay," said Rosalva, endeavouring to shake off his tremor, and force a smile, "your supposition is wrong; 'tis the fatigue of dancing and the oppressive heat that render me somewhat unwell;" then rising and taking the arm of the other, they returned to the palazzo, where they were joined by the marquis, and many of the guests, who, after spending the remainder of the night in sportive mirth, departed to their respective habitations.

Rosalva, wishing to be alone, that he might ruminate with deliberation on the discourse he had with the unknown, but mysterious mask, availed himself of the first opportunity for withdrawing, and bidding his father and aunt goodnight, retired to his own apartment.

CHAPTER VII
The Terrific Chamber

THE MARCHIONESS, when alone with Rosa, asked her the meaning of the terror which she evinced at the sight of the fancied enchantress, which she explained as follows—

"I was returning to the private path which leads to the palazzo, when I was accosted by the strange figure that yourself saw. She asked me if I should like to be made acquainted with my future destiny, and, without waiting for my reply, took my hand, which I reluctantly yielded. She looked at it with seeming earnestness, and said, 'Imprudent girl! why have you so unthinkingly, so rashly ventured to Venice? Here lives your deadly foe, the implacable, mortal foe of Rosalina St. Almo. Hasten to La Rosa, for here the assassin's hand is once more lifted to destroy.' She then left me, and glided down one of the walks, leaving me terrified almost to fainting. Signor Rosalva happening to pass near me, I requested him to conduct me to our apartments; but he laughed at my fears, and said she was only supporting the character which she assumed. But, alas! madam, it is evident by her accosting me by the name of St. Almo, and knowing that I had been in the power of assassins, that she must be well acquainted with every circumstance of my life, or possesses more than common knowledge."

The marchioness was thunderstruck at this account, and exclaimed, "Good Heavens! we are betrayed! My child, you must immediately, to prevent the possibility of danger, return to La Rosa, for whoever this strange being can be, she must certainly mean you friendly. We will depart to-morrow; but first we must inform Rosalva of this mystery, which should not, even for a moment, be treated with neglect; therefore early in the morning I will request his attendance; and now, my love, seek some repose, that you may be able to set forward with renewed strength."

Rosalina followed this wholesome advice, but could not profit by it. The mysterious words of the sorceress still sounded in her ears, and if for a moment she closed her wearied eyelids, dreadful visions flitted before her disordered imagination, which harassed her mind and prevented her rest. Earnestly did she pray that she might once more be at La Rosa, seated in the pavilion, by the side of her protectress the marchioness. Unable to sleep, she rose from the couch, and repairing to the window, endeavouring to tranquillize her feelings by gazing on the wonderful works of the Creator, for all nature was hushed in solemn stillness, save the fanning breeze wafting through the trees that surrounded the garden, at intervals caused their trembling leaves to send forth a rustling sound, which gave additional gloom to the otherwise silent scene. At length the dawn appeared, and soon as Aurora, with her empurpled rays, peeped through her casement, she adjusted her dress, and waited with anxiety the appearance of Paulina, who constantly attended to assist at her toilet, and conduct her to the apartment of the marchioness.

The latter had rested nearly as ill as herself; and soon as she thought it consistent with decency to arouse Rosalva, had sent to his chamber, requesting a few moments conversation with him.

He, alarmed and disturbed by occurrences of the preceding night, had never retired to bed, but sat in silent meditation; and on hearing the wishes of his aunt, instantly, without demur, followed the messenger.

"Rosalva," said she, soon as he was seated, "we are betrayed. The strange mask that last night represented a sorceress, addressed our Rosa by her real name, and told her that she was in the power of her mortal foes. I would not have you suppose from this that I am weak enough to be alarmed at what might be casually known, but other corroborating circumstances lead me to imagine that the mysterious mask must be acquainted with the intended act, and in friendship might take this singular method to apprise her of the danger in which she seems to stand; I am therefore determined to quit Venice directly, as the most likely mode of safety."

Rosalva coincided with the intentions of his aunt, of whom he tremblingly inquired if the unknown had mentioned to Rosa the name of her foe?

The monosyllable, no, restored him to some degree of calmness.

The marchioness then continued, "Poor child! she has been sorely persecuted! Accursed be the man, who, with unrelenting cruelty, can thus pursue innocence and virtue like hers! There is a hidden mystery in her fate which I cannot develop. She cannot be the offspring of a peasant, or her life would not thus inhumanly be sought; add to which, she has a packet of letters, found in the drawer belonging to her father's cottage, and by him, I conjecture, addressed to her mother, wherein he signs himself by the title of marquis; but the name is erased, and no where to be found. The rich pearl also that she wears on her finger, is another proof of the rank which her parents must have possessed, and undoubtedly must have been deprived of by some deed of villainy; but I trust, by the aid of bounteous Providence, she will one day attain that elevated station, her right by birth, and which her merit so justly deserves."

"I trust she will," said Rosalva, sighing at the ideal conviction that when he rescued her from the hands of assassins, he had only saved her from a fate, which, by being deferred, would fall the heavier on his heart; but endeavouring to shake off the unpleasant thoughts that clouded his mind, almost to the bewildering of his senses, he told his aunt that he would escort them some distance on their journey to La Rosa, and retired to prepare for that purpose.

The marchioness and Rosa, after making proper arrangements, waited on the marquis to bid him adieu.

He received the apology which his sister made for her abrupt departure with politeness, and again fixed his eyes on Rosa, in a scrutinizing, and, to her, a painful manner.

She shrunk from his penetrating gaze, and took the earliest opportunity to quit the saloon, and retiring to her apartment, waited with anxiety till she was joined by the marchioness, whom the marquis for a considerable time had held in frivolous conversation. The gondola soon after was announced to be in readiness, and after the usual ceremonies, they departed from Venice.

Rosa then began to feel a small degree of tranquillity, which increased as the city receded from their view.

Rosalva accompanied them a considerable part of the way, and at the moment of separation, seemed as if his heart would have burst. He took leave of them in a very tender manner, and remained upon the spot until the carriage into which he had handed them on quitting the boat, and which he accompanied on horseback for several leagues, was out of sight. A heavy sigh from the inmost recess of his bosom passed his lips, as he cried, "Adieu, sweet Rosa! may guardian angels ever watch around thee, and with interposing aid ward off the threatened danger! Accursed be the hand, that, with wanton cruelty, would shed thy innocent blood! May withering palsies unnerve the sanguinary arm of the murderous villain when uplifted against thy precious life! Ah, is not the man who persecutes thee unto death my father! Dreadful, horrid thought! it can never be! What authority have I for so thinking? the words of an unknown at a mask, no doubt an enemy to my peace, and who used that artifice to make me miserable. It must be so! My parent never can be the mortal foe of any one, much less that of an unoffending woman! But then the knowledge which the stranger evidently possesses relative to Rosa is sufficient to excite alarm in the breast of one less inclined to belief than myself. Yet it must be false; and my suspicions are base and unnatural. However, there can be no harm in being on the guard; on my return I will watch my father's conduct, and if possible come at the bottom of his heart, which I will fathom to its lowest depth."

Rosalva, buried in these reflections, did not perceive that his horse had deviated from the road, and strayed into the winding labyrinths of the adjoining forest. He checked the animal, and turning about, endeavoured to retrace his steps, but unacquainted with the different paths, he chose one which led him further still astray. Finding it impossible to regain the road, he looked around, to see if he could discover some woodman's hut, where he might inquire his way; but ere he could discern the sign of any habitation, the dusky shades of night came swiftly on, and casting a heavy gloom on the surrounding trees, (against the protruding branches of which he was every instant in danger of striking his head), obscured every object from sight, and rendered his advancing exceedingly dangerous. He now wished he had availed himself of the offer made by his aunt on their separation, who desired him not to return alone, but take with him one of her attendants, (for when he set out to accompany her, he had neglected bringing any of his own), but he positively refused taking any of her retinue, saying he did not think it necessary, as in a much-frequented road there could be no danger.

After slowly wandering for a considerable time, his eager eye caught sight of a friendly taper, whose feeble rays glimmered through the darkness of the gloomy night. His spirits revived, and dismounting from his horse, he took the reins in his hand, and endeavoured to explore the way (which he did with difficulty) towards the spot from whence he perceived the friendly sign of hospitable shelter to the benighted traveller.

On reaching the building, he was greatly surprised at not finding it, as he expected, the humble dwelling of the forest labourer, but the dilapidated remains of an ancient structure, resembling a religious house, or castle. He was astonished, for he never knew that the wood contained such a place; and from the somber appearance it exhibited, thought it might be the retreat of ruffians. The taper, that still shed its faint beams from a Gothic window over the broken portico, served the purpose of shewing the entrance to this desolated ruin, and giving it a still more gloomy look.

Rosalva stood undetermined whether to venture a knock at the gate, or remain in the open air amidst the cold and damp until the morning; but at length summoning all his courage, he resolved to explore the place, let the danger be what it would. He therefore fastened his horse to a kind of old palisado, which had bidden defiance to the power of time, (the effects of whose destroying hand were so obvious in every other part of the edifice), and ascending some broken steps, advanced to the gate, to which he applied his hand, to try whether it was fastened, but on touching it, was surprised to find it yield to the slightest pressure, and flew invitingly open. The noise of its grating hinges sounded through a spacious vaulted passage that presented itself to view, which he entered, guided by the light that shone from the heavy casement. At the end he perceived another door, which he tried with the same caution as the first, and it immediately opened, as if by enchantment. A distant receding footstep caught his ear, which convinced him the place was inhabited by beings of some sort, and following the sound, he arrived at a spacious hall, in which was a branch of lights, standing on a table in the middle of the place. He moved towards them; but his foot trod upon something that caused him to stumble, and feeling on the ground to learn what had thus caused him to fall, his hand touched some hard substance; he grasped hold of it, and taking it to the lights, perceived it was a poniard. He started, and examining it more closely, he saw engraven on the hilt the name of Augustino di Barozzi.

Cold drops of perspiration bedewed his forehead; his knees struck together, as with trembling voice he cried, "My father! Oh Heavens! my father too surely has been decoyed hither and basely murdered! The Virgin assist me to unravel this mystery, and revenge his death!"

He drew his sword, and taking a candle from the branch, turned to an entrance on the left. At the extremity was an arched door, which, as he opened, the chilly breeze that swept along the passage nearly extinguished the light. Shielding it with his hand, Rosalva advanced with some difficulty through a corridor. The unwholesome damps, which stole in lachrymal drops down its slimy walls, proved that the cheering light of day never penetrated into this gloomy recess. He advanced with great caution, but found his progress impeded by a door strongly barricadoed with massy bars of iron. He immediately applied his utmost strength to remove them, which, after great labour, he effected; then placing his hand on an iron ring which hung from the side, and pulling with all his might, dragged it open. The rushing wind forcing its entrance through the space, extinguished the light, and left him in total darkness.

At that moment a loud discordant yell broke the silence which had before, in awful solemnity, reigned within the walls of this decaying fabric. After a moment's pause, the shriek was repeated, and Rosalva, by his feelings nearly wrought to desperation, plunged forward, at the hazard of incurring the greatest danger. With his sword he explored his way along the damp mouldering wall, till he was stopped by a wooden partition, which exactly crossed his path. Striking it with his sword, it shook with the blow. This gave him hopes that it was a door, and feeling for the bolt, his hand passed across a secret spring, belonging to a sliding pannel, which flew back into a groove, and discovered to the astonished eye of Rosalva a sight that rivetted him to the spot. 'Twas the interior of a Gothic chamber. In the distant part was a bed, on which lay extended a form, clad in a long white robe, apparently the corse of a female. In the centre stood a large antique table, covered with black, on which lay various strange devices, and instruments of mystic shape. A lamp suspended from the ceiling gave a dismal light to this gloomy apartment.

Petrified with horror, and hardly conscious of what he did, he instantly pushed the pannel to its former situation, but suddenly stopped ere the secret spring had closed, to consider for a moment how he should act. "Gracious God!" said he, "what horrid place is this? surely 'tis the habitation of some demon, and the fiends of hell meet here to perform their diabolical orgies, and dance their infernal revels as they quaff human blood. That female form which I behold no doubt is a victim sacrificed to their hellish rites, and perhaps my turn may be next. Dreadful thought! How shall I proceed? Best to retire till day arrives, probably then I may be able to explore this den of wickedness with less danger."

He was upon the point of retreating, but ere the spring could shoot into its place, a loud groan struck upon his ear, which arrested his hand when in the very action of slipping the bolt, and applying his eye to the crevice he had left between the pannel and the adjoining wainscot, a sight, even more terrible than the other, bereft him of the power of moving.

A door, at a distant part of the chamber, slowly unclosed, at which entered the identical sorceress he had beheld at Venice, followed by his father, who seemed to hold her in earnest conversation.

Rosalva listened attentively, scarcely suffering himself to breathe, so fearful was he of losing a single word of the strange, incomprehensible dialogue which they held, unconscious of being seen or heard by mortal eye or ear.

"I tell you, Barozzi, you are wrong; let the girl perish, and save yourself from disgrace."

"She is so innocent," faltered the half-resolved marquis.

"So was her father," replied the hag, sternly.

"Then she is so bewitchingly beautiful."

"So was her mother," returned she, "and yet you murdered her!"

Rosalva shuddered.

"I thought you had already told me of my crimes," said the marquis, sternly; "why do you recapitulate the ungrateful theme? Will you assist me, if you possess the power, in removing this hateful serpent, that, phoenix-like, rises from the ashes intended to destroy her, and mars my peace?—Assist me, and command my services."

"Your services!" replied she, with a ghastly smile; "I've before said, I scorn, I despise them! Think you a being who possesses the potent skill of magic will regard a mortal's promise? No! I seek not your favour, nor do I dread your anger. You are in my power, marquis; you have not the means to injure me, or I had sunk beneath the poniard you so lately levelled at my breast; but I have to punish you; therefore, if you wish to secure my friendship, study my pleasure, which may be gratified in giving to me the blood of that girl. Promise faithfully that she shall be surrendered to my power, and I will offer her up a sacrifice to the deity I serve."

"The deity you serve!" said the marquis, trembling, "and who is he?"

"Lucifer," answered she, "who is both mine and yours."

"Mine?"

"Yes, yours; for he is the acknowledged deity of all murderers."

"Then why should I be a murderer?" asked he.

"Are you not one already? Think you the crimes committed sixteen years ago are blotted from the page of Heaven's judgement book? No. What have you done to expiate them? What hast thou performed to obliterate or cancel those deeds, to suppose there is pardon for thee, Barozzi?" The guilty marquis replied not. "Shallow, thoughtless man! why, thou art sunk in sin beyond redemption; then pursue your will without remorse; banquet, glut on blood, and so prove good your title to the future station you are doomed to fill."

A yell, more dreadful than the first that had assailed the ear of Rosalva, rang within the walls of this horrid fabric, whose vaulted roof re-echoed back the dreadful sound. The sorceress then waving with her right hand a wand in mystic circles round the room, and striking with her foot, the floor in part gave way and sunk. A tall female figure, clad in a white robe, ascended, bearing in her hand a scroll, on which, in letters of blood, were written the words, "Mortal, be resolute, or Rosalina shall inherit the honours of Barozzi."

The figure, after remaining for the space of a minute, descended. A loud yell, like the former, succeeded. The floor closed, and all remained as before, excepting the marquis, who, now frantic with despair, and turning to the hag, exclaimed, "Is this true?" She nodded assent. "What, shall the child of Fernando inherit the honours of my house! No! it shall never be! Sooner will I compound with fiends to dwell with them for ever! She shall die; I am resolved! To-morrow, on my return, let me behold her breathless!"

"Oh horrible!" loudly exclaimed Rosalva.

The marquis started aghast, while the cruel hag rolled her dark eyes around the room in wild affright.

"What was that?" faltered he; "are we betrayed?"

"It could be but fancy, nothing more," answered she; "then away with fear—avaunt all idle dreams! Barozzi, are you fully resolved?"

"I am!" exclaimed he; "let cowards tremble at the voice that cries forbear! It shall not daunt me; for in despite of every thing I will assert my rights, and my son Rosalva, my family's fairest hope, shall live secure, and fearless of having his fortunes blasted by the offspring of Fernando!"

"Never!" cried Rosalva, as he slipped back the pannel; and leaping into the apartment, stood before the sight of the terror-stricken Barozzi.

Chapter VIII
The Retrogression

Rodolpho di Barozzi, father to the present marquis, was a nobleman of an amiable disposition, whose riches were sufficient to keep pace with his generosity. Early in life (being left sole heir, without controul, to his father's possessions) he united himself to a lady, who possessed great beauty in her person, sweetness in her temper, and great accomplishments in her manners and education, to which was added an immense fortune.

A year passed on in great felicity and domestic happiness; at the end of that period she gave to the arms of her delighted husband two sons, at one birth.

The twins equalled each other in loveliness, and even excelled the most sanguine expectations of their enraptured parents, who mutually endeavoured to rear them in the precepts and practice of virtue, to render their minds as engaging as their persons were interesting.

Fernando was of a placid disposition, possessing great suavity of manners, and such application to his studies, that he surpassed in learning and the fine arts all his competitors.

Augustino was of a temper morose and envious; rude, but very artful. He did not aim at the possession of the accomplishments necessary for a man of rank, yet covered the defect by an artificial gloss in his manners. For learning he had an aversion, yet viewed the progress made by his brother with inward mortification, and at every praise bestowed upon Fernando, an envious dislike, almost amounting to hatred, entered his rancorous heart, which he had sufficient address to conceal, and appeared fond of him even unto dotage. So well did he play the hypocrite, if a word was spoken in slight, or dispraise of Fernando, he always espoused his cause, and became his warmest advocate; and by this means appeared not only to his parents, but to the world in general, a prodigy of goodness and fraternal love.

In this manner, days, months, and years passed on, till the twins reached the age of maturity, when it was resolved by their fond parents they should make the tour of the principal part of Europe, to gain by travelling a knowledge of the world, indispensably necessary for all those intended to move in elevated stations.

Their first route was to France, where, by the means of an ample allowance from a fond indulgent father, they entered into all the levity, extravagance, and dissipation, for which that country is noted.

Fernando's prudence restrained him from launching beyond the limits of his purse; but Augustino possessed not the least foresight; and plunging head-long into folly, was often compelled to become petitioner for a loan, and to draw on the generosity of his brother, who never refused granting the supply, though the applications were numerous. Their allowances were equally ample, yet insufficient to support the excesses and boundless extravagance in which Augustino indulged. Gaming and drinking were his chief amusements; he also was a warm admirer of the fair sex; but not satisfied with the possession of gay and depraved women, (in whose society he spent the greatest portion of his time), he sought, by his personal accomplishments, alluring address, and insinuating manners, to seduce other, who, by their virtue and modesty, he ought to have esteemed and respected.

Returning one evening from a solitary walk in the fields adjacent to Paris, meditating how to retrieve a heavy loss he had the night before sustained at a gaming-table, regardless of his footsteps, and buried in a deep reverie, he stumbled, and endeavouring to rise, found that he had sprained his foot seriously, which gave him excruciating pain, and rendered him incapable of standing without support. He was considering how he might procure assistance, when a gentle voice saluted his ear with, "Pray, monsieur, allow me to help you." Turning his head, he perceived close to him a lovely peasant girl.

Augustino forgot his anguish, while with licentious appetite he gazed on her fair form and enchanting face. She repeated her offer of assistance, and accepting her arm, he arose, and made an effort to walk. She led him along with great tenderness, while he examined minutely the person and appearance of his fair conductress.

Her stature was of the middle size, and proportionable to her shape, which was truly graceful, and rendered exceedingly interesting by the neatness of her dress, which consisted of a brown jacket, tied up the front with azure blue ribbons, a short petticoat, of the same stuff, which displayed one of the prettiest pair of feet and taper ancles in all France. On her head she wore a large straw hat, tied under the chin with a pink handkerchief, whose broad slouch shaded a pair of fine dark eyes, that rolled languishingly beneath ringlets of glossy black.

Augustino viewed her with rapture, and from that time singled her out as a fit victim to gratify his inordinate desires. With an insinuating voice he inquired if there was not a cottage near, where he might rest till he could sent to the city for a carriage, as he found it impossible to proceed much farther?

"My mother lives hard by, monsieur, though she is at present gone out; but you shall have the best accommodation our humble dwelling affords."

This was joyful news to the depraved youth, who raising her hand gallantly to his lips, returned her his acknowledgements in the most graceful manner.

The pressure alarmed the innocent girl, yet she did not withdraw it; feelings both of shame and gratification caused the mantling colour to rush in her face; a trembling seized her whole frame, insomuch that she could scarcely support herself.

This he perceived, and was resolved for the present to be less ardent; then resuming a degree of nonchalance, said his foot pained him inexpressibly, and asked how much farther was the cottage?

"It's close by, monsieur," replied the artless girl, and immediately, from behind a clump of trees, it met their view—that happy, humble dwelling, where the peasant Marian had spent fifteen years of innocence and peace.

Ah, wretched maid! why did thy guardian angel sleep?—why did he not whisper that thou wert leading to a mansion of cheerfulness and content the desolating fiend, who, by triumphing o'er thy virtue, would mar all thy future days? No more shalt thou, in harmless mirth, dance to the sweet enlivening notes of the rustic pipe; but, like the withering rose-bud, plucked from its stem by a wanton hand ere it hath reached its growth, thy loveliness shall fade and die; the canker grief shall feed upon thy cheek, and banefully destroy thy ripening sweetness.

A few steps brought them to the door, and Marian, pulling up the latch, admitted her guest.

The neatness and simplicity of the dwelling, ornamented with homely furniture, whose greatest recommendation was its cleanliness, proved at once the humble state of its industrious inmates.

Marian drew forth an arm-chair, and wiping the dust from it with a napkin, entreated the stranger to be seated; then reaching a stool, and placing on it a patch-work cushion of curious and ingenious workmanship, begged he would rest his foot on it till she could go and procure some one to send for a carriage.

Augustino surveyed every action of his fair hostess with delight; but while she flew for means to alleviate his pain, he was planning machinations for her destruction.

The unsuspecting girl shortly returned, informing him she had procured a neighbouring villager to take his mule and go to Paris for a carriage—"But who must he inquire for, monsieur, when he arrives at your residence?"

"Let him go to any hotel that he pleases, or bring one from any place he may think fit," answered he.

"Very well, monsieur," answered she, rather disappointed, as she wished to learn the name of her guest.

She thought him handsome. "Ah, I wonder if he is married; should he be so, how very happy must be madame his wife!"

Thus thought the innocent, unsophisticated Marian, while she hardly dared trust her eyes to wander towards him, lest they should betray the secret of her mind.

Augustino still kept gazing on her with longing eye; and she, to excape from his earnest regards, went into the garden, and from a luxuriant vine, whose mantling branches formed a rural alcove, plucked a choice bunch of grapes, which placing with some leaves upon one of their best earthen plates, with a low curtsey she offered to his acceptance. He ate two or three, and highly praised their flavor: "But how," added he, "can they be otherwise, pruned as they are, no doubt, by the hand of a Hebe."

"I manage the trees myself, monsieur."

"It was to you I alluded," said he, smiling at her simplicity.

"My name is Marian," said she, with an enchanting naïveté.

"Then my conjecture was right, and the rearer of those delicious grapes is more beautiful than she who fills the cup for Jupiter."

Marian did not comprehend the meaning of this, but guessing it was a compliment, and finding that he thought her handsome, it gratified the uncorrupted heart of the simple unschooled girl, who began to think the stranger exceedingly captivating.

Time past on unheeded by either party—Augustino never tired with gazing on her beauty, and Marian, though greatly embarrassed in his presence, finding a charm in his society for which she could not account. Often did she run to the window, to see if the expected carriage was in sight, and when she did not perceive it, a secret pleasure diffused through her bosom at the idea that the stranger must remain some time longer beneath the cot.

At length the unwelcome sound of wheels announced its approach, and Augustino drawing forth his purse, offered her a piece of gold, which she, with a low curtsey, modestly declined accepting, saying she desired no reward for any assistance she had been able to render—"But, monsieur, as you are so very polite, allow me to receive it for the purpose of bestowing it on my poor neighbour Pierre, who now lies sick, with a family of three children, and a wife incapable of labour."

"Then be it so," said he; "but you must accept this ring," at the same time taking it from his finger, "and when you look upon it, sometimes think of Augustino di Barozzi."

"Oh, my lord," said she, "why will you force upon me a thing of so much value? Alas! there needs not a remembrancer on the finger of Marian, while one remains in her heart."

"What!" said the joyful libertine, pleased with his conquest, "will you treasure the recollection of me in your breast?—Shall I be esteemed by you?—Will you indeed sometimes think on me?"

"I shall indeed, my lord," answered she, in great confusion, as the conviction of her having expressed more than her modesty should have allowed, shot across her guileless bosom.

He, in raptures at this confession, pressed her hand to his lips, saying, "Then Marian will not accept the ring?"

"No, my lord, excuse me if I say I will not; but if it is your wish I should take any thing, be not angry at my request; but I—" She stopped, and timidly raised her eyes to his, unable to give utterance to her wish.

"What is it?" said he; "I promise that—"

"Then suffer me to take a small lock of your hair, and when you are far distant—how—" her voice faltered, and a starting tear gemmed her silken eyelash, "ah, how often shall I think of the day when it was my happy lot to afford you assistance!"

"Sweet girl!" said he, when the simple Marian had named her wish, "why make so many words about so worthless a trifle? Take it, and perhaps, ere I return to Venice, we may meet again."

"Indeed!" said she, at the same time applying the opening clasp of her scissars to separate the treasure of her fancy, "shall I then once more behold you?"

"Do you wish to see me again, dear Marian?" said he, as his large dark eyes encountered hers. "Do you wish to see me again?" repeated he, and his polluted lips pressed hers.

She withdrew in alarm and anger, covered with crimson blushes; but recovering herself, and restraining her rage, exclaimed, "My lord, I beseech you to depart; your carriage is ready, and I entreat you will go, ere my mother returns, whom I now every minute expect."

"Say then you forgive me," perceiving she had delicacy to feel, and resolution to resent the insult he had offered to her modesty. "Wont you forgive me, Marian? I cannot leave you till you have sealed my pardon." He gently took her hand, and drew her towards him. "Will you drive me to despair, by resenting an error committed in a moment of rashness and unthinking presumption?"

She sighed. His lips again met hers, and Marian did not chide. He asked if he might repeat his visit? She could not refuse, and assisting him to ascend the carriage, saw him seated, and in a moment after beheld his departure with half-smothered reluctance. Her eyes followed the receding vehicle, and when her listening ear could no longer catch a sound of its swift-moving wheels, she sunk on a chair, and burst into tears; then looking on the lock of hair, which she had twisted round her finger, exclaimed, "Ah, how soft and pliant!—How beautiful is the colour!—What a glossy jet it is! Oh, I will never part with it! I will braid it with some of my own, and wear it next to my heart!"

"Thy heart! Ah, fond, but credulous girl! thy heart had fled in company with Barozzi; he bore it triumphantly away; thou, unknown to thy self, hast bestowed it on one, who, in return for a gift so precious, will inflict upon it the dreadful pangs of guilt and remorse. The sweet balm of peace no more shall visit it, until the mouldering sod which is to cover thy humble grave shall bury in oblivion the sad remembrance of all thy misery and thy shame!

Chapter IX
The Seduction

WHILE AUGUSTINO was thus planning the seduction of the innocent Marian, his brother Fernando was otherwise employed.

He had met at the court of France a nobleman called De Valmont, who stood high in the estimation of his royal master; but on the failure of a long-concerted plan of great importance, on which the interest of the state greatly depended, his enemies threw the whole blame upon him, and poisoned the ear of the king by exclaiming against his procedure, saying that De Valmont (who was principal in the negotiation) had prevented success, from motives that were self-interested, and that by his bad administration alone the project had failed.

'Twas in vain he pleaded guiltless of the charge. His enemies were numerous; they had long beheld his increasing favour with ther sovereign with envy, were therefore determined to crush him on the first opportunity, and this being a favourable one, were unanimous in advising his majesty to deprive him of the offices he held; to which the king consented, though with reluctance; and De Valmont in consequence was stripped of his dignity, and banished the court.

Disgusted of an ungrateful nation, that made such an ill return for all his faithful services, he formed the resolution of quitting his native country for ever, and finishing the remainder of his days under a government less prejudiced than his own.

This determination he imparted to Fernando, who, commiserating his unhappy lot, pointed out Italy as the most likely place for esteeming merit and rewarding talent, at the same time assuring him of the countenance and support of his father, who, in possession of great influence, might be able to recommend him to the notice of the Venetian Republic.

De Valmont returned his warmest acknowledgements for this solid proof of his friendship, which he should ever esteem, but declined entering into the service of any state, as he had resolved to retire from the bustle and commotion of the busy world, and seek for peace and content beneath a humble shelter—"There," said he, "blest with the sweet endearing society of my daughter, whom I will teach to despise the empty titles of pomp and greatness, she shall live in retirement, free from the vices and intrigues of the courts, like the flow-eret of the valley, which sheds its fragrant perfume, then withers on its native stalk, unplucked by the cruel hand of tyrant man. So shall pass my future days; and when it pleases high Heaven's will to call me to my forefathers, I can yield my breath with the sweet reflection of possessing a conscience uncorrupted and free from sin."

Fernando's heart bounded as De Valmont mentioned his daughter—the lovely Rosalina, who then was about the age of eighteen. Beautiful, virtuous, and innocent, he had several times beheld her at different places where he visited, and had become deeply enamoured; but as he was averse to disobedience, and knowing that his father had peremptorily fixed upon his espousing the heiress of Memni, a rich Venetian, he never disclosed his passion to Rosalina, or to her father, whose pride he knew would never descend to consent to a private mar-riage for his daughter, whom he thought, and with justice, would not disgrace the first family in France by an alliance; and in his prosperity he had refused several suitors, who had become candidates for her hand, not being of birth or rank equal to his wish, or not proving agreeable in the eyes of Rosalina.

In a few days after, they left France, in search of a peaceful asylum in another country more grateful than their own. Fernando separated from De Valmont with regret, as he entertained a real friendship for the unhappy noble, who promised to write to him at Venice, when he had fixed upon his future residence.

The gentle Rosalina sighed an adieu; the tears gushed from her lovely eyes, and with a sorrowful heart she threw herself back into the carriage. She was no philosopher; she could not tear herself from those scenes of childhood, rendered dear by many a tender recollection, without feeling the most poignant sensa-tions of grief.

Her departure quite unmanned Fernando; in spite of all the resolution he endeavoured to summon, his fortitude forsook him, and he was incapable of pronouncing a farewell; and when the vehicle drove off, a heart-breaking sigh burst from his agitated breast, and remaining on the spot from where the unhappy exiles departed, his eyes bedewed with starting tears, followed them until the last glimpse appeared in view; then retiring to his apartment, threw himself upon a couch, and strove to conquer those emotions which were excited by pity and by love. When his feelings were in some measure tranquillized, he seriously reflected on the passion he entertained for the daughter of his friend, and thinking it might be productive of unhappiness, as he was not at liberty to espouse her, entered into a determination of smothering his flame. This res-olution was no sooner formed than broken. Love, though said to bind with a silken tie, throws adamantine chains round its captives, and had entered so deep into Fernando's heart, that he found it impossible for him ever to wed another. Sometimes he was half inclined to acquaint his father with the subject, but was prevented by the conviction of uneasiness it would give that tender parent, who he knew had fixed his very soul on the union which he had proposed; and however indulgent in other respects, in this would prove inflexible.

His reverie was interrupted by the appearance of La Motte, his brother's French valet-de-chambre, saying his master requested his presence as early as possible without inconvenience.

"What! Is Augustino ill?" asked he.

"Yes, my lord," answered the other, with a cringing bow; "he has sprained his ancle severely, and is scarcely able to move."

Fernando, on hearing this, started up immediately in great anxiety, (for he tenderly loved his brother), and hastening to his hotel, found him with his foot supported on a cushion, apparently in extreme pain, at which he expressed great concern, and offered his condolence.

Augustino thanked him for his tenderness, and said, "It is not this I regard; another misfortune touches me nearer, wherein my honour may be called in question, and I sent for you purposely to know if you will befriend me?"

"You know I will," replied his brother, "therefore why do you ask?"

"Nay," said Augustino, "I never doubted your friendship, but I've applied to you for assistance so often, that it would not be surprising if you declined it now."

"My dear brother," said Fernando, "no more of that, but inform me of what causes your uneasiness, which, if I can alleviate it, will make me happy."

"Why, then, to the point at once. Two nights ago, I lost at play five hundred crowns more than I possess, and which I promised to pay on this very day. Will you lend me the sum?"

Fernando started—"Is it possible!" said he, with some degree of acrimony; "how can you game so deeply? For shame, thus to outrun our dear father's liberality! Why do you not refrain?"

"I did not send for you," said Augustino, pettishly, "to tell me of my faults—the question is, will you assist me?"

"I have already promised," said the amiable Fernando; "but it shall be for the last time, under circumstances like the present; for if you still persist in plunging in folly, you must excuse me if I decline supporting it. Be not offended with me, for I intend not to reproach you; but the repeated drafts you have made upon my purse, I cannot much longer support; of this you must be well aware."

"Well, well," returned Augustino, "you are all goodness; and when my allowance is next remitted from Venice, I will repay you."

"Nay, I look not for that," said Fernando; "you are freely welcome to it, and to all that I possess, provided it is expended in causes more worthy." Thus saying, he retired, and immediately dispatched a messenger with the required sum.

Augustino received it with a degree of thankfulness, and muttering to himself, said, "This prudent, moral brother of mine has always money, when I am poor and needy."

"Ah, my lord," said the insinuating valet, "monsieur Fernando has not the generosity as you have, my lord."

"You flatter me, La Motte."

"No, my lord, indeed I don't, for you game like a prince, and love the ladies, to whom you are very liberal. So does monsieur Fernando love the ladies too; but then he has not the noble spirit which you have, my lord."

"How do you know that my brother loves the ladies?"

"Oh, I know, my lord, he loves the daughter of De Valmont, the exiled marquis."

"Indeed! What, the pretty Rosalina?"

"Ah, my lord, she is indeed pretty, and I think she loves monsieur Fernando in return; but then she has never seen your lordship, else I think she would not; for if I was a woman, I know which I should prefer."

The vanity of Augustino was gratified by the flattery of his valet, though he was well acquainted with his character and morals, which would scruple at no vice or sin to please his employers. He once had figured in the capacity of a gambler, but finding himself in danger from being detected in the act of playing with false dice, he forsook that vocation, and took to the less honourable office of a pander to those who chose to employ him. A famous libertine count had kept him long in his service; but wishing to get rid of him, recommended him strongly to the notice of Augustino, who found him an exceeding useful tool and proper confidant in all affairs of intrigue. To this wretch he unfolded his adventure with Marian, and concluded by saying, "La Motte, cannot you officiate as a priest in this business? for I find she is not to be obtained on common terms. Money she would not accept at any rate, therefore a sham marriage is the most feasible method of possessing her, on which I am determined; but can you play the part properly?—Can you keep your countenance?"

"Can I, my lord! ah, that I can; only ask my late master the count; I married him to at least five wives whilst in his service; and I defy him to say that I ever laughed once, except in my sleeve, my lord. But why should not I be able to confine my joy within my clerical robes, when I am paid for it, as well as many old hypocrites I have seen, who, with serious faces, and joyous hearts, unite couples in the bands of wedlock, that is, to give them a lawful right to make each other miserable? Ah, my lord," added he, "many a fair creature, after enjoying the blessings of wedlock for a month, would leap out of their skins for joy, if she knew the clergyman was no other than your humble servant La Motte, and that she was free to seek another husband where she chose—don't you think so, my lord?"

"Indeed you argue the point like a true philosopher," replied the delighted Augustino; "I can't help admiring the soundness of your doctrine; and soon as this foot of mine enables me to move, I will again seek the pretty cottager."

With this laudable resolution he retired to his chamber, attended by the villainous La Motte, a fit associate for his so truly abandoned, unprincipled lord.

In the mean time, poor Marian no longer happily carolled forth her songs as she turned her wheel, or trimmed her vines—no longer sunk in calm repose upon her humble couch; balmy sleep had forsook her pillow, and the pale lily usurped the place of the damask rose, which once bloomed on her Hebe's cheek. Her garden was neglected, her fruit trees unpruned; and her flowers, unrefreshed by the watering pot's cooling drops, and scorched by the meridian sun, seemed, like their mistress, fast falling into decay.

Her mother viewed this change with grief and wonder. She knew not of the stranger's visit, for Marian, conscious of her partiality, had never mentioned his name, lest her tongue might betray the secret which fed upon her heart. Nightly she visited the spot where she first beheld him. "'Twas here," she would exclaim, as the tears started to her eyes, "that I first beheld him! He thanked me so kindly; I shall never forget it! then he gave me a lock of hair, to keep as a remembrance." She would then take it from her bosom, where she constantly wore it, press it to her lips, then replacing it, would breathe a sigh, return home, and throwing herself upon her once-welcome couch, pass the night in thinking of her soul's adored.

One evening, about a fortnight after she had beheld the interesting stranger, repairing to her accustomed place of private meditation, she seated herself at the foot of a tree, unheedful of the shades of night, which were gathering fast around, when taking the lock, and returning it as usual, she exclaimed, "Shall I never again behold the giver of this precious jewel? will he never more return?" then with her eye bent on vacancy, sunk into a train of thought.

A sigh which broke near aroused her, and turning round, she beheld at her elbow the libertine Barozzi. She started, and would have fled, but he, catching her hand, gently detained her. "Will Marian shun me?" said he. "Are you not glad to see me again?—Did I not promise to return? Come, my sweet girl, you must not leave me!—But you look pale; are you ill?"

"I am, my lord," said she, tremulously, as she suffered him to lead her towards the neighbouring grove.

The pale moon faintly glimmered through the flitting clouds; no sound disturbed the silence of the night, save a gentle rustling of the trees, which waved in murmurs to the passing breeze—"Allow me, dear Marian, to converse with you for a few moments uninterrupted," said he, seating her on a grassy bank, and placing himself beside her.

She trembled, and cried, "My lord, suffer me to return home; my mother will be alarmed at my absence—I beseech you let me go."

"Hold!" said he, detaining her, "will not Marian listen to the man who loves her?"

"That loves me! Ah, my lord, that's impossible! You cannot love one so poor, so humble as myself."

"Indeed I do; and the pain I have endured since I first beheld you is impossible to describe; and, had I not been prevented by lameness, (which I bless as the means of my first beholding you), long since would have sought you to declare my passion, which, if you will return, you shall accompany me to Venice, and be mine for ever."

"Yours, my lord! But how?" said she.

"My wife."

"Your wife! Shall I be your wife?"

"You shall, dear, enchanting girl!" said he, catching her in his arms.

His cheek met hers, glowing with fear and love. The sacred title of wife, which he swore she should bear, oppressed her senses with too-powerful a joy. Her heart for a time ceased to beat; she fainted; he triumphed, and poor Marian was lost for ever.

On her recovery, he combatted her reproaches, soothed her fears by a renewal of his oaths; then seeing her nearly home, left her to become a prey to sorrow, remorse, and misery.

Chapter X
The Fratricide

AUGUSTINO EXULTED in the accomplishment of his hellish purpose; and from that night, so fatal to the peace of poor Marian, he avoided meeting her as much as possible. His passion now was cooled; he found the endearing caresses of that deluded innocent were becoming irksome, and only wished for a plausible pretence by which he might break a connexion grown troublesome, and almost disagreeable.

Such is the end of libertine amours! Pleased only with variety, the vicious seducer soon despises his victim, then basely deserts, and leaves it to the world's scorn, and the reproaches of a guilty conscience!"

He was relieved from this dilemma by the arrival of a letter from Venice, wherein his father commanded the return of his sons, before they had finished their intended tour.

Augustino obeyed the summons with alacrity; and without the least remorse, or even breathing a sigh, he quitted France, in company with his brother, leaving Marian a prey to the horrors of poverty, infamy, and the pangs of disappointed love! 'Tis true, he went to take leave of her, and promised she should soon hear from him; but that promise he had no intention of performing; but replied to her earnest desires of accompanying him, that his father was ill, and his journey must be performed without a moment's delay. She was forced to accept his excuses, and saw him depart with a heart almost bursting with grief.

The brothers, after a safe journey, arrived at Venice, when their father communicated to them his reasons for desiring their return. "'Tis for the purpose of fulfilling a desirable plan, long since meditated, of seeing my sons, ere I may be called from this transitory life," said he, "united by honourable alliances. The ducca di Centurani has a daughter, whom I propose as a wife for Augustino. Her father has accepted you for her husband, and highly approves of you for his son-in-law, therefore nothing is wanting but your compliance—Is it agreeable to you?—Will you consent, my son?"

The dutiful youth bowed, and hugging himself in the idea of her great dowry, which he fancied he had already in his grasp, said, that whatever his father wished, he was, and ever should be, proud to obey.

His father expressed his pleasure at his seeming filial affection, and addressing Fernando, said, "My child, Victoria of Memni is to be your wife;" (he shuddered, for Rosalina at that instant crossed his recollection); "but she has solicited her father, from what motive I know not, to defer the marriage ceremony until she arrives at the age of twenty, and two years are wanting to complete that number. Her father has consented to her wish; therefore, my child, you must wait the arrival of the period when you may call her yours, with patience."

This intelligence lifted a load from the heart of Fernando, who was delighted at the idea of the marriage being deferred; but concealing his joy, bowed assent.

A few weeks after, Augustino, forgetful of his vows to Marian, led his fair bride to the altar, and at the end of nine months Rosalva first saw the light.

His birth was celebrated with great rejoicings, and Augustino doted on his boy to distraction; yet did his love not extend to a proper parental fondness, by making for him a proper provision, but continuing to mix in abandoned company, lost such heavy sums, that not only his lady's fortune was expended, but his own became seriously injured.

In the mean time, Fernando had several times visited De Valmont in his seclusion, and at a proper opportunity disclosed to Rosalina his ardent passion. She returned his flame with mutual love, and at last consented to a private marriage, which was consummated unknown to any one save a single confidential witness.

Fernando shortly after took leave of his lovely bride, to avoid discovery. At a suitable interval he again visited the cottage of De Valmont, but was suddenly called away by receiving intelligence of the serious indisposition of both his father and mother. He hastened to Venice, and found them confined to their beds by a malignant fever, which, in a short time, proved fatal to both.

On the marquis's will being examined, it appeared that Augustino had received great part of his patrimony, therefore Fernando became entitled to a much larger fortune than himself, to his great indignation and utter confusion; for it never once entered his thoughts that his father would deduct the sums, which, unknown to his brother, he had often received, but at his death make an equal division of his immense property. A proviso was mentioned, that if Fernando should die without wife or issue, his fortune should devolve to the son of Augustino. This he reflected on with gloomy pleasure. "Fernando," thought he, "probably may have no children—perhaps never marry! and if he should die, why then—"

His meditation was interrupted by the appearance of a servant, who came to announce the dangerous situation of his brother. He was in a state of delirium, having been suddenly seized with that raging disorder that had so fatally proved its baneful influence on his hapless parents.

Augustino started—"Let every care be taken of him; let no advice be wanting." The attendant left the room. "If he should die!" ejaculated he; "if he should die!" A feeling of joy shot through his guilty breast, as he hoped for his brother's dissolution. Fifty times a-day did he send to his chamber; the reports equalled his wicked expectations; the physicians had given him over, and his death was hourly expected.

Augustino exulted, and, in fancy, was counting over the possessions which must fall to him, when lo! to his astonishment and utter confusion, nature triumphed over disease, and Fernando was pronounced out of danger, to the great joy of every one else who knew him.

A change like this, so sudden and unexpected, almost overcame the prudence and forbearance of Augustino, but smothering his disappointment as well as he was able, beneath a veil of hypocrisy, he congratulated his brother on his convalescent appearance, which he said gave him indescribable delight.

Fernando thanked him for his professions of fraternal love, and said, "Had I died, there are others, my dear brother, would have regretted my loss."

"No doubt," said the other; "for the marquis di Barozzi is beloved by all."

"You do not, I perceive, comprehend me, brother," replied Fernando; "my meaning is, I should have left a wife to lament my loss."

"A wife! A wife!" reiterated the other in great astonishment; "are you married?"

"Yes, my dear Augustino; I have been married these ten months."

"Indeed! and who is your wife?" asked he.

"Rosalina De Valmont," answered Fernando, at the same time saying, "you must pardon me for having concealed it from your knowledge till now."

"Had our father known it," said Augustino, "I think he would have disinherited you for marrying without his consent, and knowing that he had provided a wife for you."

"Doubtless," answered Fernando, "he might have made some difference in my fortune at least, which was my chief motive for keeping it a profound secret; for why should I wrong my wife and child, which I might have done by disclosing it before?"

"Your child! have you then a child?" eagerly inquired Augustino.

"I have; at least I suppose so, for when I left Rosalina, she was far advanced in pregnancy; and I hope on my return to the cottage to see an heir to my estates."

"By whom was you married?" interrogated Augustino.

"By him that was once our tutor—the good father Nicholas, who, alas! is now no more. I prevailed on him, by my entreaties, to join our hands. He accompanied me to the valley adjacent the cottage, where he remained unknown, till I called for him, as De Valmont was unacquainted with our loves, and ignorant of our nuptials."

"And is he so still?"

"He is; but as soon as my strength permits, I shall go and claim Rosalina as the marchioness di Barozzi; but perhaps her father ere this is acquainted with our union, for 'tis now three months since I saw her, of course then her situation must have caused her to reveal it; therefore, my dear brother, I must request you to forward this letter," at the same time giving one into his hands, "which, by your commands, will be expedited; it will explain to her the cause of my absence, and remove the uneasiness she no doubt labours under."

Augustino took the letter, promising to see his wishes performed. He then retired, after bidding his brother be composed, and withdrawing to his own apartment, vented, in curses and execrations, the bitterness of his disappointment. Glancing by accident his eyes upon the letter, he saw it directed for Rosalina, marchioness di Barozzi. A basilisk could not have been more painful to his sight. "Marchioness di Barozzi!" exclaimed he, in a horrid voice; "damnation! Then all hopes for me and mine are vanished! Demons of hell, assist me! save me from disgrace! and let me not be a brother's groveling slave—an elder brother, who, by coming into the world a few minutes before me, possesses so great a superiority!"

The fiends he invoked obeyed his summons, for at that moment a plan so horrid struck his thoughts, that nothing but infernals could have engendered in the brain of man. He struck his forehead in gloomy joy, and pacing the room with hurried steps, exultingly cried, "It shall be so! The priest who joined their hands is dead, and none else, that I need fear, can ever prove it!—Excellent thought! The dignities of Barozzi will then be mine, and my son shall hereafter inherit his father's rights—my rights! for had my father known of this disgraceful marriage, without doubt he would have settled on me what now, through ignorance of his dereliction from duty, is Fernando's."

Thus determined upon his diabolical project, he opened the letter, and read the contents, which were tender in the extreme. With indignation he threw it in the flames, and penned another, calculated to rend the heart of Rosalina. It was couched in the following words:—

"The dying Fernando greets Rosalina; and as the shades of dissolution gleam before his closing eyes, he exerts his last remaining strength in

unburdening his guilty soul, by disclosing, ere he dies, a painful truth.
I am a villain! a base villain! You are not my wife! I have deceived
you with a forged marriage. The wretch who performed the ceremony
was no priest, but, like myself, a monster, joined in a plot to immolate
your innocence in the arms of a deceiver! He has already gone to a
place where all his deeds will meet their reward. I shall quickly follow,
to answer for my perfidy to you, of which I now heartily repent, and
wish I could atone for my offence; but to you that can be of no avail,
the deed cannot be recalled. Farewell, Rosalina! pray for, and do not
curse, the guilty

"Fernando."

This, as it was a close imitation of his brother's characters, he did not doubt it would fully convince the wretched girl Fernando was the villain which he had depicted; and applauding himself for the deception, summoned his faithful minister La Motte, to whom he found it necessary to impart his villainous project, and giving him directions how to act, dispatched this miscreant with the forgery, and then returned to the chamber of his brother with an air of perfect composure, telling him he had sent a courier with the letter according to his desire.

Fernando thanked him, and said, "Poor Rosalina! it will give peace to her heart, which must be torn with anxiety, and compose her feelings till we meet again."

Augustino could scarcely conceal the diabolical pleasure which gleamed in his eyes at the seeming success of his villainous stratagem, and his brother's simplicity.

The evening on which La Motte returned from his hellish embassy, he entered the chamber of his sick brother with apparent great concern, saying the impatience of Rosalina had caused her to set forth immediately, accompanied only by the messenger; but the carriage breaking down about a league distant in the forest, and being slightly wounded by the accident, was compelled to remain behind, while the servant came forward for assistance.

Fernando hearing the danger of his Rosalina, instantly forgot his own weakness, and set out with La Motte to her immediate relief. Thus he fell, as was expected, into the artful snare prepared for him by his cruel, bloody brother.

Night had spread her sable mantle over the heavens ere they reached the forest, which, when they entered, at an appointed spot, the villain La Motte pretended to stumble, and loudly groaning, as if he was hurt, Fernando (according to conjecture) stooped, for the purpose of raising him; at that instant two assassins rushing from behind a clump of trees, where they had lain concealed, stabbed him in the side with repeated blows, and left him weltering in his blood.

The wretch La Motte, as had been previously agreed upon, on seeing him fall, hastened back to the palazzo with the tidings, wringing his hands in pretended sorrow, and in accents of seeming grief, related the pitiful tale to his lord, who immediately ordered his servants to hasten to the spot, accompanying them himself, in well-feigned despair at his brother's wretched fate. La Motte led the way; but when they arrived at the place of slaughter, the body was no where to be found, to the great astonishment of all, and particularly to those whose guilty breasts felt a degree of fear mingled with their surprise.

As they more closely examined the ground, a track of blood was seen, which they traced to the rocks that overhung the sea, whose waves dashed against the shores of the forest's edge. His cloak and hat were discovered near, and it was concluded by Augustino and his followers, that not being quite bereft of life, he had, in endeavouring to escape, or seek assistance, clambered up the precipice, and owing to the darkness of the night, was precipitated into the devouring flood.

A palpable pretext had been made for his departure to the domestics, who entertained not the least suspicion of this diabolical distraction. Augustino had already taken care no one should ever hear of his brother's marriage; and this horrid business being concluded with such ultimate success, he assumed the title of marquis, and took possession of his dear-bought honours, without dread or fear of discovery. But he felt not happy; his brother's blood laid heavy on his conscience, and smote him bitterly with pangs of horror. Fate, as if in some measure to avenge the death of Fernando, took from him his wife, and by a severe illness, made him long despair of his son's existence. This nearly drove him to frenzy, for he dearly loved the infant Rosalva. At length it pleased the omnipotent and merciful God to restore his health, and he was graciously pleased no longer to punish the child for the offences of the blood-stained parent; and this Heaven-favoured boy was spared, that he might live to thwart, by his nobleness of mind, the wicked plans of his guilty father.

Chapter XI
The Libertine's Victim

WE WILL NOW RETURN TO ROSALINA, who had brought into the world a sweet girl, a miniature resemblance of herself. Her father had forgiven her disobedience, and she each day expected the return of her husband, whose felicity she knew would be great in beholding his infant daughter. At length the ill-fated letter arrived, and by its baneful influence destroyed the fabric of bliss which she had so long reared in fancy.

The wretched De Valmont was almost frantic. This fresh proof of perfidy, and from the man whom he thought his only friend, made him vow eternal enmity with the whole human race. In his first fit of raving, he wept and tore his hair, imploring Heaven to punish the deceitful author of his calamity. The honour of his house was now stained for ever; for by endeavouring to seek justice, he would only expose the infamy of his child.

When the first transports of his rage were somewhat subsided, he reflected that the perfidious Fernando was now no more, and that repining might increase his sorrow, but could not cure. Thus weighing the matter, he felt resolved to summon all his fortitude, and bear his misfortune like a true philosopher. This commendable resolution was aided by the consoling idea that his daughter's shame might be kept from the knowledge of the censorious world. He now sought his heart-broken Rosalina, whom, by his conciliating manners, and promises of continued affection, he endeavoured to sooth and reconcile to her fate.

This commiseration, and unlooked-for tenderness from her beloved parent, in some measure tranquillized her afflicted mind, and by endeavouring to subdue her weakness, called forth a dignified pride and energy of soul, which, until then, she knew not was in her nature. All her past tenderness and love she had felt for the cruel deceiver she banished from her breast, and strove to bury the remembrance of his memory beneath her wrongs, which she was determined to bear with a degree of stoicism. All her attention was now dedicated to her father and lovely infant, to whom she had given her own appellation, and whose endearing smiles beguiled her cares.

Thus passed her time in divided duty for several months, till one fatal night, when they had retired to rest, and in the arms of refreshing sleep sought repose, De Valmont was awoke by a piercing shriek that issued from the chamber of his daughter. He started in great surprise, and opening the door, a cloud of smoke, which till then had been confined, burst in upon him, and almost stifled him with its suffocating steams. "Oh, my child!" he exclaimed, as the devouring flames burst through various parts of the dwelling, "my child! her infant! oh Heaven, they will perish!" With distraction he rushed to her apartment, when, to his confusion, he found the door was fastened. This, added to the trepidation he felt, caused a delay of some time ere he could gain an entrance, when he found part of the flooring had already given way, and it was with great difficulty he could reach the bed, which, when he effected, he found, to his great grief and horror, that his daughter, in endeavouring to escape, had sunk into the room below, and perished amidst the dreadful conflagration; her infant still lay sleeping, unconscious of the destruction which surrounded it. Frantic with despair, he caught it to his breast, and instantly darting through the flames, which enveloped him, gained the staircase, and bore the babe off unhurt, at the moment when the room gave way with a loud crash.

Some of the inhabitants of the neighbouring village perceiving the fire, ran to his assistance, but too late to discover any signs of Rosalina, whose beloved remains were consumed in the ruins; but their exertions succeeded in preventing the entire destruction of the cottage; and his own chamber, together with some of his property, were saved by their endeavours; while some were busied in collecting what trifles were preserved, others were trying to compose the feelings of the unhappy sufferer, who was conducted for shelter to the hospitable roof of a neighbouring peasant.

While he was seated in a chair, enfolding in his embrace, and dropping a tear upon the infant cheek of his grandchild, a woodcutter from the adjacent forest having heard of what had happened, came into the house, and addressing De Valmont, said, "Signor, your cottage has been fired by some deadly foe of yours."

"Ah! how know you that?" asked the other.

"Pardon my curiosity," answered the woodcutter, "but is not your name De Valmont?"

"It is," answered the wretched man, astonished at the question, for in his retirement he had passed by another title.

"Then I am right; and had I known it before, signor, I could have warned you of your approaching calamity; for as I was returning from my labour in the forest, I heard two men, of suspicious appearance, discoursing beneath a tree;

I listened, for I thought they were after no good, as they appeared to conceal themselves from observation; I heard one of them say to the other, 'Neither De Valmont or a child of his must any longer exist, therefore I say again, that our surest method will be to fire the dwelling, and consume them altogether.'"

"God!" said the wretched man, "what have I done to merit such an enemy?"

"I know not that," said the woodcutter, "for I did not stay to hear more; and being assured they were assassins, I was fearful lest they might discover me, for if they had, no doubt but I should have dearly paid for my curiosity. This morning, hearing of your misfortune, it struck me that you might be the person to whom they alluded."

De Valmont, on hearing this account, was overwhelmed with astonishment. In vain he racked his mind in endeavouring to guess who instigated the vile incendiaries to this cruel act; but his suspicions were groundless, for he concluded some of his enemies in France had pursued him even into exile. After revolving in his mind, and forming several schemes for the defeat of their malice for the future, he adopted that which appeared the most feasible. This was, to go into a distant part of the country, and never to divulge his name to any human being whatever. By this means, he thought he might be able to shun the implacable resentment of his mortal enemies. He no sooner resolved on this but he put it in practice; and a box, containing some cash, and the most valuable part of his property, which was fortunately saved from the ruins of his cottage, furnished him with the means. He hired a carriage, and after forcing a compensation upon his hospitable entertainer, he bade an eternal adieu to a place so fatal to his peace.

After journeying several days, he passed near to Pyrano. The Valley of the Vintagers seemed calculated to afford a safe retreat, but to avoid the possibility of ever being discovered, he journeyed several leagues further to an inn, where, dismissing the carriage, told the driver he was unable to proceed farther by land, and should wait there for a vessel to take him to the place of his destination. He then procured a person to take care of his grandchild until his return, hired a mule, and proceeded to the Valley, where, finding a cottage, with a small garden, to be disposed of, he purchased them, and returned to the inn for his little charge, for whom he procured a little village girl as a nurse; and to baffle all inquiries, he passed himself as a widower, who had recently buried his wife, under the assumed apellation of Ferrand St. Almo, and father to the infant.

His days now passed on in peaceful melancholy. The tuition of the little Rosalina, and the culture of his garden, afforded him sufficient employment, and beguiled many an hour. Thus year succeeded year, and no enemy appeared to interrupt his tranquility.

In the mean time, Rosalina advanced in growth and beauty. The mystery of her birth Valmont had never unfolded to her, so that when he used to weep for the loss of her mother, the innocent girl thought he lamented the death of a wife, not a daughter.

The unhappy exile hugged himself with fancied security, and the pleasing hope of sinking unmolested to the peaceful grave. Alas! poor wretch! fate had reserved thee for a cruel death, for he fell, as related in the first chapter, beneath the dagger of Roldon the assassin.

The marquis di Barozzi was in continual dread while he knew De Valmont, his daughter and child, still existed, (for fear is ever a constant attendant of the guilty); therefore, to insure his security, he formed the horrid idea of consuming them together in their cottage.

In Venice he was not long in finding ruffians easily bought by all-seducing gold, and wicked enough to execute his dreadful purpose, in which, though they did not accomplish their full intent, they too far succeeded; and on their return, the ears of the marquis were gratified in hearing they had all perished in the flames, as the wretches he employed fully assured him.

Barozzi was so well pleased at this intelligence, that he gave them an additional reward; and shortly after, La Motte, that instrument of his guilt, was found dead in his bed, to the great joy of his master, who had long regarded him with an eye of suspicion, knowing the power which he possessed over him. Indeed some of the domestics supposed that he did not come fairly by his end, but were too wise to express their thoughts on so dangerous a subject.

The marquis now lived, as he thought, free from the danger of being betrayed, without feeling the least remorse for the blood he had shed in obtaining his unlawful wealth. Familiar with scenes of cruelty, his heart had become callous, and deaf to every feeling of humanity; and the only circumstance which made any impression upon it, was the last letter from the wretched Marian, to whom we will now return.

That poor deluded girl, not hearing from her base betrayer, as he had promised, languished, and pined away in secret sorrow; and to increase her grief, she found she was fast approaching towards that period, when she should bring into the world a living witness of her shame, to partake of her misery.

Maddened by the idea of this conviction, she cast herself prostrate at the feet of her mother.

Her heart-broken parent strove to comfort her wretched child; but, alas! she needed most that consolation which she offered, for melancholy so preyed upon her mind, that she sunk into the grave ere Marian had well recovered from the danger and peril of childbirth.

A beautiful boy, unhappy offspring of illicit love! brought to its wretched mother, with a large share of maternal affection, a load of cares how to find him food and the necessaries of life.

The landlord, at the death of Marian's wretched parent, had ordered her to quit the cottage. This harsh command she was forced to obey, as she was already in arrears for rent; and selling her little property, with her child in her arms, she sought refuge in a humble lodging at Paris. Her beauty attracted admirers even in her forlorn condition, but she was deaf to every stranger tongue, and rejected their solicitations with indignation, for she still loved her dear betrayer in spite of his cruelty, therefore was resolved never to deviate from that constancy to which she had sworn. At a shop she procured work for her needle, at which she was a proficient, and applied herself to it with indefatigable assiduity; but attendance on her child, which occupied a large portion of time, prevented her from obtaining more than a scanty pittance, barely sufficient for subsistence. Thus she dragged on life in a way, though honest, yet miserable. Often were the eyes of poor Marian filled with tears, as she contemplated the features of her darling child, who bore a striking resemblance to its remorseless father. She had frequently written to that cruel wretch, imploring his assistance; but the unfeeling marquis scarcely perused her letters, which he never deigned to answer.

To add to her calamitous situation, the infant was seized with a fever, whose malignity was soon seen in the large purple spots which covered its innocent face. Its distracted mother had no money to procure advice; giving her last farthing to a woman in the house where she lodged, to look to her babe, she set forwards into the street, for the purpose of begging. The shades of evening nearly obscured her face, when she met a good-looking female, whose charity she implored in most piteous accents of supplication.

"Why do you not work?" said she, sharply.

"Alas, madam! I cannot," replied the gentle girl, "for I have an infant perishing with a fever, and have no means to allay its agonies."

"A fever!" said the unfeeling woman; "perhaps contagious!" She hurried past her. "I have nothing for you; apply to the hospital."

Marian stood for a moment, then exclaimed, "Oh, my child! my poor babe! dear cause of my miseries, and yet my heart's greatest joy! must you perish?—Must I see you die for want?—Can your wretched mother find no friend to help her? Oh, holy Virgin! send some benevolent, humane heart to assist, to succour the distressed, yet guilty Marian! Oh, Barozzi! surely did you know my wretchedness, you would surely stretch forth your hand to save me! Oh, where shall I go for relief?—Oh, whither shall I fly?" Her strength became exhausted, and she was obliged to lean for support against the portal of an elegant hotel.

A man came forth, and seeing her stand, careless of his presence, roughly bade her begone, for she was in the way.

Marian lifted up her eyes; the tears rushed down her pallid cheeks, and she was preparing to obey the harsh command, which the man repeated in a still rougher tone, when another, coming from the same door, asked what was the matter?

"Only some bad woman," said the first; "for she cannot be any good, or else she would not be loitering about people's doors at this time of night. Ah, this city is full of them."

Marian answered not, but slowly quitted his presence, unknowing whither to bend her steps, when the second man, struck with her forlorn appearance, followed, and asked her if he could render her any service?

The poor sufferer fixed her eyes meekly on his countenance; it beamed, she thought, with benevolence; and taking courage from his proffered assistance, she said, "Monsieur, I am in poverty; I have a child dying with sickness and famine; if you are a Christian, or a charitable man, bestow from your superfluity a small trifle to save my babe from perishing!"

The stranger looked on her, and putting his hand into his pocket, presented her with a couple of livres.

Marian was overpowered by his kindness; the tear of gratitude started to her eye; she would have thanked him, but found it impossible. Seizing his hand; she pressed it to her lips with enthusiasm, then rushing down a narrow street, sought her lodging, buoyed with the hope of being able to save her child; but, alas! she was too late, for he, poor babe, was fast sinking to the grave; the cold damps of death stood upon its infant brow; and while its unhappy mother moistened its feverish lips with cordial, (obtained by the means of the stranger's charitable donation), their livid hue too surely convinced he was breathing his last.

In a state of distraction she snatched up a pen, and addressed the following words to the villain who had brought her to this deplorable situation:—

"Once more the heart-broken Marian writes to him who has been the cause of her shame, her infamy, and misery. Barozzi, if you are not bereft of all feeling, peruse this attentively. I curse you not, though author of my calamity, for you are the father of that innocent being, whose departing soul will soon appear at Heaven's judgement-seat, and accuse its sire as his murderer! Oh, Augustino, he is your son—your deserted son, a victim to famine and disease. Each groan that issues from its lips is a dagger to his wretched mother's heart, which, lacerated by repeated wounds, will soon break, and give her peace. I forgive you, and sincerely hope Heaven will pardon you also. Ah, that groan! 'tis more dreadful than the last! He is dead! Oh, unnatural father! your child is dead! My poor babe! Oh God, is it possible two parents can feel so differently! I have become a beggar to procure him food, while his rich, unfeeling father left him to die the most horrid of deaths, lingering in the jaws of hunger and poverty. My brain burns, and my bewildered fancy renders me incapable of proceeding—my heart throbs as if it would burst its confinement; yet no tears bedew my cheek; their source is exhausted. But a little while, and I shall return to my native dust. This is your work—this is your desolation. Beloved, yet cruel man, farewell! Oh, Augustino, the love I have felt for you will be extinguished but with my life. Even now I would find excuses for you, were it possible; but my babe now lies an awful witness against you, and speaks in language more terrible than words. His father is his murderer! Farewell! oh, farewell! My eyes begin to close; the icy hand of death is upon me—I feel its agonizing pangs rush through my heart—it cracks, it breaks for you. Barozzi, oh, Barozzi!"

With her last effort of remaining strength she folded the letter, and wrote the superscription of this pathetic appeal to the inhuman marquis; she then put up a fervent prayer to Heaven to receive the fleeting soul of her innocent babe, then staggering towards the bed, she lay down by the side of her child's clay-cold corse, then imprinting a kiss upon its lifeless lips, and dropping a tear of anguish on its pallid face, she yielded up her breath without sigh or groan.

Surely her sufferings paid for her crimes; they were atoned for by her repentance, and choirs of ministering angels sung a requiem for the rest of her departed soul as they wafted it to regions of eternal bliss.

The sad remains of both herself and child were deposited in one grave, by the benevolence of that humane and charitable stranger who had so generously administered to her distress; for his philanthropic heart was melted by her misfortunes, and he traced her to her lodgings, with the noble intention of lending her further aid, and, by unremitted inquiries, gained a knowledge of her hapless story.

Poor Marian! Peace be to thy remains! and may all those who pass the green sod which shields thee from reproach, drop a tear to the memory of the libertine's victim!

END OF VOL. I

Barozzi,
or
The Venetian Sorceress

A Romance of the Sixteenth Century

In Two Volumes

Volume II

Chapter I
Mysteries

THE MARQUIS RECEIVED MARIAN'S BILLET; the contents at first somewhat shocked him, but he soon recovered his spirits, by the reflection that she could now no more disturb his peace, if it was possible for a heart like his, stained with numerous crimes, to feel peace; but something like it dwelt within his breast, which was become impregnable to remorse, and cared for nothing except his riches. He again assumed cheerfulness, mixed with the gay throng at carnivals and ridottoes, drowning the thoughts of his crimes in large goblets of wine, which he daily quaffed, till hardiness took place of the fears of discovery.

Years had now passed away, and nothing occurred to alarm the guilty Augustino, till having occasion to visit an estate he possessed in a distant province, his carriage broke down in passing through the forest near Pyrano. Leaving his servants at an inn to get it repaired, and by way of beguiling the time, wandering towards the neighbouring valley, its delightful appearance caused him to survey it with particular attention, and amongst other things which attracted his notice, was the cottage of De Valmont. As he walked to it, he descried among the vines the unfortunate noble and his granddaughter. He started; for in Rosalina he thought he beheld the murdered wife of his brother; and again, looking through the hedge which screened him from their view, he was almost certain, from the wonderful resemblance, that this was the heiress whom he long since thought dead. The pangs of fear once more assailed him, and hastily quitting the valley, he returned to the inn in great perturbation of mind.

Meeting with his hostess (a talkative woman), he asked her if she knew to whom the little white cottage at the end of the valley belonged?

She answered him, "Ferrand St. Almo."

"How long has he lived there?"

He was informed, and found it tallied with the time he had supposed them consumed in the fire. "Is that pretty young lady his daughter?" he inquired.

"Why, he says so; but when he came here, she was quite an infant. But nobody knows who he is, what he is, or from whence he comes. Really I should think him a spy, only that he never has any visitors, or ever receives any letters, for the postman comes to this house, and I always ask if there is any thing for him; for you know, y lord, honest folks ought to be cautious, and upon their guard against suspicious people, and so I always tell my husband; but he, poor silly soul, says as how he thinks him some ruinated gentleman. 'Don't tell me," says I, 'about your ruinous gentleman; I know he is no better than he should be;' and I am sure, my lord," said his loquatious hostess, with a significant nod, "if he was after any good, he need not be always so retired as he is. Howsoever, he is very fond of miss, and teaches her many accomplishments: why, you must know, my lord, that she can play upon the harp like any lady; so you may swear they have not always been what they appear to be now."

The marquis agreed in this opinion with his hostess. The carriage was rendered fit for travelling, and with a disordered mind he bade the servant drive back by the road he came as he should not now prosecute his journey, his mind having changed by the delay he was compelled to undergo.

While on his return, he ruminated on the wonderful discovery he had made. "Fernando's child still lives, and should cursed chance discover the forgery of my letter sent to her mother, she will at last inherit the estates of Barozzi. Confusion! I thought all the family long since membered with the dust. Are all my stratagems proved abortive? shall my possessions be wrested from my grasp? No! sooner will I myself perish. How to prevent it then? Why, the same bravoes still reside in Venice that rid me of my hated brother. It shall be so; and though all my other measures have failed, their daggers will prove effective."

Upon his arrival at Venice, he sent to those wretches who stabbed Fernando, desiring one of them to visit him that very night, as he wished to have some private conversation upon a subject of importance. His son Rosalva at that time was on a visit to his aunt's, for the better eluding the vengeance of the marchioness Loredo, so he was not fearful of any interruption.

Roldon, the chief of the bravoes, came at the close of the evening to the palazzo, disguised under the garb of a gondolier, saying he had business with his excellenza.

The porter instantly admitted him, for the marquis had left orders that should any such person come he was at leisure.

When they were closeted together, Barozzi addressed the bravo as follows: "My brave fellow, you once gave me a proof of your fidelity, in dispatching a man who was become hateful to my sight: I now wish to employ you upon a similar occasion. There resides in the valley of Vintagers, near Pyrano, an old man of the name of St. Almo, with his daughter: she, for reasons I cannot now explain, I wish you to deprive of life; for while she exists, I never can be happy, as her offence cannot be forgiven; but you may let the father escape, for 'tis only the life of his daughter I require; therefore you need not shed more blood than the necessity of the case justifies."

"Your lordship is very considerate indeed," said Roldon, at the same time receiving a well-stocked purse, "and you may depend upon our faithful services, for if her death can afford you any gratification, your lordship may conclude it already done. I swear, when next we meet, my dagger shall be stained with her life's blood."

"Ah," said the marquis, "perform your work, and I will double the reward."

"Your excellenza was ever generous, and I love to be grateful," said the bravo. "I will instantly join my comrade Darano; then proceed to the business without delay."

"Do so, my worthy fellow," returned the marquis, "and when you have completed it, meet me at the ruined abbey in the forest: send me a billet when you shall be there, and I will not fail attending with the additional reward I have promised."

Roldon, with a low bow, took his leave, and joining his iniquitous associate, they put their hellish purpose in force, as related in the first chapter.

After the villains had escaped from the power of Rosalva, they stopped at the outskirts of the forest, when they thought themselves free from pursuit, for the purpose of consulting how to act, now they had lost their victim.

They at last concluded to meet the marquis, tell him they had fulfilled their orders, receive the remainder of the reward, and trust to fortune for the rest.

They did so, and Barozzi now thought he should be quite secure; but conscience, that awful moniter, now began to assail him with pangs of horror: his accumulated crimes now rose in terrible army, and shook his guilty soul. Marian and her infant, his brother, the daughter of De Valmont, and lastly her child, all flitted before his disordered sight, and loudly thundered in his ear—*The hour of retribution must one day arrive.* Sleep forsook his couch, or when it did for a moment close his eyes, horrid visions presented themselves, from which he would start in agony, and wiping the cold sweat from his trembling frame, try to sleep again, but in vain: sweet repose never more could be his; remorse and fear alternately smote his guilty soul; that never feeling a moment's peace, he dreaded to be alone, and scarcely suffered his page ever to be from his presence.

At length his spirits were so worn with disquiet days and agonizing nights, that he sunk into a profound melancholy. At this time he sent for his son from La Rosa, whose absence he could no longer bear; yet when he arrived, Rosalva's society was not welcome as formerly.

In this perturbed state was the mind of Barozzi when the marchioness La Rosa visited him, and brought to the palazzo that being he feared more than all the world.

His astonishment was on the point of finding vent in words, but he timely checked himself, and upon due consideration, thought he was deceived. His sister's ward, Rosa Falieri!—"Pshaw! my conjecture was groundless; it is a likeness which first alarmed me, for she can never be Rosalina: did not Roldon shew me his dagger stained with her blood? why, then, am I weak enough to start at a shadow? Hence all idle, visionary fears! my brother's child no more can blast my sight." This reflection, added to the great change in her appearance by her dress, silenced his suspicions; yet, when in her presence, they returned with double force, and caused him to regard her with so much scrutiny; but in spite of all his endeavours to the contrary, he still felt the most painful alarm. At length his eye, for the first time, caught sight of the ring which she continually wore. This circumstance confirmed his doubts, for he recognized it on the instant as the late property of Fernando, the initials of whose name it bore.

Unable to disguise his feelings, he rushed to his chamber, and throwing himself upon a couch, gave way to the following soliloquy: "Accursed fate! my fears were not without cause. 'Tis she! my brother's child still lives. Rosalina St. Almo and Rosa Falieri are both one. Damned ruffians, thus to deceive me! But she must die—she shall, though my own hand strike the blow—yes, though all the fiends of hell were—Who's there?" he cried, starting as a footstep sounded near. "Who's there?" he repeated.

"'Tis I, my lord," said a gentle voice.

His favourite page appeared.

"Ah, Julio!" said he, catching him by the arm, "how long have you been here? Did you listen? Did you overhear me, eh?"

"No, your excellenza," replied Julio; "I heard your lordship's voice, so I thought you called me."

"Indeed!" said the marquis; "I commend your diligence: retire to the antechamber, and never again interrupt my meditations. When I need your attendance, I will summon you by the bell."

Julio bowing, said—"I hope my lord is not offended? if my duty is too bold or officious, impute it to my desire of proving attentive."

"No, my boy," replied the marquis, "I am not in the least displeased, for I like your attention, which shall not be unrewarded, but at present I am very ill at ease, therefore leave me."

"I obey, my lord," said Julio, with a low bow; "but would your lordship vouchsafe to grant me a favour?"

"Name it, Julio."

The page continued—"My mother is very ill, and wishes to see me; would your excellenza allow me to go to-morrow evening, after I have attended you, to prepare for the mask?"

"Yes; you may go, and stay—"

"How long, my lord" eagerly inquired Julio.

"Why, three days."

"Oh! thank you, my dear lord!" said Julio, leaving the room, astonished at this permission so easily obtained. In truth, this indulgence did not proceed from good-nature on the part of the marquis, but he thought he would get rid of one who (though very diligent, possessed great shrewdness and cunning) he thought might be an observer of his actions while arranging his plan for the disposal of Rosalina, and which might be done effectually in the time he allowed the page to be absent.

Barozzi then strove to disguise his uneasiness between a veil of the utmost cheerfulness, and on the evening of the mask he was in high spirits, by having recourse to his usual friend, the wineflask; by repeated draughts, he grew exhilarated; this caused him to be so full of raillery with Magdalena the sorceress, but he dared not consent to her proposal. Conscious of his guilt, he felt a degree of awe at her presence, though a moment's reflection proved it ridiculous to be in dread of a character at a masked ball: and on her departure, he was again all life, having at various times received assistance from the flowing goblet, as he was seated but at a short distance from Rosalina, on whom, at intervals, he cast glances of deep and terrible meaning, though unnoticed by every one, except that all-seeing eye who views and reads the guilty deeds and thoughts of sinful man.

When the marquis retired for the night, he revolved on various methods for the seizure and destruction of Rosalina, but was unable to fix on any expedient, for he had no sooner determined on one mode as feasible, than it was the next moment rejected as dangerous and uncertain.

Agitated with fear, he started up, exclaiming—"Why should I shed more blood?—let me desist. Foolish idea! she must inevitably die, or else I have only gained my dearly-purchased honours to lose them at last; for that ring may be recognized by others as well as myself, and lead to a discovery of the whole. Accursed thought! must I then behold my son stripped of title—of wealth—a very beggar? No—sooner will I perish in the attempt of crushing this detestable worm that rises banefully to my sight, and blasts me with her presence. Ye ministers of hell, aid me to achieve this important act, and for the rest I fear not!"

A hollow moan murmured in his ear, and instantly turning, he beheld at his side the mysterious mask.

"Merciful powers! who art thou?" he cried, in fearful accents.

"Thy friend, Barozzi, and the general friend of all, who, like thee, are steeped in blood."

"Ah! what meanest thou, stranger? Beware of what you say. Knowest thou to whom you speak?" said the marquis.

"To whom! ha, ha, ha! why, to the marquis di Barozzi. Is not that one of your titles?"

"He tremblingly replied—"It is.""

"Is that the only one which distinguishes you from your fellow-beings? No, you have a superior title, for by it you have a claim to the friendship of the sorceress Magdanlena!"

"Ah! what is that?" said he.

"Why, one that sounds sweeter—oh! sweeter far—that of murderer!"

She then seized his hand, and looking in his face with a ghastly smile, while he shrunk back in terror, thundered in his ears—"*Homicide! fratricide!* these are the titles of Barozzi!"

He sunk trembling into a chair, and with a voice scarcely articulate, said— "Who art thou, mysterious being? from whence do you come?"

"Have I not already told you who I am? did we not meet before to-night in the garden, but you refused to hear me? so I scorned to intrude, therefore waited till I was summoned to your presence."

"Summoned!" repeated he; "by whom?"

"By yourself."

"By me! 'tis false!"

"Nay, Barozzi, you forget yourself; be not ungrateful for my prompt attention; did you not call to your aid the ministers of hell? then behold in me one of those demons you invoked, or, at least, one of their favoured servants."

"Oh, Heaven!" said the marquis, "what will become of me?"

"Nay," said she, "call not on Heaven; wretches like thee have nought to hope for there. If you hope for assistance, call ever, as you did, on the infernals of hell, thy proper deities—nay, fear not, for you are sunk in sin beyond all power of redemption. Then glut on, steep your hands still deeper in blood, and satiate thy sanguinary desires, for nothing now can increase your crimes— Rosalina must die."

"Ah!" said he, "thou knowest my very thoughts."

"Aye, and the thoughts of all men; but what say you? Shall Rosalina fall?"

"She shall, I am resolved," replied the marquis.

"'Tis well; then meet me at the ruin in the forest to-morrow, at the hour of midnight; there thou shalt behold her. Trust not again to mortals—they will betray you; seek alliance with higher power than bravoes, and all thy wishes shall be accomplished."

The marquis said—"Why at the ruin? 'tis the retreat of robbers."

"Barozzi, fear not, for Magdalena shall protect thee from all harm; therefore, speak, will you attend?" said she.

"I will," answered the marquis; "and for your assistance, name whatever reward you—"

"Reward!" said she, interrupting him; "weak man! think you *immortals* want gold! them I serve and please by this my attention to you. Barozzi, name not reward, but attend."

Thus saying she waved her wand, and passed through the portal, leaving the marquis standing in silent amazement. Taking courage, he followed, but he had lost sight of her; and returning, exclaimed—"'Tis well! I now am allied with ministers of hell, who will aid me in my schemes: with such powers can I fail? no. Rosalina dies, and the stem which sprung from the tree I had before crushed shall follow its parent stalk. Barozzi, rejoice! thy victory is complete; I shall conclude my life, in the world's eye, with honour; and when the grave has enclosed me, I fear not a world to come. Yet the mysterious spirit says there is a *hell*. If there should be! there must—there is! Oh, Merciful Powers! what will be the wretched Augustino?"

"*A fiend!*" replied a hollow voice.

He started in horror; his glazy eye wandered round the apartment, in search of the unknown who had answered him. No traces of a human being met his sight, and he endeavoured to persuade himself it was the effect of fancy. "Surely I am not haunted and tortured by devils in this world! yet it sounded so hollow, so sepulchral, that it alarms my very soul. I would the page were here! I am afraid to be alone. To what a miserable state am I reduced by guilt! Guilt! oh, then, let me not plunge still deeper! Rosalina shall not die. Yet, curse on my wavering, unstable thoughts, she must. Rouse thee, Barozzi, and let her sink to dust! Yet she is innocent! but not the less dangerous. Oh, conscience! conscience! why dost thou plead for her strongly—thou who wert silent on the death of her father? I cannot even pray for it. Oh, if I were but once again innocent, I would not barter my soul for the worth of empires! but alas! 'tis in vain; I cannot return, but must go farther in sin to secure the cursed wealth for which I sold my peace. The sorceress called me 'homicide! fratricide!' I am, I am! Marian—her child—my brother—all, all rise up against me, and curse me as their destroyer! Then why should I pause at one more crime? Rosalina must fall, and ensure my safety. I will live, and still will be the same in every thing— fearless of the future, and regardless of the past."

CHAPTER II
Horrors of the Ruin

Aфтеr тhe deрarture of Rosalva, the marchioness and Rosalina entered into a conversation concerning the events that had transpired at Venice, but what most excited their interest was the subject of the mysterious mask.

"Doubtless," said the marchioness, "that strange being is acquainted with many important circumstances of infinite concern to you, my child. But who the foe can be, of whom she bid you beware, I have not the most distant idea. I know not how any one can be your enemy: surely, if they were acquainted with the excellence you possess, they would forbear their malice, and cease to persecute you."

"Ah, marchesa, my kind benefactress," answered Rosalina, "your good opinion of me I prize beyond the world, and should be alone sufficient to make me happy; but I am not born for peace; I never can be at ease, but must ever dread impending danger. Would I were in my grave, free from the inveteracy of those who thirst for my blood! Oh, had I died when my poor father fell, I had been freed from this calamitous world, and followed my parents to eternal rest."

"Hush, hush! my child," said the marchioness; "do not repine or murmur at the decrees of Providence; perhaps you are reserved to be a blessing to mankind, and triumph over your enemies. My dear girl, did you never hear your father mention or hint that he dreaded the malevolence of any one?"

"Ah, madam, I do suspect indeed; but should I be wrong, I never can forgive myself; and yet I think—"

"Well, whom do you imagine? what is the name of him you suspect?" said the marchioness, with impatience.

"Ah, lady! if I thought you would not be offended, if I thought you would acquit me of being—"

"For Heaven's sake!" said the marchioness, trembling without knowing why; "I promise not to be offended; so no longer you keep me in suspense, I beseech you."

"Why, then, my lady, I think it is—I mean, I doubt—I fear it is the marquis di Barozzi."

"Rosalina, what mean you? my brother?"

"Pardon me, dear madam; forgive me; but really his looks made me tremble; indeed I know not why or wherefore, but I always was uneasy in his presence; but perhaps I wrong his meaning when he gazed on me with such particular earnestness."

The marchioness became excessively uneasy; her pride was aroused by the observations and remarks Rosalina had made upon her relative; yet she could not help thinking the same: again she thought it impossible that Barozzi could have any pique against the daughter of St. Almo. Various conjectures now succeeded each other, but all in vain, for the more she endeavoured to find some reason for his remarkable conduct, the more she was lost in a labyrinth of doubt and surprise.

Her reverie was suddenly interrupted by one of the servants, who, with a look of fear, said four men in masks were riding towards the carriage, and he supposed them to be banditti, for they were armed with cutlasses and carbines.

The marchioness was terribly alarmed at this intelligence, but not wishing to intimidate others, she attempted to assume a degree of fortitude, and said to the servant—"Fear not, good Carlo; perhaps plunder is their only aim; if so, we will yield our purses freely, with which, no doubt, they will be satisfied."

Rosalina sunk back in a swoon: the dread of more than robbers took from her the power of moving.

One of the ruffians advancing towards the driver, put a pistol to his head, and bade him stop, at the peril of his life; an argument so forcible the man thought best to obey.

In the meanwhile, another rode up to the window of the carriage, when the marchioness putting forth her hand, presented a well-stocked purse, which the ruffian readily accepted. She then thought he would have suffered them to proceed, but to her great terror he opened the door, and forcibly seized the person of the almost lifeless Rosalina.

The marchioness uttered a loud shriek, and bade them forbear—"Ah, villains!" said she, "is it the life of this helpless girl you seek? oh, spare her! spare her! suffer us to proceed, and I promise to reward you. Tell me who is the wretch that employs you?"

They made her no answer, but in spite of shrieks, tears, threats, and entreaties, they seized the almost inanimate form of Rosalina, which they placed on a horse, and galloped off with speed towards the forest.

The marchesa beheld their departure with agony. The servants, who were not prepared to act on the defensive against ruffians so well armed, were thunderstruck; and Paulina, who, till this occurance, had been in a sound sleep, for the pleasures of the fête had prevented her from reposing the preceding night, as she thought it a pity to close her eyes, and lose the opportunity of beholding so many fine sights, wringing her hands, rent the air with shrieks; but whether her grief was real or feigned, we cannot ascertain, as she was well gifted with finesse, which she often practised with great success.

Thrice did Carlo ask his lady whether they should proceed, before she was capable of replying: at last, to his repeated question, she said—"Return to Venice."

"Return! did your excellenza say?"

"Yes, return, and drive as fast as possible."

"We will, your excellenza," said the man, who could not conceive how returning could do any good; therefore, again approaching the carriage, said— "My lady, it is impossible for the horses to perform it without baiting; really they are quite unable: we are not more than a league from the inn where your excellenza proposed to rest for the night; therefore, if I might venture to advise, we had better drive there and procure fresh horses, or let those have a sufficient bait ere we return."

To this reasonable argument the marchioness could not object, so bid him proceed to the inn, from whence she was determined to return immediately to Venice, for the purpose of acquainting the marquis, and observe the changes that might be made in his countenance, or, by other concomitant circumstances, learn if there were any truth in her suspicions.

In the mean time, poor Rosalina was hurried in a state of insensibility, from which she did not recover till the shades of evening overcast the light day. On opening her eyes, she found she was placed before a rough-looking man on horseback: she gave a loud shriek, on which the ruffian bade her be silent, or it would be worse for her.

"Oh Heavens!" said she, "what will become of me? what have I done to be thus treated? where do you intend to take me? is it to—"

The marquis Barozzi, she would have said, but the words faltered on her lips.

"You will see that anon," said another ruffian, that rode near her side; "but I promise you no injury shall be offered to you, if you will suffer us to conduct you uninterrupted; but if, by screaming, or any other method, you make any alarm, to excite a rescue, we will dispatch you on the first attempt; therefore, be silent, and you will not receive the least harm."

Rosalina, finding no other alternative, acceded to the bravo's injunction, and suffered herself to be conducted in silence, while the robbers hasted towards the ruin, where they shortly afterwards arrived, and stopping at its entrance, one of them shrilly sounded a whistle, which was answered by another. Some person then came and gave them admittance.

The first sight of this lonely and decaying fabric caused the heart of our heroine to sink with fear; and when the gate, which grated on its rusty hinges, closed upon her, she thought that she had entered her sepulchre. The ruffians set her down in the hall, and without speaking a word, departed, leaving her entirely alone. "Merciful God!" said she to herself, "wherefore am I brought hither?" A stream of light glimmered through the place. "Ah, here comes my murderer!" She trembled; her heart beat violently.

The door unclosed, when, instead of an assassin, a female entered the place, who, gently taking her hand, led her into an adjoining apartment, and bade her be of good cheer, for she had nothing to dread.

Rosalina knew not what to make of this reception, which was opposite to what she expected. Falling on her knees, she besought her conductress to inform her of the purpose for which she had been so forcibly been dragged to that ruinous place.

"For your own good," answered the woman; "therefore, fear nothing, and be composed; but come, take some refreshment," added she, "and after you have supped, I will shew you to your chamber."

"My chamber!" said Rosalina, surveying the place; "I had much rather remain with you."

"Well," said the woman, at the same time laying some wine and provisions on a table, "you shall do as you please; but come, eat, for doubtless you are hungry."

"I am but little desirous of food," replied Rosalina, "yet, since you are so kind, I will partake of some."

"Do," said the woman, "and suffer me to advise you to eat heartily."

Rosalina thanked her, but nevertheless ate very sparingly: the agitation of her mind had taken away all appetite.

"Come, lady, let me prevail upon you to take a cup of wine; it will greatly relieve your spirits," said the woman, at the same time filling a goblet.

Rosalina complied, and drank off a great part of it. The liquor contained a soporific infusion, the influence of whose lethargic powers was soon felt, for, in spite of all her efforts to the contrary, she sunk into a deep and profound sleep.

In this state she was conveyed by the woman to the magic chamber, and it was she whom Rosalva saw extended on the bed.

The marquis soon after arrived, and was, by the same woman, conducted through several dilapidated apartments to the presence of her mistress, the sorceress, who, on beholding him, said—"Barozzi has not failed, then? 'tis well. Come, are you prepared to see Rosalina bleed?"

"Why, is she here?" said he, in surprise; "she left the palazzo this morning early, and I concluded that by this time she was near La Rosa."

"Shallow mortal! did I not tell you she should be here to-night? She now lies buried in an enchanted sleep, from which she shall never wake more. Come, marquis," said she, seizing his hand, "draw forth your poniard, and lend it to me, for with that shalt thou see her die."

The marquis hesitated, when snatching the glittering weapon from his girld, she said—"Coward! what! you never dare murder but by proxy! Follow me, then, and see my hand strike the blow—see thy dagger pierce the heart of Rosalina."

"Oh, hold!" said he, I conjure thee hold! I have reflected on the deed, and I must own my conscience revolts at the bare idea."

"Conscience! ha, ha, ha! Barozzi's conscience! where was thy conscience when you fired the dwelling of her mother ? where, when you assassinated Fernando? where, when you seduced Marian? where, when you knew of her poverty, yet relieved it not? where, when her infant and yours perished with famine and disease? and, lastly, where was it when the aged De Valmont sunk beneath the dagger of the bravo? All these crimes of bloody murder are written in characters of fire; and oh, you fiends of hell, who keep the flaming register, say you that Barozzi has still *a conscience!*"

A loud laugh, or rather fiendlike yell, finished this enumeration of his offences, while Barozzi stood almost petrified with horror, fear, and remorse; when suddenly snatching the dagger from the hand of the hag, he exclaimed— "Though I am guilty of all those crimes, I will not add to the black catalogue the murder of Rosalina; therefore give her me, and in a convent she shall spend the remainder of her days."

"Never," said she. "Consent to this deed, or beware how you provoke me by a refusal. Beware, I say, for if you refuse, Rosalina shall to-morrow claim her lawful rights—the titles and honours of Barozzi."

"Damned fiend of hell!" exclaimed the marquis, "who thus stands in evidence of my guilt, if thou art more than mortal, I cannot hurt thee, but if not, why, then, this to thy heart!"

Thus saying, he aimed a heavy blow at her breast; but it was of no effect, for it was as impregnable as iron. The dagger instantly fell from his hand, while a horrid yell of triumph and exultation burst from the pale livid lips of the hag, who, catching him by the arm, said—"Well, marquis, are you now convinced of my power? nay, tremble not—be not dismayed; I do not blame you, for who would not, like you, fear, and wish to extirpate, a being like myself, who is so well acquainted with your crimes?"

In a commanding voice, she bade him follow. He, as if compelled by some hidden power, obeyed, leaving the dagger behind on the place where it had fallen, and where shortly after it was found by Rosalva. The sorceress led him through innumerable cells, and various apartments; often stopping, and dancing in mystic circles, with strange gestures, and frequently sent forth horrid and discordant yells, till she arrived at the door of the magic chamber, when stopping, she told him he would now behold Rosalina.

The marquis again named his wish of immuring her in a convent; but she was inflexible, and entered the room, when the dialogue ensued which was overheard by the wondering and dumbfounded Rosalva; when this noble youth, unable to hear more, and forgetting all precaution, heedlessly leaped into the apartment.

The feelings of the different parties may be better imagined than described. The sorceress fixed her eye earnestly upon the intruder—the marquis stood aghast, confounded and dismayed, for there was not a being on earth from whom he would have concealed his crimes more than he would from his son. Turning to the sorceress, he exclaimed—"Damned witch of hell! hast thou conjured up this boy to be a witness of his father's infamy?"

The wretched woman answered—"No! neither am I acquainted with the means by which he gained admittance; but, rash mortal," added she, and turning to the youth, "if you would avoid my vengeance, instantly be gone."

"Never!" said he, impetuously. "My father, my father, oh God! is he a murderer? Is my father a murderer?"

"He is," said the hag, with a ghastly smile, "a bloody murderer!"

"Oh, powers of bliss! do I hear aright? My lord, refute this charge, or again blast my ears with the confession of your guilt."

"Presumptuous boy!" said the marquis, "be gone! hasten home, and forget what thou has heard, or I will punish thy disobedience."

"No!" replied Rosalva, with manly dignity, "I will not be gone. I will not quit this spot till the mysterious conversation I overheard be explained. Who is Rosalina, that you should fear her? This witch says she will inherit the titles and honours of Barozzi. What are her claims? oh, tell me, father, I beseech you, tell me!"

The marquis's eyes rolled in frenzy; he bit his lips, but replied not.

"You called her the daughter of Fernando! who is this Fernando?"

"Your uncle! your murdered uncle, Fernando di Barozzi!" said the hag, in a hollow tone.

"Oh God! murdered! by whom? name him, and let me be cursed at once!"

The marquis advanced toward the hag, in a threatening posture, to forbid her replying.

"Nay, speak," said Rosalva; "but you need not—I read it in your looks of horror; and can a wretch like you—a fiend who so thirsts for the innocent blood of Rosalina, feel pain at the sight of a fratricide?" He shuddered, and supporting himself against the bed, said—"Leave me, marquis; let me not curse a parent; for, oh God! thy sight is hateful to me; a murderer!—my father a murderer!"

The frenzied marquis darted upon him, and seizing him by the throat, exclaimed—"Villain! darest thou tax me with my crimes? darest thou call my actions in question? Thou serpent! 'twas for thee I plunged my soul in sin—for thee I became what I am, to procure thee wealth and honours, and thou, base ingrate as thou art, hatest me for it."

Rosalva replied—"Here, my lord, here is your dagger; I found it within the walls of this dismal ruin, and which I searched in hopes of rescuing, or to save you from danger, not expecting to find you plotting with fiends of hell against the life of the most innocent and most lovely of beings. Take it, my lord—take it—and if you have pity, plunge it to my heart, for that moment you injure the precious life of Rosalina, I will follow, though my own hand shall strike the blow. Take it, marquis, and bury it my bosom, for I am weary of existence."

The marquis quitted his hold, and said—"Well, then, she shall not die, but spend her dys in the confines of a monastery."

"What! would you imprison her—bury her within a gloomy convent—entomb her alive! No! give her to my care, and let me convey her in safety from this infernal dwelling, and I will never name you more, but quit my native land, to wander in distant climes, an exile never again to return."

At this moment Rosalina awoke from her sleep, the somniferous draught having nearly expended its power, together with the disturbance in the apartment, which contributed in arousing her from lethargy. Starting from the bed, she beheld the surrounding objects with terror and dismay. "Oh, Virgin, save me," she cried, "for I am betrayed, and sold to destruction!" She clung to the sorceress, and in supplicating accents, cried—"Oh, don't kill me! I beseech you, in pity, spare my life!"

The hag turned her head, for she could not look in her innocent face; while Rosalva, almost wild with astonishment, gazed on this wondrous scene. "She shall not harm thee, lovely maid," said he, "for I will be thy safeguard, I, Rosalva, who once before had the happiness of being the instrument of thy preservation, and who now stands forth as thy champion; therefore, fear not, for no one shall injure a hair of thy head, without feeling the effects of my vengeance. I love you, lady—fondly love you; no other shall ever be Rosalva's bride, and Rosalina shall possess the honours of Barozzi."

"Degenerate boy!" said the marquis, "what is it I hear? will you take to your arms a beggar?"

"You forget yourself, my lord," returned the youth; "she is the lawful daughter of your brother—your elder brother. If Rosalina cannot accept my proffered love, I will become her advocate, proclaim her consanguinity to the world, place her in possession of all those honours which are her right by birth and title, regardless of the shame and ignominy that must overwhelm both you and me."

"You will! degenerate viper, you will! but I'll prevent your heroic intent," said the marquis, rushing towards Rosalina, with his hand uplifted, for the purpose of plunging his dagger in her breast, when Rosalva, his body suddenly interposing, received the weapon in his own, which laid him prostrate.

The guilty parent staggered, and throwing himself by the body of his son, beat his head against the floor in frantic desperation.

The sorceress seizing the hand of Rosalina, dragged her from the room.

"Oh, he is dying!" said the wretched girl; "he is dying, and for me! Oh Heaven! till now, I did not know I loved him. Oh, Rosalva! dear Rosalva! thy Rosalina soon will follow thee: and you, mysterious woman," said she to the sorceress, who still dragged her along, "you once warned me of danger, like a friend—ah, was it only to become my betrayer?"

"Silence, lady," said the hag, in a tone of sympathy, "I am your friend: fear not, but observe my directions; keep direct along this passage until you find a room on the left. Enter without dread, for there you will find the woman you saw before: wait with her until I appear; you then shall be hence in safety, for I swear to be your protectress."

Thus saying, she left her.

Rosalina then proceeded according to her directions, but on entering the room, she found not the woman, as she expected. She looked around, and seating herself, began to consider whether she should remain, or endeavour to make her escape; when suddenly the door unclosed, and a tall spectral female figure appeared, bearing in her hand a lamp. Unknowing of what she did, Rosalina rushed past, and pursuing her way through the passage and different turnings, had the good fortune to reach the hall, when the welcome light of the moon, just issuing from behind a cloud, and glimmering through the old decayed windows, discovered to her gladdened sight an aperture in one large enough to admit her body. Of this she immediately availed herself, and pressing through, in a few moments, to her great joy, she found herself in the forest. With hurried steps she fled along till her wearied limbs could no longer support her, and sinking with fatigue beneath a tree, she found herself unable of proceeding farther. In the greatest dread of being discovered, and dragged back to the infernal dwelling, she, with an aching heart, waited for the dawn of morning.

CHAPTER III
Tortures of the Guilty

THE MARQUIS, TO HIS GREAT JOY, found the wound he had given his son was not mortal, he having only fainted through loss of blood. With a palpitating heart he raised him from the floor, and, to his infinite pleasure, he shortly after opened his eyes.

Rosalva, by his writhing and sudden snatching of his breath, seemed to suffer greatly from the pain of his wound, but not so much as beholding the room vacated by the beloved object of his soul.—"Rosalina! Rosalina! oh, where is my Rosalina?" murmured he; "oh, give me my Rosalina!"

The hag at this moment entered, and applying something styptic to his wound, she, with a large scarf, bound it up. While this operation was performing, he asked her what she had done with Rosalina?

"She is safe," answered the hag, and casting an expressive eye at the marquis.

"Then you had best keep her so, for by my hopes of mercy, should either of you injure her, the Inquisition shall have cognizance of the same; but, my father, promise not to kill her, or else this woman shall not endeavour to prolong my wretched life."

"Silence, my child!" said the marquis, "and let every attention be paid to your wound, which was dealt by my mistaken hand, and I will promise all you wish. But can you forgive me, Rosalva?"

"Yes," said the youth, "for wounding me; but had your dagger met the breast for which it was intended, my bitter curses against the wicked perpetrator should have rung throughout this infernal habitation, mocking the imprecations of the dreadful fiends who here perform their orgies; and oh, those curses would have been pronounced against a father, the author of my existence!"

He now again sunk exhausted, while the marquis, divested of every fear, except for his recovery, said—"He faints; my son! my son! your death will drive me to despair—oh, how shall I get him conveyed home, for here he will perish for want of assistance?"

"Fear not," said Magdalena; "frame but a palpable story to account for your being here when they arrive, and I promise that you shall quickly have attendants to lend you aid, in which I will prove to you the potency of my skill."

Thus saying, she left the room, while Barozzi remained in anxious expectation of their appearance. So convinced was he of the hag's power, that he doubted not her word; and she proved herself as potent as he expected; for in less than an hour, Julio, his page, entered the apartment, accompanied by two woodmen.

"How wonderful!" exclaimed the marquis; "Julio, bearu up signor Rosalva; then tell me by what means you knew of my being here?"

"By means most truly strange; but you shall know all anon," said the page, nodding significantly; "let my young lord be carried home, then your excellenza shall hear the whole."

Barozzi was silent, while the woodmen, placing Rosalva on a litter brought for that purpose, bore him away. He then followed in company with Julio, to whom he said—"Now, youth, tell me how you knew of our being here, and how you came to be so ready, for I gave you permission to be absent three days?"

"Why, my lord, methought something haunted me, and I could not rest easy in the cottage of my mother; so I set out for the purpose of returning to the palazzo. When passing, with this intent, by the edge of the forest, on a sudden a strange woman appeared to me, who said—'Julio, your young lord lies wounded in the ruin, almost at the point of death; haste, and take with you assistance to bear him to the palazzo.' She instantly vanished, while I stood amazed, and unknowing how to act, or whether to credit it or not, for I scarcely could be persuaded but that I was in a dream. At last it struck my thoughts that my not being able to rest at home was a presagement of the evil which had been communicated to me in so strange and wonderful a manner; so I went to a hut and procured those two woodmen to come to your assistance, in the hopes of being handsomely rewarded."

"They shall," said the marquis, "and you, good Julio, too, shall be recompensed for your fidelity."

"Oh, my dear lord," said the youth, "name not that, for the pleasure I feel in thinking I have rendered you assistance is, of itself, more than a sufficient reward: but say, my lord, how came you into this horrid place, and how came my young lord so terribly wounded?"

The marquis felt greatly embarrassed by this inquiry, but endeavouring to put a good face on the matter, said—"I and my son having passed our day in the neighbourhood, late I the evening took a stroll in this forest; but we wandered so far, and night coming on, we were unable to find our way back. At last we happened to discover this ruin, which we thought was inhabited, and knocking at the gate, for the purpose of requesting shelter for the night, when we were instantly surrounded by robbers, whom we endeavoured to resist, and in the scuffle Rosalva received the wound which you see."

"Well, that is good," cried Julio.

"What is good?" said the marquis, surprised at this exclamation.

"Why, did not your lordship say that you and signor Rosalva walked into this forest?"

"Yes," answered the marquis; "why do you ask?"

"Because, my lord, yonder, tied to a tree, is the steed which my lord Rosalva generally rides; from that, any one would suppose that the signor came alone; but perhaps the witch who sent me with the woodmen, at the same time sent the horse, on purpose to carry my young lord." A sarcastic smile crossed his features, and a look of meaning glanced from his eye, as he unbound the animal, and led it to the confounded marquis, who now had no doubt that this was the method by which Rosalva came to the ruin, though he had before attributed it to the sorcery of Magdalena. He knew not what answer to make to the shrewd youth, who seemed to enjoy and triumph in his confusion; therefore he avoided replying, and in silence proceeded till they reached a gondola, which carried them to the palazzo, where medical assistance being procured, the wound of Rosalva was pronounced not dangerous, provided a fever did not ensue.

This was a cordial balsam to the disordered mind of the marquis, who felt more remorse at this sad event than for all the united crimes he had committed in his life. He never quitted the chamber of his son, even for a moment, but nightly watched by his side. At last unfavourable symptoms appeared, and in spite of all the physician's efforts to resist it, a fever ensued, attended with a delirium.

Rosalva, in his fits of frenzy, would call upon his father, bidding him beware of shedding more blood; then he would threaten the sorceress with the Inquisition; then he would call Rosalina by the name of martyred innocent, to the great astonishment of the domestics, and confusion of the marquis, who, fearing the incoherent expressions of his son might excite suspicion, undertook the office of attending him solely himself, and strictly forbade any one, except the physicians, approaching the chamber, so great was his precaution. Guess, then, how terrible must have been his dismay, when the marchioness, on her return, without having her arrival announced, or the least ceremony whatever, entered directly the patient's apartment with abruptness, and seeing him wounded, testified her great surprise; then addressing the marquis in a manner rather stern, said—"My lord marchese, what is the meaning of all this, for I cannot comprehend it? Indeed, the complicated events which have so recently transpired, utterly confound me. Do you know, my lord, that my ward, Rosa, when on our journey, was forced from the carriage by ruffians, employed, without doubt, by some enemy? Have you heard any tidings of her?"

As she put this question to him, she fixed her eye steadily on the marquis, who turning pale with conscious guilt, faltered out—"I—I—heard of her!—what do you mean by asking me?"

"Nay, my lord, be not offended," said she; "I only thought that rumour might have brought you some intelligence; nothing more; but I have returned for the purpose of having the matter properly investigated; for I will employ all the officers of justice in Venice, so resolved am I to have her discovered, in which, if I am fortunate enough to succeed, the villainous perpetrator of the crime shall meet the condign punishment of our laws."

Barozzi became agitated; the marchioness perceived it, and was resolved, as soon as her nephew became sensible of her presence, to question him concerning his hurt, of which she had heard a strange incomprehensible account; neither could she help thinking but that it was in some measure connected with the fate of Rosalina.

When she had retired to her chamber, (the same which had before been appropriated to her service,) while the physicians visited Rosalva, Paulina, who attended, said—"My lady, what does your excellenza think Julio, the page, told Erasmo? Why, my lady, he said, that an enchantress appeared to him, and bade him hasten to some ruins in the forest we passed, for that my lord Rosalva were there; the latter she said was expiring: so Julio went and procured some woodmen to go to their assistance. How very strange! was it not, my lady?"

"An enchantress!" said the marchioness, as the strange character which she had seen at the mask recurred to her mind; "I can scarcely believe it; fetch the page hither; I will question him concerning the affair."

Paulina departed for that purpose, when quickly returning, she said Julio had fled from the palazzo, and borne away with him some papers belonging to my lord, who was almost distracted at the loss. "He has also taken," said the girl, "a small box, originally the property of the late lord Fernando, in which, I fancy, there are deeds and bonds, and I don't know what; but this I know, that the marquis has dispatched servants every way in pursuit, who have orders to bring him back, either dead or alive."

"You astonish me," said the marchioness; "but indeed I observed, when I first came here, there was something about that youth which I did not like; he seemed to pry into every body's actions, and used to fix his eyes so earnestly upon the poor child who is missing, that I almost suspect he had some concern in her disappearance; and yet that is impossible, for too surely she is in the power of more potent enemies than Julio."

Thus did she canvass this strange affair, till she again sought the chamber of Rosalva, whom, to her great sorrow and surprise, she found raving on the subject of the wonderful occurrences that had so recently transpired; but from his unconnected words she could gather nothing that might serve to develop the mystery, but only increase her amazement.

The marquis was compelled to leave the chamber of his son, on account of the great alarm he felt at the absence of the page, and the robbery. The box he knew contained letters, deeds, and documents, of great consequence to his late brother, which he feared might lead to a discovery of his marriage, and other circumstances that he could wish were buried in oblivion; indeed he had often been on the point of examining the contents, but was deterred by conscious guilt, which, when he ever essayed to open it, palsied no riches, he desisted from his attempts. That Julio, of all things else, should take a fancy to this, and leave untouched so many valuables, whose intrinsic worth were greatly superior, was to the marquis an incident of great astonishment, for he placed such reliance on the boy's integrity, that he would have confided any thing to his care. Indeed, the way in which he met with him, the great indulgence he received, and the youth's consequent ingratitude, raised in the breast of Barozzi much indignation, and had he been taken while this fit lasted, he doubtless would have sacrificed him to his resentment.

The marquis was now the most wretched of human beings; he every moment dreaded detection, and each step he heard approaching his apartment he feared were the officers of justice coming to apprehend his person, for he knew the servants had noticed the expressions of his son, from which, though very incoherent, a sufficiency might be selected, that would authorize them in laying against him an information upon suspicion of murder. Of this he was well aware, which caused him to pass his time in the greatest state of agony. The servants lurked about him, regardless of his orders, eyeing all his actions. An awful dulness reigned throughout the palazzo, except when, at intervals, its silence was broken by the shrieks of Rosalva, whose disorder, however, at the expiration of a few more days, took a favourable turn, and gave hopes to his afflicted aunt and wretched father. The latter had again ventured to the ruin, which he explored in hopes of discovering Rosalina; but all was desolate and solitary; no human form met his eye; from which he concluded, she must have perished beneath the poniard of the sorceress. This he would have rejoiced at, but he felt at a loss how to appease his son, whom he knew, soon as his strength allowed, would make every search for her recovery, and no doubt criminate him, as an accessary in her disappearance.

Rosalva now slowly recovered, and one day, when he was able to support himself in a chair by the side of the marchioness, he motioned the attendants to withdraw; then, with a feeble, faltering voice, he thus addressed her—"My dear aunt, did you ever know Fernando di Barozzi?"

"Most assuredly I did; the marchese's eldest brother," replied she; "why do you ask? and why have you so often uttered his name? he could never have been known to you."

"No; but, my dear madam, he is our Rosalina's father."

The marchioness gazed on him, and began to think a return of his disorder caused this strange expression.

He guessed her thoughts, but proceeding, said—"Pray, madam, how did he die?"

"He was assassinated in the forest," replied she.

"Oh God! do I live to hear it? Know you who was the instigator of this hellish crime?" His eyes rolled wildly as he asked this.

The marchioness replied—"No, but it was supposed, as he was never known to have any particular attachment for our sex, that it was to revenge some neglect or offered slight."

"Ah, madam, too surely it was not a woman's work, which Rosalina full well knows to be true."

"Rosalina, did you say? how should she know it? and what did you mean by saying she was the daughter of Fernando?"

Rosalva now imparted to her all that happened at the ruin.

The marchesa, during this recital, was dumb with horror, and at the conclusion she clasped her hands together, and ejaculated—"Oh, the Virgin deliver us from such sin! but how, my dear nephew, came you to be wounded?"

He was unwilling to criminate his wretched sire, so answered it was inflicted by the hand of the sorceress.

"Indeed! and where is the dear girl all this time?"

"Alas!" he replied, "I know not, as to the truth; but my father says she is safe within a convent." He sighed, while the tears found way to his eyes, and cried—"Oh, hapless maid! beloved Rosalina! heiress to the honours of Barozzi! you shall possess your inheritance, though I become a beggar."

"A beggar you can never be," said the marchioness; "you know I always garded you as my intended heir, which I promise you shall be: but, my dear nephew, there must be some mistake in this; Fernando was never married, but always in a state of celibacy; add to this, she lived with her father when the villains sought her, beneath whose daggers he met his death; this is a contradiction to your account. But endeavor to compose yourself, and if you can prevail on the marquis to disclose to you the place of her concealment, my consent shall not be wanting to your union, even were she no other than the daughter of a peasant, but that I am pretty well sure she is not. There is a mystery in the fate of that hapless girl which neither you or I can develop: but say, Rosalva, would you take her for your wife?"

"My wife!" a gleam of joy shot across his pallid face, which was instantaneously succeeded by a look of the deepest despair, as he uttered, in frenzied accents—"Oh God! Rosalina can never wed the son of her father's murderer! the sorceress accused him, and I heard him confess the horrid deed. Would I had died long ere that dreadful night, for now my life will ever be most truly miserable!"

The marchioness shuddered, and when she quitted the apartment, gave to the marquis notice of her intention to leave Venice immediately, which she did, without even seeing him. So great was her disgust towards him, that she never again could endure his sight; but she left a billet for Rosalva, entreating him, as soon as his strength would permit, to follow her to La Rosa.

The marquis felt the full force of this slight, which he attributed to its real cause, his becoming the object of her suspicions. His life now was become truly burdensome, and had he possessed worlds, he would have freely given them to recal his crimes; but, as this was impossible, he was determined to meet the issue, let the event be what it would, with firmness. Of this he soon stood in need, for in a few days after he was cited to appear at the bar of justice, to answer a charge laid against him for committing murder on the person of his brother, Fernando di Barozzi.

Chapter IV
The Hospitable Shepherds

ROSALINA LAY IN AGONY, till the rising sun, tinging the tops of the trees with its golden rays, announced the new-born day. She arose, but knew not what course to pursue, or whither to fly for assistance: should she be even fortunate enough to discover a habitation, she thought her appearance, which was now become strange and wild, might subject her to insult. Her hair was dishevelled, her robe rent in many places, and her arms torn and scratched by the briars that grew around the Gothic window, which greatly impeded her escape from the ruin; but so eager was she to quit that dreadful place, that she felt not at the moment the wounds they made.

On her quitting Venice, she had about her two or three pieces of gold; she felt in her pocket, and had the good fortune to find them there still, (as the ruffians had not rifled her person,) with the ring on her finger. She took it off, and tying it up with her little treasure, secured them in her garments.

Almost parching with thirst, she cast her eyes anxiously around, in hopes of beholding some rivulet, and searching strictly, her ears were greeted by a gurgling stream, which rushing down a gentle eminence, glided in murmurs along the declivity, and gave an appearance truly pleasing, and the most picturesque imaginable. Rosalina proceeded to its brink; she drank from the runnel, which greatly refreshed her drooping spirits, and bathed her arms, whose wounds appeared angry, and festering for want of care; then divesting herself of a loose scarf that she wore across her shoulders, while the transparent brook served for her mirror, she bound beneath it her disordered tresses, and dropped upon its glassy surface tears as crystalline and pellucid as itself.

After thus adjusting her dress, she ascended one of the highest steeps, in hopes of descrying some woodman's hut, where she might procure a morsel of bread to appease the attacks of hunger, which now assailed her forcibly; but no such place met her longing eye. She descended, and again proceeded, unknowing whither to bend her weary steps.

At length, growing sick and faint for want of food, she sunk upon a grassy bank. She had not long remained in this situation, when the sound of soft music wafted along the air attracted her attention.

Starting up, she endeavoured to discover the source from whence it came. At last, to her great joy, she beheld a youthful shepherd playing upon his pipe, regardless of every care, except attendance to his fleecy charge, which was quietly grazing at his side.

Rosalina stopped, in hesitation for a moment whether to advance or recede; but summoning her courage, and stifling her innate delicacy, that would scarcely suffer her to appear in her present garb before a stranger, she went close to him, and in a gentle manner, said—"Friend."

The youth instantly snatched the pipe from his mouth, to listen to the superior melody of her enchanting voice; but when he beheld, he was struck with admiration, and rising, saluted her in a manner the most respectful. Indeed the lad did not at first sight know whether she was a mortal, or a nymph of the woods or sky, whom, by his ravishing notes, he had called down to the earth, and with his cap in his hand, he begged to know her commands.

"Friend," said she, while pride and suffering nature combatted within her gentle breast, "have you any thing in your scrip which you can give me to eat, for I am well nigh famished?"

The youth replied not by words, but opening his bag of homely fare, spread it before her on the grass, inviting her to feed heartily, which she did, and uncorking his leathern bottle, poured out a horn of simple wine; this he presented with great good-nature, at the same time gazing on her most earnestly, to the great confusion of Rosalina, who, to break the prevailing silence, asked a few innocent questions, and amongst others, if he could inform her of any cottage where she might repose her weary form, and be sheltered from the heat of the noontide sun?

"My father and mother live hard by," said the shepherd; "if it would please you, lady, to go to them, they will let you have a couch to rest on, and make you welcome to whatever their house contains. I have a sister too, who will render you every assistance in her power, as you are distressed. I beg pardon, lady," said he, confused, "but you seem to me to be in distress."

"I am indeed, good youth," answered Rosalina, as the tears started to her eyes; "I am in great distress."

The shepherd boy then called his dog, and gathering up his flock, left the faithful animal as a safeguard, while he conducted our poor heroine to his parents' humble cot.

The little family were enjoying a repast of fruits and milk at the door, beneath an arbour of twisted jessamine and vine, whose intertwining tendrils and luxuriant foliage served as a canopy; while the purple store, which in clusters hung around, gave pleasure to the sight, and yearly gladdened their hearts by the produce of their luscious beverage.

When they beheld Rosalina, all of them instantaneously arose; but she, in a voice of sweetness, bade them resume their seats, which they did, after a little hesitation, gazing alternately at each other and at the fair stranger, who addressed them as follows:--"Friends, I doubt not but my appearance must excite your surprise, for it cannot be very prepossessing: in escaping from an inveterate foe, my dress became thus disordered, and my arms thus lacerated: this implacable enemy, from what cause I know not, still pursues me, and I am compelled to fly for my life. Will you, for a short time, afford me a concealment in your dwelling, until I can hear from a dear friend near Pyrano, who will reward your hospitality? indeed I am not absolutely without the means of affording you some recompense myself."

Thus saying, she produced one of her pieces of gold, and offered it to the old shepherd, who replied—"When we have served you, 'twill be time to think of a reward; in the meanwhile, make yourself easy, for you are heartily welcome to what our humble cot can afford, for though I am but poor, yet the door of Alberto never was shut against the unfortunate."

Rosalina thanked him for his kindness, while her welcome was repeated by the wife and daughter; the latter a pretty girl of eighteen, called Marcelina, and the former a good honest housewife, of about forty, who strove, in her plain way, to express her sorrow at the misfortunes of our heroine, who was soon after conducted to a couch, rather mean, but exceedingly wholesome and clean, and nature being almost exhausted, she quietly sunk into a profound, refreshing slumber; while Marco, the youth she had first beheld, returned to his flock, deeply interested in the fate of the fair stranger, whose image he could not for a moment banish from his mind, but earnestly longed for the evening's approach, that he might again behold her.

When Rosalina had withdrawn, the honest cottagers entered into the following dialogue:—

"Well," cried Marcelina, "of all the pretty creatures I ever saw, this surely is the most so; and when I tucked her up comfortably in bed, she thanked me so kindly, and the tears rand down her cheeks in such a way, that I declare she made me cry too. I wonder who or what she is! I really should, of all things, like to know."

"I dare say you would," replied old Alberto, "for your curiosity is always afloat."

"Ah! and well it may," cried Beatrice; "'tis enough to make the child curious, when a person comes from no one knows where, but springs up, as a body may say, out of the very bowels of the earth; and indeed;" added she, with a very important look, "Marco said as much, for he told me slyly, that he never saw from whence she came, but thought she might be a fairy or sprite."

"Ha, ha, ha! don't you be so silly, wife. A fairy! egad, I don't know which is the simplest, the boy or you. If she is a fairy, how came those scratches on her arms, to which you applied some of your famous basalm? No, no, she is real flesh and blood, I warrant; besides, fairies seldom eat with mortals, and she, I believe, partook of some of Marco's fare in the forest, and drank some of his sour wine; so, if she is a fairy, she is a very condescending one at least. Ha, ha, ha!"

"Well, well, you need not laugh," said Beatrice, somewhat piqued, "for I am not the first that fairies have visited, indeed, husband; but however, fairy or mortal, she is welcome to what our roof affords, and I only wish, for her sake, it was better; but to such as it is, she is heartily welcome."

"That she is, I know," said Alberto, pleased with his wife's hospitality; and giving her a hearty kiss—"Beatrice had always a heart to feel for the unfortunate, or else I never should have loved thee so well as I have."

This well-timed praise soothed the rather nettled feelings of the superstitious housewife, who, addressing Marcelina, said, as the stranger's clothes were almost tattered to pieces, she had better ask her, when she awoke, if she would like to put on some of hers, "for," added she, "your last new gown will, I think, fit her; and your straw had will look very pretty over her fine dark eyes; though I think your eyes are as handsome as hers, though I should not say it, because I am your mother; yet I do say it, that your face is as pretty as any signora's in Venice."

"Silence, wife!" said Alberto; "you'll make the girl so vain, she'll not know what to do with herself. Do you think she can't see? what do you suppose she looks so often for in the glass, fi it wasn't to see her face? It pleases her, no doubt."

"Ah, and somebody else too," said her joyful mother: "Reuben loves her, and this day begged of me that he might have her for his wife. I told him that I would ask you, and, of course, you've no objection, for Reuben is well off in the world, for he has flocks and vineyards, and a cottage too."

"Well," replied Alberto, "if the girl loves him, I can have nothing to say against it; what say you, Marcelina?"

The blushing girl looked on the ground, and said—"You know, father, I love Reuben ever since he sought my kid that strayed a long way in the forest; and when he found it, he brought it to me: then he spoke so kind, and said—'if I had not the good fortune to have found it, you should have had one from my flock, for I cannot bear to see you weep, dear Marcelina.' Now this was so good, that of course I tendered him my best thanks, and afterwards I—"

"Afterwards you loved him?" said her father.

The blushing girl replied not, but nodded an affirmation, while her little heart bounded with joy. She then left the room to look out her habiliments, for the purpose of offering them to Rosalina.

The latter slept for the space of several hours, and awoke greatly refreshed, when looking on the chair, she beheld Marcelina's best attire, placed, as she conjectured, for the service of herself; but not choosing to make to free, she gently knocked, and the young shepherdess appearing, in a gentle voice asked if she could do any thing to serve her? "for look, lady," added she, "here are my clothes, if you will put them on, while my mother and myself make yours clean and tidy, fit for your ladyship to wear."

Marcelina concluded the offer of her services by a low curtsey, of which Rosalina gladly availed herself; and when she was arrayed in the russet gown, and bodice laced up with blue, recalled to her memory the happy days she had passed with her father in their own little cottage; and while the tears fast rolled down her cheeks, she was half resolved to return to honest Gerrard in the Valley of Vintagers, instead of writing to the marchioness. "Good Heavens!" said she, "what a chequered scene have my days represented since my dear father fell! Was he my father? He was—he must have been my sire, and yet Rosalva said I was heiress of Barozzi, the child of Fernando, brother to the marquis! if that indeed be true, there is a wonderful mystery hangs over my early days. Rosalva, dear youth, who twice has saved me from death, dost thou still live? or has thou fallen a martyr to thy nobleness of mind? Ah no, for guardian angels, that watch over goodness like thine, will save and protect thee from farther danger; but I, alas! though I've now escaped, must one day fall beneath the persecutor's hand, unpitied and unknown. No father shall mourn over my grave, no mother's tears shall moisten the pillow of my deathbed, nor wilt thou, dear Rosalva, ever know that thy Rosalina so tenderly loves. Were I to apply to justice, what could I do? who would believe me? No one would stand against so powerful an opponent as the marquis; and though his dagger was raised against my breast, no one witnessed it but Rosalva and the mysterious woman. The former could not appear to criminate his father, and the latter would not, though she once professed to be my friend; but her conduct afterwards proved her wicked, and that she deals in magic was evident, by her wand and the wonderful chamber. 'Tis also plain Barozzi must have had recourse to her aid, to get me into his power; but then how the dear youth who stood my champion came into that infernal dwelling, is beyond my penetration."

This soliloquy was interrupted by Marcelina, who came to tell her their evening's repast was almost ready, and that her mother expected her to partake of it; then looking at her dress, expressed her admiration at the method in which the body and coat were laced. "Well, lady," said she, "how much it does become you! I declare I shall always like it better than ever, now I see how nice it looks upon you; but then your waist is so nice and slim, and your neck so white and fair, while mine is sunburnt, that I never can expect to look so beautiful in it as you; and I dare say Reuben will soon perceive the difference between us."

A half-smothered sigh escaped her lips as she uttered this, which Rosalina observing, said—"Pray, who is Reuben?"

"Reuben, lady!—oh, Reuben is—is—Reuben."

"So I should suppose," said her interrogator, smiling at her confusion; "but why do you think he will make any remarks upon our difference? and what if he were?"

"Why, lady, because Reuben loves me, and says I am the prettiest girl in all this part of the country. To be sure, there are not many hereabouts, and so, perhaps, what he said might be true; but he had not seen you, and when he does, I fear he will no longer think poor Marcelina handsome."

"Fear not," returned Rosalina, "for I may not stay very long with you, and whenever Reuben comes, if you think me so dangerous, I will keep out of his sight."

"No, no, I don't desire that; but I am sure he, or any one else, must be blind not to see who is the prettiest. Come, lady, and make yourself free with our homely fare."

She tripped down the steps, leaving our heroine to follow at her pleasure, who mentally exclaimed, as she thought of the foregoing conversation—"So I find the bosom of an obscure forest maid is as susceptible of jealousy as the first lady's who figures in the most elevated sphere."

She now descended to the lower apartment, where she found the good folks seated beside a table covered with a clean napkin, on which were placed their wholesome viands, with part of a kid cheese and brown bread, a plate of fine grapes, and a flask of their best old wine, which had been saved by Alberto for some particular occasion.

She was invited to join them with a hearty welcome, and sitting down, endeavoured to please them, by doing as much honour as possible to the regale, eating with a tolerable appetite, quenching her thirst with some fine milk, which Marcelina served out in a clean earthen bowl.

After their frugal meal was ended, they removed into the garden, and remained in the open air till the shades of evening drew on, when Rosalina strayed into a distant part, to indulge in solitude those thoughts that would intrude upon her mind, maugre the good intentions of her host and hostess to dissipate them.

She stood leaning on a fence which enclosed the garden, looking at the fine surrounding scenery, when her cogitation was disturbed by some one, ere she was aware of it, putting his arms round her neck, and giving her a smacking kiss. She turned round indignantly, and with a voice and look of majesty, which petrified the intruder, demanded the cause of such insolence.

The man stared for a moment, and then, without answering a word, rushed down the nearest avenue that led to the cottage, while Rosalina, dismayed, and wondering at such unpardonable conduct, followed. When she came within sight of the door, she beheld him in earnest conversation with her host and family, who seemed to laugh very heartily at what he was saying.

Marcelina seeing her approach, flew to meet her, saying—"Ah, lady, you look angry, but do forgive poor Reuben."

"Reuben!" said Rosalina.

"Yes, lady, 'twas Reuben that kissed you, but I dare say he would not have given a pin to have done so, only," said Marcelina, blushing at her blunder, "lady, he thought it was I, because he saw your back, and knew the gown."

Rosalina smiled at the mistake, and holding forth her hand to Marcelina, said—"Tell your lover I am not offended, now I know the innocent cause."

"Ah but, lady, do tell him so yourself; yonder he stands, and he will not rest until you have pronounced his forgiveness."

Our heroine suffered the shepherdess to lead her to Reuben, who, with a multitude of bows and apologies, said he hoped she'd pardon the liberty he had taken unintentionally, "for you must know, lady, I came in the back way, and seeing you stand there, I thought to myself this is Marcelina; I will surprise her; and so I kissed you in her stead; but when you turned round, perceiving the face of a stranger, I verily thought I was bewitched, as I knew the garment and hat to be Marcelina's, for that blue ribband was a gift of mine, and the straw of my plaiting—was it not, Marcelina?"

"Ah, that it was, Reuben," said she, smiling; "but you need not say any thing farther about it, for the signora will think no more of it; so she told me."

Reuben bowed, and again began a whole string of apologies, till Rosalina, finding he could not be easy in her presence, good-naturedly withdrew, to the great joy of Reuben.

Alberto having given his consent to their union, fixed that day se'nnight for their marriage. This was communicated to Rosalina by the intended bride, who said she hoped she'd not go before the arrival of that time, but would grace the ceremony with her presence.

Our heroine thanked her, and after indulging the pretty Marcelina, by praising the person and manners of her destined husband, retired to her chamber to compose a letter, which she intended to dispatch by the first opportunity to the marchioness La Rosa.

Chapter V
The Fugitives' Return

POOR MARCO, ONCE SO ANXIOUS to behold, was now forced to avoid her presence, for he found he loved her, and no longer doubting but that she was by birth a lady, could not indulge the hope of calling her his own. After returning from his occupation in the forest, he would take his evening repast, then wandering in the garden, ruminate on his hopeless passion, which he strove to conquer; but in vain, for the stranger had taken possession of his heart. His faithful dog no longer received his caresses; his pipe hung by his side neglected; and nothing dwelt in his thoughts but the image of Rosalina, who, endeavouring to make herself as little burthensome as possible to the honest cottagers, spent her hours in making ornaments for the decoration of Marcelina on her wedding-day.

Thus passed the time, till one night a gentle tap at the door gave signal of some one's approach. Alberto opened it, and Rosalina recollected the voice of Julio, who was requesting shelter till the morning: her colour forsook her cheeks, and she was near fainting when she heard her host bid him welcome. She sat like the image of death, as she had no doubt but he was searching for her.

The youth followed the hospitable shepherd into the cottage, seemingly both weak and faint. This Beatrice perceiving, offered him her chair, as being the most easy. He thanked her, and then said—"Good people, have you seen a lady, within these two or three days, pass this way, dressed in white?"

The peasants looked confused, and fixed their eyes upon the agitated Rosalina.

The quick glance of the page followed their sight, and in spite of the disguise, instantly recognised her; when starting up, he exclaimed—"'Tis she! she lives! she's found! Oh, blessed Virgin, accept my thanks!"

He sunk on his knees, and raised his hands to Heaven, while Rosalina expected every moment to be surrounded, and dragged into the presence of the marquis.

Alberto, seeing her alarm, cried out—"Fear not, lady, no one shall harm thee. At your peril, I charge you not to touch her; she is under my protection;

therefore, abuse not my hospitality while beneath my roof, for I will not tamely stand by to see her delivered into the hands of her enemies."

"Her enemies!" said the youth; "her enemies are Julio's. I sought you as a bosom friend. Rosalina; listen to me; you must immediately return to Venice!"

"Return!" said she; "oh, never, never; what! return to Barozzi?"

"Fear him not; he can no longer harm you," said Julio.

"What, is he dead then?" asked she.

"No, he still lives; but this is foreign to the purpose. Was the memory of your father ever dear to you?"

"Was it! oh Heaven, bear me witness!"

"Then you must appear as the accuser of Barozzi."

"What, Rosalva's father!" said she; "oh, I cannot!"

"Recollect, Rosalina," replied Julio, "that he murdered yours; and will you suffer a childish passion that you entertain for his son to prevent you from punishing a homicide—a dealer in sorcery and hellish spells? If you say you revere the memory of him to whom you owe your existence, delay not, but accompany me to Venice."

"Go with you, Julio! how do I know to the contrary but you may deceive me? Are not you a confidential servant to the marquis? Then why attempt to impose upon me by feigning to sympathize at my misfortunes?"

"If," said the page, seizing her hand, "the aged Ferrand was ever dear to you, or if you have been taught by him to remember your unfortunate mother, do not skreen from the hand of justice a villain—the worst of villains, who, in cool blood, can murder and destroy! Oh, do not, I conjure you, Rosalina!"

"Strange young man!" said she; "how know you all this? How can you tell that Ferrand St. Almo was Fernando di Barozzi?"

"They were not the same," replied he.

"Then how can I be heiress to the honours of the marchese, or wherefore does he fear me?"

"Ferrand was not your father, but your grandsire," said the page.

"Oh, then I surely am Fernando's child, and kinswoman to Rosalva! Then can I wound his noble heart, by appearing against his father? Oh, Julio, does he still survive? does he still exist?"

"He does," replied the page.

"The blessed Virgin receive my thanks! Julio, that wound was received in my defence."

"I know it was," replied the page, "intended by his guilty father for your breast. Can you then, knowing him to be so vile a wretch, even for a moment hesitate in bringing him to condign punishment? Will you not, when the morning dawns, suffer me to conduct you to Venice?"

"Oh," said the wretched girl, "I know not how to act."

The page then seizing her hand, in an impassioned manner exclaimed—"Oh, Rosalina! beloved Rosalina!"

She started, imagining Julio entertained a passion for her person, and by stratagem was endeavouring to get her in his power, but, by this unguarded action, had betrayed himself. Under this supposition, she resolved not to entrust herself with him, and rose from her seat, while the confounded youth seemed sinking to the ground, overpowered with confusion at his precipitant, unguarded manner.

Old Alberto looked on him with an eye of anger, and Marco with envy. Beatrice and Marcelina had, from the foregoing conversation, concluded that their guest was at least a marchioness, and with a thousand apologies for their not being able to discover her nobility, entreated her pardon for having used so little ceremony.

Our heroine was not in the humour to listen to their ill-timed excuses, but turning to the page, in a voice of resentment, said—"'Tis well, youth; I now plainly perceive your flimsy artifice; you are not well skilled in deception, or prudence would have kept a guard upon your actions till you had gained me entirely in your power."

Thus saying, she retired to her chamber, in spite of his efforts and entreaties to the contrary; but ere long, Marcelina followed, and gave such a description of his unhappiness at her anger, that she was induced to return, when the offender addressed her as follows:—"Lady Rosalina, I am exceedingly sorry that you should impute my desire of serving you to a premeditated design of insult, which. Heaven bear me witness, was foreign to my intention. I no longer request you to accompany me to Venice, but that you will suffer this good peasant and his son to conduct you; under their escort you need not fear any danger. You may procure a carriage in the adjoining valley, and here is a purse containing a sum sufficient to defray the expences. You will pardon this liberty, and if you do not wish the shades of your departed parents to look down and condemn your improper lenity, fail not to attend the public tribunal that is to be held, in two or three days from this period, and declare all you know of the marquis's diabolical conduct towards yourself." He now assumed a tone of command, and said—"Marchioness di Barozzi, will you follow my injunction?"

The half-irresolute Rosalina, struck by his singular method of address, promised compliance.

Julio now took her hand, and respectfully pressed it to his lips; then turning to his host, begged to be accommodated with a corner to repose in for the night, which the old shepherd showing to him, he retired.

Rosalina now began to repent the extorted promise, but finding she ought to perform it, she agreed that Alberto should accompany her on the following morning, and that he should rise early, for the purpose of hiring a carriage.

At this arrangement, Marcelina seemed rather discontented; but on Rosalina's promising to return ere the day appointed for her nuptials, she endeavoured to set her heart at rest.

Our heroine once more returned to her chamber, but not to sleep. Julio's strange conduct, and his earnest entreaties to prevail on her attendance at the ensuing trial—that he could seem to feel for the wrongs she had suffered, and how he should be acquainted with so many different circumstances of her fate, were enigmas she could not solve; but when she reflected on his words—that a parent's death ought to be avenged, she could not but acknowledge the justice of the observation; and though she had never known either of them, she felt that as an injured daughter, she was in duty bound to prosecute the murderer of her father. Thus determined, she offered up a fervent prayer to the Virgin, to support her with fortitude under the trial, and then endeavoured to address herself to sleep; but in vain, for with her eyes fixed upon the humble lattice, she waited for the approach of morn.

Soon as the ruddy goddess, peeping from her eastern chamber, shed her bright influence o'er the shepherd's cot, Alberto went in quest of a carriage, and soon returning, our heroine, Julio, and himself, (Marco, not being sufficiently reconciled to the idea of losing the beloved object of his soul, pleaded illness as an excuse for not attending,) set forth from the cottage, to proceed to the valley, where the carriage waited for them, and their departure was accompanied by the prayers of Beatrice and Marcelina for their success.

Soon as they reached the appointed place, they entered the carriage, and the driver giving his whip to the horses, they with all possible speed came in sight of the city. On the outskirts, Julio alighted from the vehicle, giving to Alberto a direction where to proceed to, at the same time promising to be with them without fail by the evening.

The carriage then went forward, and Rosalina shrunk close behind, to avoid a discovery. At length the driver stopped at the place to which he had been directed, where they found their arrival looked for with anxiety. Our heroine procured fresh apparel, as the dress of Marcelina was too rusticated for her to wear in Venice, which was more than usually thronged with nobility, attracted by curiosity to witness the extraordinary trial.

In the evening, Julio made his appearance, to whom Rosalina said—"Now, youth, of what importance can my evidence prove? I never knew my father, therefore what I may alledge against the culprit can be of very little avail."

Julio answered—"You must wait till you are called upon; then answer as your truth and honour, or the reverence you owe to the memory of your parents, may dictate."

Rosalina admitted the propriety of this procedure, and waited for the important day with a degree of expectation mingled with dread.

In the mean time, Julio endeavoured to rally her spirits, and prevent her from thinking so incessantly on the unhappy youth Rosalva, who, she had no doubt, was nearly distracted at this public disgrace of his father.

CHAPTER VI
Wonderful Occurrences

THE WRETCHED BAROZZI, now an object of pity, passed his hours in all the bitterness of despair and guilt: he dreaded the approaching trial, as he had no doubt of the issue proving against him; neither could he endure to meet the eye of his son, who cursed the hour that gave him birth, and wished he had perished beneath the poniard, rather than live to witness such an indelible stain of infamy to blot a line of ancestry hitherto so illustrious. This, added to the fear he entertained for his father's life, nearly drove him to madness. In some of his calm moments, he'd call upon the name of his dear Rosalina, saying—"Beloved, yet unfortunate maid, surely thou wilt not appear against my parent—my guilty, but miserable parent!"

On the morning of trial he shut himself in his apartment, and waited the result in a gloomy kind of stupor, with a dagger before him, inwardly resolved, if his father's infamy were proved, not to outlive the event, for he could ill brook to be a wretched object for the unfeeling world to treat with scorn.

In the mean time, the guilty marchese was led to the bar, and his accusation being read, he was called upon to declare what he had to say against this dreadful charge. In a faltering voice he pleaded innocence.

Rosalina sat in an obscure part of the court, where she had been placed by Julio, watching all that passed with anxious eye, and a heart throbbing with various sensations. Near her was placed Alberto, who served as her protector.

The marquis, attempting to assume a tone of dignity before the vast concourse of nobles there assembled to witness this important scene, haughtily demanded the name of his accuser.

Rosalina started and shrunk back, fearing she might be called upon, when the president summoned the evidence to appear in court, and to the amazement and terror of our heroine, she beheld the assassin Roldon, who fixed his eyes on the marquis, while the latter started aghast at the sight of this unexpected adversary, and could scarcely withstand the sudden shock.

The bravo seemed to enjoy his evident alarm, and exclaimed—"My lords, I am the man who struck the first murderous blow aimed at the heart of Fernando di Barozzi, to which act I was induced, together with my comrade, by a rich reward from his brother, who now is before you."

"'Tis false!" said the marquis.

"Nay, my lord," replied Roldon, calmly, "why should I utter falsehood? I am a prisoner, as well as yourself, and as there is no chance of either of us escaping, I have confessed my crimes; do you do the same, and, like me, throw yourself upon the mercy of the court."

The miserable Augustino gnashed his teeth on hearing this, and could scarce contain his fury within the bounds of moderation, by the bravo thus reducing him to a level with himself, who was a very outcast of society, and turning to the president, he cried—"How, my lord, am I arraigned on the evidence of a wretch like this? Is this your only proof? 'Tis the first time I ever beheld him."

"Then, my lord, as it is well known Fernando fell beneath the assassin's steel, had you never suspicion of the real offender?" said the president; "for though, I am exceeding sorry to observe, in this city crimes of this deep dye are too frequent, though, indeed, you are accused of shedding a brother's blood, yet few are so hardened as to murder merely for amusement; 'tis generally interest or revenge directs the blow. Now, you, marchese, who was so well acquainted with his friends or enemies, as at that time you both dwelt under the same roof, cannot you guess who was on terms of animosity with him, and by that means surmise who might be the perpetrator of this horrid act?"

The marquis faltering replied—"No."

"And did you never hear that Fernando had a wife and child?" added the president, looking earnestly in his face.

The marquis again answered—"No," as his countenance betrayed evident marks of confusion, the paleness of his cheeks quickly changing to a deep crimson.

"Then who is Rosalina St. Almo, and on what account have you pursued her with your unceasing hatred? Come, come, my lord, confess; you know she is the heiress of Barozzi, therefore, as some atonement for your great and manifold offences, resign to her the inheritance which is her proper and lawful right."

"Never, my lord president, will I give up the legal titles that I have to the honours of Barozzi. I am my brother's heir by law, for I declare he was never married."

"'Tis false!" exclaimed a loud voice, and, to Rosalina's amazement, the sorceress appeared.

The marquis supported himself on a gentleman next him, and in tremulous accents uttered—"Oh Heaven! this woman here! what means she? Do you, wicked fiend, appear against me, you, vile demon?—My lords, let that wretch be secured; I accuse her as a professor in magic; one who dwells in darkness, and at her will can call forth spirits of hell."

The president was prevented replying, by a loud voice calling—"Hold! the prisoner is innocent of the crime imputed to his charge!"

Rosalina directed her eye to the entrance of the hall, and beheld Rosalva, pale and disordered, followed by a man in a Turkish habit.

The marquis gazed for an instant, then sunk insensibly to the earth, for in the person of this stranger he recognised his long-supposed murdered brother Fernando.

The sorceress uttered a loud shriek, and ere she could be restrained, rushed from the assembly.

An awful silence reigned throughout the throng, who knew not what to make of the appearance of this stranger, when Fernando, pulling off a large turban, and, turning round to the numerous spectators, said, "Has sixteen years of slavery altered my features so much, that no one recollects, beneath this disguise, Fernando, marchese di Barozzi?"

Rosalina started from her seat, in spite of the entreaties of Alberto, and falling at the feet of the speaker, cried, "Oh, stranger, if you are indeed he, behold in me your child!"

He gazed on her for a moment, then said—"You are my daughter, for I behold the very lineaments of my beloved Rosalina, my lawful wife: come, my child, come to my bosom, and receive a father's warm embrace: as for this wretched man, my brother, though he ill deserves it, as I still live, oh, join with me, offspring of my beloved Rosalina, in supplication for his pardon! I know the wrongs you have received from his hands, but if you resemble your sainted mother; you will forgive."

She was about to reply, when a loud shriek from Rosalva prevented her, who exclaimed—"My father is no more! he is dead! he is dead!"

The concourse of people that were gathered to witness the trial now arose in alarm, but upon examination, it appeared that Augustino was not dead, though nearly so, occasioned by the shock he so unexpectedly received by the sight of the injured Fernando. He was conveyed home, and placed upon a bed, when medical assistance being procured, he was with great difficulty restored to life. Meanwhile Rosalina was embraced by her father, who conducted her to the palazzo, accompanied by her friends. As soon as they were left together, he questioned her on the subject of her past life, which she related to him with great sweetness and simplicity.

Their conversation was interrupted by an attendant saying a woman particularly requested an audience with the marquis Fernando.

"Admit her instantly," he replied.

The door of the apartment was then thrown back, and to the great terror of Rosalina, the sorceress made her appearance. "Health to the marquis di Barozzi and his beauteous daughter!" said she; "but there wants another who I could wish to see."

"Who is that?" asked Fernando, amazed at her strange manner and appearance.

"Your wife, the marchioness Rosalina."

"Woman, forbear!" replied he; "drive me not mad by the remembrance of my loss, for alas! she is dead—she perished in the flames—miserably perished! Oh that she was still alive, that I might once more behold her—she whom I have for years prayed to behold again—for whom I so desired to be released from slavery, that I might once more clasp her to my heart! but, alas! she is now no more."

"She still lives," said the sorceress.

"How, my mother"—"My wife"—"still exists!" burst at once from the lips of Fernando and Rosalina.

"She lives," repeated the hag.

"Ah, beware how you trifle with me; do not raise my hopes, to crush them with despair."

"I will not," replied the hag; "but have not sixteen years obliterated from your memory the semblance of Rosalina de Valmont?"

"Oh no," answered he; "she will for ever live in my heart; and this child revives her recollection still more, for she is her very counterpart."

"She is indeed," said the mysterious woman, "but I can show you a still stronger likeness. Behold it in me," she said, and plucking off the veil of mystic figures and long false hair which half-concealed her face, discovered, in the countenance of the dreaded sorceress, the still lovely bride of his youth, his long-lost Rosalina.

Fernando starting, cried—"Oh, do not mock me with illusion! yet, hold, and let me gaze! Gracious Powers! 'tis she! yes, thou art my wife!"

He rushed into her arms, and pressed her to his throbbing heart; then turning to the wondering girl, said—"My child, embrace your mother;" but she stood aloof and replied not; when the marchioness, as we shall now call her, guessing her reason, said—"My daughter, my beloved child, come to my bosom; let not the thoughts of the past embitter this blessed hour; for oh, my love, when, joined with the marquis, I appeared most your foe, I was your greatest friend; bound by the strongest ties in nature, I hazarded my life for the preservation of thine, in assuming the character of a witch, an innocent artifice to gain the confidence of Augustino."

"Thou art all a wonder," said Fernando: "my wife! my child! oh God, accept my thanks for these thy bounteous blessings!"

He clasped them both in his arms, while tears of joy moistened the cheeks of each.

Henri, Rosalva's servant, now came to inform them that Augustino was restored to his senses, though dying, and requested to see his brother, to make confession of his crimes, and implore his pardon ere he breathed his last. A tear stood in the eye of the youth as he continued—"I fear my master is dying too, for he raves as much as his father did. Will it please you to go and see them, my lord?"

"I'll attend directly," said Fernando, "and try if I can give ease to the afflicted conscience of my wretched brother. Come, my Rosalina, and you, my daughter, come, and join me in this laudable intention, for never can I forget how dear this brother once was to me, how we both were reared in precepts of virtue by our beloved father, and grew like a twin ear of corn upon the same stalk, united in the bonds of fraternal love, till cursed avarice crept into the heart of one, and, like a baneful worm, destroyed the love of years and all our future peace. Avarice, destructive fiend! what misery hast thou caused, not only to me and him, but unto those we love dearest on earth, for if I mistake not, the youth Rosalva is noble and affectionate, and most poignantly feels the disgrace of his father!"

The heart of Rosalina burned at this panegyric on her lover, as she accompanied her parents towards the apartment where, in bodily torments, and agony of soul, did lie the guilty Augustino.

Chapter VII
The Repentance

WHEN THEY REACHED THE ANTICHAMBER, Fernando expressed a wish that the marchioness would remain there till called upon, lest the unexpected sight of her should prove fatal to his brother. To this she willingly consented, while the marquis and his daughter entered the apartment where Augustino laid, writhing in the pangs of death. At this affecting sight, Fernando forgot all his wrongs, and gently approaching the bed, took hold on the clammy hand of his brother.

The miserable wretch shrunk from his touch, and in convulsive accents cried—"Ah, Fernando, dost thou come to mock me with a show of kindness! if thou wilt pity or give me ease, curse! oh, curse thy miserable brother, who, like Cain of old, repaid thy kindness by murder—thy brotherly affection and confidence by consuming in flames thy beloved wife! Oh that dreadful pang! Oh fiends! fiends! already do I feel you at my heart! There is not—there cannot be a hell like this, for oh, my brother, if I may be allowed to call you by that tender name, my conscience now repays your sufferings by pangs unutterable! Your Rosalina died a death most terrific, and oh! her murderer will, like her, meet flames and fire, but not, like her, to rise from them to heaven! endless must be my punishment, nor that inadequate to the enormity of my crimes!"

A loud groan succeeded this exertion, and he sunk exhausted.

A tear bedewed the eye of Fernando as he exclaimed—"Oh, my brother, live—live to repentance, for I can administer a cordial to thy wounded heart, by informing thee that my wife still exists!"

Rosalva, who sat at a farther part of the room, absorbed in grief, now started up, exclaiming—"Hear that, my father, the marchioness still survives!" but his joy was damped by perceiving his father insensible, and he again relapsed into a fit of frenzy, to the great grief of Rosalina and his uncle, who already began to love the unfortunate youth.

They both attempted, and at last with success, to restore animation to the wretched Augustino, who, on opening his eyes, cast them wildly round the room, and cried—"Did I dream that you said your wife still lives, or is it really so?"

"It is true," said Fernando, unclosing the door, "and she is here to pronounce your pardon."

As he spoke the marchioness entered, dressed in a rich habit, becoming her dignity and native excellence of person, having divested herself of the robe which she had worn when as Magdalena, so that Augustino could not discover the least trace or faint resemblance of the dreaded sorceress. In a voice of sweetness, she tendered him her forgiveness, adding, that she hoped Heaven would pardon him also; and approaching Rosalva, greeted him by the title of nephew.

The miserable dying offender put up his earnest thanks to that gracious Providence which had preserved her life, and freed his guilty conscience from one crime more. Then calling to Rosalina and his son, he took a hand of each, saying—"There, my children, live in the bonds of amity and friendship; but you never must expect to be united, for Fernando cannot wed his daughter to the offspring of a wretch like me."

"What," said the marquis, "do they love each other?"

"Yes," replied Augustino, "Rosalva long has loved your daughter, but I divided them, and aimed a poniard at her heart, which he received in his breast; therefore, if you think the blood he shed in her defence can give him a claim to her hand, oh, let them be united, for my son is noble, and inherits none of my vices, but is every way worthy your esteem! Can you consent to this, my much-injured brother? and you, marchioness, daughter of the unfortunate De Valmont, who, through my means, was untimely cut off? yet, I swear before Heaven, it was not my intention to destroy him, nor knew I of his death till chance revealed it to me."

Our heroine, at the mention of her grandsire, burst into tears. Her parents sought to console her, and both joined in consent to her union with Rosalva.

A ray of joy illumined for a moment the pallid cheek of Augustino, and catching the hand of his brother, he cried—"Forgive, oh forgive!—my son—my Rosalva, come near, and let me once more clasp you to my heart! Curse not my memory, and avoid my crimes, which damned ambition, and a thirst for power, first engendered in my breast: remember this, my beloved child, and pray for thy guilty father!" He then sunk back, and with a loud groan expired.

Rosalva's grief was now beyond measure, and it was with great difficulty he could be prevailed upon to separate from the inanimate corpse. After the first transports of sorrow were somewhat subsided, he assumed fortitude sufficient to appear tranquil in the presence of the marchesa La Rosa, who shortly after arrived, for even there rumour had spread the report of Augustino's death in the hall of justice, together with the wonderful discoveries which had taken place.

She condoled with her nephew, and by her soothing arguments soon weaned him from despondency, for he was not of a disposition to feel long such poignant anguish: by nature lively, his sensations, though always violent, were never lasting.

When the marchesa La Rosa was led to the presence of our heroine, they both indulged in the most unfeigned congratulations. Fernando received her with the utmost tenderness, and joined with his lady in expressing their acknowledgments for her goodness to their daughter, though only known to her as a peasant.

She replied—"My lord, I soon perceived in that peasant an inestimable jewel, which, like a precious brilliant in its native quarry, had long been buried in obscurity; nor was I the only one who beheld this excellence, for my nephew, though he attempted to conceal it by a shew of indifference, soon felt the force of the charms belonging to the rustic cottager;" (Rosalva and his fair relative both blushed at this remark of the marchesa;) "and I hope," continued she, "your disinterested passion will now be rewarded, for I am well assured the marchese Fernando is too noble to punish the misdeeds of the father in the son."

The marchioness di Barozzi now informed her of the promise made to the deceased Augustino relative to their union, upon which she congratulated the youthful pair, and expressed her intention of making her nephew heir to the honours of La Rosa; adding—"Peace to the sad remains of my sister's lord! I would not, by any observation of mine, rouse an unpleasant feeling in either of your breasts, but I must say, my nephew always resembled his mother more than your excellenza's brother, to whom I cannot sufficiently admire your charitable conduct. But, my dear sister," said she, addressing the marchioness Barozzi, "suffer me to call you by that title, pray inform me by what means, after so long being supposed dead, did you appear at the moment so truly critical? There is a strange story rumoured among the domestics, that no one saw you enter or heard of your arrival—nay, Erasmo says he let in an ugly being, who wished to speak with the lord Fernando, who was shortly after changed into a beautiful lady; and Paulina tells me, that it is thought you are only a spirit; and will shortly make your exit into the airy regions from whence you came."

The marchioness smiling, replied—"There is some truth in the report, my dear lady, but as soon as the obsequies of the unfortunate Augustino are past, I will recount to you all my sad eventful history."

This was what Rosalva much wished to hear, as he had not yet learned how, or by what means, the marchioness had arrived at the palazzo; and on his aunt's mentioning the metamorphoses that had taken place, a vague idea ran across his mind concerning the sorceress, a character which is ever connected with mystery.

Several days had now elapsed, when Rosalina finding it impossible to attend the nuptials of the pretty shepherdess, sent for Alberto, who had since remained within the palazzo, and by desire of her father, on being made acquainted with his generous hospitality, presented him with a handsome compensation, and several valuables as bridal-gifts to Marcelina, and gave him permission to return home as soon as he might think it convenient, which he being desirous of, did the same day; but previous to his departure, she spoke with him in private, saying—"Alberto, hast thou ever, since the morning when I first beheld my dear father, seen the page Julio? has he ever inquired for, or sent to you?"

"No," replied Alberto, "and it has often raised my wonder, for he certainly was interested in your fate, lady: sometimes I think he probably may have returned to my cottage till he hears from your excellenza."

Rosalina thought the conduct of the page exceedingly strange, but said nothing, and kindly bidding Alberto adieu, proposed in a short time to pay a visit to the cottage. With this mark of her condescension he departed, after promising, that should he see or hear of the page, to dispatch a messenger with the tidings to the palazzo.

In due season the body of Augustino was inhumed, with all the funeral pomp becoming his rank. The noble Fernando, in attending with Rosalva as one of the chief mourners, proved to the world he had forgot his brother's crimes, and only remembered that he sprung from the same stock with himself.

In a few days all in the palazzo was at peace. The youth Rosalva began to forget his suffering sorrows by the sweet society of his intended bride, whom he found endowed with qualities so excellent, that princes might have disputed with him for her hand. The marchesa La Rosa one evening reminded the marchioness Barozzi of her promise, to relate her eventful story, and turning to Fernando, said—"Your excellenza has never informed us how you escaped from the forest, where you were left for dead; but I imagine you have communicated to each other all these wonders; but for our benefit, promulge those miracles, for miracles indeed they are, or else you could not have been preserved and brought together at so important a period."

A loud ringing at the gate of the palazzo prevented the marchioness replying, and the servant announced a lady who wished to pay her respects, upon which she arose, and introduced her as madame De Verencourt, a French lady of distinction.

They all saluted her with marks of the greatest respect, and the marchioness continuing, said—"My dear Isabella, you are just come in time to hear the relation of my story, and as you are somewhat concerned in it, perhaps our joint asseverations may convince those inquisitive ones of the truth of many events, that on my bare word might not be believed."

"For shame, marchioness!" said Isabella; "this noble company must be well convinced that nothing is impossible to the sorceress Magdalena."

Rosalva started—"Magdalena!" cried he.

"Restrain your impatience, dear youth," said the marchioness, "and you shall hear of things most strange, most wonderful, and yet most true."

Chapter VIII
The Marchioness of Barozzi's Narrative

To you, my beloved lord, I need not describe the keen anguish which rent my bosom on the receipt of that vile forgery, which contained the poisonous intelligence of your falsehood; but thinking you unworthy of my regret, I strove to banish the remembrance of our loves, and think only of your villainy, in which resolution I was aided by the sympathetic condolence of my beloved and affectionate parent. Some time had now elapsed, when one evening, after we had retired to rest, I thought I heard footsteps in the garden beneath my chamber window; a sulphureous smell seemed to arise, and I fancied I heard a whispering of voices. I started from my couch, and unclosing the casement, I beheld just beneath a heap of straw and other combustible matters, which a man with a torch was in the very act of firing, with the base intent of destroying us in the flames. A loud shriek burst from my lips, and I instantly shrunk back with affright, when he, I should suppose, thinking he would be discovered, by the assistance of his fellow-ruffian, immediately vaulted in at the window, and seizing me violently, placed a bandage over my mouth, at the same time commanding me to be quiet, for he wished to save me.

"In spite of all my efforts and struggles to get extricated, he forced me to the casement, through which he thrust me, and the wretch who accompanied him caught me in his arms. 'Oh God, my child,' thought I, 'and my father are now perishing in the destructive element!' Urged by desperation, I struck my head repeated blows, and endeavoured to tear off the scarf in which they had muffled me; but they soon stopped my violence, by pinioning my hands, and then placing me on a horse, maugre my despair, I was borne far, far away from my babe, my father, and my home.

"Pardon me," said she, wiping away the tears which started from her eyes, "but even at this moment the agony I then felt is fresh in my memory, and causes this unwelcome interruption."

Her auditors could not refrain from weeping in unison, and it was a considerable time ere she could resume her narrative, which was as follows: "A happy deprivation of my senses succeeded the first transport of grief, and several hours had elapsed ere they returned, when I found myself reclining upon a

113

decent couch, within a gloomy apartment, and the rays of the declining sun, which gleamed through the Gothic casement, served only to render it more dismal, for the tapestry figures, with which this place was ornamented, seemed by this partial light starting from their situations. My returning senses brought with them a recollection of the preceding evening's sad events, and a friendly shower of tears coming to my relief, I left the couch, and repaired to one of the windows. A prospect bleak and dreary met my view. The loud roaring sea dashed its foaming waves against the dilapidated walls of the ancient fabric in which I was confined, and by their tremendous noise, seemed to threaten destruction to its decaying foundation. No vessel or friendly fisher's bark appeared upon its agitated surface; my soul sickened at the dismal sight, and I turned to the opposite side of the apartment, where a huge forest appeared to my disappointed eyes, in which in vain I endeavoured to distinguish some sign of human habitation, and convinced me I was devoid of hope.

"In despair I threw myself upon the couch, and gave way to sorrow. My child, my parent, were pictured to my distempered fancy perishing in the most excruciating torments; and as a shriek of anguish burst from my agonized breast, my senses fled, and for several weeks, as I was afterwards informed, I became a maniac.

"On the first dawn of sanity I found myself in the same chamber, on the same couch, but bound down with cords, as I suppose in my ravings I had been dangerous, and they had apprehended I might commit some act of desperation. I lay patiently for some length of time, when at last I heard some one open the door, and calling another to follow. A strange thought suddenly occurred, and I closed my eyes. I resumed my situation, hoping by this stratagem to hear something relative to myself. I was not deceived, for these intruders approached the bed. 'She's asleep,' said the first; 'come, this is well. She looks handsome even now; don't she, Rodolpho?'—'Ah, that she does,' replied the other, 'and I am glad we have saved her, as our chief has never yet seen one so beautiful; indeed he says so himself; for he came in to look at her when he was last here.' I trembled, and wished that moment was my last, for I now found a fate far worse than death awaited me.

"The man then continued.—'The marquis di Barozzi would be very much displeased if he knew she was alive; but I assured him of all their deaths, which he never once doubted, but gave us our reward, and a handsome one it was, for I gained more by this business than any in which I was ever concerned; but I am glad I saved this pretty creature, however, for it would have been a pity to let her have fallen, though her ambition did soar so high, to marry Fernando, the marquis's brother, who was lately assassinated by his order. I suppose he wants to get all the riches of the family within his grasp.'"

At the conclusion of this sentence, Rosalva arose from his seat, and left the room in visible confusion. Rosalina looked at her mother, with an expression that seemed to condemn her enlarging on the crimes of Augustino; but she did not comprehend the meaning, or else her sufferings had blunted the delicate feeling of her naturally excellent heart, for she made no apology, but continuing, said—"From the foregoing, and other sentences which they let drop, I discovered the whole of the diabolical plans which had been laid for our joint destruction. How I restrained my feelings, or how I avoided, by any involuntary movement or exclamation, letting them know my sleep was only feigned, I cannot tell, but so I did; and after unloosing the cords by which I was bound, thinking, I suppose, that all danger now was past, they departed. I then started from my bed, and sinking on my knees, made a horrid vow of vengeance against my destroyer, should opportunity ever offer, in which attempt I called upon the shades of my murdered child and father to lend me aid. In a few minutes after a woman made her appearance, who seeing me seated on the side of my couch, with my hands at liberty, would have retired, but with a voice somewhat calm, I bid her not be afraid, but come nearer. She did so, bearing in her hand a medicine, which she persuaded me to take; I complied, resolving to dedicate all my future days—do not despise me for the confession—to revenge, and to that end I took the means of prolonging an existence otherwise painful.

"The woman finding me thus tractable, entered into a conversation, in which I sought to win her affection, thinking that by making her my friend, it might be one step gained towards emancipation. I thought I had so far succeeded, and I then assumed an air of cheerfulness, that I might the better deceive my persecutors, and elude their vigilance; but a fresh circumstance caused me to relapse into my misery; this was, the expected appearance of the chief for whom my wretched person was designed. At length the unwelcome tidings of his arrival, and a command for me to prepare for an interview, aroused an energy which long had lain dormant, and assuming an appearance of pride, and superiority, I gave consent to his admittance.

"Never was I so astonished as on his entrance, for instead of the ferocious bandit I had expected to behold, a mere youth appeared, with an aspect somewhat pleasing. I descended from my high demeanour, which I changed into condescension, and briefly relating my unhappy story, threw myself upon his clemency. How did his answer delight me, as, with an air of assumed dignity, he said—'Rinaldo is no ravisher, lady; displeasing must that object be, who is obtained by force, therefore, be not alarmed.'

"'Then will you give me freedom?' said I, falling at his feet. 'Oh! complete your generosity, by restoring me to the society which best befits my rank and sex!'

"He gently raised me up, but frankly said that was impossible, for the interest of his followers was his greatest pride; 'and give me leave to add, lady, that, in appearance you must be mine: nay, start not,' he continued, 'but rely upon my honour. I swear never to betray the secret; but if you reject my proposal, a fate more desperate than the realizing this project will await you.'

"I comprehended his meaning, and finding how impossible it was to escape, was obliged perforce to consent, trusting to his integrity; and oh, my Fernando, never did he give me cause to repent this reliance on his virtue. He treated me with all possible respect, and every thing was at my command, except the greatest of all earthly blessings, dear liberty.

"Years passed on in the same manner without danger or discord; but at last the numerous depredations of the band caused the government to take cognizance of them. Troops were appointed to watch their motions, and they found they could no longer remain safe in their retreat, the ancient fabric in which I was imprisoned; but fearing to retire in a body, they divided, and by different routes at last arrived in the adjacent forest, where the ruin proved an admirable receptacle; and I believe they had frequently resorted thither as a place of rendezvous, when separated on their excursions. I was removed by night, and in a manner which prevented the possibility of my escaping, and I found myself immured in a fresh confinement, where all hopes of enlargement were as much frustrated as in the first; but fortune afforded me some solace in the society of this lady, madame De Verencourt, who fell into their power by accident, on the particulars of which I shall not dwell, as I know it will renew her sorrows. We mutually condoled each other on our misfortunes, and loved like sisters.

"About this period the old woman, who was formerly my gaoler, fell sick and died, which to us was a great loss, for we both were obliged to submit to some of the menial offices, in despite of the captain's authority, for the men refused to serve us, declaring that women were in duty bound to wait on men, their lords and masters.

"The worst misfortune which I thought could occur, soon after took place; this was no less than the death of the chief, who was one night brought home dreadfully wounded; and there being no hopes of life, he called me to his bedside, and in the presence of his band, desired that I might inherit his share of the riches which had been a long time accumulating. My feelings revolted at the idea of possessing plunder, part of which, perhaps, had been obtained by blood; but I did not name my objections, and, was accordingly, by the unanimous consent of the band, awarded his heiress to property of considerable amount. The unfortunate Rinaldo soon after breathed his last, and was buried with civil honours by his faithful followers, who revered and loved him for his strong attachment to their interests.

"Not many weeks after his demise, the officers of justice again got scent of their rendezvous, when finding Italy no longer afforded them a safe retreat, they one night called a council, to determine on the safest method of proceeding, in which it was decided by a majority of votes, that after a fair division of their spoils, the band should separate, and depart to different countries, which they did, leaving us to our fate, first extorting from us an oath not to discover ourselves for the space of three months, and then resigning to me a just proportion of their booty, as left me by the generous Rinaldo.

"Thus you perceive," said she, addressing her auditors, "the danger of placing confidence in villains, who think no longer of their oaths than while they can serve themselves as well as their employers. So it was with the band to which I perforce was many years an associate; for finding that Augustino could render them no further good, they left me to employ my freedom against him as I might think proper, and this I put in practice at the first opportunity.

"For some time after their departure, I concerted numerous schemes for gaining access to his presence, as I well knew applying to justice, unfriended as I was, without witnesses, or even a certificate of my marriage, could be of no avail, but that I should probably be treated as an impostor, and perhaps a second time fall into the power of my enemy. Unfixed in my aims, I yet retained a thirst for revenge, and having no child or parent to whom I could fly, I resolved to dedicate my life entirely to this darling object, unless by any chance, which I thought impossible, I might procure evidence unquestionable that would be sufficient to substantiate my claims. My friend at last suggested a plan that appeared feasible, which was to offer myself as a servant to the marquis. This I instantly adopted, and procuring male attire, for the better concealing my person, I arrayed myself in it, to see if the deception was passable, and had the satisfaction of finding it answer equal to my wish: my appearance being rather juvenile, I made use of a liquid which gave a florid hue to my complexion, and thus disguised, my friend named me Julio."

"Ah, Julio!" exclaimed Rosalina, unable to contain her emotions.

"Yes, my dear child, that identical Julio who offended your delicacy in the cottage of Alberto, forgetting, in the ecstasy of my joy at beholding you again, my boy's disguise, which conveyed with my delight sinister designs on your person. But to proceed: I only wanted an opportunity of gaining admittance to Barozzi, and various methods were devised by myself and friend for that purpose. Often have I lingered about the door of the palazzo, with an intention of addressing him, but at his sight my courage always failed, and I once again returned dispirited, hopeless of success. At last fortune seemed to favour my design, for one day, as he was mounting a spirited steed which he usually rode, the animal growing restive, by a sudden plunge threw him to the ground. I ran to his assistance, and helped him to rise ere Erasmo, whom he dispatched on some message, returned. He thanked me for my aid, and offered me a piece of money, which I refused. Whether he was pleased at my disinterestedness, as he of course thought it, I know not, but he eyed me attentively, and said—'Thou art a strange youth: who are you? and what is your name?'

"I answered that I dwelt in the forest with my mother, and that I was called Julio. 'Indeed,' said he; 'it is a pity you should live in such obscurity.'

"'Ah, your excellenza,' I replied, 'willingly would I serve as a page, could I be so fortunate as to procure a situation.'

"He looked at me again, and after a little more conversation, I had the pleasure to be received by him in that capacity. By paying great attention to his wishes, I in a short time became a favourite, and he seemed lost without me, when by any chance I was absent.

"His mind I soon perceived was very miserable, and his unhappiness gladdened my heart, which rankled with the most settled hatred against this destroyer of my peace. Whenever he was out, or engaged with company, I used to go to the forest, and recount to my dear friend the manner of my proceedings.

"Thus passed the time till Rosalva returned from La Rosa, whose adventure in rescuing Rosalina from the ruffians, her being adopted by his aunt, and the change in her name, was whispered amongst the servants, although much precaution had been used to keep it concealed. I knew the appellation of Rosalina was common, yet at the recital of this incident, there was a strange fluttering at my heart, for which I could not account; and hearing that the marchesa La Rosa had brought her ward with her to Venice, I was wild with impatience to behold you, my dear child, and, when I did, thought I saw my own image, for such was my appearance when at your age. But I could not be assured you were my daughter, till I beheld that jewel on your finger, which on the first glimpse I knew was your father's, and bears the initials of his name, and which convinced me of your identity. I need not attempt to describe the joy this discovery gave me, which to be known must be felt.

"I now watched the conduct of Augustino more narrowly than usual, and from some expressions which inadvertently escaped his lips, found he still persecuted our unhappy family with unceasing hatred. So desirous was I of gaining a knowledge of his inmost secrets, that I had nearly betrayed myself one evening by listening, too closely, but with a piece of finesse I warded off his suspicions. Just previous to the mask, a stratagem darted on my imagination, which was to assume that character which struck so much terror to his guilty conscience; and for the better management of this artifice, I obtained permission of absence for the term of three days; but I then, did not know of its being of any advantage, farther than the gratification it would afford me in the tortures he might endure by my taxing him with his numerous crimes: the knowledge of one, I gained by finding a letter in his escrutoir from an unhappy girl in Paris, whom he had seduced, and abandoned to misery. In one of my interviews, I feigned to be his dearest friend, and, my child, your bitterest foe, undertaking the charge of putting a period to your existence. By this I hoped he would consign you to my care, when I intended, in company with my friend, to fly to France. To do this effectually, I found it necessary he should suppose you deprived of life, for if he ever doubted it, I well knew he would pursue us to the earth's utmost verge. For the accomplishment of this, I suggested a method which appeared practicable.

"After my interview with Augustino on the night of the mask, when he had agreed to meet me at the ruin, I quickly threw off my strange attire, and resumed the page's habit, in which character I procured men to waylay and bring you to the abbey, as the knowledge of your return I had gained by overhearing from a closet adjoining the apartment appropriated, for the use of the marchesa, your kind protectress. I took the precaution to prevent shedding blood, by promising the men who I employed an additional reward if they refrained from violence. Your reception is already known, and that of Augustino was conducted in such manner as to give him a high opinion of my power as a sorceress: one convincing proof of my art was his failing in his attempt to pierce his poniard in my breast, which I had fortified, in case of such a circumstance, with a plate of steel concealed under my garment. In his confusion the weapon fell from his hand, which, by an artifice I had before endeavoured to obtain, lest, on coming to the mystic apartment, he should indeed attempt to destroy you, which office I wished him to resign to me, hoping he would not have the courage to witness it, but leave you to my pretended revenge. For the better prevailing upon his fluctuating mind, my friend, as had been concerted, at an appointed signal, ascended from a trap habited like a spectre, bearing in her hand a scroll, the purport of which urged him to consent to my wishes.

"Every thing seemed to answer my expectation, when the sudden appearance of Rosalva frustrated all my designs. He and you, my child, have no doubt already informed the marchesa of the events which afterwards transpired, and your alarm at beholding the fancied supernatural appearance, which was no other than my friend, whom I expected you to find ready in the apartment to receive you; but she delayed casting off her habit, as had been proposed, conjecturing mischief had ensued by the confusion she heard, occasioned by the entrance of Rosalva, who being afterwards wounded, I hastened to a chest left by the robbers, and found a styptic liquid, used by them in similar cases, which I applied to the bleeding youth. Then, promising to send Augustino proper assistance, I retired to an adjoining chamber, and changing my dress to the page's, immediately went in search of those woodmen, who I procured so quickly, that he still supposed he was indebted to the power of Magdalena, and which I further corroborated by the fabrication of a tale he did not scruple to believe. I then accompanied him to the palazzo, not entertaining the least shadow of a doubt that you, my dear child, was safe in the company of madame De Verencourt, therefore was perfectly easy in regard to your security.

"Augustino was almost distracted at the danger of his son, From whose chamber he was seldom absent, leaving the care of his household to my charge. One day, when his mind was greatly agitated, he left unlocked one of his private drawers: this was a singular circumstance, for he was at all times extremely cautious in rendering them secure, and I never knew him before neglect them. The instant he quitted the room, I gently drew it open, and in it perceived a small box with the name of Fernando di Barozzi engraven on the lid: my heart gave a sudden bound at this discovery, and I exerted my whole strength to force the lock, hoping to find some documents of our union. After repeated attempts, I at last effected my purpose; but how shall I describe my joyful feelings, when amongst other papers of little consequence, I found some letters of my own writing, and the certificate of our marriage! I did not hesitate a moment, lest I should be deprived of this unlooked-for treasure, but throwing on my cloak, and passing through the gate of the palazzo, hastened to the president, to whom I unfolded the whole affair, represented my claims, and produced the certificate as an authentic proof of the truth. He was greatly surprised at my communication, and expressed his wish to see the daughter I had mentioned, and to this I consented.

"As we were further discussing the business, a servant came to inform him of the seizure of a notorious assassin, and added, that the prisoner was particularly importunate to see his lordship, as he had something to communicate which was of great import. I begged that my affairs might be no obstacle to other business, and the president handed me into an adjacent apartment, while the villain was brought to his presence, who I overheard make confession of being my husband's murderer, having been employed to perpetrate this crime by his brother Augustino, whom he would accuse, if permitted, in open court—'Not that I do it in hopes of saving myself,' said he, 'for I am well convinced the cause for which I am apprehended merits death, and since I must fall, why, I will drag down others who are as wicked as myself, who being rich rogues, are not suspected. He is also guilty of other crimes,' added the villain, 'for he has sought and does still seek the life of Rosalina St. Almo, a peasant girl, which I can irrefragably prove.'

"After owning to several other enormities, he was conducted to prison, and the president calling me forth, proposed that the apprehension of Augustino should immediately take place, upon the charge of murder, and that at the trial I should appear as the sorceress, for I had given him a brief account of all my transactions, conjecturing that the sight of so unexpected a witness would force him to confession, which otherwise might not be extorted, and he would not be adjudged as guilty upon the evidence of an assassin already a prisoner. It also was necessary my daughter should be interrogated, respecting his intention of depriving her of life, and I repaired to the ruin for the purpose of acquainting you with this; but oh, my child, how shall I express the anguish I felt on learning you had fled! I made a strict search in the forest, and inquired of several wood-cutters; but no one could give any intelligence of you. I continued my strict endeavours to recover you for several days, but finding all my efforts fruitless, I waited upon the president, to acquaint him with this accident. He informed me that the trial of Augustino would take place in three days at furthest, the tribunal being already convened, and it could not be deferred, whether you were found or not.

"I was dejected on hearing this, and returned to the ruin in great despondency. My friend used all her rhetoric to console me, and at last thought you might be at Pyrano. This appeared a likely suggestion, and I immediately set forward to the next village to procure a conveyance for my journeying thither. Passing through the forest with this intent, I lost my track, and was benighted. Blessed chance at last conducted me to the cottage of Alberto, where, in a moment the most unexpected, I discovered the object of my search. What since occurred, you already know.

"When my dear long-lost lord appeared in the court, 'twas with great difficulty I avoided fainting through joy, so much was I overpowered; but wishing to prove whether his affection for me was unabated, was my reason for discovering myself in a manner that excited so much amazement. By this you learn the merciful goodness of Heaven, whose decrees, though dark and intricate, are ever wise and just. The prisoner is restored to freedom, the widow has gained her husband, and the parents their child. So the poor mariner, after encountering the perils of a storm, escapes with life, and returning to the bosom of his family, gazes in ecstasy on those whom his soul holds so dear. Impressed with gratitude for his present happiness, he forgets his past sufferings, and thinks only on his future bliss."

Chapter IX
The Marquis of Barozzi's Narrative

VARIOUS WERE THE SENSATIONS excited in the breasts of the auditors by this narration, and all expressed the gratification they received by its recital, which was an elucidation to those strange occurrences whose mystery they knew not how to solve.

Rosalina returned her grateful thanks to Providence for being restored to the bosoms of her affectionate parents; then addressing her father, begged he would recount the manner of his miraculous preservation, to which they all joined their entreaties; and the marquis, without further ceremony, thus began:—

"On the fatal evening when La Motte, by his subtle wiles, deluded me into the forest, under the pretence of meeting with my beloved wife, two bravoes, rushing from a place of concealment, gave me several stabs with a poniard, and then fled, leaving me as dead, for the violence of the blows, and loss of blood, caused me immediately to faint; but fortunately the weapon had not penetrated any vital part, and the cold in air checking the flowing of my wounds, it was not long ere I regained my senses, when I found myself on the same spot where I first fell, but all around dark and silent.

Exerting all my remaining strength, I crept upon my hands and knees, and endeavoured to explore my way in the best manner I was able towards the path I knew to be most frequented; but missing the proper track, I wandered to the cliff that overhangs the sea, from which I fell headlong into the briny deep. Fortunately the water was calm and unruffled, so with a slight motion of my hands, being an able swimmer in my youth, I contrived to float upon its surface, and was drifted by a gentle current to a considerable distance. My whole strength was exhausted, and seeing no hopes of relief, I commended my soul to Heaven, and each moment I expected to give up the ghost; but gracious Providence was pleased to prolong my existence, and sent me succour in the time of peril. A fisherman was coasting about in search of the fiimy tribe, and hearing something disturb the water, he made towards the place from whence the noise proceeded, and at last perceived me, though very imperfectly. He then demanded who was there, but was unable to reply, and answered him only by a faint struggling noise. Guessing the cause, he stretched forth his arms at the very moment I was sinking, and dragging me into the boat, saved me from a watery grave. Nature was now at its last gasp, and I was fast yielding up my life, when extending me upon a coat, by chafing my temples with some spirits, and applying it to my lips, he recalled that animation which appeared fled for ever. My eyes now unclosed, and continuing his application, I began gradually to revive. As I grew warm, my wounds began to bleed afresh. My kind preserver bound them up, by tearing up my linen as well as he was able, and cheered me with the hope of being quickly better, and forced some liquor down my throat; but in spite of this honest creature's humane efforts, I found life was ebbing, and my dissolution inevitable.

"Perceiving this, he made towards the shore, in hopes of still saving me; but we were several leagues from the place where assistance might be obtained; and ere we could reach the wished-for land, the wind began to veer, which tempestuously increasing, and a contrary tide flowing, he with all his might plyed at the oar, and strained every nerve to stem its force in vain; it soon blew a hurricane, full in our teeth, and we were driven into the main ocean. Finding it fruitless to resist or combat with its violence, he was compelled to abandon the vessel to its fate, and we rode at the mercy of the waves, which bandied us about with great fury.

"The little skiff was but slightly timbered, ill calculated to sustain the boisterous billows, which alternately lifted us mountains high, or sunk us into a deep abyss; and to complete our distress, the seams of our shattered vessel were now starting open by the force of such a heavy sea, and it began to fill with water. The poor fisherman each instant expected we must perish, and gave all up for lost, as it was impossible the skiff could outlive the storm. He sunk upon his knees, and presented to Heaven a humble petition to preserve us, while I, groaning with the anguish of my pain, lay nearly insensible of our imminent danger, and almost regardless of my fate.

"The honest fisherman at last discovered a light right ahead: he hailed it, and it proved to be an armed galley. They answered us by a speaking trumpet, and learning our distress, let down one of their boats to our assistance; then grappling with us, my preserver leaped on board them, and assisted in hauling me in. This with difficulty they accomplished, in the very crisis of danger, for in a few moments after the sides of our skiff were stove in, and she went to pieces. The boat's crew rowed with all their might to regain their vessel, into which we were at last all safely received.

"I know not to what perils we were exposed during the continuance of the tempest, for it was several hours ere my senses were restored, when I beheld myself surrounded by several men of ferocious aspects, and to my great grief found I had escaped one dreadful fate only to be exposed to another, for the ship on which we were aboard was an Algerine corsair, that had been upon a cruise in search of plunder. Harsh treatment, and endless slavery, I now found was to be my lot; however, contrary to my expectations, they used us kindly, administered remedies to my wounds, and promised to set us on shore, when they should reach the land; but this was only an artifice to prevent my dying with despondency, for the vessel was fast bearing from the Italian coast to that of Algiers.

"As soon as I was able I remonstrated with the captain, a Spanish renegado, whom I besought to release us, telling him my name and rank; but this, instead of moving his compassion, excited only his avarice, for by detaining me he might hope of gaining an immense ransom for my liberty. I expostulated with him, and promised him a handsome reward to land me; but the perfidious wretch affected a pretended sense of honour, saying he would not be seduced from his duty, and if I wished to be released, I must explain it so to his master, Ali Ben Hassan, whose slave I now was. Finding all my rhetoric ineffectual, I desisted from further persuasion, and consoled myself with the hope of being liberated as soon as I could write to Venice for a sufficient sum to purchase my redemption.

"The vessel, with prosperous gales, continued its course, while all my thoughts were bent upon the idea of my beloved wife, and the pangs she would endure for my absence; but I strove to repress my anguish, by the consolation she would receive from my brother, whose affection I never doubted, much less did I think he was my direst foe.

"My wounds were now nearly cured, and in due time we arrived at our destined port, when I was by the renegado captain conducted to the presence of Ali, whom, by the assistance of an interpreter, I made acquainted with my situation, and bade him name the ransom he expected for my emancipation. He eyed me sternly, and said he would consider of my request, but he could not consent to it at present, and I had better remain in my present state.

"Enraged at this refusal, and forgetting my prudence, I aroused his choler, by dignifying him with the epithets of robber, and breaker of Heaven's laws, in seizing and making slaves of his unoffending fellow-creatures, particularly those whom, by the rights of hospitality, he ought to protect, for we were not taken in battle, but wounded, and in distress, by which alone we had claims upon his compassion; but humanity was not to be found in the breast of a merciless barbarian.

"The natural ferocity of his disposition was kindled into passion by my contumelious reproaches, and summoning his guards, ordered them to convey me to a dismal dungeon, which he said would lower my lofty mind, and teach me to pay proper respect to my lord and master. I was instantly seized, and loaded with heavy manacles and fetters, then rudely thrust into a loathsome cell, where the blessed light of the sun never yet entered. What became of my kind preserver I know not, but I suppose he fell to the renegados share, who sold him on the bavarambla.[1]

"In despair I threw myself on the cold damp floor, and gave way to the most poignant anguish, calling upon the dear names of Rosalina and Augustino. Then, being wrought to desperation, I frantically struggled to break my chains; vain attempt! for my strength was nought, opposed to my vile, disgraceful bonds. My time was spent in fruitless complaining and excruciating torments. I never saw a human being except my keeper, a ferocious Mussulman, who every day brought me a scanty share of coarse food and a small jug of water. He seemed, by the expression of his countenance, to enjoy my sufferings, and as we did not understand each other, I seldom heard the sound of his voice, save when he seemed to execrate me, by pronouncing some phrases, which I since understand were—'Vile unbeliever, Christian dog,' &c.

"Three weeks, as near as I could guess, had elapsed since my interview with the cruel Ali, when one night I was alarmed by voices seemingly in earnest conversation at the portal of my dungeon. I concluded my executioners were coming to rid me of a life become truly burdensome, and I waited the event with all possible firmness. The key was applied to the lock, the massive bolts drew back, and the heavy-barred door unclosed, when my gaoler entered, followed by a youthful Moor of noble appearance. He pointed to my fetters, to which my surly keeper applied an instrument, and in a few moments I was released from those galling irons which had almost worn me to the bone. I knew not what was to follow this strange ceremony, when the youth, with an air of dignity, motioned the rough Yusef to depart. This he instantly obeyed, and the stranger in a silver voice addressed me in my own language—'Christian, fear not, but rise, and listen to what I shall say.'

"I did so, when my visitor, throwing off a cloak, discovered to my astonished eyes a lady of exquisite beauty. This unexpected sight bereft me of the power of utterance, and she in a voice of melody thus continued—'I see thy surprise: know 'tis a friend who addresses you; I am not empowered with the means of giving you liberty, yet I have that of making your bondage lighter, and the heavy hours of solitude rendered less disagreeable, by the administration of those comforts to which no doubt you always have been used.'

---

1   A place where markets are held [Smith's note]

"She then gave a signal—Yusef appeared, bearing a mattrass and covering, which he spread in a corner of my cell, and again departing, quickly returned with a basket, containing various delicious viands; then respectfully bending his body, retired.

"I gazed in wonder at this unexpected sight, and could scarcely credit the evidence of my senses, when the lady, resuming her discourse, said—'Tis the reverence I feel for your religion, and love I bear to your countrymen, that excite my compassion. A Venetian, called signor Montaldo, once was fond of poor Selima, and I returned his affection with mutual warmth. He was a slave as you are—nay, do not look angry at my using that vile term, for I meant not to offend you.' I bowed, and she proceeded. 'He was betrayed to wearing the yoke of ignominy: his placid manners won the hearts of his taskmasters. I, conjecturing he was not of the common stamp, felt an interest in his fate, and feigned to my father a wish of being initiated in the rudiments of his language, which granted, he became my tutor. This was a great alleviation to his misery. I need not dwell upon it; suffice it to say, we loved each other; we often met in private. A trusty slave of mine was privy to our passion, and by her means our interviews were contrived. At length my father become acquainted with our stolen meetings, and one fatal night, just as the unfortunate Montaldo had separated from me, and was passing as usual through the garden, he was by the order of my cruel parent assassinated.' The tears flowed quickly down the face of the lovely Moor, as she uttered this. From that time, the remorseless Ali has persecuted the Venetians with mortal hatred, and to that cause may be attributed the greatest part of your sufferings; for had you but been of any other nation, signor, the ransom would have been preferred to your confinement. My father greatly thirsts after riches, yet he is more revengeful than avaricious: then, since I, though innocently, was the first cause of incensing his implacable hate, it ever shall be my care to ease the sufferings of all who are objects of his resentment. Yusef, your gaoler, has no respect for any thing belonging to Christianity, but as he is entirely devoted to my will, often suffers me to ease the captive of his galling chains; but as for liberty, it is neither in his or my power to give; nevertheless, all I can grant you shall command. Signor, farewell, and ere the silver moon's pale beams have thrice shone upon the castle's turrets, you again shall behold Selima.

"I tendered this lovely infidel my warmest acknowledgments, who again enveloping herself with her cloak, departed; and the door closing, the ponderous bolts were replaced, and I once more was barred from all human intercourse.

"Months passed on, with lazy, leaden strides, as usual, except at proper intervals, when I received the friendly visits of the beautiful Moor, who so greatly alleviated my sufferings.

"At length a slave's habit was brought for me, with orders to equip myself, for I had too long lain in a state of inactivity, and must now share the toils and drudgery of my fellow-slaves, by labouring in the Moor's garden, and other servile offices. I own my soul, instead of revolting, felt pleasure at these tidings, for confinement had tamed my indignant spirit, and I panted with desire again to breathe the pure air, and behold the glorious light of heaven, even in that ignominious capacity. I equipped myself in the disgraceful habiliments with such alacrity, that I perceived it excited astonishment in the eye of the messenger, who no doubt expected reluctance or opposition. This ceremony performed, I was conducted and placed amongst the herd of miserable wretches who, like myself, were condemned to inglorious servitude, and dreading the scourge of our inhuman masters, were daily compelled, beneath a burning sun, to carry burdens fit only for senseless brutes to bear, or to deck the earthly paradise of our imperious tyrant. I soon acquired a sufficiency of the language to comprehend them, and be understood by my yoke-fellows; and years of galling slavery dragged heavily on, till, worn by fatigue, and scorched by the parching heat, my countenance became so changed, that it would have been impossible to have traced in the brown visage of Ali's lowly slave, the features of the unfortunate Fernando Barozzi.

"The lovely Selima oftentimes passed me while at my labour, and though by language she dared not, yet her sweet pitying countenance fully expressed the sorrow she felt at my bitter fate. About the fifth year of my captivity, her hand was sought in marriage by a Moorish general, but she continued stedfast in her refusals, and true to the memory of the deceased lord of her heart, the unhappy Montaldo. Her rejection exasperated the temper of her stern, obdurate father, who, to force her to compliance, had recourse to rigorous methods; and the miserable victim of his rage at last, being urged by desperation, put a period to her existence by swallowing poison. In her last moments she confessed the deed, and declared her reason for this dreadful act was a wish to preserve her affections pure and unviolated; for she could love none, or ever would wed any of her father's choosing, for her heart was buried in the grave of the unfortunate Venetian.

"Ali, though rough and flinty, tenderly loved his child, and when he found she was lost for ever, he wept, tore his beard. and raved like a maniac, vowing to wreak his vengeance on all Christians who were so unlucky as to fall into his power. This oath he verified, and I severely felt its bitter effects, for upon the most trivial occasion, or slightest neglect, I was most inhumanly scourged. Life became truly burdensome, and if it had not been for the friendly aid of hope, I think I should have been wrought also to put a termination to my wretched being, by some violent means; but the sweet idea of again being restored to the dear inestimable blessing of liberty and my native land, gave me fortitude to endure my miserable lot, with a resignation becoming our blessed religion.

"One day, as the malignant Moor passed near me, when laboriously toiling in his garden, I rested on my spade, and once more ventured to remind him of the ransom I had offered for my emancipation, which I besought him to accept, and suffer me to return to my own country, from whence I had been detained against all laws, both divine or human; at the same time mentioned how derogatory it was to the feelings of any man to bend to servile offices, who had been used to hold an exalted situation in life.

"He cast upon me a ferocious look, then sternly replied—'Vile unbeliever, think not of regaining freedom, but toil, and grovel on, and delight my soul by seeing thy proud spirit humbled with the dust, fit employment for all of thy persuasion: by our holy prophet, great Mahomet, I swear I would not barter the pleasure which I feel in witnessing thy degradation, not for the wealth of all Algiers. No, thou Venetian dog, I have sworn eternal enmity to all of Christian race, especially those of thy accursed nation, whom I will persecute with unceasing revenge, for it was one of thy vile countrymen that seduced, by his hellish wiles, the affections of my daughter, whose loss I can never forget, and my sorrows only can be mitigated in beholding the miseries of all those upon whom my power can inflict them; of that number thou art one, and were thy life prolonged till age or infirmity render thee incapable of labour, yet, if I should survive, still would I hold thee in bondage." Thus saying, he left me, while sparks of fury flashed indignantly from his fierce black eyes, and murmuring dreadful imprecations of still increasing torments to me, and all of Christian belief.

"Some time after this, another wretched captive was added to the number of miserable slaves, who, like myself, proved to be a Venetian: unhappy man! hard was thy lot to bear a life of ignominious toil beneath the command of cruel barbarians; but he, finding resistance vain, submitted without a murmur. Oftentimes did I observe this man regarding me with an eye of great scrutiny, as if he before had seen me, and I frequently wished to speak with him; but our inhuman task-masters prevented any intercourse between the miserable captives, during the hours dedicated to labour, and at night we were confined in separate cells. One day, however, passing close by him, when I thought we were unobserved, I said to him—'Friend, are you lately from Venice?'

"He started at the sound of my voice, and again fixed his eyes upon me most earnestly. 'What is it you perceive in my countenance so astonishing?' I inquired; 'have you ever before seen me? am I known to you, that you betray such agitation?'

"He answered—'You greatly resemble, in person, voice, and countenance, a man I once knew; and if your complexion was not so embrowned, you would bear to him a perfect likeness: do, signor, favour me by pulling off your turban.'

"I immediately complied, when he exclaimed, as if involuntarily—'Merciful powers, he still exists!'

"I felt greatly moved at this, and said—'Whom do you suppose me?'

"He replied—'You are Fernando, marchese di Barozzi.'—'I am,' answered I, immediately; 'and pray who are you?'—'One entirely unknown to you, though I am well acquainted with all your house,'—'Indeed! and know you whether my brother is still alive?' I eagerly inquired.—'He is, or at least he was, a few months ago,' he replied.—'Of course he supposes me dead?'— 'Aye, no doubt, and it is a very natural supposition too, permit me to say, when he sent two assassins to kill you.'—'How! my brother Augustino hire murderers to deprive me of life? impossible! he loved me affectionately.'—'Ah, very likely,' said the man, 'but he loved your title and riches much better, I promise you.'—'Good Heavens! can it be? but my wife, did she not claim the honours of Barozzi? for were I really defunct, Augustino has no lawful right to my possessions, as long as the marchioness Rosalina, daughter of De Valmont, and her child exists.'— 'Ah, but he took care of that, for she was removed, together with her infant and father.'—'What!' said I, petrified with astonishment; 'it cannot be! 'tis false.'—'You'll find it true, however,' said he, calmly, 'if you should ever return to Venice.'—'How know you all this?' I again inquired, still hoping to find him wrong, while the circumstance of my being beset in the forest carried with it a full conviction of its being true, which, as the cold chill of death, seemed to creep across my heart, stopping the current of the vital drops, which froze with horror, grief, and indignation.

"He then informed me how he once had belonged to a gang of bravoes, two of whom had been employed to assassinate me, and that shortly after, my wife, child, and her father, were all together consumed in their cottage, which no doubt had been set on fire by the order of my unnatural brother. How I lived to hear the end of this dreadful intelligence I know not, but at its close I sunk insensibly on the earth, apparently dead, and when my senses returned, I found myself stretched on the straw which served me for my bed. I remained a considerable while in this state, struggling with a fever, which succeeded the anguish of my tortured mind; but my constitution yet remained good, and in despite of my wishes to the contrary, I recovered.

"The first tidings communicated to me, on my return to a state of convalescent appearance, was the death of the cruel Moor, who had been suddenly seized with a malignant disorder, which in a few hours carried him off, to the great joy of all my fellow-slaves, as well as myself. His heir came to take possession of his inheritance, and him I had the happiness to find totally opposite to his predecessor, for Hamet was noble, humane, and benevolent: his first step was a mitigation of the hardships imposed upon the wretched captives, an action truly praiseworthy; and when he heard my unfortunate story, he not only gave me freedom, but provided me with a passage on board a vessel bound for this country. After thanking him in the best manner possible, I set sail, and by the blessing of Heaven, arrived at Venice at a crisis so truly important; and thus you perceive, that though the hour of retribution was long deferred, it has it last arrived, and after wearing so many years the galling yoke of captivity, I at length am restored to the sweets of liberty and love."

Chapter X
The Conclusion

O FTEN DID FERNANDO BEGUILE his auditors of tears, while recounting his hapless story, but particularly the marchioness and his daughter, who felt inexpressible anguish at this relation of his suffering and vile captivity, amidst all of which he had still retained the affection of father and husband, unabated by time or calamity. On its conclusion. Rosalina took an opportunity of quitting the apartment in search of Rosalva, whom she anxiously sought throughout the palazzo, but in vain. She then strayed into the garden, where she discovered the object of her affection in an arbour, seated in a cogitating posture. She stepped lightly, and placing her hand upon his shoulder, with a voice of sweetness, said—"Rosalva!"

He stalled, and exclaimed—"Ah, my beloved Rosalina, why do you seek out an unhappy wretch like me? 'twere fit you shun me, for have you not just heard a recapitulation of my father's crimes? then it is impossible you should ever love or esteem one sprung from that guilty man; therefore leave me, I beseech you, leave me."

"Unkind youth," she replied, as a tear started to her eye; "is this your opinion of Rosalina? Do you think she does not estimate you for yourself alone? Ah, dear youth, can I forget when you saved me in the forest, or when your breast received the poniard meant for mine? Oh, Rosalva, never, never shall the obligations of the peasant St. Almo be forgotten by the heiress of Barozzi; and here, by yon azure canopy of heaven, I swear, if you do not partake my fortune, and share those honours, a cottage would be preferable to the gilded palazzo, solitude more agreeable than the parade of rank or pageantry."

"Indeed!" said the enraptured youth, eagerly catching her hand.

"Yes indeed, dear Rosalva," she replied; "but come, suffer me to conduct you to my father and mother; they wait for you, and the dear marchioness La Rosa feels not easy at your absence. Come, my love, come."

She led him to the saloon, but the cloud of sorrow still hung upon his brow, which being perceived by the marquis, he, with a view of dispelling his melancholy, and diverting his oppressed mind, entered into a conversation upon the subject of the intended nuptials, and appeared so free and convivial, that pleasure and cheerfulness once more assumed their jocund reign within the walls of the palazzo of Barozzi; and for the purpose of beguiling the time till the period proposed for their union, the marchesa La Rosa proposed paying a visit to the cottage of the good old shepherd Alberto: to this all parties immediately acceded, and the next day was fixed on for the commencement of this excursion.

Early on the following morning the carriages were ready at the gate, and every arrangement being prepared, they set forward. In the first rode the marquis di Barozzi, his lady, and madame De Verencourt; in the second, Rosalva, Rosalina, and the marchesa La Rosa, with their retinue following in the rear; and after a pleasant ride, they beheld the neat cottage peeping from the foliage with which it was surrounded. The situation prevented a near access of carriages; from these they then alighted, and walked the remainder of the way, leaving their horses, which were unharnessed, and cropping the sweet herbage which grew around in great abundance, to the care of their attendants.

The noble visitors soon arrived at the humble dwelling, to the joyful confusion of Beatrice, who was all in a flutter at the conferring of this honour, and with a thousand curtseys, and as many apologies, ushered them in.

Marcelina, who had been tending the flowers in the garden, and from the choicest had selected a bouquet for her Reuben, came in at the back door, chanting a merry air, unconscious of the presence of so many exalted personages who had honoured her roof. She had advanced halfway into the room, with her eyes fixed upon the little gift, which she was disposing with great taste, when her mother, in a voice rather angry, cried—"Plague on the girl, what ails her? is this your behaviour to their worshipful honours?"

At this address the pretty cottager looked up, and seeing herself surrounded by so much elegance, to their great mirth let fall the flowers, and began to stammer an excuse about Reuben and her father, who, she said, had desired her to prepare a nosegay of roses and jessamine; "so I thought, as no one was here, why, I—I—would make it—as pretty as I could."

Rosalina, pitying her confusion, approached her, saying—"What! has Marcelina then forgotten me?"

"Oh, Holy Virgin!" exclaimed the astonished girl; "pardon me, madam, you are the marchioness of—of—somebody—but I forget what that bold youth called your ladyship, though I endeavoured to keep it in my head, and bid Reuben do the same, for he used to have a better memory than I; but somehow or another, since we have been married, his has been so strangely affected, that he can remember nothing."

"Indeed!" said Rosalva, laughing; "and pray what, my pretty rustic, has affected your husband's head so suddenly?"

"Oh, joy, my lord," said she, blushing still deeper, and dropping a low curtsey: "but look, my lady, here comes Reuben; oh, how glad he will be to see your honourable ladyship, and all their worshipful honours who accompany you!"

Her new-made husband now entered the dwelling, and with a rusticated bow, greeted the noble visitors of his father-in-law; but perceiving Rosalina, the mistake he had committed on his first beholding her occurred to his memory, and the fault now seemed more terrible than ever, seeing her arrayed in splendid apparel, and surrounded by her friends. The poor youth, while twisting his hat about, and turning it backwards and forwards, began making an apology, saying—"I hope your ladyship's goodness has forgot the rudeness I committed when I first saw your honour; but indeed, as I then told your ladyship, I took you for Marcelina—I did indeed, your excellenza."

"Pray don't mention it any more," said Rosalina, "for, good Reuben, I am perfectly convinced of your innocence."

"What is it to which the young man alludes?" inquired the marquis, noticing the confusion of his daughter.

"Oh, nothing, my lord," said she, "a mere trifle."

"Oh no, my lord, it was not a trifle; only her ladyship's goodness pleases to call it so, for really it was so great a crime, that I never shall forget it, and so I'll tell your lordship all about it." He then related the whole affair of his saluting Rosalina so freely, supposing her to be Marcelina. This communication afforded great mirth to the whole party, except her whom it most concerned.

Beatrice, who during this relation had slipped out in quest of Alberto, now returned in company with the honest shepherd, who, in a hearty, frank, and yet respectful manner, bade them welcome while a repast of the choicest grapes and finest fruits his garden could boast were quickly spread upon his homely board, of which they all partook.

After this refreshment they retired into an arbour, and sat several hours, tasting, at intervals, their host's best wine, the produce of his own vintage. The marchesa La Rosa and madame De Verencourt were delighted with the manners of the unsophisticated cottagers; and on their departure, the former presented Marcelina with a well-stocked purse, as a marriage present, and left another for her brother Marco, who was in the fields at a considerable distance, tending his flock.

The visitors now bade adieu to their humble entertainers, and departed, almost overwhelmed with their good benisons, and thanks in profusion, for the gifts which every one had presented to them, as tokens of remembrance.

On their return, they beguiled the distance in discoursing of the pleasure they received in witnessing the happiness, felicity, and domesticated cheerfulness, which reigned throughout the family and inmates of the peaceful cottage; and in good time they all reached the palazzo.

The following day, a long-proposed intention of the marchioness di Barozzi was put in force. She thought she never could fully know peace, till the remains of her beloved father, the unfortunate count De Valmont, were removed into consecrated ground, and inhumed in a manner becoming the exalted dignity of his rank and birth. Therefore, though it was a cause of renewing both her own and daughter's sorrows, she set forth for Pyrano, accompanied by the marquis and Rosalina, appointing to meet the marchioness La Rosa and her friend at the castle of the former, together with Rosalva, who could not remain an hour in Venice after it was evacuated by the lovely and amiable object of his affections.

They performed the journey without meeting with any accident, and again beheld the once-loved cottage in the Valley of Vintagers, where they were received with great joy and surprise, by honest Gerrard, his son, and daughter. The first, with a low bow, inquired if signora Rosa was going to increase their happiness, by again residing amongst them?

The marquis, in a manner brief as possible, informed them of the strange events that had taken place, and mentioned the marchioness's intention in having her father's ashes conveyed to an adjacent monastery, and interred with due solemnity and funeral rites.

The honest peasant, on hearing this, brushed a tear from his eye, and led the way to the garden, and pointing to the humble grave, retired, leaving them uninterrupted.

Rosalina's grief was renewed, and she was forced to be conveyed from the place by her father.

In a few days the mournful ceremony was performed, and they saw the last remains of the unfortunate count deposited in hallowed ground, and a monument raised to his memory. They then proceeded to the castle of La Rosa, and were cordially received by the generous mistress of that hospitable mansion.

After such lapse of time as decency required, the long-wished-for union took place between Rosalva and Rosalina. By this tie, the ancient family of Barozzi again flourished with its former greatness, benevolence, and honour.

Henri and Paulina, by their mutual desire, and consent of their lord and lady, made another happy pair, and spent the rest of their lives in the service of their noble employers.

Roldon perished on the rack, and soon after his villainous comrade, Darano, was taken and condemned, together with some other bravoes belonging to the same inhuman crew, which had been too often employed by the deceased Augustino.

Madame De Verencourt returned to France, and found her husband, whom she had long supposed dead: they had mutually wept for the loss of each other during their long separation, but now at last, by the kind interposition of Providence, were restored to each other's arms, to finish their days in connubial love and harmony.

The meretricious marchioness Loredo, after being deserted by her favourite paramour, Flodiardo, swallowed poison, and thus wickedly terminated a life of licentiousness and guilt.

The marchioness di Barozzi distributed the wealth awarded her by Rinaldo, chieftain of the band, amongst the peasantry and woodcutters who inhabited the straggling cottages on the skirts of the forest, as a recompence for the losses they had sustained by the depredations committed by those unlawful plundering banditti.

Rosalva and his fair bride were in due time blessed with a numerous offspring, sweet pledges of wedded love; and while the delighted marchioness listens to their innocent prattle, and views the increasing happiness of her darling child, she blesses the hour when fortune inspired her with the thought to assume, and Providence gave her strength to support, the arduous and dangerous character of the sorceress Magdalena.

FINIS.

Timeline of Gothic Fiction and Historical Context

1756, May:	Seven Years War between Britain and France begins
1760:	George II dies and is succeeded by George III
1764:	*The Castle of Otranto* by Horace Walpole – arguably the first Gothic novel
1765:	Americans begin to revolt following Parliament's issuing 'stamp' taxes
1772, June 22:	Slavery is effectively outlawed in England
1775, April 18:	American Revolutionary War begins
1777:	*The Old English Baron* by Clara Reeve, published originally as *The Champion of Virtue*
1783:	American Revolutionary War ends
1789, July 14:	The Storming of the Bastille, start of the French Revolution
1793, February 4:	England goes to war with France
1793, October 16:	Marie Antoinette executed by guillotine
1794:	*The Mysteries of Udolpho* by Ann Radcliffe
1796:	*The Monk* by Matthew Lewis
1797:	*The Italian* by Ann Radcliffe
1799:	End of the French Revolution
1801, January 1:	Act of Union creates the United Kingdom
1807:	*The Misanthrope Father, or The Guarded Secret* by Catharina Smith
1810:	*The Castle of Arragon, or The Banditti of the Forest* by Miss Smith
1811:	***The Caledonian Bandit, or The Heir of Duncaethal* by**
1815, June 18:	Napoleon is defeated at Waterloo
1815:	***Barozzi, or The Venetian Sorceress* by Mrs. Smith**
1816:	*The Vampyre, A Tale* by John Polidori
1818:	*Frankenstein, or The Modern Prometheus* by Mary Shelley
1818:	*Northanger Abbey* by Jane Austen, published

	posthumously
1820, January 19:	George III dies and is succeeded by George IV
1830, June 25:	George IV dies and is succeeded by William IV
1837, June 20:	William IV dies and is succeeded by Queen Victoria, marking the beginning of the Victorian Period
1840:	*Tales of the Grotesque and Arabesque,* a collection of short stories by Edgar Allan Poe
1886:	*The Strange Case of Dr. Jekyll and Mr. Hyde* by Robert Lewis Stevenson
1890:	*The Picture of Dorian Gray* by Oscar Wilde
1897:	*Dracula* by Bram Stoker

* marks books that may have been authored by the same person who wrote *The Caledonian Bandit* and *Barozzi.*

Suggested Further Reading

Dacre, Charlotte (alias Rosa Matilda). *Zofloya; or, The Moor: A Romance of the Fifteenth Century.* Longman, Hurst, Rees, and Orme, London 1806

Heller, Terry. *The Delights of Terror: An Aesthetics of the Tale of Terror.* Chicago 1987

Lathom, Francis. *The Midnight Bell.* H. D. Symonds, London 1798

Lewis, Matthew. *The Monk.* London 1796

Parsons, Eliza. *The Castle of Wolfenbach.* Minerva Press, London 1793

Polidori, John. *The Vampyre, A Tale.* First published by Colburn in the New Monthly Magazine with the false attribution "A Tale by Lord Byron." London 1819

Radcliffe, Ann. *The Mysteries of Udolpho.* G. G. and J. Robinson, London 1794

Radcliffe, Ann. *The Italian.* G. G. and J. Robinson, London 1797

Smith, Eleanor. *The Orphan of the Rhine.* Minerva Press, London 1798

Spencer, Jane. *The Rise of the Woman Novelist: From Aphra Behn to Jane Austen.* Blackwell, Oxford 1987

Walpole, Horace. *The Castle of Otranto.* First published under the title, *The Castle of Otranto, A Story. Translated by William Marshal, Gent. From the Original Italian of Onuphrio Muralto, Canon of the Church of St. Nicholas at Otranto.* 1764

www.ingramcontent.com/pod-product-compliance
Lightning Source LLC
Chambersburg PA
CBHW022023240626
47154CB00007B/2229